M000211711

KOTIMAA: HOMELAND
By Mark Munger

Cloquet River Press
Publishing Stories from the Lake Superior Basin
www.cloquetriverpress.com

First Edition
Copyright 2019, Mark Munger

All rights reserved, including the right to reproduce this book or any portions thereof, in any form, except for brief quotations embodied in articles and reviews without written permission of the publisher. The opinions, observations, and references herein are those of the author alone.

This story is fiction. Places, characters, organizations, or incidents are products of the author's imagination and are used fictitiously. Any resemblance or reference to "real" people, places, organizations, living or dead, is used by the author as part of the artistic license inherent in a fictional tale.

ISBN: 978-1-7324434-0-2
Library of Congress Number: 2018908614
Published by: Cloquet River Press
                  5353 Knudsen Road
                  Duluth, Minnesota 55803
                  (218) 721-3213

Edited by Scribendi
Photos by Marie Kobe, SA-kuva, and Shutterstock
Visit the publisher at: www.cloquetriverpress.com
E-mail the author at: cloquetriverpress@yahoo.com
Printed in the United States of America

ACKNOWLEDGMENTS

I would like to thank the following individuals who served as readers for this project: Walter Mondale, Gerry Henkel, Mark Rubin, Hannah Erpestad, Irina Björklund, Jim Kurtti, Jill Eichenwald, Roman Kushnir, Ron McVean, Olavi Koivukangas, Bruce Laurich, Polly John, Thom Chartier, Randy McCarty, and Molly Tynjala.

Without these dedicated family, friends, and professional scholars devoting their time and effort to reading the manuscript, the content and flow of this novel might be vastly different—and more than likely, vastly inferior.

Special recognition must be afforded two individuals. First, as I type this, I am mourning the passing of the man who had the most influence on me as a person, lawyer, writer, and human being. My father—Harry Leonard Munger—always stood in my corner, cheering me on in my writerly exploits, even when things weren't going so well. I miss you, Dad.

Additionally, this book is dedicated to Gerry Henkel, Finnish American, friend, and the person who has done more to promote my Finnish American novels than any other human being. I miss Gerry's intelligently crafted newspaper, *The New World Finn*, where Gerry took the time to expose new artists, writers, and musicians with Finnish roots or themes to the world. Thanks, Gerry, for fifteen years of friendship and encouragement.

Lastly, a word of thanks to my wife, René. Many days and nights have been lost to the family while I type away at the keyboard, struggle with revisions, or sleep in my chair because I've been up at five in the morning working on this book. Her patience through the duration of this project is much appreciated.

Mark Munger
2019
Duluth, Minnesota

Dedicated to my friend, Gerry Henkel and to my father, Harry Leonard Munger.

The Lord will roar from on high,
And from his holy habitation utter his voice:
He will roar mightily against his fold,
And shout, like those who tread grapes,
Against all the inhabitants of the earth.

The clamor will resound to the ends of the earth,
For the Lord has an indictment against the nations,
He is entering into judgment with all flesh,
And the guilty he will put to the sword.

(Jeremiah 25:30-31)

KOTIMAA: HOMELAND

THE FAMILIES

Alhomäki

Anders Alhomäki: Son of Marjatta and Mikko Salminen. Adopted by Jorma Alhomäki. Immigrant from the Kainuu region of Finland. Boxer. Worked in the Røros copper mine in Norway, iron ore mines in Minnesota, and the Quincy Mine in northern Michigan. In love with a Gypsy, Anneli Balzar. Lived with Elin Gustafson. Married Heidi Genelli and ran Wolf Lake Logging Camp in northeastern Minnesota. Has children.

Mikko Salminen: Married to Marjatta. Father of Urho Salminen and Anders Alhomäki. Failed farmer.

Jorma Alhomäki: Finnish farmer. Married Marjatta after she was widowed. Adopted Anders. Two daughters with Marjatta: Helmi and Ronja. Brother to *Wachtmeister* (Sergeant) Alvar Alhomäki, The Elf Warrior, soldier in the Russian Army.

Marjatta Alhomäki: Married to Mikko Salminen. Two sons: Urho and Anders. Widowed. Married to Jorma Alhomäki. Two daughters: Helmi and Ronja.

Alvar Alhomäki: The Elf Warrior. Brother to Jorma. Uncle to Anders and Helmi and Ronja. Great-great-grandfather of Master Sergeant Jere Alhomäki, disgruntled Finnish soldier. Married a Russian war widow. Has children.

Jere Alhomäki: Soldier who served in Africa with the Finnish Defense Forces. Anti-Muslim. Seeks to assassinate a prominent Finnish official in charge of Syrian immigration to Finland. Not married. No children.

Gustafson

Karl Gustafson: Swedish-speaking Finnish immigrant to the United States. Married to Laina. Widowed. Remarried Sofia Wirtanen. Father of Elin Gustafson and Alexis Gustafson. A lawyer and a conservative.

Laina Gustafson: Finnish-speaking immigrant to the United States. Mother of Elin Gustafson. Married to Karl. A suffragette and progressive activist.

Sofia Wirtanen Gustafson: Mistress (later second wife) of Karl. Mother of Alexis Gustafson. A maid in the Gustafson household before her marriage to Karl.

Elin Gustafson Ellison Goldfarb Peltomaa: Daughter of Karl and Laina. Born in Duluth, Minnesota. Lover of Anders Alhomäki. Wife of Horace Ellison (divorced). Widow of Hiram Goldfarb. Widow of Matti Peltomaa. A teacher and journalist. Raised her half-sister Alexis as her own daughter.

Alexis Gustafson Tate: Finnish American daughter of Karl and Sofia Gustafson. Born in Duluth, Minnesota. Treated by her half-sister Elin as a daughter. Medical doctor. Married Elmore Tate, MD. Two children: Josiah and Janine Tate.

Elmore Tate, MD: African American physician. Married Alexis Gustafson. Two children: Josiah and Janine. Founded clinic in Harlem with Alexis.

Josiah Tate: Grandson of Elin. Son of Alexis and Elmore. Registered nurse at a nursing home in Lakeville, Minnesota. Brother to Janine. Married. Has children.

Janine Tate Tanninen: Granddaughter of Elin. Daughter of Alexis and Elmore. Sister to Josiah. No children. Married to Finnish engineer Olavi Tanninen. Plastic surgeon serving as a volunteer at the Kajaani Refugee Center in Kajaani, Finland.

PREFACE: The Warrior's Story. December 1, 2017 (Helsinki, Finland)

They come even though they aren't welcome. They enter our homeland on the thinnest of excuses and permissions. They are not us. They are not Swedes. They are not Russians or any other Christian branch of the human race. They are Muslims: believers in Allah and Muhammad and practitioners of self-immolation at the slightest suggestion from their Mullahs, and they do not belong here. They will never belong here. For you see, these immigrants to my country are like an unwelcome cancer that needs to be excised, and, like a malignancy of skin or organs or bone, discarded into the trash. But unlike a cancerous tumor, there is no need to evaluate or study these blasphemers sliding unhindered across our borders, welcomed and protected by a secular and liberal government's corrupt abandonment of Christian faith. No, there is nothing to learn from talking to or evaluating or examining the unwanted immigrant men, women, and children infecting our country. There is only this: a message must be sent. What happened on 9 March 2015 near the Tapanila railway station can never, I repeat never, happen again. What were the sentences handed out for degrading one of our women? A year and four months as the longest punishment? A year for another of the scoundrels? Two acquittals? Even the prosecutor on the case recognizes these sanctions are a joke, an embarrassment. And the cancer is spreading. On 23 November 2015, another attack. Another rape by an immigrant. A fourteen-year-old girl walking home in Kempele was sexually abused by a Muslim foreigner, a beast allowed in from the backwaters of Afghanistan. Perhaps his skin was a shade paler than The Others who betrayed the government's misplaced trust at Tapanila. But his soul, ah, that was no brighter, no cleaner than that of those who committed unspeakable acts near the Tapanila railway stop.

There's also this: my brother's death—his murder by suicide bombers while traveling on business in Russia. A tragedy. An undeniable atrocity. But I choose not to dwell on my personal loss. Rather, I'm focused on the bigger picture, the societal instability Muhammadan immigration is wrecking upon my beloved Finland.

What can one say about the recent events in Turku, where a Moroccan Muslim, a cur who shall not be named, attacked and killed two innocent Finnish women and wounded ten others, sending many of them to the intensive care wards of local hospitals with life-threatening injuries? All because he was denied asylum by my country? Again, I fault my government for inviting Muslims into the Finnish homeland with full knowledge that many who follow Islam have one thing and one thing only on their minds as they accept the generosity of my people: the complete and utter destruction of Christianity and our way of life.

And what of my fellow nationalists, my brothers in arms within the Sons of the Raven? What has been their response to all of this? Have they taken any action to salt the leeches sticking to our national skin, to tamp down the tidal wave of foreign interlopers taking advantage of our social safety net? Have any of my comrades in the Utti Jaegers, the unit I served in—from my enlistment at age eighteen until my discharge after putting in twenty-plus years—those brave men who deployed with me to foreign lands, taken steps to address the disease afflicting our beloved homeland? No, they have not. A handful of us acting together could make a statement that our nation and the world can't ignore. But my former comrades sit on their hands in their lake-cottage saunas, pitifully naked, enjoying cold beer, thinking about their own futures, their women, their pensions, and their precious civilian jobs with no concern for what is happening to the country they once swore to defend with their lives.

Well, that's not me. I am different. My Christian faith fortifies me, strengthens my resolve. Having risen to the rank of master sergeant in the Jaegers, having connections with patriots in other European countries who understand such things and who have access to the tools I need—plastic explosives, ammunition, a Sako TRG-42, and an Arsenal semi-automatic—I am equipped to do God's work on my own. One man. One journey. One result. I will deliver a message similar to the one Anders Breivik tried to send to the authorities in Norway, but one that will, as God is my witness, not indiscriminately take the life of any Finn, with one purposeful exception.

That was Breivik's folly. Instead of targeting the source of his upset—Norwegian liberal politicians—he chose to take the lives of innocent children; children who were most certainly being led

12

down a primrose path by their misguided liberal parents and educators, but children capable of redemption. I'm not making that same mistake. I will, with God's steady hand and the clarity of Christ, intentionally take but a single life, the life of the woman overseeing the insane resettlement of The Others in my beloved homeland.

And so, I have assembled my cache of explosives and weapons. They are hidden in the winter camping gear I've crammed inside my military duffle and surrounded with clothing, a mess kit, a sleeping bag, dehydrated food, a lantern, a stove, and fuel canisters. I sent the heavy canvas bag ahead by delivery truck. The tools of destiny await me in Kajaani.

The train trundles along. Because it's early December, there are few passengers. Steam obscures the window as I clutch my stainless-steel travel mug of hot coffee and watch the ghostly landscape slide by. The sky is gray. The sun is absent. Clouds threaten. It's afternoon. Soon, the day will set behind the weather. An observer might, if incapable of understanding what it is I am about to do, think that the bleakness of the afternoon replicates the ugliness of my task. But that is not true: I am not some homegrown terrorist, deranged and unhinged by what I saw in Central Africa where I spent a year clearing mines and trying to keep the peace between Muslims and Christians. To ascribe my current mission as being directly related to what I witnessed in Africa would be too simplistic. My present quest, such as it is, initiates from the horrors of Central Africa and from an innate, core belief that each segment of humanity—from my people occupying the very height of religious evolution to The Others, who may, one day, after generations of progress, break free from their reliance upon Muhammadan fables—must keep to its own. That is why I am on this train. That is why the Syrian men and women and children being processed in the Kajaani Refugee Center must witness the assassination of their most vocal advocate. God's message must be delivered, and I am his Messenger.

BOOK ONE: THEN

CHAPTER ONE: December 1893 (Paltamo, Finland)

A strong wind blew from the west, originating in the North Sea off Norway, gathering velocity as it crossed Sweden, accumulating moisture over the Gulf of Bothnia before encountering the Finnish coast. At landfall, the warmth of the ground caused the sky to release snow. From Paavola, just in from the sea, to Paltamo on the northern shore of Finland's fifth largest lake—Oulujärvi—low, fat clouds deposited a fluffy white blanket: the sort of snow children dream of during Christmas holiday.

A boy stood atop a ridge. The landscape descended from a hillock of pines and birches where the child and his mates scrutinized the ground's pitch from forest to frozen lake. There were two girls in the group—two blond-headed, fair-skinned, blue-eyed girls—the Noskinen sisters, Eeva and Inka, and three boys: Eino and Eero Tulainen and the smallest of the five children, the lone boy who stood apart from the others. The girls, whose father and mother were the most affluent parents of the assembled children (the Noskinens owned a dry goods store and boarding house in Paltamo) sat on a wooden sled. The sled was a luxury that the boys, whose fathers were ordinary farmers and whose mothers were common homemakers keeping the hearth warm and the floors swept in cramped dovetailed pine log cabins built decades earlier by the paternal grandfathers of their families, could only dream of owning. The solitary boy, ten years old and of wiry build, his head covered in kinky black hair, his expectant face accented by deep-set brown eyes, and his comrades (who were also ten years old and, like the girls, displayed Nordic complexions and indigo eyes) negotiated the hill on their fathers' birch skis. The skis were too long, and the leather bindings were too large for the boys' boots. The boys used a single ski pole—a stiff birch shaft punctuated by a point of smithy iron surrounded by a leather basket—to climb from Oulujärvi to the top of the rise. Squalls obliterated the landscape. The children disappeared from view until the wind calmed between gusts. Thumb-sized discs of white descended, creating a layer of powder that, as the day grew longer, accumulated above the knees of the laughing, squealing, happy children. Waltzing flakes stuck stubbornly to the children's winter clothes. The Noskinen sisters wore smart-fitting navy pea coats, dresses, and matching leggings to ward off the chill. The boys wore hand-me-down clothing that was ill-fitting and ragged. All of the children save the smallest boy wore stocking hats. The Tulainen brothers wore woolen hats knitted by their mother whereas the girls' flaxen hair was covered in factory-made hats selected from their father's store. The lone boy started the day wearing his stepfather's woolen stocking hat—the hat too large for the child's slender head. But he'd lost the hat in a crash at the end of a run. The boy and Eino Tulainen had dug and dug and dug in the deepening snow for the lost hat without success. The boy knew his stepfather would be upset. They were a poor family—his stepfather, mother, and toddling twin sisters—especially given that the twins were colicky, requiring visits from Henri Nevonen, the neighborhood healer. Money was in short supply. The boy's parents barely made ends meet, working land that was scrubby, rocky, and infused with stubbornness. Their potato crop had failed. Their rye had withered because, for much of that summer, too little rain had fallen. Late-August storms helped save what would have been a disaster. Carrots and peas and rutabagas were salvaged such that the family would not starve. And with dehydrated reindeer strips in the larder, an ample supply of dried berries and nuts in the root cellar, two fine, fat hogs ready for butchering, and fresh eggs from a dozen hens also available to the family, they would get by. But the luxuries of a simple life—coffee, salt, sugar, wheat flour, and occasional pieces of hard candy from the Noskinen store—all of these were relegated to rationing and, by Christmas holiday, mere memory.

"Anders!"

The call was distant and faint, but the boy recognized his mother's voice. Though not yet three in the afternoon, the sky was already dark. Dinner would be ready. Anders Alhomäki would eat before commencing his evening chores. Because of the season and the northerly latitude of the family farm, the boy's work with the hogs and the chickens and the family horse—Aake—would be done by the light of a barn lamp. Kerosene was in short supply, but as the only source of light available for work after dusk, the lamp was essential to the boy's labors. He would kindle the cotton wick, light it with a match (another store-bought item limited in quantity), and place the clear glass reservoir filled with amber fuel on a steadfast perch as he mucked out the horse's stall, fed her last summer's hay, and brushed her golden flanks with tenderness. He'd ridden the filly occasionally—bareback, using a rope for a bridle—without his stepfather's permission. As a foundational horse in the line that would become the *suomen hippo* (the Finnhorse), Aake was far too valuable as a draft animal, as a machine to break soil, rake hay, and cultivate ground owned by Jorma Alhomäki to risk injury during some ill-conceived romp involving a ten-year-old would-be cowboy. And so, Anders concealed his exploits from his stepfather, though, if truth be told, Jorma and Marjatta Alhomäki had an inkling of what the boy was up to when they weren't looking.

Hearing his mother's voice, Anders turned towards his companions, wiped snow from his hatless head, and nodded with solemnity.

"Mother's calling," the boy said, pushing off with his ski pole, breaking a trail for home. "See you tomorrow?" he asked, tossing the question over his shoulder to the Noskinen sisters and the Tulainen boys.

"Ya, sure!" Eero Tulainen yelped. "Right here, after morning chores."

Anders made no reply. Across the bleak land, a lantern twinkled in a window. He moved quickly; the rhythm of skiing as innate as walking to a young boy of the north. He knew, without having been told by his mother, what awaited him at the rough-hewn family table: the warmth of a wood fire burning in the crudely constructed stone and mortar fireplace; hot rabbit stew, fresh rye bread; and cold milk his mother had obtained by bartering fresh eggs with another farmer's wife, Kaija Järvenpää, the Järvenpääs owning a dependable cow—an extravagance the Alhomäkis could not afford. The thought of eating a hot meal, completing his evening chores, and clambering into his warm bed in the loft of the log house to read a few pages from Kivi's *Seven Brothers* by candlelight compelled Anders to lengthen his stride as he skied home.

CHAPTER TWO

Anders sat on a wooden bench staring out a window overlooking a snow-covered field next to the boys' elementary school. There were ten other boys seated on three benches facing the instructor, Miss Kekkonen, a broad-shouldered, squat spinster who, though she lacked formal training as a schoolteacher, did not let that deficiency alter her truth: she *knew* herself to be the smartest person in any room she graced with her presence.

"Mr. Alhomäki," the plainly featured matron said sharply, "please tell us what today's passage from Lönnrot's *Kalevala* is trying to illuminate for its readers, if you will?"

The question startled the child. "Ma'am?"

A scowl crept across the teacher's perpetually pinched face. "You have read today's assignment, yes?"

I don't want to admit to her that I was so caught up in reading Seven Brothers *that I forgot to read my assignment. If I do, it will likely be "Get to the front of the classroom, drop your trousers and your long underwear, bend over, and take your punishment," which means the yardstick. God, how I hate the yardstick! It's supple, like a whip, and Miss Kekkonen wields it harshly. Last time she gave me ten lashes with that birch ruler, I couldn't sit down for two days! Better to lie. At least that way, maybe I can buy myself some time.* "I did."

"Good." The teacher walked with determination across the planked floor of the drafty schoolhouse. Her skirt and petticoat sashayed as she moved. Miss Kekkonen stopped in front of Anders, adjusted her eyeglasses, and scrutinized the trembling boy. "So then, please explain the passage to us, Mr. Alhomäki, the one that you were assigned and have declared you've read thoroughly."

Anders's eyes welled. His face contorted. His focus was not on the woman's stern countenance but on the yardstick hanging from a nail against the board and batten wall at the front of the classroom. Anders swallowed. Pine logs crackling and popping inside the school's woodstove attracted his attention. But respite was fleeting. Tears came. Anders hung his head in shame, yielding to the authority of the teacher without protest. *My goose is cooked.*

"Alhomäki, you are such a donkey!" Erno Karppinen chided as Anders stood next to Jari Järvenpää, who, like Anders, was in the third year and ten years old. Jari was smaller and skinnier than Anders, whereas Erno, solidly built, eleven years old, and as mean as his drunken, abusive father Luukas, had the classic physique and demeanor of a bully.

The younger boys had been clutching tin lunch pails, holding their schoolbooks, and talking about the upcoming Christmas party at St. Thomas Lutheran Church, the parish church they attended. They had not been looking to interact with Erno. In fact, knowing that Erno was likely, by virtue of the black eye and goose egg prominently displayed on his temple, ready to dish out the sort of punishment he'd received from his out-of-work father, Anders and Jari had exited the schoolhouse and found shelter under a grove of pines to talk. Their efforts to avoid the bully were for naught. Erno Karppinen—accompanied by two of his closest friends, boys older but no bigger than Anders and Jari—had spied the other boys and approached them with determination.

"A smarty-pants like you," Erno continued, planting himself in front of Anders, hands on hips, striking a menacing pose, "is supposed to know *everything*."

Anders swallowed and adjusted his books under his right arm. Wind swept across the field surrounding the schoolhouse. Shards of old snow, hard-edged and propelled by the breeze, stung Anders's face. "I forgot to read the passage Miss Kekkonen assigned," Anders whispered. The child had received ten lashes with the yardstick for idleness. Pain pulsed up and down his rump and legs where the ruler had raised skin. "She did what she had to do to make sure I don't forget again."

A flash of understanding swept across Erno's face. Anders hoped it was enough, that he'd endured his punishment, and, beyond a few harsh words, the bully would let him be. But Erno's demeanor changed. The dark mood—the mood every boy at the Paltamo Boys' Public Elementary School dreaded—returned. Before Anders could drop his books and lunch box to defend himself, Karppinen's bare fists—the bully's mittens forgotten or lost—lashed out, striking the smaller boy in the face, splitting

21

Anders's lip, and breaking his nose without warning. And the pummeling didn't end with Anders splayed across snowy ground.

"You dumb ass. You walk around ..." another blow landed, boxing Anders's right ear, "... with your belly full and your head stuffed with bullshit memorized from some goddamn book." A boot landed in the small of Anders's back. "I'll show you how it is to learn something useful," Erno added, slamming his big boot again and again into the defenseless boy.

"Stop it!" Jari cried out, tears flowing down his cheeks. "Stop hurting Anders!" he screamed, dropping his lunch pail and books onto frozen ground.

Jari Järvenpää lunged at the bully. But Jari was too slow. Erno sidestepped the boy's rush, extended his size-eleven boot—a discard of his father's far too large for Erno's foot—and tripped Jari. The boy tumbled, struck his head on a frozen pine, and was stunned senseless by the impact.

"Serves the little asshole ..." Erno was cut off in midsentence as Anders, blood gushing from his nose and his lip, his eyes nearly closed from swelling, smashed the Alhomäki family's leather-bound copy of the *Kalevala* on top of Erno's head. Anders hoped the blow would drop the bully but, though the attempt staggered the brute, it did not bring him to his knees.

"What the hell happened to you?"

Anders had limped home, his legs and buttocks sore from corporal punishment administered by his teacher, his face a mottled mess of blood and leaves and twigs and dirt, his hands and fingers scraped and bruised from fending off Erno's blows. His lunch pail had been left behind, crushed under the heel of his enemy's hand-me-down boots. His mathematics, Finnish grammar, and history texts, though wet from snow, were intact. But the family's cherished leather-bound copy of the *Kalevala*, the multicolored cover dangling from the book's abused spine, was in tatters. Erno had not been satisfied with rendering his foe inert and unable to respond; he had smacked the hefty Lönnrot—an expensive gift to the family from Anders's Uncle Alvar—against Anders's head until the book burst at its seams and the boy was no longer a threat. Anders said nothing to his stepfather as he stood at the threshold of their farmhouse. The boy's eyes were so swollen he could barely make out the silhouettes of his stepfather and his mother. Marjatta held Anders's half-sisters—one on each matronly hip—as the family stared at the boy from the warmth of the familial home, their faces a blur, their expressions invisible.

"Out with it, boy, what the hell happened to you?"

"Jorma, let him be. He will tell us by and by, once I clean him up," Marjatta Alhomäki said tenderly, lowering the girls to the floor, pushing her husband aside, and urging their eldest child into the house.

After his cuts and bruises were treated with healing liniment and herbal salve applied by his mother; after his stepfather—without warning as Anders sat on a stool waiting for further ministrations—grasped the boy's crooked nose and jerked it back in place, sending a jolt of pain through Anders that nearly knocked him to the pine planked floor of the kitchen; after sitting silently next to the hulking, sweating, muscular frame of his stepfather in the family sauna, the moist heat of the bathhouse permeating the boy's skin and his soul; the boy told his parents what had happened at school.

"The lashes from Miss Kekkonen, those you deserved," Jorma said as he puffed on a cherrywood pipe, clouds of sweet tobacco smoke rising in the kitchen, the intimate space illumined by the inconsequential light of an oil lamp. "But what happened at the hands of that bastard ..."

"Husband, watch your tongue! Ours is a Christian home and the girls have just gone to bed. They might hear you. We do not use such expressions in this house!"

Anders, his face still swollen and painful, managed a weak smile. "But Father is right, Mother. Erno Karppinen is the biggest bastard in Paltamo, maybe in all of Kainuu!"

"Still, that's not language we use in this family."

Jorma puffed his pipe. "You got a few blows in?"

"Don't encourage such nonsense. Violence never solved anything," Marjatta added softly, the former edge gone from her words.

The boy grew nostalgic. He thought of his dead brother, Urho, and his dead father, Mikko, both bearing the surname Salminen. *If Urho was alive and heard about this, he'd find Erno Karppinen and kick his ass. Father wouldn't intervene. He was always drinking. That's why he and Urho are gone. That's why Momma and I moved from the shores of Vilpusjärvi to this place, a farm owned by my stepfather, which according to him, will one day be mine.* Anders didn't dwell on the fact that he didn't want to be a farmer. Instead, he concentrated on remembering his dead brother. *It wasn't like Urho cared about me. He would've hunted down Erno and beaten him silly to defend the family name. He wouldn't have done it out of love, that's for sure. Hell, Urho himself beat me on a regular basis, passing down from Father the blows and kicks and punches that Father delivered whenever he thought there was a need to correct Urho or ensure Urho understood who was in charge ... Funny,* Anders thought as he closed his eyes against the pain, *I don't think about Urho or Father much. In fact, until this moment, I hadn't thought about them more than a handful of times in the three years since they passed. I wonder why.*

"Bullies don't understand negotiating, Marjatta," Jorma declared, interrupting the boy's reminiscence. "They understand brute force. I'm not suggesting Anders go looking for trouble. But when a man is cornered—when he cannot retreat—knowing how to defend oneself is a valuable skill."

The woman sighed. "It doesn't look like your assessment served our son well in this instance. Just look at his face. That beautiful smile. His nose. His rosy cheeks. All displaced and distorted." She paused to forestall tears. "I was married to a man who thought he could settle every dispute with his fists," Marjatta whispered. "I don't want Anders to follow the example of his dead father or his dead brother. Anders is too bright a light for that."

Jorma took a long sip of coffee from a chipped cup. "Anders, you never answered my question."

The boy tilted his head, so that his left eye locked on Jorma's wide face, and grinned. "I clobbered him over the head with the *Kalevala.* Does that count?"

Jorma guffawed. "I know a man. Otso Olson. Half Finn. Half Norwegian. Runs the tannery at Mieslahti. His name fits him: as strong as a polar bear from the Barents Sea. Not just a big man, but fast on his feet and with his fists. Once knocked out the heavyweight champion of Karelia in a bar fight."

"Husband! Enough!"

"Calm down, woman. I'm not suggesting that Anders become the boy who torments him. I'm only suggesting that, after a few sessions with The Bear, given Anders's hard head, well, the next time Erno Karppinen comes looking for trouble, he'll be in for one hell of a surprise."

The boy nodded. "I'd like to learn how to box, Momma. Just in case."

Marjatta sighed, shook her head, and looked at a wind-up clock on a shelf above the fireplace. "It's past nine. Morning comes early," she said in a defeated tone.

CHAPTER THREE

The boy met The Bear in a warehouse. The large, open room was, like so many indoor spaces in rural Finland, heated by a fieldstone fireplace and lighted by kerosene lamps placed around the building's barn-like interior. The former tannery was constructed in the traditional way—of logs squared and notched by hand. Though the space had been repurposed into a gymnasium, Otso Olson could not afford a formal boxing ring. Four birch posts secured by iron straps to the plank floor, the varnish of the boards scuffed by the boots of men and boys—their footwear inappropriate for the ring but the best the combatants could afford—and thick hemp ropes, repurposed lanyards from an Oulu shipyard passed through holes drilled in the birch pillars, defined the fighting space. Galvanized pails sat on the floor next to wrought-iron stools designating opposing corners of the ring.

Morning broke. Sunlight—yellow and fragile—streamed into the gymnasium through a window. Though it was after dawn, lanterns still glowed. Muted light cast shadows onto the floor and into the open rafters. A large man opened an interior door constructed of pine boards neatly joined and held together by iron strapping that swung noisily on iron hinges. A towel was draped over the man's right shoulder as he shuffled into the room. He wore brown woolen trousers cinched around his ample gut with a belt (assisted by redundant leather suspenders) a blue and white patterned wool shirt, distressed work boots—the laces tied halfway up the ankles—and rumpled black socks. A hand-rolled cigarette was clamped in his teeth. A vapor of vice trailed the man as he moved with cautious strength. He carried a bucket filled with cold water in his right hand, stopped in a corner of the homemade boxing ring, and poured water from the bucket he carried into a pail resting on the floor before turning his head to address the sound of approaching footsteps.

"Come in!" he bellowed. "It's unlocked."

Winter rushed into the room as a door opened to reveal a man and a boy standing in daylight.

"Alhomäki, my old friend! Get a move on. The lad will catch a cold standing outside," Otso Olson commanded. The gymnasium proprietor set the empty bucket down before walking across the gritty floor, his enormous right hand extended in greeting.

Jorma approached Otso and returned the handshake with vigor. Anders followed his stepfather into the gymnasium and shut the door. The weather changed. The sun disappeared. The wind ramped up and it began to snow. Otso's bulk shrouded stepfather and son in shadow as the building creaked and moaned.

"Good to see you, Olson," Jorma said evenly, avoiding overt affection for the man who'd been his friend since they were toddlers. "This is the boy I was telling you about, my only son, the heir to the Alhomäki fortune," he added with a sly wink, the day-to-day existence of the Alhomäki family clear in the threadbare clothing worn by the man and the boy. "He's been having a tough time at school because of a bully—a big fellow with a mean streak. I thought maybe a few lessons with you might be of use."

Anders's attention was drawn to a framed poster hanging on a wall. The boy studied the lithograph depicting two men circling each other, boxing gloves poised to strike, a crowd cheering in the background.

"Just got that," Otso said. "That's Gentleman Jim Corbett and world-champion John L. Sullivan. They fought a few months ago in America. New Orleans, I think. First time Sullivan boxed with gloves under the Marques of Queensberry Rules."

"I read about that in *Päivälehti*," Jorma said, joining his son next to the lithograph. "Sullivan lost."

Otso shook his head. "You best be careful reading that nationalist trash. The czar's agents are always watching!"

Jorma looked at Otso, fierceness raging in the smaller man's eyes. "Fuck Alexander," Jorma said tersely. "He's nothing but a woman in a man's clothing."

Otso touched his right index finger to his lips. "Shush. You'll get us both in trouble with those damnable Russians. Plus," the man added, gesturing for his guests to move towards the ring, "you're teaching your son some very bad words!"

Though young, Anders understood the reality of Finland's existence as a semi-autonomous Grand Duchy within the Russian Empire. His father, Mikko Salminen, had been a socialist who spent much time at the Puolanka Socialist Hall engaged in dialectics. Though a church-going woman, Marjatta often accompanied Mikko to those meetings, meetings that an intellectually curious farmer from Paltamo periodically attended. When Mikko and Urho died, an event that shook Marjatta Salminen to her core, the farmer from Paltamo began calling upon the widow and her surviving son, eventually wooing Marjatta to remarry and move south to live on the Alhomäki farm. Anders had listened intently to adult conversations around the dinner table and, though young, appreciated the cautionary tone of Otso Olson's reproach.

Nothing further was said regarding the czar or politics as they moved towards the ring.

"You know, Ahlomäki, you introduced me to the lad before. We bumped into each other in town. He was tagging along and I made his acquaintance. So, it's not like I don't know the lad or know that he's your only son," the big man added matter-of-factly. "In any event, hang your coats on those chairs," Otso said, pointing towards two hardwood chairs snugged to a pine table outside the ring. "Boy, slip those on," he added, gesturing towards a pair of boxing gloves on the table. "They're likely too big but they'll do. Join me at the heavy bag," Otso concluded, casting an eye towards a canvas sack hanging by a cotton clothesline from a rafter.

The stepfather and son deposited their coats. Anders stood in the room's briskness, his trousers worn at the rump and knees, a loose-fitting tunic of wool hanging off his slender frame, his black hair shiny and flattened from tonic, his deep cocoa eyes defiant and fierce. His brown boots, the leather cracked but newly polished, dripped water as he slipped boxing gloves over his hands. Jorma tightened the laces. Melt from the boy's boots left a trail across the floor as Anders approached the heavy bag. The poor lighting did nothing to diminish the sapphire of Otso's eyes as he scrutinized his newest pupil. Jorma arrived at the bag and stood behind his stepson.

"These are swell," Anders said, smacking the gloves together.

"Made 'em myself," the tanner said matter-of-factly, his thick, black beard moving with each word. "Moose hide. Tough as iron. Sewed the heavy bag from an old sail I got from Oulu.

Stuffed it with sawdust from the Paltamo sawmill." Otso nodded. "Give it a smack."

Anders tried to mimic the boxers on the poster. He held his skinny, prepubescent arms away from his torso and landed an awkward blow.

"No, no, lad. You don't pound on the bag with the side of your fist. You strike hard and fast between the first and second knuckles," Otso said, correcting the boy's positioning. "Like this."

With a speed defying his bulk, Olson lashed out with his left, then his right, repeating the strikes until his bare fists drummed a cadence. The demonstration lasted only a minute but the exhibition winded Otso Olson. The knuckles of his hands were raw from pounding the heavy bag's abrasive surface. "Now you try."

Jorma smiled as his stepson threw a punch with his left glove.

"Better. But faster," Otso observed. "Don't worry about how hard you're hitting your target. Worry about speed. You're a little fellow. You'll not win fights against bigger boys because you're stronger. You'll win because you're quicker, in better condition, and know how to move."

"Move?" Jorma asked, the air of the big room pungent with lingering smells of animals, tanning chemicals, and death.

"Two-thirds of boxing, as Gentleman Jim proved in beating Sullivan—the bare knuckles champion of the world—is knowing when to move in, when to move out. Corbett gave up fifteen kilos to Sullivan and yet, because he was smarter, faster, and knew how to move his feet, he prevailed over a bigger, stronger, more experienced man. It can be the same for Anders; that is, if he listens to The Bear!"

The boy threw a quick right and then an even quicker left. He followed the combination with repetitive strikes that mimicked his teacher.

"Good. Very good. The lad is smart. Adept at listening. Don't find that in many of my pupils. But he's getting too tired too fast. We'll need to work on conditioning as well. We'll get him doing calisthenics and roadwork."

Anders stopped, his face lined with sweat, his black hair moist from effort. "Roadwork?"

"Running, lad. Running. You do a mile or two every day in those big boots of yours, well, in no time, you'll be able to outlast even the randiest young buck in the schoolyard."

Jorma chuckled. "Now who's teaching the boy expressions that his mother would not want repeated at the dinner table?"

Otso Olson smiled. "Let's get into the ring, shall we? I want to see how steady he is on his feet."

It was noon when the boy and his stepfather clambered aboard the family wagon. Jorma held leather reins in his gloved hands and studied the grizzled face of his old friend as Otso stood next to Aake, the stout horse chewing her bit and waiting patiently for a command. The snow had stopped but the sky remained close, the white land merging with low gray clouds to create a seamless monochromatic world interrupted only by the painted buildings of Mieslahti's main street and the dark green of the surrounding forest.

"Next Saturday, my friend," Otso said, his face ruddy from the sauna.

The men and the boy had stripped naked after an hour in the ring and had purged themselves in the swelter of a log sauna building located twenty paces from the back door of the tannery.

Jorma nodded. "Thanks for the steam bath. And thanks for taking the time to teach my son." The farmer nudged the boy.

"Yes, thank you, Mr. Olson," Anders said with childish deference.

The big man smiled, exposing gaps in his teeth where hard luck and hazelnuts had taken their toll. "You did well, lad. But don't go trying to size up that bully just yet. We've got much work to do, and, as I said in the ring, a man needs to be patient, to wait for his moment. Your time will come and when it does, that bastard in the schoolyard won't know what the hell hit him."

"Heehaw," Jorma said, snapping the reins. "See you next Saturday," he said as Aake began pulling the wagon west. Behind them, Otso stood in diffuse light, his right hand waving in the crisp air. "Anders," Jorma whispered as the wheels creaked and bounced over frozen gravel, "best not repeat what you heard today in front of Mother. Agreed?"

There was no response. Exhausted from the workout and the sauna, Anders, his thin frame protected by a winter coat, his hands balled inside woolen mittens knitted by his mother, his head covered by a raggedy blue stocking hat, was snuggled against his stepfather's side, fast asleep and snoring.

CHAPTER FOUR

The Alhomäki family: Jorma, Marjatta, Anders, and Anders's twin half-sisters, Helmi—ebony haired, brown eyed, and of dusky complexion—and Ronja—golden haired, indigo eyed, and milky skinned, were a typical Finnish peasant family living under the rule of the Russian czar. Before Sweden's defeat during the Napoleonic Wars, Finland had been a part of Sweden since the middle of the 13th century. But in contrast to other monarchies, such as Germany and Russia, where peasant farmers worked the land as tenants or serfs under the harsh supervision of rich landlords, in Finland nearly a fifth of all farmers were freeholders—men owning the small plots of land they tilled, planted, and harvested.

Such had not been the case with respect to the land Mikko Salminen toiled upon near Puolanka. He and Marjatta did not own the farm and did not earn wages for their labor; they were tenant farmers plowing, planting, and harvesting crops for an absentee owner. Julius Sternberg, the Swede who had purchased the farm from Mikko's father after a famine in the mid-1800s, allowed the Salminens to use a portion of his land to grow crops and livestock that the tenants could use or sell. It was a subsistence living at best, one destined to keep the family impoverished.

Sternberg had only seen the farm once, the day he signed the purchase agreement, and then, having made a verbal arrangement with Mikko to run the place, the Swede went back to his law practice in Stockholm with full confidence that the farmer would protect his investment.

In contrast, Jorma Alhomäki's land had been passed down from father to eldest son over many generations. Most Finnish farms were transferred in this manner. Familial plots were not sliced into pieces and shared equally by heirs but became the property of the eldest son. Jorma had inherited the family farm—thirty hectares of plowed field and twenty hectares of standing timber outside Oulujärvi—a region featuring difficult soil, long winters, and a short growing season. As a consequence of Finland's unbending inheritance laws, Jorma's younger siblings left the farm when they became of age: three sisters to Oulu, Helsinki, and Vaasa respectively, and Alvar to Viipuri, where Jorma's younger brother was posted as a soldier at an old Swedish fort manned by Finns in the service of the Russian czar.

Three difficult years—years of slight rain, immodest sun, and early frost—plagued the farm as the decade of the 1890s entered its middle years. During this interval, Anders completed his six years of formal education—the standard for Finnish children at the time—becoming fluent in reading and writing the Finnish language, achieving competence in mathematics, and obtaining a basic understanding of Finnish history. Entering his teens, the boy grew taller, developed sinew, and his voice deepened. But although Anders dutifully worked the land with his stepfather and mother, the teenager was not content. He envied the lives of dashing adventurers and gallant soldiers he read about in books, casting a longing eye towards the heroic example of his favorite relative, Uncle Alvar—The Elf Warrior—who, at nearly two meters tall, weighing over a hundred kilograms, and boasting a fiery mane of thinning red hair, did not fit his namesake in any manner but vocation.

Alvar Alhomäki had risen to the rank of *wachtmeister* in the Russian Army and, on his infrequent visits home, struck a dashing figure in his resplendent uniform sitting in the Alhomäki kitchen sipping hot coffee while describing the intrigues of empire.

When Alexander III passed away in 1894 due to kidney disease, the possibility of a violent, more serious conflict in Europe became the topic of familial discussion. Anders sat rapt and in awe as Alvar explained the realities of late-nineteenth-century European politics.

Before Alvar was born, Czar Nicholas I—driven by an insatiable desire for territory—had engaged in a fruitless, expensive, and devastating war in Crimea. Nicholas did not survive his war, perishing in 1855 as the struggle for control of the Crimean Peninsula on the Black Sea between the Russians and the French, English, Turks, and Sardinians went badly for the Empire. Nicholas was succeeded by his son—Alexander II—who sued for peace. By the mid-1890s, the embarrassment of the Crimean War was a distant memory. But innuendo of renewed conflict and the sharpening of international rhetoric caused discomfort amongst the empire's citizenry.

Catastrophic losses such as those experienced by Russia in Crimea were but small, painful steps in Europe's inexorable march towards Armageddon. It was, in the view of most Finns, only a matter of time before the powder keg of petty grievances fueled by dynastic connections blew fragile alliances apart and engulfed Europe in a cataclysmic war.

In addition to international uncertainty, a series of famines in the mid-1800s caused Finns to flee their homeland for the United States and Canada in larger and larger numbers. The 1890s alone witnessed the emigration of nearly 60,000 Finns. This trend accelerated until over 250,000 Finns—ten percent of the Grand Duchy's population—embarked on similar transatlantic passages. The lack of available farmland and good-paying manufacturing jobs; the advent of required military service for adult Finnish men in the czar's army and navy, and a retreat from the reforms put in place by Czar Nicholas II caused the displacement of thousands of Finnish men whose yearnings for better lives were, in time, imitated by Finnish women and children until the exodus reached a crescendo.

Among those who left were Finnish miners working copper deposits in northern Norway. These miners immigrated to North America, drawn by grandiose newspaper ads promising instant wealth from the underground copper mines of Michigan's Upper Peninsula. These Finnmark miners were followed by others: the younger sons of Finnish farmers for whom there were few options given they could not inherit ancestral land; Laestadians seeking freedom to practice their severe brand of Lutheranism; and free thinkers and socialists who had little love for the czar or his mad dashes into war riding upon the flesh and bones of his subjects.

Amidst this tidal wave of leaving, Anders Alhomäki would attempt to stand his ground and remain in Finland. He hoped to one day find glory and honor by serving in the Finnish Army just as his uncle had done. But the young man's *sisu* and loyalty to his birthplace could not overcome his wanderlust.

CHAPTER FIVE

There were Gypsies living near Paltamo. Known as the *Kale* in the Finnish language, this northernmost branch of an ancestrally nomadic people—recognized collectively as the Roma—had been present in Finland since the sixteenth century.

Anneli Balzar, a dark-haired, wide-eyed, compact vision of burgeoning womanhood, one of the eight living children of Amadeus and Fiinu Balzar, did not attend school or church. Being Kale, she was destined to marry young, procreate often, and travel throughout Finland with her husband as he plied whatever skill or craft he'd learned, tending to an ever-enlarging brood of children until age rendered her barren. In her matriarchy, Anneli's standing within her community would ascend; old women's wisdom being the highest form of knowledge available to Gypsy families. Though most Kale women were illiterate, they were venerated as guardians of their race's culture and history as they reached old age.

To Anders, the olive skin, ebony hair, ample chest, wide hips, and deep brown eyes—pools of near black that gleamed whenever Anders caught the girl's gaze—manifested an exotic quality that spoke of mystery and the distant mountains of the Indian subcontinent where the forefathers and foremothers of the Roma once lived. The forbidden aspect of a strait-laced, school-taught, Lutheran-raised Finnish boy carrying a torch for a *Kale* girl elevated Anders's emotional turbulence. In 1890s Paltamo, such longing harbored by a Finnish boy for a Gypsy girl was forbidden. And yet each time Anders passed Anneli, her skirt sashaying as she walked with her father and mother or her younger siblings down the gravel streets of the town to acquire necessities at the Noskinens' general store by trading Amadeus's handcrafted leather goods and *puukkos,* Anders could not help himself.

She is the most beautiful girl I have ever seen, the boy would think, lowering his eyes to avoid the wrath of Anneli's father.

Rumors of blood feuds and criminality abounded concerning the Roma and the boy did not wish to find himself indicted by Amadeus Balzar for some unintended slight or disrespectful gesture that led to the boy's disappearance from the

35

forest outside Paltamo where the Balzars and other Gypsy families camped.

The wandering families came and went from Kainuu in four-wheeled carts pulled by teams of stout horses. The Kale would travel from town to town, from village to village throughout the summer and fall, their encampment near Paltamo being one such temporary stop. As the air chilled and leaves fell, the families would make for the warmer climes of southern Finland to overwinter, staying put long enough to avoid the tumult of spring when the dirt lanes and roads and cart paths of rural Finland were reduced to impassable mud.

And so, out of a sense of respect for the clannish ways of the Kale, and out of fear of reprisal—despite having grown into a wiry, well-muscled young man whose good looks, diligent work ethic, and native intelligence made him an attractive choice, Anders did not act on his feelings for Anneli.

The thought of one of Amadeus Balzar's puukko blades pressed to my throat is enough to make me mind my own business, the boy reminded himself whenever he passed by the demure, though flirtatious, Gypsy girl.

Throughout the years following his beating at the hands of Erno Karppinen, Anders trained under the watchful eye of Otso Olson, until, having learned all that The Bear could teach him, Anders began fighting publicly throughout Kainuu. It was rare for Anders to be knocked to the canvas by an opponent. And he was, through dozens of bouts, never rendered unconscious. Most often, Anders fought adult men of similar size; men whose fighting prowess relied upon a quick rush at a foe followed by a flurry of blows. Anders Ahlomäki took Otso's admonitions to heart: he did not forget the Norwegian's patient approach. Instead, as Otso had taught him in the drafty confines of the old Mieslahti warehouse, Anders concentrated on speed and avoiding an opponents' gloves, using footwork and endurance, coupled with jabs and the occasional stinging blow to the head and gut, to dispatch his enemy. He was a skilled boxer who, time after time, bested brawlers sent into the ring as local favorites.

Venues for these athletic contests were gymnasiums and workers' halls throughout Kainuu, though the most boisterous and rowdy and enthusiastic crowd Anders drew was at a match held outdoors during the Paltamo Midsummer celebration. Contestants fought in a makeshift ring erected in the center of town beneath a sweltering summer sun. It was there that the young boxer battled twenty-four-year-old logger Risto Erkko, besting the welterweight champion of Finland on points despite giving up significant weight to the older man. The victory, though technically an exhibition and not a sanctioned bout, resulted in Anders being proclaimed—at least in Paltamo—as the unofficial welterweight champion of his people.

At the end of his fight with Erkko, Anders noticed the girl. The bruised but triumphant boxer saw the remarkable face of Anneli as she led three of her younger siblings along a wooden sidewalk behind cheering spectators. The girl emerged from the unruly crowd to stand with her kin in the shadow of the town's hardware store where shade provided respite from the heat. Anneli watched the referee raise Anders's right arm in triumph, sweat streaming from the boy's ebony hair onto his face and chest, his right eye blackened and closed from a left hook that Risto landed late in the fight. The boxer, embarrassed by the girl's appearance and reluctant to acknowledge the crowd's admiration, did not smile or wink or nod. He remained stoic despite the Kale girl's unexpected manifestation. But as Anneli scrutinized Anders's disfigured face from across the village square, she concluded that his taciturn aspect was only bravado, an act of indifference meant to conceal the truth: Anders Alhomäki was smitten with her.

CHAPTER SIX

Erno Karppinen's comeuppance did not occur immediately. Though the brutal attack on Anders took place during Anders's fourth year in school, it was not until the younger boy had concluded his sixth year of schooling that he finally made his stand. It happened this way.

It was the summer before Anders became acquainted with Anneli Balzar. School was out. In fact, for Anders and Jari Järvenpää, having reached the age of thirteen and having completed grade six, school was over. This was the summer between being children and becoming men, even though, for both boys, adolescence was slow to make its appearance. When the boys gathered at the Alhomäki farm to collect *matoja* to use as bait, intent on fishing Pynnölänlahti, a bay on Oulujärvi not far from the boys' homesteads, they dreamed of big-bodied *zanders*; frisky and delicious members of the perch family that schooled along the reefs of the big lake where clouds of bait fish sought refuge. They were not thinking of Erno and his band of roving thugs, or that there would be a confrontation between the bully and the fishermen. And yet that is exactly what happened.

"Oh boy!" Anders had exclaimed, holding the two-meter-long *paju* limb he'd fashioned under the tutelage of his stepfather into a fishing pole, the flax line taut and running from the dark waters of the lake to the bending tip of the willow stick, through a series of iron eyelets, before terminating at two wooden pegs affixed to the base of the makeshift rod. Excess line wound around the pegs created a stubborn anchor against the fish; a three-kilo zander that made the mistake of attacking a night crawler impaled on a hook suspended beneath a floating wooden bobber. "She's a beauty!"

Three zander and one *taimen* had been landed by the boys. None of the fish was more than thirty-five centimeters long, but all would eat well when fried in the cast-iron frying pans of the boys' respective log homes. The captured fish swam lazily in the shallow, cold water lapping the stony shoreline of the enormous lake, a rope strung through their gills and tied to a pine tree. There were no limits on fish, no need for the boys to purchase a license; the bounty of the lake was theirs to harvest without restriction. Fish was a staple on the dining tables of Finnish families. The addition of tasty fillets to the repetitive diet of the Finnish common man and woman—the fish covered in white sauce or butter—was a diversion from epicurean boredom that delighted the mothers and wives of the boys and men who contributed fresh fish to the family table.

"Don't lose 'er," Jari chided, his own hook lodged between stones, the snag demanding attention so as not to break the line and lose the one and only steel hook he'd been allowed by his father. "Your mother will want to bake that big one up for Sunday dinner."

Anders waded into the lake, his woolen trousers absorbing the water's chill, his bare toes feeling their way across a carpet of stones. Thigh deep in the lake, Anders stopped to play the big *zander*. "Damn," the boy cursed, holding tight to the willow pole that was bent nearly in half, "she still wants to run."

"Careful! You don't want to break the line."

Anders nodded and returned his attention to the fish, which had switched tactics from running deep and was instead making for a tree hanging over the water. "Oh no, you don't," Anders muttered, moving quickly to turn the fish away from catastrophe.

"She's a monster," Jari said reverently as Anders coaxed the exhausted fish onto gravel.

The fish emerged from the lake thrashing, its red gills opening and closing in desperation.

Anders placed his rod in tall grass at the water's edge and picked up the big fish with both hands. He dislodged the hook from the walleye's boney lip and held it high. "She's a fat one," he agreed as he stepped back, drew the stringer holding the captive fish to him, untied the rope, slid the tip of the makeshift stringer through the zander's gills, before retying the rope to the tree.

As he turned to release the now-secured fish into the water, Anders heard rough talk from behind a thicket separating the lake from an adjacent meadow.

"Shit," Alhomäki whispered, recognizing the loudest, the most obnoxious voice in the approaching group. "It's Erno."

Three boys, all much bigger, rougher looking, and older than Anders and Jari, emerged. Erno Karppinen stood at the top of the bank, his body blocking the rising sun, his hands on his broad hips, his shoulders jutted in defiance, his face ruddy from effort, and—by the smell of booze wafting off the boy—having consumed vodka stolen from his father's stash.

"What do we have here?" the bully said as he picked his way down the hillside, his big boots tripping on stones and rocks with each drunken step.

Anders bit his lip. He recognized the boys accompanying Erno as the bully's cousins. He couldn't remember their names, but he knew they were trouble, just like Erno.

Erno stabbed a dirty paw into the lake and lifted the stringer into the air. "Ah. I see you and the little queer have caught us supper."

Anders squinted. "Put the fish down," he said firmly, balling his fists. *Steady. Remember Otso's lessons. This is the place. This is the time. Breathe. Watch him closely. Do not be afraid.*

"Ha. And just what are you going to do about it?"

As Erno bent to untie the stringer from the tree, Anders dipped his right hand into cold water and secured a plum-sized stone. He raised the rock behind his left ear. "Put the rope down or this rock will meet your skull!" he threatened.

Erno stared indignantly. "Really? You think one rock is all it will take, pussy boy"

Anders threw the rock. But Erno Karppinen, despite the vodka, despite his bulk, was athletic. He anticipated the throw and turned his head. The stone glanced off Erno's skull with little effect except that the bully released the stringer. Anders watched dinner swim towards deeper water, the black and yellow-banded back of the big zander leading the escape. "Get the fish!" Anders yelled.

Jari grabbed the end of the rope before it disappeared.

"I'll deal with you," Erno said through clenched teeth, looking at the shaking, shivering, upset Jari with menace, "once your friend gets what's coming to him."

Erno advanced. His cousins smirked, amused and fully confident that Erno was about to dispatch the smaller boy without compunction. Despite their loyalty to Erno, the cousins didn't encircle Anders. Their inaction made it clear that this was a matter between Erno and Anders: that it was none of their affair. As Erno's boots met water, Anders moved towards shore. Without warning, Erno rushed Anders, hands clenched, head down, like a bull charging a matador.

Anders raised his fists.

"What the hell is this?" Erno stopped short of Anders, his face expressing bewilderment. "You've got to be the stupidest cow in the pasture," the bully chided, balling his fists and raising his hands. "When I'm done with you, Alhomäki, your mother won't recognize you."

Anders said nothing. Erno was impatient. He was drunk, or, at the very least, tipsy. His reflexes were impaired, though, because of his size and hard head, he was still dangerous. Erno launched a left hand destined for Anders's jaw. Anders ducked the blow and landed two quick jabs, striking the stumbling, confused boy in the gut and on his cheek. Neither punch was fatal but, from the amazed look on Erno's face, Anders knew he'd surprised his enemy.

The fight moved to shore. Erno circled menacingly. He threw a right jab that nicked Anders's left ear. Two lefts hit Erno's belly and caused the bigger boy to gasp. Anders didn't put much behind the punches, just enough to buy time. Another haymaker was launched by the bully—a wild and uncoordinated punch that completely missed its target. The effort exposed Erno's face. Anders sent a right and then a hard left, a punch he'd been loading up to deliver, into Erno's face. Blood exploded from Erno's nose.

"Goddamn it, you little shit!"

The bully stumbled forward, intent on tackling Anders so he could use his bulk to pin the smaller boy to the ground, where, Anders knew, he would be beaten to a pulp.

Patience.

A vision of Otso Olson, the big man standing in the middle of the makeshift ring in his gymnasium, the colorful poster of John L. Sullivan and Gentleman Jim Corbett illuminated by sunlight, Anders listening intently as The Bear taught him cunning and strategy, came and went as Anders gauged his enemy. Just when it looked to the cousins and Jari as if Erno had the smaller boy in his grasp, Anders danced away, tagged the bully with a quick right and a beautifully timed left that struck the very point of Erno's jaw. There had been the sound of something cracking, like the noise made when a dog chews bone. Erno's eyes opened. His arms sought to clutch his foe. But Anders moved out of harm's way. As Erno flailed, Anders delivered a swift kick from a hand-me-down boot to Erno's ass that sent the bully sprawling.

"Get the little bastard!" Erno screamed from disgraced repose.

But the cousins had seen enough. "You made your own mess," the eldest cousin said, "and we sure the hell aren't going to clean it up for you." The boy nodded to Anders. "Where'd you learn to fight like that?"

Anders, his breathing labored, his adrenaline up, his heart racing, held his fists at the ready. "In a tannery," he answered flatly.

Both cousins guffawed.

"That's rich," the younger cousin said, "seeing how you certainly *tanned* Erno's hide!"

The older cousin stepped forward. Anders tensed, ready to defend himself. "I'm not gonna fight you, Alhomäki," the boy said in a reassuring tone. "I'm just gonna collect what's left of Erno. Looks like he might need a doctor the way his jaw's off-kilter." The older boy reached down and, with assistance from his younger brother, brought the bully to his feet. Erno started towards Anders but was held back by his cousins.

"Enough, you dumb shit. He hits you again in your jaw and you'll be sipping broth for a year. Fight's over."

Jari remained shin deep in Oulujärvi, holding the stringer, the big zander pulling inexorably towards the depths. Anders lowered his hands. His heart began to calm, and his breathing started to slow as he watched his nemesis retreat.

"That's enough fishing for one day," Anders said as he retrieved his rod and secured the steel hook to an eyelet. "Come on," he added, his voice edged with the lingering excitement of the contest as he picked up Jari's rod. "Let's get these fish home."

CHAPTER SEVEN

As he negotiated adolescence, Anders's desire to secure a future for himself akin to the perceived exotic life enjoyed by his Uncle Alvar increased with the exponential rise of testosterone. *I want,* he thought, based upon his naive understanding of a soldier's life, *to see the world in service of Finland.* Never mind that such positions came with a caveat: that though the unit Alvar served in had once been independent of the whims and caprices of the crown, with the abolishment of the Finnish Army and the incorporation of its soldiers and officers into the Russian military, the czar once again dictated when and where Finnish soldiers and sailors fought and died.

As the son of a peasant farmer, Anders lacked the depth of comprehension needed to make wise and sound decisions regarding his future. Anders realized this limitation such that, even though he wanted to leave the family farm, he stayed with his mother, stepfather, and twin sisters working the land, repairing fences, feeding livestock and the family chickens, mucking Aake's stall and the pig pens, and harvesting the farm's reluctant crops. He got along well with Jorma. There was no quarreling between them. And though Anders did not outwardly display affection for his stepfather—for that was an outpouring of emotion unusual for the boy except with regards to his mother and, on occasion, his little sisters—a bond grew between Anders and Jorma that was more reciprocal and honest than any connection Anders ever had with his own father, Mikko, or his brother, Urho. But still, the draw of the exotic, the call to find purpose, to seek a noble, heart-stopping life as depicted in the books he read beneath the glow of a tallow candle in the loft of the old farmhouse while the rest of his family slumbered, clawed at the boy's psyche, unrelentingly calling upon him to act.

Changes had occurred in the Grand Duchy. In 1898, Czar Nicholas II, mindful of his great grandfather's disastrous handling of the Crimean escapade, charted a revisionary course, a course unpopular in Finland but one designed to unify the Empire and curb Finnish autonomy. To accomplish the goal of re-establishing Finnish subservience, Nicholas sent Nikolai Bobrikoff as

Governor-General of Finland to Helsinki to oversee the contraction of Finnish freedoms. Half a million Finns supporting Finnish political integrity signed a petition against Nicholas's edicts. As protests within the Finnish educational, artistic, and professional communities increased, the czar reorganized the Finnish Army, replacing Finnish commanders with Russian officers. This Russification of the Finnish military also infused existing units—like the one Uncle Alvar served in at Viipuri—with new soldiers procured through conscription. But the Finns did not take the czar's insults to their autonomy lightly: fully half of the Finnish conscripts refused to report. Throughout this turmoil, Wachtmeister Alvar Alhomäki, who had learned to speak and write Swedish and Russian, remained at his post.

On a visit home, after eating a home-cooked meal and while smoking expensive, imported cigars with his brother, Alvar and Jorma and Anders, joined by Marjatta—after the twins were put to bed—sat around the family table, the day's light failing, the weight of gravy and carrots and potatoes and moose roast and lingonberry pudding seducing the participants towards slumber, and engaged in a lively debate about history, the Finns' future as a people, and not incidentally, young Anders's love life.

"You lick the boots of the czar, brother, in a way that I never thought possible," Jorma observed through a cloud of smoke, the pungency of cigars noxious in the close quarters of the Alhomäki ancestral home. "I never thought you'd bow to the likes of Nicholas or Bobrikoff."

The hulking, gregarious soldier, his recently issued Russian uniform freshly pressed, his wachtmeister's stripes displayed prominently on the sleeves, did not reply to his brother's insult except to smile and wink at his nephew.

"Jorma," Marjatta said softly, her eyes fixed, her chin regally poised, "is it wise to denigrate those who hold all the power, to teach our son such disrespect?"

Alvar nodded. "Exactly. My brother's nationalism, something I thought you shared with him, Marjatta, while certainly sincerely held, will only lead to complications for his family." The big man grinned and took a puff from his stogie. "Far better to work inside the system, to curry the favor of those of Finnish blood who one day might lead our people out of bondage than to whine and curse and protest things which we, at present, cannot change."

"And how are you, a soldier in the czar's army, managing to 'work within the system' for change?" Incredulity colored the question. Jorma was skeptical of his younger brother's loyalty to Finland now that Alvar's unit had been incorporated into the Russian Army. Though never a soldier himself, Jorma understood the creed of loyalty and service that military men adhere to and doubted Alvar's independence of thought.

Alvar reached across the table and patted the arm of his nephew. "Tell me about the girls of Oulujärvi, Anders. Are they pretty? Have they blossomed in their years like wild roses in the field? Is there a special girl, someone you fancy, someone you have your eye on?"

The teenager blushed.

"He has his eye on a little Kale princess, but that one, ah," Jorma replied, resting his smoldering cigar on the edge of the table so that the ash would fall to the floor, "she's more trouble than she's worth, I'm afraid."

Anders remained silent as he studied his stockinged feet.

"Hush, now, Jorma. That's mere infatuation, a passing fancy. Anders is a good Lutheran boy. Why, just last year he completed his catechism and was confirmed," Marjatta scolded. "He's not about to wander off into the forest with some illiterate unbeliever. No, no. He's destined for better things in the arms of a sweet, innocent Finnish girl."

The boy's face flamed. "Mother!"

Alvar tilted his head and smiled. "That's alright, Anders. I've heard told that Kale women are passionate lovers, that their desire to please a man is overwhelming."

"Alvar!"

Jorma winked at his brother and shook his head at his wife's upset. "Facts are facts, my dear wife. The women of the caravans are known to bed down with anyone, even broken down wachtmeisters in the czar's army whose heads are filled with nothing but Russian straw."

"You two are incorrigible," Marjatta spewed, standing up from the table and picking up her empty coffee cup and saucer. "Talking such dirt in my home!"

Alvar's tone turned apologetic. "I'm sorry for asking the question, dear sister-in-law. It was very impolite of me to query Anders about his intentions. Let's get back to politics ..."

"I'm going to bed," Marjatta muttered, placing her dirty dishes next to the porcelain sink, a pail of cold well water standing on the counter ready for warming on the wood cookstove. "Anders: make sure you wash and dry the dishes before you climb into the loft. And don't stay up too late reading those books your uncle has provided ..." Her voice trailed off as she opened the pine door leading to the home's only bedroom and disappeared.

"She's a keeper," Alvar noted wistfully. "The sort of wife I've never been able to find."

Jorma nodded, placed his cup back in its saucer, and returned to puffing his cigar. "That she is. Best woman I've had the pleasure to meet. That's why I married her; that, and the fact she had one of the smartest sons I've ever encountered." The farmer reached across the table and mussed his stepson's dark hair. "And he just so happens to also be one hell of a boxer. Isn't that right, Anders?"

Anders smiled. "I was hoping we'd get back to hearing about Uncle's views on the czar's attempts to make Finns into Russians."

A frown crept over Alvar's face. "Careful, boy. The walls have ears."

Jorma chuckled. "I thought you said you wanted to talk politics!"

Alvar nodded. "Within the bounds of propriety, brother. With care and deference to the fact that, at least for the foreseeable future, Finland is tied to the Empire and must, unless and until something catastrophic occurs, accede to the wishes of Czar Nicholas." The soldier paused. "He is, after all, my commander in chief, the man who makes the decision if and when I must go to war."

"Uncle, have you met anyone of importance while serving in Viipuri?" Anders asked, breaking the tension between the brothers.

"Indeed, I have. There's this one officer, a *poruchik* in the Chevalier Guards: Mannerheim is his name. A Swede-Finn who speaks fluent Russian and Swedish but not a lick of Finnish.

A big, strapping fellow in charge of the Tsar's stable. Came to Viipuri looking for horses."

Jorma guffawed. "A poruchik? Hardly a person of importance."

Alvar shook his head and, having reached the end of his cigar, stubbed the butt out on the china saucer holding his cup of lukewarm coffee. "Ah, but he is much more than an officer in the czar's elite guard. He's married to a Russian-Serbian aristocrat and comes from Swedish aristocracy himself. But truth be told, though publicly he says all the right things—supporting the policies of Nicholas and Bobrikoff—in private, despite his societal status and Swedish roots, he's a loyal Finn. One hundred percent."

Jorma's eyebrows rose. "He talks of these things with you, a wachtmeister at Viipuri whom he does not know from a stray lamb wandering down the lane?"

Alvar touched his right index finger to his left ear. "No. But these big ears hear things meant to remain private. I heard him talking to my captain—Veksa Mikkeli. The poruchik is concerned, very concerned, about the constriction of Finnish rights, about the course our czar is charting."

"Don't call him 'our czar,'" Jorma Alhomäki scolded, shaking his head. "You may claim him; I do not."

"Fair enough. Anyway, Mannerheim is, in my estimation, a man to watch. I had one brief conversation with him when he stopped to admire Gauri, my horse, and wanted to purchase him. We spoke Swedish, of course. I told him, 'No, my horse is not for sale, not even to the czar,' which he accepted as the end of the matter. But we also talked briefly about the coming storm, how Japan is rattling its envious saber on our eastern border, and about the likelihood of war. He revealed no details concerning the actual status of these things, at least not to a lowly wachtmeister! But I sensed intelligence and contemplation in the man, the sort of seriousness that one desires in a leader. I'd keep an eye on Carl Mannerheim, if I were you. He's destined to be a force in Finland."

"Bah," Jorma said. "Hogwash. He's a Swede dressed up in a Russian uniform. Likely only in it for himself—like all the fancy men are. Ander: don't listen to your uncle's bullshit. It's as deep as Aake's leavings in the barn!"

Anders snorted as he tried to forestall a laugh.

"Something funny, Kale lover?" Alvar chided with a smile. "Let's get back to talking about women."

The boy retrieved his cup and saucer, stood up from the table, and carried his dishes to the sink. "I'm tired," the boy said, leaving the dirty dishes on the counter, ignoring his mother's instructions. "It's time for bed."

CHAPTER EIGHT: Before (Vilpusjärvi, Finland)

November 1888. Mikko Salminen and his eldest son, Urho, are fishing a reef, pulling nets filled to the brim with *Corgegonus lavaretus nilssoni*—lake whitefish, a silvery, succulent, and easily smoked member of the *salmonidae* family. They are standing in an open boat, balanced on the pine ribs of a leaky pram, the craft a mere three meters in length, Mikko at the stern, Urho in the bow, the two of them slowly raising a net from the shallows near Säikänsaaret, an island located just off Härkinniemi, a wide, fat peninsula along the south shore of Vilpusjärvi only a few kilometers from the Salminen farm. Marjatta and Anders are at home digging rutabagas. A near-winter wind descends as Urho and his father retrieve their catch—dozens of spawning fish, nearly all identical in size—from the lake's rocky bottom.

"Lift, you lazy little shit!" Mikko shouts, gusts stirring the black waters of Vilpusjärvi into a frenzy that batters the little boat. "There's a storm coming, and we need to make Talvilahti Landing before it hits!"

Urho looks west. Forbidding clouds sweep across the forests and fields of Kainuu. The boy's distressed and multi-patched woolen coat is buttoned up against the weather. His hands are bleeding from hauling in flax line made heavy by birch floats, lead weights, netting, and abundant fish. Urho Salminen glances at his father as they strain. The boy's left eye is swollen and blackened from a blow delivered by his father for sneaking a sip of the old man's vodka from a bottle hidden in the family barn. The son's surreptitious gaze takes in the besotted eyes of his unrepentant father.

How in God's name did Mother ever end up with this asshole? the boy thinks, drawing upon a vocabulary he'd been taught by his father. *I'd love to pull up the anchor, tie it around the old man, and toss him over the side. That would solve a lot of problems for me, Mother, and that piss ant brother of mine.* But Urho knows his father's strength, knows that there is no way that, at ten years old, he can take on the old man. The boy doesn't reply to Mikko's admonition. Urho simply does what he always does: he holds his tongue, works harder, and bides his time. *One*

49

day, the boy thinks, *one day when he least expects it, it will all come to an end.*

As father and son drag the flopping, dripping, silvery mess of whitefish over the gunwale of the boat, a bolt of lightning, followed by a crack of thunder, slashes and echoes from above. Thunderheads—low, dark, and ominous—race across the lake. The pram remains fixed in place, its anchor holding despite the increasing waves, as the last of the catch slides into the bottom of the pitching boat.

"Now that's what I call fishing!" the old man squeals in delight, reaching out and slapping his eldest son on the back. Mikko slips a calloused right hand between the buttons of his foul-weather coat, the waxed canvas impervious to rain, pulls out a flask, the tin canister dented from hard use, pulls the cork, and drinks lustily. "You want a snort?" Mikko asks, extending the container in his trembling right hand. "Vodka's good for young boys. It'll grow hair on those pimples between your legs you call balls."

Urho shakes his head. Swells heighten. Heavy rain falls. The boy pulls on the anchor rope with chafed hands. "It won't budge," he says, straining hard to dislodge the anchor. Weeping sky merges with boiling lake, causing the ghostly silhouette of the adjacent island to disappear. Mikko stands up and takes a step towards his son. A rogue wave hits the pram, showering the fishermen with lake water. "Goddamn it boy, pull in that anchor or this piece of shit will flounder!" Mikko Salminen screams, dropping his precious flask onto the undulating mass of whitefish in the bottom of the boat.

Another wave hits the aft of the boat. Urho struggles with the anchor until it breaks free. "It's off!" the boy yells, glancing over his shoulder towards Mikko. But the old man is gone. "Father!" Urho cries out, standing in the boat to search the tumultuous lake. *Nothing.* There is no trace of the drunken farmer. Urho feels panic well inside his young heart but despite his fear, draws upon experience to consider his options. The boat is only seventy-five meters from the island, a short distance to row. Urho Salminen has little time to decide his course of action. *If I turn the pram around to search for Father, I'll capsize. Better to row for the island. With any luck, the waves will carry Father to land.*

Urho steadies himself on the boat's gunwales as he seeks the middle seat of the boat, where oars and oarlocks await. The boy leans forward. He plants his boots against the ribs of the boat's hull, intending to slide onto the seat, grasp the oars, pivot the pram, and row like hell for the island, but another wave slams into the boat before Urho can act.

The bodies are recovered, prepared, and posed for viewing at the front of the Puolangan Kirkko. Marjatta's family—the Komulainens—comprises most of the mourners in attendance. Anders is six years old. He cries for his brother and his father despite the fact that neither one had been kind to him. But the simple caskets—the pine lumber freshly sawed and unstained—do not, as one would expect, frighten the child. The stiff, unnatural bodies of the deceased—dressed in the best clothes Marjatta could find in the impoverished farmhouse that her father-in-law had lost to the wealthy Swede—do not trouble Anders as he wipes tears and steals himself against sadness. The holy man expresses a faith in the Almighty that is far beyond a child's ken while elegizing Mikko Nante Salminen as a loving father and husband, convincingly rehabilitating the drunk into a sober, industrious laborer for the Lord.

Lies, the little boy thinks sitting beside his mother. He glances at his mother's face. It strikes his young mind as odd that Marjatta appears to accept the pastor's falsehoods. *Pastor's telling lies in church!*

The service includes the Eucharist. The child, not yet old enough to receive the consecrated bread and wine, stands next to his mother, who, for whatever reason, has lost her calm and begins, as Pastor Torvinen hands her bread to dip in the chalice of red wine held by a sullen acolyte, to cry. Anders's attention isn't focused on his mother but on Pastor Torvinen. The boy studies the reverend's movements and decides there's a bit of chicanery, some sleight of hand being exhibited in the drafty confines of the old church.

If God is so great, the boy muses as he watches his mother weep, tremble, nod, receive the host, dip it in wine, and then move off, her hand sweaty and tight in his as she leads him back to their pew, *why did he take Urho?*

51

Sitting in the front row, watching others receive communion, Anders's musings continue. *Father was mean. God needed to punish him. Urho was mean too, but he was only ten. He could've changed. Mother would've seen to that. But he's dead, lying up there in that wooden box, just like Father. I don't understand why God took Urho too.*

After the prayers for the dead and the committal are said and the mourners join in singing a familiar hymn, the caskets are closed and the pallbearers, men from the Komulainen family—Mikko having no friends or male relatives interested in escorting him to his final place of rest—do their duty and haul the bodies away, the caskets adorned with fir branches, the pallbearers wearing white gloves out of respect for the dead. Anders and his mother follow Pastor Torvinen and the coffins out of the church, across the lawn, and into an adjacent graveyard where the mourners stand silent, waiting for more inconsequential words from the preacher, a graceful blanket of snow beginning to fall upon Kainuu.

CHAPTER NINE: Autumn 1900 (Paltamo, Finland)

She's vibrant, exciting, and untouchable. That was Anders's assessment, his predicament, as he watched Anneli Balzar lift the hem of her skirt, exposing her ankles, legs, and knees to wade the cold waters of the Kiehimänjoki, the river flowing between Liljärvi and Oulujärvi north of Paltamo. Anders sat thirty meters from the girl on the east bank of the slow-moving river where the Kiehimänjoki empties the Ruutinlampi—a widening in the river created by a crude earthen dam—his stepfather's sixteen-gauge shotgun resting across his knees, studying the girl as she moved gracefully in the shallows.

It was the autumn of Anders's seventeenth year. The new millennium had arrived. The birches and willows and aspens abutting the river were in full color. The sun stood high and golden above the idyllic scene as the boy drew a piece of cheese and a chunk of smoked salmon from a pocket of his jacket. Anneli had not yet discovered his presence. The boy watched the girl dance and dip and curtsy—as if she was an actress in an imaginary play—as he pulled a tin of water from another pocket in his stepfather's hunting jacket, removed the cork, and gulped. He would replace the water in the tin with water from the river before leaving the Kiehimänjoki. He would find a gurgling section of the river near the village of Alia—where his stepfather would be waiting for him at dusk with Aake and the wagon after delivering hay to a distant neighbor—from which to refill the tin. Alia was located on the opposite riverbank. Anders would follow the eastern bank of the wide river, cross the rudimentary dam at the south end of Ruutinlampi, follow the Kiehimänjoki upstream, and meet up with his stepfather to catch a lift in the family wagon.

As he watched the beautiful girl move animatedly and uninhibitedly, Anders felt the weight of two mallards in the jacket's game pouch and smiled. *Two shots. Two greenheads.*

The boy re-corked the tin and swallowed the last of the salmon before emerging from concealment. Anders's sudden appearance startled the girl despite the expanse of river between them.

"Oh! Alhomäki! I didn't see you hiding there!" Anneli shouted, drawing back from the water's edge at the boy's manifestation and lowering her petticoat in modesty.

Anders cradled the shotgun. "Didn't mean to scare you. Just taking a break from hunting!" he yelled. Without prompting, he placed the shotgun on dry ground and pulled the ducks from the game pouch and held them high in the air by their necks for the girl to see.

"What sort of birds are they?" she asked.

"How's that? I didn't hear that last part?"

"THE BIRDS. WHAT SORT OF BIRDS ARE THEY?" she yelled.

"Ducks! Two big, fat, grain fed mallards!"

The girl tucked her hands beneath the armpits of her sweater, uncomfortable that the boy had been watching her without disclosure. "For supper?" she asked, trying to maintain a tone that didn't reveal her true feelings. *He shouldn't be sneaking up and startling girls,* she thought. *But he is, despite being slight of build and not much taller than me, very handsome. Stop that,* she admonished. *Father would take a switch to me if he knew what I was thinking.* "For tonight's dinner?"

Anders shook his head. "No. Mother will likely save them for Sunday." He returned the ducks to the game pouch, cradled the shotgun, and studied the girl. *Those brown eyes are remarkable even from across the Kiehimänjoki! And that figure, her bosom, her legs, her shape. My God, I've never seen such a girl other than on the pages of a magazine.*

"Well," Anneli finally said, casting furtive glances into the forest, "I best be going. Father and mother will wonder what's become of me. There's work to be done before leaving for Turku."

"Turku?"

She nodded. "That's where we're wintering. Father has work in a leather goods shop until spring. Through a friend of a friend—that sort of thing. We leave for Turku on Monday."

A lump formed in Anders's throat as he watched Anneli turn to climb the gentle slope behind her. *You may never see her again,* the boy thought. *Ask her before it's too late.* "WOULD YOU LIKE TO GO ON A PICNIC WITH ME BEFORE

YOU LEAVE?" he shouted, blurting out the words in a confused flurry.

Anneli stopped, turned towards the river, and studied the boy on the far bank of the Kiehimänjoki. Her natural inclination, as instilled in her by a strict and clannish culture—reinforced over the years by parental corporal punishment—was to decline the boy's invitation. But there was so much emotion, so much hormonal anxiety and uncertainty churning inside the young woman, she hesitated.

A picnic is harmless, she thought. *Mother and Father don't need to know. I can find a few hours of time—say that I am going to town to buy some things for our journey—to meet this boy. I haven't spoken with someone my own age for so long; to do so would be a comfort and a joy. Yes, that is something that I can do, that I* <u>must</u> *do, for myself.* "When?"

A lump formed in Anders's throat. Anxiety was replaced by an overwhelming feeling of joy followed by an adrenaline surge that nearly buckled his knees. "How about this Saturday? I'd say 'Sunday,' but it's our turn to host Pastor for dinner."

"What time?"

"Eleven?"

"That's fine. Where?"

The boy considered the situation more fully. "Will this cause problems with your parents?"

Anneli smiled, exposing clean, white teeth not visible to her suitor. "Yes. But let me worry about them. Where shall we have this picnic?"

"The park in town? It's after season and it should be empty."

She nodded, and, believing he could not see her acceptance, yelled out, "THAT'S FINE. ARE YOU MAKING LUNCH?"

The boy replied boisterously, "YES! I CAN DO THAT!"

"Good. My parents might ask questions, questions that I don't really want to answer, if I start making lunch for two. I'm not a big eater so such actions would lead to a conversation that I don't really want to have!"

The boy waved. The girl turned away. "Eleven on Saturday. In the park. I'll bring food and drink!" Anders confirmed. There was no reply. Elation nearly toppled Anders

Alhomäki into the brumal, slowly churning waters of the river as Anneli Balzar disappeared.

CHAPTER TEN

"We could write each other, continue our friendship through letters," Anneli suggested as they sat beneath a leafless birch tree, the grass of the park's lawn brown from drought.

Anders's left hand firmly—yet tenderly—embraced the girl's delicate right hand as they sat on a blue blanket, the crumbly remains of lunch scattered across wool, and looked into the atramentous eyes of the girl. *She is more striking than I imagined*, Anders thought, evaluating the fullness of Anneli's mouth, her caramelized face, and her subtle, less-than-angular cheekbones as he pondered a reply. "I thought Kale children didn't attend school. How is it you know how to read and write?"

The girl smiled, exposing the small, blazingly white teeth Anders had been unable to see from across the Kiehimänjoki. "Mother. Despite Father's tribal ways, Mother's a bit of a modern woman. Mind you, she doesn't parade her beliefs around. But she's made certain that all her children know how to read and write Finnish and, at least with us older ones, comprehend a bit of Russian as well."

Anders considered the girl's revelation. "So, your father ..."

"Didn't have a clue. Mother is very good, as most Kale women are, at keeping secrets." The girl nodded as she gathered her thoughts. "He knows now, knows that all of us are able to read and write," Anneli added wryly. "But it's too late. The genie, as they say, is out of the bottle." She paused and looked away from the boy before continuing. "Could we write to each other?"

Anders was nervous being so close to, being so connected with, beauty. He did not immediately answer.

"My, you certainly are talkative," the girl teased, pecking him on the cheek.

As Anneli's lips brushed his skin, Anders's face flushed. *She kissed me! The most wondrous girl in all of Kainuu kissed me!*

"I have your parents' address. I'll send you a letter when we get to Turku," Anneli whispered. "I'll include the address of my mother's sister, Pritta Paasikivi, so you can respond. She lives in Turku, near where we'll be staying. She's very much like Mother: she can keep secrets too!"

Anders remained tongue-tied.

"You are such an engaging conversationalist," the girl teased, her grin slowly turning into a frown. "Is something wrong?"

Instinctively, Anneli believed that her demonstration of affection, as innocent as it was, might have been too personal, too intimate, for the circumstances. But she was too unschooled in the ways of men and women to give voice to her suspicion. She was also, true to her role as the eldest daughter of Amadeus and Fiinu Balzar, a virgin at eighteen despite the fact that she was past the age when most of her contemporaries married. Anneli knew, through conversations with her mother and other girls, the basics of coupling and child making. She had long ago passed into womanhood. She was shy about such topics and unwilling to break the bonds of propriety with a boy she was seeing for the very first time. But she did so much desire intellectual stimulation and conversation with a young man of her own age, something that the recalcitrant Finn seemed impossible of accommodating.

He looked away, released the girl's hand, and pointed to a place of transition, where the park's yellow lawn gave way to green, piney forest. "Look," Anders said, attempting to divert Anneli's attention from more weighty topics, "a bear!"

Though common in eastern Finland, brown bears were infrequent visitors to Kainuu. Seeing the lumbering, cinnamon-colored omnivore skirting dense foliage, its snout elevated to detect scent, alarmed Anneli. Panic caused the girl to wrap her arms around Anders, constricting his diaphragm, making it difficult for him to breathe.

"Don't worry," Anders whispered. "She knows we're here and she's not the least bit interested in us. She's looking for her next meal; a yearling roe deer or a young moose—something to tide her over until spring."

Anneli's eyes widened. There was fear, distinct and unnatural etched on her face. "Are you sure?"

He nodded. "See?" Anders replied as the big sow waddled off. "She smelled us, took a look, found we weren't interesting, and went back to hunting."

Despite the bear's absence, Anneli did not release her embrace. They sat on the blanket, their hearts racing from the bruin's apparition and from hormonal plateaus they dared not act upon, as a breeze stirred.

When her fear abated, Anneli removed herself from the embrace, stood up, smoothed her red, yellow, and white skirt, adjusted her yellow wool sweater and the red cap atop her thick, inky hair, and smiled. "I think my parents will be wondering what happened to me," she said casually, as if nothing had occurred. "I'd best get back. I still have packing to do."

"I'll walk you to the trailhead," Anders offered, standing up and adjusting his own rumpled fedora before brazenly tucking an errant strand of Anneli's luxuriant hair behind her left ear.

Though unnerved by the familiarity of the gesture, the girl did not protest but stood quietly, allowing him his moment, all the while staring at the opening in the forest that had swallowed the bear. Anneli's inclination was to refuse Anders's assistance, to simply let things stand as they were: she'd kissed him, she'd embraced him, and was now safe from the clutches of the bear. Rationally, there was no reason for Anders to walk with her. And yet, the image of the animal, its big head swaying menacingly from side to side as it searched for its next meal, was frozen in Anneli Balzar's mind.

"That would be lovely," she said, trying hard to suppress her anxiety, desperate to sound grown up and brave in the face of irrational fear.

Anders placed empty jars that once contained preserved fruits and tepid coffee, wadded up pages from *Päivälehti* used to wrap the pork and cheese sandwiches they'd enjoyed, and tin cups into a wicker picnic basket. They folded the blanket until it was small enough to fit inside the basket. Their hands touched unintentionally—an intimacy that was electric and overwhelming. Constrained by the mores of the day, they did not act upon their subconscious desires beyond Anders kissing Anneli as a brother might kiss his sister. The boy's lips brushed the girl's forehead, briefly wetting wrinkles caused by an unrehearsed frown. But Anneli's reaction did not express upset; she wasn't offended, though she was surprised by Anders's sudden boldness. Instead of protesting, Anneli closed her eyes. Once the boy's lips vacated her skin, her eyes opened to reveal expectant, unending pools of shimmering ebony. A sedate smile spread across her face.

Anneli's reaction left Anders with the impression that her feelings for him were encapsulated in a single, glorious word: *someday.*

CHAPTER ELEVEN: April 1901(Oulu, Finland)

"He's an experienced fighter, lad," Otso Olson said, eyeing an older, taller, muscular man climbing into the ring. "Watch out for his combination; he throws a wicked left jab, a short right—not a big, sloppy roundhouse like some of those rubes you're used to mixing it up in Kainuu—before coming back with another left loaded up like Ilmarinen's hammer. He's like a coiled spring, this one is. You've not been up against the likes of him."

The opposing boxer claimed a stool in the far corner of the ring and stared, his murky blue eyes seemingly vacant and unwavering, at Anders. Anders sat on a four-legged wooden stool inside the ropes. Otso stood behind Anders, his powerful hands rubbing the boy's shoulders, trying to exorcise pre-fight tension from the boxer's joints. Anders diverted his eyes, unwilling to engage in a stare-down with his opponent, a man who, at twenty-five and zero, had never been beaten in a professional fight. Anders had lost three bouts fighting in and around Paltamo. This was to be his first sanctioned match against a seasoned fighter. The test was certain, immediate, and as Anders considered the laces of his new, black leather boxing shoes—shoes that Otso had purchased, shoes that complimented the satin boxing drawers and jersey, the name "Alhomäki" stitched carefully across the back of the tunic by his mother—was about to become very real. He sought to avoid his enemy's gaze but found it impossible not to fix his eyes on the prominent jaw, rabid eyes, and shaved head of the lightweight champion of Ostrobothnia. Later—when their gloves touched in the center of the ring after Anders and the older, more experienced man were summoned to parlay with the ring official— Anders would become intimately acquainted with Pekka Pakkanen. But from a distance, the boy knew the man's reputation and, try as he might, Anders was unable to dispel the gloomy feeling occupying the pit of his stomach.

Things had not gone well between Anders and the Kale girl. The spring following their clandestine, long-distance courtship, Anneli Balzar, her siblings, her parents, and three other Gypsy families set out by wagon for Kajaani with the intention of spending summer near Oulujärvi. But in the process of the caravan's slow, northward journey from Turku to Kainuu, something occurred that destroyed any possibility of a meaningful relationship between the girl and the boxer.

Somewhere outside Lapinlahti, on the road to Kajaani, Amadeus Balzar got wind of the letters his eldest child had received over the course of the winter through Fiinu's sister, Pritta Paasikivi. While Anneli had exercised discretion in corresponding with Anders through her maternal aunt, collecting his letters and secreting them in a dark and distant corner of the family's rolling home amongst her personal things, Lali—Anneli's ten-year-old sister—had watched the older girl's cautionary movements with suspicion: mistrust allowed curiosity to get the better of her, which culminated in Lali reading Alhomäki's passionate and indiscrete revelations. It wasn't as if Lali read Anders's love letters aloud or, after reading them, ran tattling to their father to reveal the simmering affair. It was simply an unfortunate accident that, while rummaging through her sister's personal belongings to replace a letter she'd perused, Lali was interrupted by her father with a stout, "Child, what do you think you're doing, going through your sister's things?" which caused the girl to drop the envelope and enclosed letter at her Amadeus's feet, her charcoal eyes wide, her heart beating in fear of what might come next.

"Nothing, Father."

Amadeus had studied the carefully addressed envelope resting on the planked floor of the family wagon, sunlight creeping into the space from an open door leading to stairs at the rear of the narrow chamber. "Nothing? This certainly looks like something to me, young lady," the family patriarch said as he bent at the waist to retrieve the purloined letter. Amadeus opened the envelope and removed two pieces of crisp, linen paper covered in fine script.

My Dearest Anneli ...

Amadeus found his oldest daughter outside the wagon, hanging laundry on a clothesline running between two birch trees. A faint, southernly breeze stirred damp shirts, breeches, blouses, skirts, dresses, stockings, and undergarments. The girl shuffled along dewy grass, dragging a heavy basket of wet clothes behind her, stopping to remove items from the hamper and pin them to the line with wooden clothespins before moving forward.

"What the hell are these?" Amadeus barked at Anneli, the tone of her father's voice so severe, the young woman snapped to attention like a soldier. Amadeus held a small leather satchel, a purse that he'd made for her, stuffed to the brim with love letters, in his thick hands as he addressed his eldest child. "What the hell have you been doing behind my back?"

The girl trembled.

"I asked you a question. I expect an honest answer."

Anneli cast her dark eyes to her shoes, the black leather caked with dust. "It was harmless. Just notes from a boy ..."

Amadeus dropped the satchel, reached out, and slapped his daughter. The blow opened her lower lip. Blood oozed onto Anneli's chin and dripped onto the clean, white linen of her blouse. The girl raised her hands to defend against another slap from her father's huge, calloused, right hand. But a second blow never came.

"You and Mother will write to this ..." the father hesitated, considering whether to add a viperous adjective, "... this Finnish boy you've apparently acquainted yourself with in ways that are shameful, intimate, and unacceptable. You will tell him in no uncertain terms that any further letters will be returned and, if he does not cease his pursuit of you, I will find him and make him stop this nonsense."

Anneli grinned, a gesture at odds with the fear she'd displayed immediately after being slapped. "I'd like to see you try to make Anders Alhomäki do anything he doesn't want to do!"

Amadeus's eyebrows narrowed. His face reddened. "How dare you speak to your father as an equal!" The man raised his right hand again but before he could bring it to bear on his daughter's cheek, his arm was arrested.

"Enough, Amadeus," Fiinu said in a quiet, even voice, her left hand holding her husband's wrist in a vice-like grip. "No more hitting. She is a young woman, not some little girl you can take across your knee. That is in the past. We will write the letter as you ask and put an end to it. There is no need to strike her again."

Amadeus did not immediately accede to his wife's command. *I am the man of this family,* he thought. *And now I have two women telling me how things should be. First, my eldest, a girl who should be married and having babies sneaks around behind my back with some ordinary Finn of low morals and little*

63

means. Then my wife, in front of that very daughter, rebukes me.
Amadeus looked into his wife's eyes. *But she is serious. And the
commotion has brought some of the little ones to see what's the
matter. I don't want to start an argument with Fiinu in front of the
children. Better to lower my hand and let her deal with the
situation.*

Amadeus nodded. His wife released his wrist and scowled
at their daughter.

"Come with me!" Fiinu barked. "We will write a letter to
this Alhomäki character together. But it will be the last letter you
send to him. Do you understand?"

Anneli's eyes welled. "But I love him."

"Bah!" her mother said derisively. "You're eighteen years
old. You know nothing of men and women or love. Come, we will
talk about these things, have a cup of tea, and write the letter.
Then we will discuss which of the many young Kale men you are
acquainted with might be a suitable match for you. It is past the
time you married and gave us grandchildren!"

The girl did not reply. She knew she was defeated, that
the dream she'd cultured and nurtured of leaving her meandering
life, settling down with Anders to birth little Finn-Kale babies, and
living a life of domestic normalcy was over.

When the letter came, Anders expected that it would announce
news of Anneli's imminent return to Paltamo, where the two
young people would rekindle their relationship. The handwriting
appeared to be that of his confidante but the message inside the
envelope was foreign. The words were all there, in proper order,
creating cogent sentences and paragraphs. And yet, Anders
deduced, as he read Anneli's dismissal of their love, that the hand
of another, perhaps Amadeus, perhaps Fiinu, had guided the pen.
He was warned, in the plainest of terms, not to attempt
reconciliation. Consequently, he tried to forget her. And yet,
images of them in the park, eating and drinking and laughing and
holding hands and, for a brief interlude, becoming intimate
through the tenderness of an innocent kiss, would not dissipate.
But there was nothing to be done about it: Anders knew that the
girl's father would not tolerate a Finn boy suddenly showing up in
camp, professing love. Razor-sharp Swedish blades secured to
hand-carved hilts of bone and wood by craftsmen such as

Amadeus Balzar—*puukkos* Anders and every other Finn salivated after when spread out for sale on felt tablecloths in Finnish marketplaces—could disembowel a man. *I must move on,* Anders finally admitted with reluctance. *It is simply not to be.*

Bronze skin. Long tresses of ebony held in place by colorful ribbons. A round, pleasing face with generous red lips. Sculpted calves and demure ankles ...

"Alhomäki, where the hell are you?"

The Bear's deep, resonant voice called the boxer back to his predicament.

"It's time to fight."

Anders looked up at Otso and nodded.

"Keep away from his combination. Use your speed to stay out of reach. He has you by ten centimeters. That's an advantage you can't let him utilize, understand?"

Anders stood up, smoothed his trunks with his gloves, and stared across the ring. Several hundred patrons stood around the gymnasium, a space that had once been a warehouse for storing barrels of pine tar destined for export.

For centuries, Finland's greatest contribution to the world's economy had been pine tar, a product cherished by great powers as waterproofing for the hulls of wooden sailing ships. But when steam replaced wind as a means of powering ships, as steel supplanted wood in shipbuilding, the world's hunger for Ostrobothnia tar declined, and, by the mid-1800s, disappeared. The end of the tar trade saw thousands of so-called "tar Finns"— men who turned pine sap into tar through a labor-intensive process involving burning pits and charcoal—out of work and clamoring to emigrate. The tar warehouses of Oulu, such as the one hosting the boxing match, soon emptied.

The majority of the lower-class women in attendance—likely ladies of the evening since few respectable wives or girlfriends would attend such an event—stood near men in workingmen's clothes;. However, there were also—in contradictory fashion—a handful of elegantly dressed ladies escorted by dapper gentlemen in expensive business suits, the men's hair slicked with tonic, the women sporting the latest fashions from Paris or Rome, their hair

65

fixed in the newest styles. These were the aristocrats, the Swede-Finns, folks who controlled the city and its commerce at the expense of the rougher, less polished Finnish speakers. But Anders did not differentiate or identify such cultural stratification as he stared blankly into the crowd as his mind had wandered again.

Too bad Uncle Alvar couldn't be here. He'd planned to ask for leave. Said so last winter when he was home for Christmas. This fight was arranged by Otso as my big break. If I win, if I beat Pekka Pakkanen, or simply go the distance, I'll be set. We'll likely meet again and fight for the title somewhere down the line. Though Uncle said he wouldn't miss it for the world, Jorma wouldn't hear of it. He said, "I got you boxing lessons with The Bear so you could defend yourself, not get yourself beat to a pulp by real fighters. I'll not encourage this bullshit!" And Mother, despite stitching my name on my tunic, was of similar accord. "I can't stand thinking of what might happen to that beautiful smile, those straight, white teeth, that angelic face." My parents are not here, and I think that with my stepfather, there is something more to the story. I am fairly certain he sees this as my stepping away from the farm, as a continuation of my emancipation from servitude to the land. The lot of a Finnish farmer is all work and sweat and uncertainty. There is little leisure or relaxation or enjoyment of life, beyond occasional afternoons spent fishing or hunting or Sundays occupied by the consideration of God, to the lot in life Jorma and his ilk have drawn. I'll not have it. I want adventure, to see the world, to have money in my pocket, to be, as Jorma pejoratively says, "a big man." If I win this fight or make it to the final bell, I will become what I have been dreaming about for years. It's too bad Alvar can't be here to see this. He's been sent to Manchuria—as a translator—because he's fluent in Russian. I wish Uncle Alvar a safe return. Enough! I best get my wits about me and concentrate on this fight.

The bell sounded. The debate inside Anders's head subsided; visions of grandeur were replaced by a steely determination to win. Anders strode towards the center of the ring, mindful of Otso Olson's admonition: "Use your legs, your endurance. Stay away from his combination. Many have tried to Pekka Pakkanen. All have failed. He has experience and strength and reach on his side. You have only *sisu* and youth. Use them to your advantage and you will do well."

Anders nodded at the clarity of The Bear's advice, tucked his chin into his chest, and raised his gloves.

CHAPTER TWELVE

Walking along a wharf in Oulu inside a warm spring rain Anders felt a pain deep in his gut. "I think I'm going to be sick," he moaned, stopping dead in his tracks, doubling over and vomiting onto the pine planks of the dock.

"Is that blood?" Otso held his young protégé around the shoulders, keeping the boxer on his feet as the contents of Anders's stomach splatted the pier. "I thought you told me you were alright!"

Anders's only response was another convulsion. Morning porridge sprinkled with specks of red was expelled onto the wood planking. When the spasm ended, Anders stood up, his balance precarious, his mind woozy, and shook his head. "I thought I was. That bastard hit me pretty hard on the noggin a few times, especially in the eighth, when I went out cold." Anders wiped spittle from his mouth, his breath foul and sour from vomit, as he tried to stop the pier from shifting beneath his feet.

"I told you to keep moving, to use your speed. But no, you had to get into it with that maniac. He was too savvy, had too much experience for your skills. I shouldn't have pushed this fight," The Bear admitted. "Maybe in a year, you would've been ready, you would've had enough patience and maturity to listen to your teacher."

Anders tried to reply but found that the nausea had returned. Another spasm buckled the boy, but as he strained and strained and strained to release the contents of his stomach, only a thimbleful of bile dribbled from his mouth. The rain intensified. Gray, misty sheets cloaked Oulu harbor making it difficult to identify the steamers and schooners and brigs and fishing skiffs secured to piers jutting into the sea.

"Christ I'm sick," he moaned.

"Did he bruise a kidney?"

Anders shook his head.

"A low blow to the groin?"

Anders repeated the gesture.

Otso looked into the young man's eyes. "He tagged you pretty good with that last right, the one that put your lights out. Maybe a bruise to the brain?"

Anders disagreed. "I've got a slight headache. My eye hurts, but given how he tagged me, that's to be expected. It's this damn pain in my joints, in my low back. Every fucking joint aches like someone put shards of glass in it," the boxer moaned, using an expletive Olson had never heard Anders utter.

Otso nodded. "Still, you've got a pretty good shiner going where he planted that big right hand of his and put you down. You need to see a doctor."

"There goes the money we made from the fight," Anders moaned. "It would have been a hell of a lot better to win, to claim a thousand Finn marks, than the three hundred I earned for taking a beating. Now we're gonna spend it all on a doctor. That doesn't seem fair. Especially to you, since you paid for my shoes, tunic, shorts, robe, and our stay in Oulu."

Otso kept the boy upright as they walked against rain. Their clothes were soddened. Anders wore a wool robe with his name stitched across the back, the stitching identical to the work his mother had done on the tunic. The robe became heavier and heavier as the storm unleashed its fury. The old man wore a black wool jacket that leached rainwater as they trundled along. "I didn't get you into this to make money. I did it because I saw something in you that first day in my gymnasium. You have heart, 'spunk,' as the English say. It's not often I run across such internal strength. I knew you had the makings of a boxer. But I rushed you. I should have waited. A year—maybe two. Let you develop ..." Otso stopped talking as they passed a gaggle of boisterous sailors. "You boys know of any doctors close by?" he asked.

A lanky seaman, insignia of the Russian Navy displayed on his storm coat, boasting mousy hair and a freckled face, his eyes dull and gray, stopped and smiled. "Hey, isn't he the kid from Paltamo?" the sailor asked in Finnish. The sailor's companions stopped behind him as he addressed Otso. "We just got done watching Pekka Pakkanen wail the snot out of your boy," the sailor continued, slurring his words and rocking unsteadily on his feet after too many shots of Swedish vodka or too many bottles of Finnish beer.

Otso nodded. "Poor coaching on my part," he said quietly, sizing up the drunks. "He needs a doctor. Do you know of any?"

The sailor grinned. "Old Doc Attiokoski's just around the corner. He cured me when I came down with the clap from one of those god-awful Oulu sluts. He should still be sober since it's not past seven. Get to him after seven and he'll likely be stone drunk."

"Appreciate it," Otso said agreeably. "Perhaps he can help my young friend."

The sailors ambled on, more interested in finding their berths and sleeping off their celebratory mood than causing a ruckus.

"From the looks of this rash on your left flank," Lakku Attiokoski said, "and the symptoms you're describing, I'd say we're dealing with typhus."

Anders's robe and tunic were removed and tossed in a heap on the examination room's floor. The physician's glasses were poised on top of his bald head, his wizened eyes peering at a host of red bumps cascading from the boxer's left armpit to the waistline of his shorts.

"Shit."

Otso's response caught Anders off guard.

"What's that mean, Doc?" Anders asked.

Before the physician could respond, Otso interjected, "It means, lad, that you're infected. That you'll need to be quarantined. Likely several weeks in the hospital. Am I right, Doctor?"

Attiokoski nodded and placed his stethoscope on the boxer's well-muscled back. "Pretty accurate prognosis. Where did you get your medical degree?" The physician stopped talking and listened to Anders's heart. "Seems unaffected. Very low rate, which one would expect in an athlete of your age and conditioning. Breathe in and out, deeply and slowly, please."

Otso chuckled at the doctor's suggestion. "No medical degree, Doc. Just a long life and many experiences."

"You can put your shirt back on."

Anders complied and resumed sitting on the examination table, his sinewy calves dangling in the air, his vomit-stained shoes barely touching the floor.

"What sort of medicine should he take?"

Attiokoski frowned. "Unfortunately, we don't know the cause of typhus. Some think it's from bad water. Others, from fleas dispersed by rats. We just don't have a definitive answer at this point as to what causes it. And if we don't know what causes it, we don't have medicine to cure it. The best you can do, Mr. Alhomäki, is be confined to hospital, get plenty of rest and fluids, and, with any luck, the bug will run its course and you'll recover."

"How long?"

"Likely several weeks as Mr. Olson predicted. Depends, but that's a good guess given the level of symptoms. You're in excellent shape, which gives you a fighting chance to avoid what happened to Napoleon's army."

Otso's eyebrows furrowed. "Napoleon's army?"

"I won't keep you long. The short version is that, while it's true that weather and food shortages played a part in defeating the French, it's more likely that the Little Corsican's misguided attack on Russia was done in by typhus. That's the speculation raised in medical journals."

"I feel sick," Anders moaned. The boxer leaned over to expel bile and blood into a bucket the doctor shoved in place with a deft left foot. The spasms continued for a few minutes until, exhausted and humiliated, Anders wiped his mouth and sweaty forehead with a clean towel that Dr. Attiokoski provided. Anders detected a faint smell of used booze emanating from the man's breath. *Good thing we got here before seven*, the boxer thought as he sought to return the soiled towel.

"No, you keep it," Attiokoski said, shaking his head. "You're likely contagious. Just toss the towel in the garbage when you're done using it."

Otso assisted Anders to his feet. "What hospital would you suggest, Doctor?"

"Gustavus Adolphus Lutheran. It's clean, relatively cheap, and close by. They have the expertise for a case such as your young friend's."

"Excellent,' Otso said, reaching into a trouser pocket for his billfold. "What do I owe you?"

The old physician replaced his spectacles on his nose. "Fifty marks."

The Bear Man nodded, withdrew soggy bills in the proper denominations, and handed them to the doctor. "Come on, kid.

71

Let's find you a bed," he said, replacing the billfold, looping his right arm around the fighter, and urging Anders to his feet. "I need to get back to my tannery in Mieslahti, and you need to beat this nasty bug."

The doctor pocketed the cash as he walked across the room and opened the door. The rain had stopped. A full moon waxed over the city. Steam rose from cobblestones as Otso urged Anders across the threshold. The physician waved goodbye, a gesture the trainer and the boxer did not see as they confronted an empty city.

A random thought struck Otso, a notion, an inkling that had nothing to do with the fight or the illness afflicting Anders, as the men walked towards the hospital. "Say, whatever happened between you and the Kale girl?"

Anders's only response to the question was a groan, the dismissive flip of his right hand, and profound silence.

CHAPTER THIRTEEN

They saw each other once more before Anders left for Norway. It was a meeting of happenstance. It was a brief interlude, an uncomfortable and truncated connection between two people denied happiness by culture and society that played itself out on a dusty alley in Oulu where Anders Alhomäki had taken up residence following his recovery from typhus.

Jorma and Marjatta were disappointed in their son's decision. "That boy's making a grave mistake," Anders's stepfather had muttered when the family received Anders's single-page letter written in uncertain cursive. Jorma and Marjatta sat at the wooden table in the family cottage, wringing their hands and lamenting the choice made by their only son as they considered the news. "He says that The Bear has a job lined up for him in a copper mine in Norway. Well, that's a fine 'thank you' for adopting the boy, promising him this farm, this house, this life. I never thought dragging Anders to boxing lessons with the Norwegian would corrupt the kid's thinking. Clearly, I was wrong."

Marjatta served her husband good Swedish vodka to dampen his upset. The family rarely kept alcohol in the house; the wee bit that could be found tucked away amongst the fruits and vegetables preserved by the woman from the family garden was generally reserved for medicinal purposes. "Here," she said, pouring a dram of liquor into her husband's empty coffee cup, "drink this, take a deep breath, and calm down. What's done is done. He's made his choice, for good or bad. He's a man now so there's little we can do. Better that we let him spread his wings, attempt to fly, and fail than try to restrain his spirit."

Anders's letter had set out a plan that he conceived after learning that The Elf Warrior had been posted for the second time in Asia. As related in correspondence Anders received from his uncle in late 1904, Wachtmeister Alvar Alhomäki had been plucked from Viipuri to accompany *Podpolkovnik* (Lieutenant Colonel) Carl Gustav Mannerheim on a lengthy deployment to the Far East. Mannerheim sought combat experience: he understood that a soldier's chance for promotion increased dramatically upon surviving enemy fire. With promotion as his goal, Mannerheim transferred from the highly regarded Chevalier Guard to the 52nd Nezhin Hussars, a less prestigious cavalry unit but one destined for the front line. The reason for the *podpolkovnik* being dispatched to Siberia was simple.

Convinced that Czar Nicholas II desired to expand his empire, Japan preemptively declared war on Russia on February 8, 1904. Elements of the newly Westernized Japanese fleet surprised Russia's ill-prepared navy at Port Arthur and, in swift and unexpected fashion, dispatched Russia's Pacific Fleet, sending Admiral Stepan Makarov and many sailors to their deaths. With the surviving Russian warships bottled up in port, Japanese troops swarmed into Manchuria, attacked Russian outposts, and overran Russian defenses. Finnish indifference to the conflict led to the Finnish press ignoring news from the Eastern Front. By June 16, 1904, the situation in Finland had deteriorated to the point where Eugene Schuman, a Finn working as a clerk in the Finnish Senate, approached Governor-General Bobrikov—the czar's emissary in Finland—and shot the hated Russian three times before committing suicide. Bobrikov, the enforcer of Nicholas's edicts in Finland, died the following day, and within the year, Russian conscription of Finnish men into the Imperial Army and Navy died as well. None of this political upset deterred Uncle Alvar from continuing his service to the czar: The Elf Warrior was a career soldier who understood that czars and governors general come and go like flotsam on the Baltic tides, but that duty and honoring one's commitments define a man.

Mannerheim considered the events in Finland and determined that his best course of action was to surround himself with loyal adjutants including Finnish-speaking soldiers plucked from the ranks of the former Finnish Army. Alvar Alhomäki's fluency in Finnish, and a utilitarian comprehension of Russian and Swedish, made him an invaluable addition to Mannerheim's inner circle.

Additionally, Alvar's rural upbringing and his ability to diagnose and doctor equine maladies were godsends for Mannerheim, whose primary mount was a six-year-old thoroughbred—Talisman—the offspring of a racing champion: a horse of incredible speed and strength but one prone to frequent affliction.

Uncle Alvar's pronouncement, that he was once again headed east on the Trans-Siberian Railway in the service of the czar had rekindled Anders's wanderlust. At first, Anders considered joining the army. But a quick reconnoitering of the situation, coupled with Anders's unrequited affinity for Anneli, led him to approach Otso Olson about other options. It was The Bear's suggestion that, instead of risking his neck by enlisting in the army, Anders take advantage of steady work available in the copper mines of Røros, Norway, where he could accumulate enough capital to convince Amadeus Balzar of his worth as a suitor.

To this end, The Bear offered to fund Anders's voyage across the Gulf of Bothnia from Oulu to Sundsvall, Sweden. Train fare from Sundsvall to Trondheim, Norway, and from Trondheim to Røros would be covered by Anders's new employer, the Røros Copper Works. His plan was to work for a year in Haakon's Mine, a warren of underground tunnels beneath Røros, earn his grubstake, return to Finland, seek out Anneli, and convince her headstrong father of his veracity and worth. After their marriage, the couple would depart Oulu on a transatlantic steamer to seek new opportunities in the Upper Peninsula of Michigan where Anders knew there was steady work for experienced miners in the copper mines surrounding Houghton, Hancock, and Calumet. While Anders Alhomäki's vision did not include military service akin to the glorious legacy of his uncle, his plan—a plan he had yet to share with the object of his desire—did afford the young Finn a modicum of adventure, fulfilling in him the desire to change course, to redirect his life and purpose.

"Anneli is here, in Oulu?" The question had been posed by Anders to an acquaintance—a young woman he'd met in a greasy spoon eatery along Oulu's waterfront. Vabu Agres Ståhlberg was tall, bucktoothed, hipless, and unattractively thin. But she had a glint of mischief in her eye and a kindness to her manner that endeared her to Anders, causing him to consider her in a favorable light whenever she waited on him at the lunch counter in the Café Bothnia.

It was a Saturday in early September. Anders had just finished his shift as a night warehouseman at the Kantonen Brass Works, a foundry located a short walk from the one-room flat he'd rented around the corner from Dr. Attiokoski's clinic. He ordered scrambled eggs, a side of ham, rye toast, and a pot of tarry coffee, knowing that, despite a need for sleep, he was due to meet a recruiter for the Røros Copper Works at the company's Oulu office at nine o'clock that morning to sign papers.

"I've sent three letters to her aunt in Turku in hopes of getting a response. Nothing. Not one word."

"Aren't you supposed to stay away from the girl? Hasn't her father made his objection to your intentions perfectly clear, as any Kale father would if he knew an outsider was smitten with his precious daughter's charms?" Vabu winked as she asked the question.

"You're a fine one to talk, Mrs. Ståhlberg. You married a Swede—a man outside your tribe—and yet you condemn me for wanting to do the same?" Anders's food arrived. The young man picked at his eggs with a fork as he waited for the woman to respond. But anxious to learn more about Anneli's presence in the port city, Anders interjected before the waitress could reply. "Where did you see her?"

Vabu smiled, exposing front teeth that nearly touched her chin. "At the fish market. Buying cod. She's staying with a cousin. The rest of her family is camping outside town, getting ready to move south as winter approaches."

"I must see her."

The waitress nodded, reached for a coffee pot, steam wafting from the container's spout, and refilled the Anders's cup. "I told her you'd say that. But she's pretty firm. She's made her peace with her family and is engaged to a nice Kale boy. A tinsmith. The wedding's in a month."

The news hit Anders like a left hook from Pekka Pakkanen. A frown captured the young man's soft, whiskerless face. Sorrow invaded his dark eyes until it appeared to Vabu that Anders, whose emotions were normally concealed and well contained, was about to cry.

"I'm sorry," she whispered.

Anders shook his head. "It's my own damn fault. I'm a coward. I should have taken a chance, made my pitch to her father when the opportunity arose. Now," he stammered, regaining his composure, sipping coffee, and nodding tersely, "it's too late."

Vabu placed warm fingers on Anders's left wrist. "There will be another girl, a girl whose family will welcome you as kin. Of this, I am certain."

Anders shook his head but did not otherwise respond.

Two weeks later, they chanced upon each other in an alleyway ten blocks from the café. When he saw the strong, supple walk of the woman ahead of him on the planked sidewalk leading to a row of apartments overlooking the harbor, Anders thought he was dreaming. *Can it be?* But as his breath quickened, as his heart raced, as he increased his gait to cover the distance between them, he knew: *It is her!*

When the woman stopped at a doorway, shifted the brown paper package she was carrying from her right arm to her left, reached inside a pocket of her coat, and retrieved a key, it gave him the opening he needed.

"Anneli." He said her name with such reverence and care and tenderness that when she turned to face him, the upset and scorn he expected due to his abrupt approach was absent from the woman's kind face.

"Mr. Alhomäki."

Her voice was touched by warmth, as if she still carried affection for him. And yet, her eyes, wide set and dark and honest, betrayed the impossibility of what he was seeking.

"I was hoping we could talk."

She nodded and looked him over. "We are talking."

He kicked a raggedy work boot against the brick wall of the apartment building. "I meant in private."

She looked up at the gray, drizzly sky that entrapped the harbor, the bank of slender rain and fog making it difficult to determine where the land ended and the sea began. "I don't think that's possible. We have nothing beyond pleasantries to say to one another. I am due to be married. To a good man. A Kale man. My fate is sealed. You need to forget me and move on with your life."

Gently, so as not to provoke fear, the boxer reached out his left hand and placed it on the woman's right shoulder. "You don't mean that."

A tear slid down her cheek. "I do. What we thought was possible is not. It's that simple. There is nothing more to be said."

She removed his hand and pursed her lips as if to forestall saying something she might regret.

She wants to say more. But tradition and custom and honor and family dictate that she cannot. "You still care for me, don't you?"

Anneli shook her head but there was no sincerity in the gesture.

"Anneli, I have a job. In Norway. For good wages." The young man swallowed hard before blurting out his proposal. "Marry me! Come with me. I leave Friday for Røros. One year in the mines and then we can take a ship across the ocean to America like we planned."

The door to the apartment opened. A craggy-faced woman of considerable age, shorter in stature and wider of hip and trunk than Anneli, peered at the two young people. "Who are you talking to, cousin?"

Anneli answered without emotion, "A friend, Lavinia."

The old woman frowned. "Seems to be more than a casual acquaintance by the sound of things," she replied with gruff candor. "I'm pretty sure your father, not to mention your fiancé, would not approve of you talking to strange young men in public!"

"Mr. Alhomäki was just leaving. We have concluded our greetings. He's on his way—later in the week—to Norway. To work in a copper mine."

Skepticism clouded Lavinia's face. "Well then," the older woman said, "he best be getting to his own business, hadn't he?"

There was no opportunity for goodbye. There was no kiss on the cheek, no tender hug of regret. Anneli Balzar turned away from Anders Alhomäki and disappeared into the apartment, her sudden departure punctuated by the slamming of the solid, pine door, leaving the boxer to wander back to his flat as cold rain wept from the ashen sky.

CHAPTER FOURTEEN: March 9, 1905 (Manchuria, China)

The Elf Warrior waited behind snow-covered, hastily shouldered earth. Alvar and the other hussars in the podpolkovnik's entourage had dismounted and formed a skirmish line.

It had been a long, arduous journey from St. Petersburg to Manchuria on the Trans-Siberian Railway requiring multiple changes of locomotives and cars and a trip aboard the *SS Angara* across Lake Baikal. The track connecting the western shoreline and the eastern shoreline of the mammoth lake—by virtue of the Circum-Baikal link—was incomplete. Even after finishing the track around the southern edge of the big lake, the *SS Angara* would remain in service until 1916 due to the instability of the tracks skirting the marshy lakeshore.

Wachtmeister Alhomäki kept watch through binoculars. A small stream separated the Russian line from the Japanese position. The wachtmeister studied the enemy with the reluctant knowledge that, despite bravado and a stubborn willingness to fight for the czar, the Russian effort in southern Manchuria was doomed.

Port Arthur was in enemy hands. The seaport's surrender had freed up tens of thousands of Japanese troops as well as artillery batteries and machine gun units to turn north, towards Mukden, where Alvar and his mates were dug in. The great relief—the Baltic Fleet that had departed St. Petersburg fully outfitted to circumnavigate the globe in hopes of reinforcing the beleaguered Russian forces—would arrive in May of 1905; too late to save Port Arthur. The Russians' naval misadventure had been delayed by weather, lost the element of surprise, and was opposed by a formidable foe. Most of the Finns serving as sailors in Russia's Baltic Fleet would never see their homeland again; Admiral Tōgō's ships would intercept the armada and, in decisive and swift fashion, send over twenty Russian warships to the bottom of the China Sea. Only three relief vessels would survive: too little and too late to impact the war's outcome.

This future was, of course, unknown to Alvar and his comrades as they defended Mukden. General Kuropatkin had ordered his troops, including Mannerheim's hussars, to dig in south of town with full knowledge that swarms of Japanese reinforcements—freed by Port Arthur's capitulation—were on the way.

Most of the engagements Alvar and his mates experienced prior to Mukden had been mere skirmishes between the Russian cavalry—sent to reconnoiter enemy positions—and Japanese foot soldiers manning hastily erected fortifications. During one such fight, Mannerheim, mounted on Talisman and leading the charge, rode hell-bent-for-leather into a hail of Japanese bullets. The result of the podpolkovnik's brashness was the death of his favorite steed. Though stricken, Talisman carried the unscathed officer back to friendly lines before collapsing. A rumor made its way back to St. Petersburg that Mannerheim had died in battle. Though such murmurings of his demise were untrue, he *was* incapacitated as the Japanese advanced.

"Karasov," Alvar whispered as he scrutinized the Japanese trench system across the shallow tributary of the Yalu River separating the combatants, "how's the podpolkovnik?"

Alexey Karasov, a medic assigned to Mannerheim's staff, held a Mosin-Nagant rifle loosely in his right hand and adjusted his soft cover with his left against the burgeoning sun of early spring. The ground was thawing. The snow was melting, filling the bottom of the trench with water. "Fever's high. There's a danger of delirium. Fluids and rest seem to be helping but he's not out of the woods yet."

Alvar nodded. Another hussar raised a scarecrow wearing a Japanese uniform into the air. The mannequin's penciled-in lips, hastily drawn eyes, and straw-filled breasts appeared above the rim of the trench.

Craack!

A sniper snapped off a round from distance.

Twaatt!

The bullet hit the scarecrow and showered the Russians with straw. The prankster lowered the target.

"Nice shooting!" he yelled, poking a finger into a bullet hole located squarely between the straw woman's eyes. "Best keep your head down, Finlander," the prankster advised Alvar "or you'll end up ventilated like Olga here."

Alvar snickered, removed a pre-rolled cigarette from a pocket of his coat, drew the head of a match against his belt buckle, lit the cigarette, and pulled heavily on tobacco. "No shit, Narikov," he replied.

Narikov, a slender, frail-looking boy of no more than eighteen, leaned the dummy against muddy earth and studied the Finn. "How's that wife of yours?"

The reference was to a Russian war widow, Tatianna Teshenko, who'd traveled east on the Trans-Siberian Railway to be at the bedside of her wounded husband. Unfortunately, the woman arrived in Vladivostok two days too late. With no money to fund her return to Moscow—having spent the last of her savings on an Orthodox priest, a casket, and a funeral for her husband—the twenty-two-year-old widow, weary and ragged from her travels and travails—settled down in the port city, making ends meet by doing what soldiers and sailors desired her to do. Tatianna was comely and fit despite her languor, and Alvar took a fancy to the woman, who was a full decade younger than the Finn. He made her acquaintance, bought her a beer in a seaside pub—fully intending to pay for her favors—but in an unexpected turn, ended up falling in love and asking Tatianna Teshenko to marry him.

"No," Tatianna had responded to Alvar's initial proposal. "I am a widow in mourning. I am also a woman of poor reputation who doesn't deserve your attention or your affection. Choose someone better suited, with better credentials, Mr. Alhomäki, to be your wife."

But the big Finn persisted, showering the widow with jewelry and silk stockings and French perfume, spending nearly all of his meager pay on the fallen woman in hopes of changing her mind. And, in the end, he did just that. They were married by the same Orthodox priest who'd buried Dmitri Teshenko, secured a one-room, cold-water flat overlooking Vladivostok Harbor, and made love twice a day until Mannerheim's orders came through and the hussars galloped off to Manchuria. That was two months ago, and the single letter Alvar had received from Tatianna in the interim brought him impossible, improbable news: his new wife was pregnant.

"She's good. Safe and quiet in Vladivostok until the war ends. The Japanese haven't the resources or the nerve to attack Russian soil."

Karasov tilted his black, Cossack-style Persian lamb-wool hat off his brow to better see the Finn. "Isn't she pregnant?"

Alvar, displaying teeth stained by tobacco and chipped from hard use, smiled and inhaled smoke before responding. "She is."

"Wasn't she a whore?" Narikov asked.

Alvar scowled and tossed his cigarette into melt pooling in the bottom of the trench.

"What the hell kind of question is that to ask?" Karasov interjected before Alvar could reply. "Mind your manners, little one, or your nose might end up on the receiving end of a Finnish fist!"

Alvar forced a smile, the gesture filled with weariness yet patience. "It's alright. He's heard the rumors. Let's just say that when a soldier's wife finds herself without her soldier in a war zone, she must do what she must to survive. Wouldn't you, Private Narikov, do the very same if you were in her shoes? No money. No job. No food. No shelter. No one to care for you. No way to return to your family in Moscow. Put yourself in the place of such a woman before you judge her. To do otherwise is unfair, and, as Karasov says, unwise."

Narikov pursed his lips and looked across the stream at the enemy. "Understood, wachtmeister. It was unfair of me to think ill of her. I apologize. I'm certain she is a fine and upstanding woman now that she is your wife."

Boom!
Boom!
Boom!

Enemy artillery commenced a barrage. Shells landed short of the Russian trench but, as the hussars hunkered against sloppy earth, they knew it was only a matter of time before the enemy corrected the miscalculation and began dropping ordnance on them.

"It's about to begin," Alvar said plainly, leveling his Mosin at the enemy. "They're going to drive us to Mukden, encircle the city, lay siege, capture us, and end this war."

Karasov nodded. "Let the bastards try. I've still got plenty of fight left inside of me."

"But do our comrades?" Wachtmeister Alvar Alhomäki asked as an artillery shell exploded just outside the Russian trench showering the Finn and his companions with moist, fertile, Manchurian dirt.

CHAPTER FIFTEEN

The situation became untenable. General Kuropatkin's optimistic view—that reinforcements would arrive on the Trans-Siberian Railway or that his position would improve when Marines landed at Port Arthur—was unfounded. Though the Baltic Fleet had not yet met its unfortunate fate as Japanese Field Marshal Ōyama gave the order to destroy the Russians at Mukden—the naval battle taking place in May, nearly two months in the future—it was clear by early March that the fleet would not arrive in time. And the alternative scenario, that Kuropatkin's forces would be reinforced by rail, was equally unlikely. The single track linking the western and eastern portions of the Romanov Empire was insufficient to save the Russian Army.

"We've been ordered to withdraw," Podpolkovnik Mannerheim advised his hussars. Wachtmeister Alvar Alhomäki was seated on his mount at his commander's side, the hussars ready to move as the fever-afflicted podpolkovnik surveyed the smoldering carnage that had once been the Russian trench. "There's going to be hell to pay for it, I assure you," Mannerheim continued, addressing his men in Russian. "General Kuropatkin has ordered all units to *simultaneously* withdraw to the railway station. Trains are waiting to take us Gonzhuling where we're expected to regroup and make a stand."

A short, thin-legged Russian captain, his clean-shaven, handsome face disfigured by a fierce scar slicing across his left cheek—the imperfection likely the result of a duel, the wound long-healed but distinctive—shook his head. "Goddamned Kuropatkin. He could fuck up a one-buggy parade!"

Mannerheim scowled. "Captain Petrov, mind your tongue. We have our orders. Whether we agree or disagree with them, we will all, I repeat, *all* follow them. Is that clear?"

Petrov smiled impishly. "Perfectly, podpolkovnik. But I can't help but reflect that *you* were the one who called attention to our leader's foolishness. What commander in his right mind orders everyone, tens of thousands of troops, horses, artillery, and support staff, to pull out all at once? With no one left behind to cover the retreat? It's madness. Or cowardice. Or stupidity. I'll leave it for you to choose."

The podpolkovnik leaned over and patted the left flank of the big roan he was riding. The horse, christened Ukko by Alvar Alhomäki after the thunder god of the *Kalevala*, was fast as the wind, but fidgety—a trait that Mannerheim was learning to curb by constant reassurance. "Fair enough, Petrov. Just do what is asked of you and we'll get out of this mess just fine. Trust me on this."

"It's not you, podpolkovnik, whom I mistrust. I'll do my duty. I'll lead my men with a steady hand. But damn it all, something needs to be done about the general."

Mannerheim frowned. "I'm afraid that's a topic for folks in St. Petersburg. Nothing you or I can do about it. Griping about what we cannot change gets us nowhere," the podpolkovnik concluded. "Now, let's see if we can't catch a train, shall we?"

Wachtmeister Alhomäki knew that, once the hussars made their way north to Harbin on the train, he'd be in a position to seek Mannerheim's blessing and ride his horse, a sturdy, well-muscled mare named Kuu—the mythical goddess of the moon—to Vladivostok to reunite with his pregnant wife. He and Tatiana would, presuming the Trans-Siberian Railway remained undisturbed by the Japanese, board a westbound train and, if everything went according to plan, arrive in Viipuri, where Alvar would rejoin his old unit, settle down, and live in relative peace with Tatianna and their child. But before Alvar could approach his commander with his proposal, there was one small matter to be dealt with: Japanese forces had surrounded the Russians, meaning that the enemy stood, machine guns and bayonets waiting, between Alvar Alhomäki and love.

The 52nd Nezhin Hussars clambered down a dirt road. Mannerheim had determined that, with only disorganized chaos and bitter hand-to-hand fighting to be had between the hussars and the railway station, rather than attempt to break through the strength of Ōyama's army, the Russian cavalry would ride parallel to the Japanese defenders probing for weakness and turn towards the railroad only when they encountered impotence in the Japanese line. The hussars would make a beeline for the rail station where empty cars and steaming locomotives waited. It was a risky maneuver, one that would bring the unit under heavy fire. But given the suicidal retreat ordered by General Kuropatkin, Mannerheim's approach appeared to be the only prudent course of action.

"We're going to be in for it, Finlander," Mannerheim said tersely, holding leather reins firmly in his right hand as he looked north. "We're exposed, open to fire from anyone and everyone. Our only advantage is our speed."

Alvar nodded and shoved his soft cap, the fabric damp from drizzle, the snows and the below-zero cold of March having given way to rain and intermittent spring, onto his head. He studied the distant enemy knowing that in less than five kilometers, the hussars would face a decision: retreat and return to their original position to await capture or charge willy-nilly into the enemy in hopes that their horses could outrun bullets unleashed from Hotchkiss machine guns and Arisaka rifles. Either prospect was numbing, gut-wrenching, and unnerving. And yet the Finn rode on, his little mare matching the pace of Mannerheim's big gelding, his eyes forward, his heart rate accelerating as the enemy line came into focus.

Custer. Not Custer at Gettysburg or at Winchester or in the Wilderness. But Custer at the Little Big Horn. The image of a troop of cavalry smashing headlong into a superior force, the imprudent attackers rebuffed and harassed until they claimed final repose atop a lonely, treeless, dusty vista of the American Plains, struck Alvar as remarkably similar to what he and his comrades were about to experience. He became sad at the notion that he might never see his child, never know the color of his or her eyes, never experience the joy of his or her first halting steps across the kitchen floor he deigned to share with Tatiana in Viipuri. *Viipuri. Safe, quiet; a Finnish seaside town bathed in sea breezes and salty air. The perfect place to live out one's life.* A vision of Tatiana bent at the waist in the family sauna, hot steam curling her chestnut hair to a frizz, sweat sliding down her small, white, breasts, tawny nipples retracted from heat, her deep chocolate eyes closed in contemplation, the baby asleep in a wicker basket on the cedar slats of the steam bath's floor, interrupted the soldier's melancholy. *Something to live for, that.*

Crack!

Rat-a-tat-tatt!
Crack!

They were within range of Japanese small-arms fire. As the hussars spurred their mounts, moving from canter to gallop, the enlisted men unsheathing their swords, the officers readying pistols or brandishing custom-made sabers, the Japanese did not unleash their artillery. Instead, the enemy relied upon concentrated small-arms fire to repel the Russians.

"We're in for it now, men. Charge!"

Mannerheim, unaware that he was being promoted from podpolkovnik (lieutenant colonel) to *polkovnik* (full colonel) as he led his men into battle, raised his blade and urged Ukko into a gallop. Mannerheim's hat flew off his head, but he did not slow to acknowledge the loss.

Alvar kicked Kuu in the ribs, pushing the little mare to her limit. Bullets whizzed past the Finn and his horse. The *wachtmeister* retained his cap, its soft fabric shoved so far onto his head that it folded his ears in half. "Let's get through these bastards, boys!" he urged.

On the left—a private known to Alvar—took a bullet in the neck. Blood spurted from the man's carotid artery, but the hussar did not release the reins guiding his mount. The stricken man raced forward until he and his black gelding were surrounded. The horse's hooves flailed as enemy soldiers hacked and stabbed and thrust without mercy. In short order, both man and mount fell to the muddy earth, inert and unredeemable.

A poruchik—an intelligence officer who was part of Mannerheim's inner circle—spurred his horse with vigor, only to be struck by a volley from a Hotchkiss. Bullets from the machine gun cleaved the man's right arm from his torso. The officer's newly liberated limb fell to the ground with the sword still clutched in its right hand. Blood sprayed from the poruchik's stub as his mount crashed into the enemy. The Russian lost consciousness, toppled from his saddle, and fell into a crowd of enemy soldiers where a bayonet thrust ended his life.

Alvar rode next to Mannerheim, the two men slashing their way through the heart of the enemy. They were nearing the end of a horrific gauntlet when a young Japanese officer lunged out of the mass of humanity and stabbed Alvar's left thigh with a short sword. Before the soldier's compatriots could join in, halt

Kuu's progress, and drag the wachtmeister from his saddle, Captain Petrov raced up, pointed his revolver at the offender, and blew the man's brains out the back of his head. The Japanese surrounding Alvar were taken aback. The shock of witnessing such intimate carnage provided a diversion that allowed the Finn to escape. His sword lost, his cap gone, the wachtmeister and his horse followed Petrov and his white stallion over a low stone wall, the last barrier between the enemy and Russian troops securing the railway. Arriving inside the Russian line, Alvar turned in his saddle to verify that Mannerheim had also escaped. In the process of searching for his commander, Alvar exposed himself to enemy fire. An Arisaka round slammed into the Finn's back, exited his chest, grazed Kuu's muscular neck, and caused the mare to stumble.

CHAPTER SIXTEEN: June 1905 (Røros, Norway)

It was cold, damp, and claustrophobic in the rat-infested underground mine. Anders was on the cusp of his twenty-second birthday as he worked with a crew of five including his boss, Raimo Wirkkala, in a low-ceilinged section of Haakon's Mine. The mine, named after Norway's first Christian king, exploited one of Norway's most productive copper deposits. Wirkkala was an untrustworthy, foul-mouthed, hard-drinking, failed dairyman who'd lost his family's ancestral land west of Alakylä—on the banks of the Kiiminkijoki—to predatory bankers. That had been twenty years earlier, around the time of Anders's birth. Wirkkala had left Finland impoverished, but with the promise of steady work and honest wages—a better lot than he was facing as a bankrupt farmer in Finland. The man had no compunction about relegating his timid, nervous wife and two malnourished babies to the Oulu slums, promising to send for his family once he became established in Norway. Anders learned the very first day he lit a candle and inserted it into the metal holder of his wide-brimmed, cloth mining cap that Wirkkala was as lazy as sin, had little use for the truth, and held to an over-inflated opinion of his standing with God. Anders also learned, from speaking with the other Finns on his crew, that Raimo Wirkkala never reclaimed his family, a circumstance that did not seem to bother the man as he boasted about his new Sami wife and their growing brood of little Norwegians.

A Laestadian, Raimo Wirkkala did not, in any fashion, practice what he preached. Lars Levi Laestadian's brand of Lutheranism included absolute sobriety, the avoidance of pre-marital sex, disdain for birth control, prohibitions against secular music and dancing, a dislike of tattoos, and a fervent abhorrence of curse words. Wirkkala's penchant for engaging in spiritual sleight of hand, including a pontification of values and doctrines that he professed but never adhered to, was, to Anders, an astounding thing to behold. Anders had never met a man who could proclaim such personal sanctification while engaging in the very sort of behavior he denigrated. But Wirkkala was brutish, a towering presence who exuded menace, and Anders decided early on that it was better to hold his tongue and let Raimo Wirkkala engage in charade than end up in a brawl, one Anders would likely win given his pugilistic savvy, but one that would leave him bruised, battered, and sacked.

Better to allow the man his hypocrisy than lose my job and wind up penniless in this godforsaken Norwegian town!

The five-man crew Anders worked on also included Edvin Koivu, a sad-faced, desperately thin man from Turku who'd tried his hand at seafaring and failed, and two brothers, Poju and Fredrik Pöysti, who though Finns, were—like Wirkkala—Norwegian citizens. But unlike their boss, the Pöysti brothers had been born in Norway. Five years before Anders and Edvin arrived in Røros, Wirkkala and the Pöysti boys had migrated from Kåfjord, a copper mining town in the Finnmark region of Norway located above the Arctic Circle. Known in Norway as the *Kven,* these Norwegian Finns had learned their mining skills from Cornish immigrants brought to the frozen north by the English owners of the Kåfjord mine. In addition to Norwegian fishermen plying the frigid waters of the Alta fjord—the main body of water linking the Norwegian coast with the Arctic Ocean—several hundred Finnish and Cornish miners and families of indigenous Sami (who fished, hunted, and herded reindeer for subsistence) lived in and around Kåfjord.

The wages paid by *Altens Kobberverk* were low, but the work was steady until the copper ore being excavated from the stubborn Alta Mountains began to run out. As the operations in Kåfjord wound down, Wirkkala and his companions made their way to Røros, lured south by promises of continued work, better pay, safer conditions, and a less brutal climate. The latter proved true: away from the Arctic, the winds and snows and blizzards were less frequent; the summers, more temperate and longer in duration. But it was as nearly as cold in Røros as in the Arctic, sometimes plunging to minus forty or fifty degrees Celsius in winter, and the wages were no better than what the Finnmark miners had left behind—a mere seven Norwegian kroner per day for the average miner, the equivalent of one U.S. dollar for twelve hours of rock breaking and digging and shoveling and lifting and pushing each workday, six days a week. As a crew chief, Raimo Wirkkala earned slightly more—ten Norwegian kroner a day—but his hours were as long and tedious as those of his fellow workers.

90

The handbills posted by the Røros Copper Works in and around Kåfjord to lure Kven miners to Røros, were also displayed in the labor halls and saloons along the Oulu waterfront by less-than-honorable agents of the mining company. Recruits who signed employment contracts and showed up for work in Røros generated tidy sums for the agents. Otso Olson had trusted the word of an acquaintance, a warehouseman he'd done business with who also moonlighted as an agent for the Røros Copper Works. The candid optimism of Olson's contact led The Bear to convince Anders that a stint in the copper mines of Norway, after struggling for three years as a laborer on the docks in Oulu, would provide the nest egg Alhomäki needed to fund his dream of emigrating to North America.

The voyage across the Gulf of Bothnia aboard the Swedish steamer *Överflöd* (*Abundance*) had been Anders's first experience at sea. As a consequence of the broiling, crashing, tumult of the crossing, the Finn spent the majority of his time aboard the coal-fired paddle wheeler upchucking tasteless meals of salty cod and overdone rutabagas. With only a rudimentary understanding of Norwegian, having been schooled by Otso as to the basics (how to ask for the toilet and how to say please, thank you, hello, and goodbye), the young Finn kept to himself, speaking only with fellow Finnish travelers such as Edvin Koivu.

Despite disparities in age and physical condition between the men—Edvin was nearly forty, his health suspect, his skin hanging from his cheeks and his upper arms as if he'd been starving, which was, in fact, the case—the two men hit it off. Anders learned from the skeletal older man that he was a widower, his wife having died years before in childbirth, the child—a premature daughter—dying with her mother, leaving Koivu despondent and inconsolable.

"Eevi was the most beautiful girl in any room she walked into," Edvin had lamented as a crisp winter wind buffeted his forlorn, anguished face. "Long, silky, yellow hair and steely gray eyes with flecks of blue that, when light struck them, seemed to mimic ice on a winter morning."

"It sounds like she was striking," Anders said as the two men stood alongside the port rail of the little paddle wheeler, the modest steam engines of the vessel assisted by billowing sails.

The older man nodded. "Indeed. And she would have been the best mother. But it was not to be." As the man remembered, his body trembled.

It had been clear to Anders that his new friend would never recover from the shock of losing his wife and child. "Life is not always fair," Anders offered, "but we must go on."

Such flippant advice appeared to trouble Edvin. A flash of upset had crossed the man's salt-and-pepper-bearded face. But the uncomfortable moment vanished, leaving behind a pallid, emotionless, defeated expression that seemed to proclaim: *What's the use?*

"I'm sorry to upset you," Anders said in a placating tone. "I meant no disrespect."

Edvin nodded. "Understood. You are young, my new friend. Very young. You've not felt the sort of ripping apart of your heart I've experienced." There was a pause before the old man concluded his thought. "And I hope you never do."

Anders wanted to object, to proclaim that, in losing Anneli Balzar, he had an inkling, an insight into the distress ailing Edvin Koivu. *No, that's not right,* he thought. *We had nothing between us but possibility. An illusion of a future, a future that was never going to come to pass. What Koivu experienced was very real and likely cannot be overcome. I can go on. I can love again. But Edvin Koivu? I think his days of falling in love are over.*

The young Finn did not make the same mistake twice. He held his tongue, removed his hand from his friend's shoulder, and returned to watching the sea.

A year after arriving in Røros by train from Trondheim, Anders was bone weary, ragged, and near exhaustion. Constantly wielding hammer and pick to free copper-bearing rock from the earth's grip, shoveling ore into mine carts, and pushing the heavy cars on narrow-gauge steel rails into the cage of the elevator in the main tunnel of the Haakon's Mine was far more arduous than any training regimen The Bear had insisted Anders adopt when preparing for a fight. Six days a week the miners worked to exhaustion in the cold and damp, their meager clothing insufficient against the chill, the fabric of their jackets and slacks and caps and any exposed skin or hair covered with the dust of excavation. And six days a week, they were supervised by Raimo

Wirkkala, who spent the majority of his time studying The Bible by the bright glow of newly installed electric lights in the mine's main chamber or by candlelight in crowded, oppressively narrow, newly excavated side tunnels. Wirkkala only engaged in physical labor when he heard the approach of the crew's Norwegian foreman, Lars Pettersen. Occasionally—when not reading scripture—Wirkkala would also lift a pick and demonstrate proper technique or direct the crew's efforts to a particular vein of ore, or, rarest of all, get behind a loaded ore car and add his muscle to the crew's effort to budge a stubborn vehicle. But once the wheels of the mine cart began to turn and the load began to roll towards the mine's central shaft and its electrically powered elevator, Raimo would resume reading scripture, though, as assessed by Anders, the boss had a difficult time converting apostolic theory into Christian behavior.

Anders was perceptive. After intermittently being in the presence of Raimo Wirkkala and his Sami wife—Salgjerd, a diminutive and proud woman whose most prominent physical trait was a dimple neatly dividing her chin—the young Finn understood Raimo's game. It was clear that a faithful, dedicated adherence to Laestadianism was engrained in Mrs. Wirkkala and that Raimo mimicked his wife's piety as a matter of acquiescence. By paying lip service to his young wife's beliefs, Raimo kept domestic discord to a minimum. He'd learned to placate Salgjerd's religiosity by studiously reading scripture and concealing his love of aquavit and his pejorative use of the Lord's name from his better half.

But Salgjerd wasn't stupid. She recognized her husband's razor-thin faith, his failings, and his weaknesses, and when appropriate, she chastised Raimo with an eye to correcting his moral failings. Ten years younger than her husband and unintimidated by his physical stature, Salgjerd Wirkkala knew the power of her sex and used it to wrangle from the stubborn, immoral man a marital truce that struck Anders, despite his youth and inexperience with women, as remarkable.

She holds the cards of her figure, her looks, and the fact that their children adore her. She plays that hand with skill, Anders thought after studying Raimo's and Salgjerd's interactions. *She's far cleverer and more deliberate than her boorish husband,* the young Finn concluded. *The sort of woman who can toy with a man like a cat plays with a crippled mouse.*

Anders watched his boss relaxing, reading scripture or dozing—the candlelight didn't afford accuracy as to detail—as Anders and the other miners sat on cold stone, leaned against rock, kicked at scurrying rats, opened their lunch buckets, removed cold pork, salted herring, or cheese and thick slices of rye bread, sipped fresh milk from tin cups, and enjoyed brief respite from their toil. After wolfing down his food, Anders removed an envelope from his dusty wool jacket, unfolded a two-page letter and began to read by candlelight.

May 13, 1905
Viipuri, Finland
Dear Nephew:

Well, these things were certainly unexpected. I survived my wounds and you have left Finland. It was with astonishment I learned from Jorma that you gave up the fight game to try your hand at mining. That, quite frankly, was a move I never saw coming. But then, as you proved in the ring, you are adept at bobbing and weaving in unexpected ways! I understand wanting to seek adventure and a change in scenery. Have I not done that very thing? Of course, in my situation I really did not have much choice, now, did I? The farm was always destined to be Jorma's. He is firstborn. That is just how things are. So, I had to find a different path. With no money in my purse and no connections to make my journey easier, with no possibility for me to become a farmer on my own, and with no interest in working the woods, I chose the army. Despite the wounds I received in service of the czar, I remain convinced that it was the right choice for me. I always thought you might follow my example in this regard, but I guess I was mistaken.

I hope things are going well in Norway. It is not easy being in a place where you do not know or understand the language or the people. I experienced much the same on my long journey with Mannerheim. There's a man who is as adaptable as they come, except he still cannot speak passable Finnish. On that score, he has much to learn!

I am disabled and no longer in the army. The wound to my thigh healed without any permanent consequence but the bullet to my back and chest caused much damage and left me weak—too weak to march or ride a horse. What general wants a hussar who cannot ride or a soldier who cannot march? I am now working for the postal service, not as a postman but as a clerk, a position that allows me to sit for most of my shift while sorting mail.

I should tell you that, while in the east, I married a Russian woman. Her name is Tatiana, and you would like her. We are having a baby in November and if it is a boy, we will christen him Kari. We have not yet agreed on a girl's name. I am leaning to Kukka, but my wife, being of much stronger faith than I, is holding out for Kirsti. Given my wife's Russian stubbornness, I think she will eventually win this dispute if the child happens to be a girl.

We live not far from the sea in a modest two-bedroom flat with our own bath—a luxury, I will tell you, after sharing facilities with immodest soldiers for much of my army career. Things are going well here, and despite the abrupt end of my military service, I am at peace with the lot God has chosen for me.

Your parents are worried about you. Of course, your sisters miss their big brother, but they are growing up so fast that when I was last at the farm, I hardly recognized them. They are getting taller, talking constantly, and dart hither and yon with exuberance. They will, when they hit their stride as young ladies, give old Jorma quite a run for his money! The farm is, as always, a constant source of struggle for your father, more so now since he has been forced to replace you with a paid man. Your father employs that bully you once taught a lesson, Erno Karppinen, fulltime. Karppinen has, since you last encountered him, changed a great deal. I think it has to do with his complete abstinence from alcohol and being away from his old man, away from the abuse that fueled his anger and unkindness towards boys smaller than himself. He is living in the bridle and harness room of the barn and gives your folks no trouble. The girls adore him, and he dotes on them like they were his little sisters. Your mother has also taken a shine to the reformed Erno, and, perhaps, in some small way, she has substituted him for you to fill the empty space in her heart. And Erno is working out splendidly, though the small wage

Jorma pays the lad makes it hard for your folks to make ends meet.

How are things with you? Are you saving your wages, making prudent use of your time in Norway to sock away kroner to fund your dream of immigrating to the States? I am assuming you are doing so. While your parents have expressed concern over your conduct, I do not share their worries. I applaud your willingness to take a risk, to allow God to decide your fate. I just hope you are making wise decisions and staying away from aquavit and Norwegian whores! Either one will divert your attention from your goal. So, keep your eyes on the horizon and, when you get to America, make sure you write and tell me if the streets are indeed paved with gold!

> *With fondness,*
> *Your uncle,*
> *Alvar Alhomäki*

"Time to get back to work," Raimo Wirkkala grunted, closing his Bible with authority. "Copper doesn't jump out of the ground on its own!"

The miners stood up, wiped the dust off their pants legs, put new candles in their caps, lit the candles from a shared match, and began walking towards the dig. Anders tucked his uncle's letter into its envelope, slid the papers into a pocket of his wool jacket, and wiped snot from his nose with his sleeve. He had bested the typhus that laid him out in Oulu but was fighting a nasty head cold, the result of insistent winds and pesky subterranean drafts that carried the Norwegian landscape's forbidding cold into the depths of the mine. He fell in behind Poju Pöysti as the miners returned to work and pondered the remarkable spell Salgjerd Wirkkala, a sprite of a twenty-something Sami girl, had cast upon her husband.

As Anders considered this paradox, he grinned, knowing that the woman's tenacity was rooted in her heritage. A fiercely independent spirit of nomadic tribalism had nurtured Salgjerd all her young life. He knew, from casual conversations he'd overheard in Røros, that Salgjerd's uncle, Aslak Haetta, had been one of the leaders of the Kautokeino Rebellion in 1852. Haetta, along with his conspirator Mons Somby, were, like Salgjerd Wirkkala, devout followers of Laestadius. An abhorrence of alcohol caused the two men to ransack a trading post owned by Carl Ruth. Unfortunately, during the raid, Ruth and a deputy sheriff were killed. Citizens captured Haetta, Somby, and a dozen other Sami involved in the protest.

Anders picked up his hammer, worked the wall of the stope, and pondered the unpleasantness of the murders within the context of extreme religiosity colored by legend. Haetta and Somby had reportedly endured their executions in the Alta town square without protest. An apocalyptic vision of the two Sami martyrs marching headless into heaven convinced the young Finn that Raimo would never best his wife in any contest of faith, determination, or will. Anders's realization—that Salgjerd would always have the upper hand in her marriage—caused him to smile as he slammed steel against stubborn Norwegian rock.

CHAPTER SEVENTEEN October 1905

"**I** hear you're a boxer," Lars Pettersen said to Anders as the miners nursed beers in the *Hammeren og Velg* (Hammer and Pick) tavern on Kjergata Street.

Anders stared into his mug as he waited for Fredrik Pöysti to translate. The difficulty for Anders was that while Fredrik and his brother Poju spoke Finnish, their version of the language was colored by being a generation removed from Finland. The Pöystis had learned the Finnish language from their parents, parents whose Finnish had been corrupted by their time in Norway. Anders listened carefully to the nuances of Fredrik's translation so as to catch the gist of what Pettersen said.

"I was," Alhomäki replied. "But not anymore," he added with finality.

Pettersen, a man nearly as large and burly as Wirkkala, but genuinely kind and, despite the power of commanding thirty-plus men, easy and friendly in his speech and manner, shook his head as he listened to Anders's translated response. "Too bad."

Fredrik looked around the tavern, gaslights hissing in the ceiling, the bartender the only other person in the place, before fixing his eyes on Anders. "Why?"

Anders didn't want to be sidetracked by history. "Doesn't matter. I'm out of the game."

Fredrik translated.

Pettersen slapped Anders on the back. "Aren't you the one who's always dreaming of America? At least, that's the complaint Wirkkala makes against you. Says you daydream instead of work, take too long to get the job done because you have your head in the clouds, searching for visions of Utopia across the sea."

Fredrik answered for Anders. "Raimo's a jealous asshole. Alhomäki outworks the rest of us." Fredrik considered the liability of admitting that he, his brother, and Edvin Koivu were less dedicated to task than Anders Alhomäki. Despite this potential liability, Fredrik plunged ahead. "Wirkkala's a henpecked fraud. Struts around like he owns the place when you're nearby but, when you're gone, he rarely breaks a sweat or takes his eyes off that damn Bible he keeps in his shirt pocket."

Anders had no idea what was being said. Instead of complaining about being left out of the conversation, he watched the bartender clean the back bar with a rag. Pettersen drained his beer and raised his mug. The barkeep, John Schultz, a German who'd married the local pastor's daughter when she was on holiday in Munich and had followed her back to Røros, snatched Pettersen's empty mug, moved with grace despite an enormous, gelatinous belly, opened the tap, and started a pour.

"He's a fighter?" Schultz asked, his own version of Norwegian heavily colored by Germanic roots.

Pettersen nodded. "Heard he was once on his way to fighting for the Finnish welterweight championship. Got beat to a pulp in Oulu and then caught typhus. That was over a year ago. Hasn't fought since."

Schultz slid a mug of cold lager towards Pettersen. The Norwegian dropped a two-kroner silver piece on the bar. "I'm buying."

Fredrik translated.

"*Takk*," Alhomäki said.

Pettersen tapped Fredrik on the shoulder. "Ask the boy how much he's saved towards his ticket to America."

Fredrik miner translated again.

"Not much," Anders admitted.

There was no need for Fredrik to interpret. The despondency in the young miner's voice was evident.

"Well, then. He needs to know this. With the mine in Kåfjord about to close, more Kven will be headed this way. One of them, Antti Swedberg, half Swede, half Finn, used to be the Swedish lightweight champion. He hasn't fought since the Swedish government banned the sport, but he's trying to get back in shape for the All Scandinavian Boxing Championships to be held in Copenhagen in the summer of '07. He's got his eye on the Olympics as well. Some well-heeled Englishmen, owners of the Alta mine, are willing to put up eight hundred kroner for anyone who goes twelve rounds with the brute."

Fredrik relayed Pettersen's message.

"Not interested," Anders said, draining his beer, standing up from the bar stool, nodding at the barkeep, and leaving the tavern.

CHAPTER EIGHTEEN December 1905 (Viipuri, Finland)

The child was a boy. As agreed, Alvar and Tatianna named him Kari. He was a large-headed, thick-limbed, chubby mound of pink flesh, the sort of baby a stranger can hold without being intimidated. The fact that Kari was born virtually hairless wasn't unusual: many newborns enter this world without abundant hair. But the child's near baldness was humorous to the Finn and his Russian wife because the infant's situation mimicked the bald plate that now defined his father's head. Seemingly overnight, whether due to his injuries triggering something in his body or simply the march of time, The Elf Warrior's red hair had fallen out in clumps until Alvar resorted to having Tatianna shave his head.

"He looks just like me," Alvar would say with a chuckle as he rubbed soft, nearly invisible tufts of red down on the child's significant cranium. "But that means he's a bright lad. It's been said that grass cannot grow on a busy street!"

Tatianna looked at her husband as he sat in a rocking chair in the parlor of their apartment, day's light fading, the last of a Saturday afternoon fleeing to the west, the lazy sun of early winter barely illuminating the room and smiled. "But unlike your hair, husband, Kari's will eventually grow and, given my side of the family, be thick and long ..." here, she hesitated for effect, "... and permanent!" She stood up from the davenport where she'd been engaged in darning socks, studied the child, and nodded. "But right now, he needs to be fed."

Alvar extended the child wrapped in swaddling to Tatianna. "That's a task you're better suited for than me," the Finn said through a smile, his eyes locked on his wife's bosom, her breasts engorged with milk and barely constrained by the thin fabric of her camisole, the undergarment peeking out from beneath her silk blouse, the blouse a luxury Alvar had purchased when they were in Siberia. "Perhaps later, you will allow me closer inspection ..."

"Husband!" Tatianna's response was part of a game they had recently conceived. "I'm in no condition to lay with you so soon after bringing your son into this life," she continued in

100

Russian. Despite the admonition, Tatianna wasn't seriously objecting to her husband's carnality and, in fact, having healed from the birthing, wished to return to their lovemaking despite the heaviness in her breasts and the weariness in her bones from caring for a demanding infant. "It's too soon to talk of such foolishness!"

Tatianna held Kari in her arms, the child's weight clear in the mother's sagging shoulders. Alvar reached out with his right hand. For a moment, Tatianna thought Alvar's intention was to stroke the baby's rosy cheeks. But instead, Alvar tweaked the lobe of his wife's left ear.

"You're a vixen, Mrs. Alhomäki," he whispered. "It seems to me that you're sufficiently recovered; that it's time we enjoyed each other's company."

She shook her head and stamped a small, bare foot against the pine floor. "Enough of your nonsense!" she replied. "This baby needs to nurse."

Tatiana reclaimed the sofa, opened her blouse to the dusky skin of her right breast, lowered the snuggling baby to the nipple, and closed her eyes as Kari began to suckle.

Alvar watched the interplay of mother and child without comment, his pride and love and dedication to them clear in his silence, his quietude compelled by reverence. *Beautiful.*

28 November 1905
Dearest Uncle:

Thank you for the letter and the news of Kari's birth. I was happy to receive your announcement here in Røros, which is a pretty boring place. Besides working and drinking and sleeping, there's not a lot to do in this town. There are no single women. No cinema. No civic events to divert one's attention. With this exception: I have agreed to fight again, in February, in Trondheim. Englishmen who run mines in Finnmark have proposed that I spar with Antti Swedberg, the former lightweight champion of Sweden. Despite working twelve hours a day in the mines, six days a week, I've put on some weight and am more of a middleweight, but the organizers don't care. They want to sponsor an exhibition with someone who can take a punch and deliver a punch but someone who isn't likely to wreck their champion.

Swedberg hasn't fought in two years and is getting ready for a tournament in Denmark. He'll fight as a Norwegian, not a Swede, if he makes it to Copenhagen. I'm to be his first test. I'm hoping I can get in shape quickly so that I don't embarrass myself. It's been a long time since I fought. Who knows? He might just knock me out. He's undefeated and has dropped twenty of twenty-five opponents. There's a pretty good chance he'll do the same to me!

You might be asking why I'm willing to take a risk and get back into the ring after what happened in Oulu. Well, Uncle, the answer is simple: money. After a year of working in the mine, I'm still without significant purse. I find that the cost of food, lodging, and an occasional beer at the local tavern leaves little for savings.

The Englishmen funding the match are putting up eight hundred Norwegian kroner: five hundred just for stepping into the ring and three hundred more if I go twelve rounds with Swedberg. You'll note that he's got a Finnish first name. He's what the Norwegians call a Kven—*a half Swede, half Finn—who has lived here a considerable period of time. It's funny that a boxer with Finnish blood and a Swedish name is being promoted as the champion of the Vikings, but that's just how it is. So, the reason behind my lacing up the gloves and endangering my noggin is this: eight hundred kroner pays for a ticket to America with enough left over for a grubstake. It's that simple.*

I'm sorry that I've not had the chance to meet your wife and son. I'm unsure if I'll be able to visit Finland. The cost of travel, the time involved, and the fact I have no idea what the future holds for me once I arrive in America all complicate thoughts of returning. So please give Tatianna and Kari my love and treat them with the same kindness you've always treated me.

I'm sending a separate letter to my folks. I trust they too are doing well, that the farm is productive, and that my father has calmed down some since the czar has modified Bobrikov's restrictions and allowed more freedom for our people.

I'll write again after the match with Swedberg. That is, if I haven't broken my writing hand on his thick skull!

Sincerely,
Your Nephew
Anders Alhomäki

The rocker ceased moving. The subtle rooting of Kari's mouth on Tatianna's breast was, other than significant snoring from Alvar, the only sound in the parlor. The pages of Anders's letter were settled in the postman's lap. Tatianna's kind, dark eyes studied the reflection of gaslight highlighting Alvar's bald head. She considered what she would wear to Transfiguration Cathedral, the Russian Orthodox church she attended in Viipuri, for Sunday morning service. *Someday,* she thought, adjusting her son on her breast, *I'll get Alvar to attend. For now, he's reluctant on that point. But I'll work on him and perhaps, with some encouragement in the bedroom, I can elicit a promise that he'll attend a service or two. Extracting such an oath will, given what my husband saw in the war, take time: time to convince him that God cares about people despite all the blood and slaughter and death Alvar experienced. Father Garisnikov is a kindred soul. He too went to war as a chaplain in the czar's army. If I can get my husband to church, I think Father will do the rest.*

The woman nodded as she completed her thought. She was satisfied. She would convince her husband that his soul needed the moral guidance only Christian prayer could instill. Her eyes closed. The child stopped pulling on her nipple and fell asleep, his small, moist mouth nuzzling Tatianna's breast as mother and baby joined Alvar Alhomäki in a late afternoon nap.

CHAPTER NINETEEN: January 1906 (Røros, Norway)

Though Wirkkala's crew worked a side tunnel of Haakon's Mine by hand, breaking copper-bearing rock free of the walls of the shallow tunnel by hammer and pick, the steady pounding of Ingersoll mining drills could be heard in the distance. The machinery—newly purchased and implemented—was pneumatically powered by compressors located above ground. Pipes connected the compressors to reserve tanks adjacent to the drill sites. Rubber hoses brought pressurized air from the reserve tanks to the drills where the miners worked ore. The din of mechanized drilling echoed within the close quarters of the mine, drowning out voices and commands and small talk between miners. The noise was deafening and dehumanizing and deprived Wirkkala's crew of comradery as they cracked open the secrets of the low-ceilinged room they were working.

Anders didn't dwell on danger. The subterranean world he inhabited for a paltry wage, a wage that would never accumulate and set him free of his toil, was not a coal mine. The stopes the miners worked were solid rock, hewn from the Løkken volcanogenic copper–zinc deposit, the result of ancient tectonic and volcanic activity. The mining done at Haakon's Mine was hard-rock excavation, where the threat of cave-in was virtually non-existent. Protective measures were only implemented, when, after inspection by Sig Olafson—the Norwegian mining engineer overseeing all of the mines owned by Røros Mining—instability was noted. In the rare instances when shoring was required, iron bars were bolted across unstable rock to prevent cave-ins. But the methodology of mining applied at Haakon's Mine did not include the installation of the familiar wooden timbers utilized in soft-rock mining. The ceilings of the stopes in the copper mine were universally stable and pillars of standing ore functioned as columned supports—pillars which, when the excavation of a particular room was completed, were removed as the miners forged ahead. The stope Anders's crew worked did not, in Olafson's opinion, require shoring. There appeared to be no need to expend additional time, effort, or expense to ensure the safety of Wirkkala's crew.

It was not fear of death by suffocation or by the inadvertent detonation of the dynamite sometimes used by blasters to free up ore—a technique used sparingly at Haakon's Mine—that weighed heavily upon Anders's mind as he shoveled rock into a tin bucket, carried the heavily laden pail into an access tunnel, and dumped rock into a waiting ore cart. It was the fact that, no matter how hard Anders strained, no matter how fast he loaded ore into the little wooden cars that transported the raw ore to the mine's elevator and hence, to the surface, his wages would always remain insufficient for him to leave Norway for America.

Fighting in Trondheim is my only hope for salvation from this hell, Anders thought as he bowed his head to avoid the roof of the stope, leaned on his short-handled shovel, and took a deep breath of the fresh air being supplied by ventilation shafts cut through the rock above them. The shafts not only served as air exchanges; they were lined with iron ladders and functioned as escape routes in the event of a catastrophe. If the power went down, creating a bottleneck of panic at the darkened decline or at the elevator station, or if a section of ceiling gave way, cutting a crew off from the surface, the ventilation shafts provided the possibility of escape. Alternatively, the shafts also served as entrance points for rescue workers or, if time ran out, for the extraction of the dead. As Alhomäki inhaled fresh air, he did not dwell on such possibilities. He removed a red cotton handkerchief from the pocket of his woolen trousers, wiped dust and sweat from his face, and considered the impossibility of America.

"Finlander, stop loafing and get back to work!" Raimo Wirkkala shouted from somewhere out of Anders's view. "You don't get paid to fuck the dog!"

Anders tucked his soiled handkerchief into the pocket of his woolen trousers and moved towards the far end of the cut. Wirkkala's crew was assigned to work the deepest location in the mine, a tunnel far from the decline, the central shaft, electric lighting, and the drills. And yet, the hustle and bustle of the mechanized portion of the mining operation still invaded their workspace as industrial noise. Anders made his way into the stope, his back bent to keep his head from striking the ceiling, and stopped next to Edvin Koivu. The yellow light of miners' candles flickered and danced across the walls of the claustrophobic space. Edvin sunk the business end of his pick into the rock. The older

105

Finn grunted from the effort, the simple task seeming to exhaust the emaciated man after just one swing.

"That bastard wouldn't know what work was if it bit him in the ass," Edvin said quietly. "You outwork the three of us combined and deserve a break now and again," Edvin said as he studied a portion of the stony wall in front of his face. Without warning, Edvin changed the topic. "Hey, take a look at this, would you? Never seen anything like it."

Anders moved closer. Wavering, uncertain candlelight revealed a bright, red scar—smooth and polished—a naturally occurring vein of copper beneath the gray rock that Edvin had been working. "That's got to be a hundred percent pure! I wonder where the vein goes from here?" Anders queried.

Edvin chipped away portions of the surrounding rock with his pick. "Can't tell for sure, but it looks like it continues overhead."

"I don't like the looks of the vein once it hits the ceiling," Anders observed. "Doesn't look stable. Maybe we should get Wirkkala to take a look."

"You think that lazy bastard gives a good goddamn about it?" Edvin asked. "Olafson might but he's not on site today. I say I follow the vein and if I'm right, we'll make the owners of this shithole very, very happy."

Anders studied the wall and ceiling. "Your call, Edvin. Just don't bring the whole damn thing down on us."

Anders returned to his labors. Anders and Edvin worked in close proximity to the Pöysti brothers, each man in the crew using his hammer and pick to free rock from the stubborn grip of the mountain.

"Shit," Edvin exclaimed a few moments later.

"What's wrong?"

The business end of Koivu's pick was embedded in the wall near the old man's head, the details of the scene illumined by a stub of a nearly exhausted candle on his cap. "Damn thing is stuck. The vein continues into the ceiling. I thought one strike would loosen it up. I took a good swing and now the damn rock won't let go."

The Pöysti brothers remained silent save for the sounds of steel slamming stone. Wirkkala was outside the chamber, either asleep or reading his Bible, and would be of no assistance. Anders studied the blaze of scarlet revealed by the thin man's efforts. The coppery seam stood out from the metamorphic rock surrounding it. There was something odd, something different about the deposit Koivu was working. Anders couldn't pinpoint the anomaly, but it was there, nonetheless. *Edvin's right: if we call the boss, Wirkkala will simply tell him to free his own damn pick and get back to work. Olafson isn't available to assess the stability of the vein. It's up to me to help.*

"I'll get a pry bar," Anders said. "Maybe we can wedge the seam open enough to release the pick."

"Do that. I sure as hell can't get it to budge," Edvin agreed.

Anders kicked at a rat. The animal chirped and scurried away. The Finn leaned his pick against the rock, slid into darkness, and returned with an iron bar. The Pöysti brothers stopped working to watch Anders and Edvin's efforts.

"Got 'er stuck, eh Koivu? Poju asked.

"Maybe if you weren't so old and broken down, you'd have the strength to pull it out yourself, like King Arthur and that sword!" Fredrik joked.

"Funny, boys. Maybe you two should mind your own business and break some rock before the boss gets wind you're lollygagging," Edvin retorted, pulling hard against the oak shaft of the pick, his effort failing to dislodge the tool.

Anders held the pry bar horizontal to the ground with both hands. The heavy rod had a tapered blade at one end. "If I slide the tip in here," he said, gesturing with the bar towards the seam, "and apply pressure, you should be able to pull the pick out."

Edvin nodded. Anders jammed the narrow end of the rod into the fissure. "On three," he said firmly, widening his stance. "One, two, three!"

Craaack!

The ceiling gave way. Tons of rock fell when Anders applied leverage, burying the two miners. Dust filled the chamber. The Pöysti brothers raced across the tunnel and discovered that only Anders's left boot remained free of the screedy pile.

BOOK TWO: NOW

CHAPTER ONE: June 2017 (Lakeville, Minnesota)

Josiah Aristotle Tate, CNP was tired. Tired of caring for old people. Tired of politics and the divisive nature of American discourse in the era of The Donald. Tired of his marriage to Maggie Ann Beumont Tate, his wife of thirty years, a woman who had started their run as pretty and overly optimistic but had descended into staleness and pessimism after the birth of their second child. Tired of writing checks for his kids—Amy Lee and Dexter—both in their late twenties and still in school. *Perpetually in school*, he thought with annoyance.

Josiah was—in ways that his father, Elmore Abram Tate, MD would (had he still been amongst the living) condemn as self-centered and in violation of the family's Baptist faith—ready to toss in the towel. The Tate Family had started out as Lutherans but, in a bow to his father's African American heritage, the family became Baptists. Josiah, never enamored with tradition, was on the precipice of ditching the whole mess, buying an airplane ticket, and beginning a long-dreamed-of "'round-the-world trip" by visiting his younger sister—Dr. Janine Tate Tanninen, and Janine's husband, Olavi—in Kajaani, Finland where the couple volunteered in an internment facility housing Syrian refugees.

Sis must be like what, Josiah thought as he stood outside the assisted living facility on break and took a long drag from a smoldering Marlboro, a habit he'd picked up while serving in the First Gulf War as a hospital corpsman in the United States Navy attached to the Marine Corps, *one of the only black people in Finland! Why my African American, Finnish American sister would go off and marry a Finlander and then up and move to his homeland, a place where dark-skinned folks are viewed with suspicion, I'll never understand.* Josiah drew heavily, flaring the Marlboro against dusk as the nurse ruminated on his sister's deep, personal connection to The Savior, a level of belief that had eluded Josiah for the entirety of his life. At sixty-five, on the cusp of retirement and with the opening of a vast void of indifference between himself and his wife, Josiah Tate was ready for change. He tossed his smoke onto the sidewalk, crushed it beneath a rubber soled Nike, retrieved the butt, and deposited it in an ash can. He pulled his iPhone 8 from a pocket of his scrubs, glanced at the time, and found a seat on a wrought-iron bench. *Ten minutes left.* He watched a pair of pheasants, the rooster alert and brightly colored, the hen cautious, inconspicuous, and subservient in her movements, peck gravel. His eyes left the birds. He scrolled through e-mails. There was a new message from Janine. Curious as to why his highfalutin plastic-surgeon-sister would be sending him an e-mail in the middle of her night, Josiah opened the message and began to read.

Ari:

Hope this e-mail finds you in good health. I'm well, though right now, for some reason, I'm wide awake. I just took an Ativan so hopefully, sleep is coming!

Olavi is well. All is fine here in Kajaani as we work with the Syrian men and women and children Finland has chosen to accept for resettlement. There are new faces appearing in the camp—living in the clean but modest barracks of this facility—every day as the fighting between Assad and the rebels and ISIS and the Kurds grows more brutal. The word atrocity is too small a term, I think, for what is happening to the innocent civilians of that very ancient land.

The Finnish government spares nothing trying to make the immigrants feel at home despite the fact that very few of them have ever seen pine trees or snow! These are people who have lost everything and who have, in the case of the children, many health issues. I find my medical and surgical skills constantly challenged. I've been called upon, through SmileTrain, an international charity, to perform a dozen or so cleft lip and palate procedures, all funded and paid for through donations. The results are remarkable. Kids who would not smile, would not laugh because of disfigurement, are now grinning at the slightest tease or joke. It's astounding to think that medical care so simple, so elementary, is unavailable in Syria. It makes my heart sing to see the results. God is indeed at work here.

My medical knowledge is challenged every single day. There are only three doctors working in the camp. A British internist named Doaks Hampton, Julie Chambers, a Canadian OB/GYN, and me. From that roster you can see that I am the only surgeon posted here through the United Nations refugee agency, UNCHR, the same agency that the government is working with to bring an estimated thirty thousand Muslim refugees from Syria, Iraq, and Afghanistan to Finland for resettlement. Given that most of Finland's population—except for some Somalis who immigrated here twenty years ago and the indigenous Sami and a few roving Gypsies—is of typical blond, blue-eyed, Nordic stock, there's some discomfort over the government's acceptance of dark-skinned immigrants. Well-publicized assaults committed against Finnish girls by Muslim men have increased tensions. Those attacks have ratcheted up hate speech from nationalist and isolationist groups. But that sort of xenophobia has been dismissed as baseless noise by many Finns, including my husband.

Being the only surgeon in camp has been quite a learning experience. I've found myself assisting Dr. Chambers on difficult C-sections and other OB/GYN cases. I even performed a complex delivery on my own when Chambers was off on holiday. I've also worked with Dr. Hampton on a plethora of medical conditions requiring surgical intervention, including the removal of three appendixes and a couple of gall bladders. And of course, I've ended up treating any number of adults and children for complications related to bullets, shrapnel, and burns. We refer the most difficult cases to the local hospital. But UNCHR has provided us with a fairly complete, modern, and sterile operating room located in the camp's infirmary from which to dispense care so the number of such referrals is quite small.

The scenery here in central Finland is something you would recognize. Remember when we visited Helsinki and Pietasaari and Turku with our parents? We came to see Grandma Elin. That was quite a trip! I'm sure you remember it well and remember that kindly old blind woman who, it turns out, wasn't really Mother's mother at all, but her half-sister. Thanks, Grandmother Elin for waiting decades to reveal that little family secret! Anyway, the setting here in Kajaani would be familiar to you. The woods and lakes and swamps and topography are reminiscent of Minnesota. I never understood why you left New York City until I retired from practice and started volunteering to work in the far corners of the world through the National Baptist Office of Disaster Management. Now, having spent two years in Olavi's native country surrounded by reflective lakes, flowing rivers, and piney forests I get why you choose to live where you do. But the Twin Cities isn't my point of comparison here. Rather, I'm thinking of those forested and wild regions of northern Minnesota where our Finnish ancestors tried to mine and farm and raise families, when I make comparisons. I'm finding that the Finn in me is at home in such lonesome places even if my more urban, African American side longs for inner-city excitement. For now, Olavi and I have our work, and I'm content to, in the warmer months, hop on my mountain bike or, when the snow falls, step into my cross-country skis and explore this place. Never having had children, having considered my work to be my calling and my passion, I'm content giving back to my fellow man and enjoying a reflective life amongst folks who need my help.

Speaking of children, how are my niece and nephew? Has Amy Lee taken her MCATS yet? There's a slot open for her at McGill, courtesy of her auntie's connections, if she does well. Of course, the U of M isn't a bad place to land if McGill proves too distant or expensive. Dexter, I understand, is finishing up his master's in engineering at St. Thomas. Isn't he due for deployment through the army reserves as well? Here's hoping he stays safe wherever he is sent.

Well, that's about it from here. Oh, I did want to tell you this: there's a slot opening up here for another certified nurse practitioner. UNCHR has freed up funds to pay for a second CNP in hopes of lessening our caseload. I know from our telephone conversations that you and Maggie are having a time of it. Sorry if that remains the case. But if you're looking for a place to contemplate and consider life, a stint in Kajaani might serve you well. It's a volunteer position so the pay is non-existent but living and meal expenses and travel are covered (a warning here: the food at the commissary is for shit!). With retirement looming, I thought that maybe we could finish our careers working together. It's been a long time since we broke bread, Ari, and I'd dearly love to see you again.

Think about it.
Love,
Thena

Josiah closed the e-mail. He stared into the oak and maple forest surrounding the sprawling, single-story assisted-living complex. He loved that Janine still called him by his nickname, a shorthand

114

version of "Aristotle," an expansive and important middle name his father had insisted upon. His sister's middle name, "Athena," came with a similar air of imperiousness—evidence of a haughty pride Dr. Elmore Tate had exuded. Their father had never countenanced Janine calling Josiah "Ari" or Josiah calling Elmore's tall, lanky daughter "Thena." Those were unsanctioned sobriquets the Tate offspring had used when addressing each other out of their father's presence. Despite the fondness he felt for his sister, Janine's e-mail seemed to emanate a presumptuousness of concern and caretaking for Josiah that, quite frankly, had always annoyed the elder child of Elmore and Alexis Tate.

Damn it, Janine. It's like you can read my mind. You've been screwing with me like that since we were kids. How the hell did you know I was thinking of paying you and that big, dumb oaf of a Finlander you call "husband" a visit?

Josiah's break was over. It was time to return to work. He slipped the iPhone back into his pocket, stood up from the bench, and walked towards the front entrance to the building.

Finland, he thought. *That bat-shit crazy sister of mine wants me to pull up stakes and fly off to Finland to take care of some goddamned Muslims. For free! She must be out of her mind.*

The nurse reached for the door, pulled hard on the stainless-steel handle, entered the building, and tried to focus his attention on the old folks inside.

CHAPTER TWO: (Kajaani, Finland)

Dr. Janine Tanninen sped down a rugged trail on her mountain bike, her lean body folded over the handlebars as she pumped her legs like a madwoman. Sweat poured from beneath Janine's helmet and slid down her coppery face, her skin tone more akin to a good Scandinavian tan than the dark, serious African complexion of her older brother. Another racer—a woman— haunted Janine's rear tire. Two men bounced along ahead of her. Other than the three riders near Janine, the other entrants in the fifty-kilometer cross-country bicycle race were spread out along the course. Janine and her group were somewhere near the head of the pack, in the hunt for medals depending upon their respective ages.

In her youth, Janine Athena Tate had won countless 1600- and 3200-meter foot races, finishing fourth her senior year at Long Island Prep in the New York State High School cross-country meet. By pushing her own personal envelope, by running five miles a day—every day, rain or shine, from eighth grade through her senior year in high school—she'd turned a languid body into a machine. Janine went on to run varsity cross-country at Columbia, but once she began medical school at McGill in Montreal (her mother Alexis's alma mater), Janine tucked away her running shoes and used a portion of her hard-earned residency stipend to buy a good road bike. Like many kids, she'd owned Schwinns and other off-the-rack mountain bikes during her youth but, due to limited time and an obsessive/compulsive striving to be the best runner she could be, Janine's pedaling time had been severely limited until Montreal.

The mountain bike she rode outside Kajaani was a Finnish blue, Trek Top Fuel 9.8, a bike retailing for more than six thousand dollars—*before* customization. Her ride boasted shock-absorbing technology and twenty-nine-inch wheels to fit her nearly two-meter frame and had the durability of an Abrams tank. It was one of four bikes that the doctor owned, two of which, the Fuel 9.8 and an Émonda SLR 9 (also a Trek and also custom painted in Finnish blue and retailing for more than eleven grand) accompanied her to Finland. Even when not competing as part of the Kajaani *Kanit* bike team as she was in this race, her scarlet

116

Spandex jersey boasting the team's logo—a buck-toothed, crazy-eyed hare on a bicycle—Janine made it a point to ride every day possible, though she hadn't yet made the switch from cross-country skiing to riding a fat tire in snow. There was something in the Finnish heritage gifted to Janine by her mother Alexis (who'd passed away from dementia in 2001, eleven years after Janine's father Elmore was killed by a drunk driver while crossing a street in Harlem) that compelled her to ski. But the day was coming, in Janine's estimation, when she might give up her skinny skis and bike year-round.

That is, if I can stay away from a complete replacement of my left knee, she ruminated, glancing at the bulky brace she wore below her scarlet Spandex biking shorts as she pedaled. The brace kept pain at bay and allowed her to pedal on. *But eventually ...*

As she aged, she needed more training, more consistency, more time on the bike to remain competitive. But the knee, an old injury that had started when she ran the New York City Marathon on a dare from her best friend on the Columbia cross-country team, was problematic. She knew that someday she wouldn't be able to continue, that the knee or old age or another injury or cancer or, like her mother, dementia would claim her athleticism. But she would try, as best she could, to suspend time by wearing the damnable brace and by working her slender ass to the bone.

The trail widened. *Three kilometers to go. Time to make my move.* Janine dug deep and sought residual strength to pass the men in front of her. "On the left!" Janine shouted in Finnish.

The rider leading Janine's group, a heavy-set fellow decked out in a black Spandex riding outfit accented by the yellow and orange lettering of his club, *Helsingin Hellions* and a fluttering, red-and-white numbered bib with his race number, 101, snuck a peek at Janine over his left shoulder and nodded. The rider drafting the leader, a short, diminutive man wearing bib number five, did the same. Janine moved out as quickly as her legs would allow and felt the woman following her, a thirty-something bundle of nervous energy with short cropped blond hair and monstrous calves—Milla Aho—accelerate in kind. As Janine summoned another internal gear to fend off Aho's challenge, she felt a familiar twinge in her left knee. *Shit.* Despite the pain, Janine assumed the lead of her little group. Milla also passed the men, settled in behind Janine, and matched the doctor's pace as they climbed a steep hill. *She's biding her time, seeing what I've got left in the tank.*

Janine sought distraction from her knee. She thought back to her long journey from New York City, a place her mother, Alexis, and her grandmother/aunt, Elin Gustafson Ellison Godlfarb Peltomaa, had called home after leaving Duluth, Minnesota in 1918. Her mother had been an infant, the product of an illicit affair between Janine's great grandfather, Karl Gustafson, and Karl's housekeeper-turned-mistress-turned-second wife, Sofia Wirtanen. Sofia and Karl both died unexpectedly— Sofia from influenza and Karl from a massive heart attack. She knew this history because Grandmother Elin kept letters she received from friends and relatives, along with an informal memoir she had written depicting her life, as she moved first to the Finnish Cooperative in the Sunset Park neighborhood of New York City and then to Finland, where she ultimately survived the Winter War, the Continuation War, and the Lapland War to marry fellow Duluthian Matti Peltomaa. The letters and memoir documented Elin's pilgrimage from America to the Gustafson ancestral homeland. This history was entrusted to Alexis when Elin passed away in her sleep in a Pietasaari nursing home and was gifted to Janine upon Alexis's own death.

Grandma kept everything!

The boxes of letters and newspaper articles and diaries and documents—including the handwritten memoir—were filled to the brim with family lore. The archive revealed long-hidden Gustafson secrets, including the truth about Alexis's conception and birth and the fact that, as a young woman in America, Grandmother Elin had been a newspaper reporter for the radical Finnish American press, had been involved in a torrid affair with a Finnish immigrant miner that was ended by an edict from Great Grandfather Karl, and described in bitter detail Grandma's failed marriage to Duluth businessman Horace Ellison. That union ended in divorce about the time Alexis was born and her parents died, giving Grandma Elin the courage and the impetus to leave Duluth for New York City where she married Socialist newspaperman Hiram Goldfarb.

Janine was fascinated by the past. Though she had made her mark in the world using math and science to become a top-

118

notch plastic surgeon, the old stories, the family sagas, the grist of her forming and being kept her engaged in self-discovery. The fact that Grandma Elin and her Jewish husband had left America with Alexis in tow, hoping to chronicle the reverse migration of Finns from America to Karelia, enduring hardship, difficulty, danger, and—in Hiram's case—death at the hands of the NKVD, stirred something in Janine's soul. This piquing of interest compelled Janine to investigate the historic forces that drove her grandmother to risk it all such that, when offered a posting at the Kajaani Refugee Center, Janine jumped at the opportunity to spend time in the homeland of her maternal ancestors.

These reflections clouded Janine's mind as she fought discomfort fomenting beneath her left kneecap. She stood on the pedals, pumping as hard as her long, muscular legs would allow, trying to forestall the inevitable. *I can feel her breathing down my neck.*

It happened at the crest of the hill. Exhausted from the climb, knowing that only a downhill cruise and a flat expanse of river bottom remained before crossing the finish line, glimpses of other riders' vibrant outfits visible through the birch and pine and spruce forest crowding the trail ahead of her, Janine understood that she was bested even before Milla shouted, "On the left!" and passed Janine as if she was standing still. Janine's only solace was that the men had completely failed the test: they were behind the women, walking the trail, pushing their expensive bikes towards the hill's summit, and totally spent.

"Hell of a race," Janine said evenly, her breath catching. "Hope you place."

Milla nodded but did not reply.

Janine watched the younger woman downshift and move off with speed. The trail followed a narrow ridge for half a kilometer before descending onto the floodplain of the Kivijoki. Just ahead, the trail widened to accommodate four racers riding abreast, the added space allowing contestants to sprint to the finish line. As the front tire of her Trek hit the muddy flats, the grassy surface obliterated by churning tires to reveal rich, brown Kajaani soil, Janine noted that a woman and three men constituted the group directly ahead of her. The four riders were tightly bunched, riding neck and neck, leaving no room for trailing riders to pass.

119

Janine glanced over her shoulder. Another female racer close to Janine's age was gaining on her. *I don't know if I'm in first, second, or whatever,* Janine thought, returning her attention to the looming finish line, *but I'll be damned if I'm going to let anyone else pass me!*

Janine's Spandex top and cycling shorts were dappled with mud. Her left knee screamed. She gritted her teeth, downshifted, and pushed herself. "On the left!" Janine called out, her Finnish clear, though spoken with a New York accent—a legacy of learning the language from her mother—as she drafted the female rider in front of her. The woman glanced over her right shoulder, her dark brown eyes and black hair evincing Sami blood, her body thick and muscular, but her breathing deep and struggling as she sought to keep pace with her group. For a moment, Janine thought the woman was going to ignore her request and block her. "On the left!" Janine repeated with more authority. The woman glanced to her right, slowed her pace, tucked in behind one of the men, and let Janine pass.

The woman behind Janine started to accelerate.

Damn. I didn't think she had enough left in her to make a push. My knee isn't going to last much longer. God, give me the strength to hold her off.

Janine's helmet slid down her nose and obstructed her view of the trail. Her nubby salt-and-pepper hair was slick from sweat encouraged by the humidity of an approaching storm. Broiling clouds closed in from the west. Janine gleaned that the woman behind her was gaining ground, but she resisted the urge to turn her head and check. To do so would cause Janine to lose momentum and possibly, the slight edge she maintained.

Fifty meters. Fifty damn meters. Janine's Baptist soul cringed at the curse.

The front tire of the pursuing bike appeared in the periphery of Janine's vision. A bolt of lightning lit up the sky. A boom of thunder welcomed the women as they began one last, desperate sprint through pouring rain.

A gold medal dangled from a white and blue lanyard against Janine's flat chest. Mud covered her tunic, shorts, limbs, and face. Olavi, his golden hair flecked at the temples with gray, his icy eyes clear and searching, left the crowd milling around the finish line.

Olavi found his wife pushing her bike across a muddy field flanked by birches and willows that defined the limits of the Kivijoki. The rain increased, but as the sky let loose, the thunder and lightning dissipated.

"Nice race," Olavi said, water dripping off his blond mane, the storm soaking his clothing as he fixed his gaze on his wife's uneven gait. "Knee acting up?"

Janine nodded. Olavi responded with a bear hug.

"Hurts like the devil," Janine admitted as she separated from Olavi's embrace. "I think this might be it."

Olavi Tanninen shook his large head. He knew the fiercely competitive spirit that fueled his wife's passion for medicine, for athletics, and for life. They remained sexually compatible despite the physical changes imposed by maturation, the process of aging requiring creativity that younger folks wouldn't understand. An environmental engineer by training possessing an analytical mind, and a realist by nature, Olavi could not imagine his wife forsaking the adrenalin rush she received from competition simply because of age. *She's adaptable as all get out*, he thought as they walked side by side towards a Volvo station wagon parked in the gravel lot, pushing the lightweight bicycle with one hand as he guided his wife towards the car with the other. "I doubt that very much, Thena," he replied, uttering a nickname for Janine that only he and Josiah used. "You'll sauna, rest a bit, take some Ultram, have a few glasses of wine, and all will be well."

She studied him. "You're such an optimist," she said without conviction.

Olavi smiled, removed a key fob from a pocket of his sodden khakis, pushed a button, and opened the Volvo's hatch. "Not at all; I'm a pragmatist. I know you, know your nature. I don't see you, as that Welshman once said, 'going gently into that good night.'"

Janine shivered. She stood alongside Olavi, constant, tumultuous rain penetrating already-soaked Spandex, watching him hoist the Trek over the car's rear bumper into the station wagon. "Great. Now you have me dead," she quipped between chattering teeth as she opened the Volvo's front passenger door and slid her wet, sweaty, tired, aching body across leather.

CHAPTER THREE

Of the one hundred and ninety-two asylum seekers from Syria screened by Finland's Immigration Service in the six months after Dr. Janine Tanninen arrived at the Kajaani Refugee Center, seventy-five of the applicants—thirty-two adult women, thirty-seven children, and six adult men—were accepted by the Finnish government and placed in the camp. The newcomers were assigned housing in antiquated, wood-framed, metal-roofed barracks pained forest green once used by the Finnish Defense Forces for reservist training. Families were housed in the former barracks, retrofitted to provide private rooms. Single men were housed dormitory-style in a smaller, cement-block building that had once been the armory. The recently arrived joined an existing cadre of 205 other Syrian refugees whose applications for asylum had been approved. But the Syrians already at the center when the newcomers arrived were languishing: forced to be patient, to bide their time waiting for housing, jobs, education, and new lives. The men, women, and children who escaped civil war and ISIS incursions into their homeland had been, in some cases, waiting over a year for resettlement while braving an unfamiliarly cold, snowy, rainy, wet, mosquito-afflicted reality.

"How goes it today, Venla?"

Janine asked the question of a nursing student, Venla Balzar, a short-limbed, squarely built woman in her mid-twenties; the student's Kale heritage evident in her exotic complexion, black hair, and dark brown eyes. The young woman hailed from Rovaniemi and was a second-year student at the Lapland University of Applied Science seeking her Bachelor of Health Care in Nursing. Janine suspected, by virtue of Venla's place of origin and her bearing, that the young woman also had ancestral ties to the Sami, the indigenous people of the far north formerly known as the Lapps.

Venla was forearms deep in a sink of warm, soapy water laundering her underthings—utilitarian bras and panties without frills—as well as other clothing. The sun burned above the camp. It was unnaturally hot for summer in central Finland. A clothesline ran from an exterior wall of the staff's quarters to a steel post anchored in the yard. The clothesline had been erected by Olavi Tanninen—the unpaid volunteer overseer of the camp's physical plant. "Fabulous, Doctor. Doesn't this look like a great way to spend a Saturday afternoon?" Venla teased. She moved the wet clothes—the waistbands of her white panties stretched out, reminiscent of the twenty pounds she'd lost since coming to the center—from the basin into a tub of hot rinse water. "Isn't this what every single Finnish girl should be doing: washing her delicates while waiting for Prince Charming to call?"

Janine—casually dressed in a tank top, denim shorts, and expensive sandals—stood alongside the stainless-steel sink and matching counter affixed to the exterior of the building. She held a ceramic mug advertising *Stora Enso*—the Finnish papermaker where Olavi last worked as an engineer—in her right hand. A U.S. firm had bought out Stora's North American affiliate, compelling Olavi to retire early, prompting the couple's extended visit to Finland.

Their mission to Kajaani was seen by them both as only temporary; they maintained a rent-stabilized apartment in Greenwich Village, the artsy New York neighborhood they'd called home for the better part of a decade, giving them options for when their posting at the refugee center was over. But whether they would leave Finland and return to New York to spend their "golden years" in the Village or live somewhere more temperate was left unsaid.

Steam rose from Janine's coffee mug despite the afternoon's balminess. She smiled. "Prince Charming? Isn't he English? Shouldn't you be holding out for a Prince Anti or an Aleksi or an Aukusti?"

Venla twisted panties to remove excess water before dropping the underwear into a wicker basket. She repeated the process with a bra. In short order, Venla had her clothes ready for hanging. Janine sipped coffee and followed Venla across newly mown grass. An insinuation of womanhood shifted beneath Janine's tank top as she walked. Janine watched as the Kale woman hung wet clothing on the line with clothespins.

"You know, you could use the washer and dryer," Janine advised. "It'd be quicker."

"I find doing laundry by hand serves two purposes, Madam Doctor," Venla replied regally as she flipped a migrant

123

strand of thick, black hair away from her eyes. "First, it's therapeutic: gives me time to think big thoughts. Second, it saves energy. I fill up the sink, fill up the rinse basin, and that's the only hot water I use. We have to think about these things, you know, with global warming being a concern."

Janine's face took on a questioning aspect. She was a staunch Republican. She'd voted for Mr. Trump, not because she thought he was the answer but because Mrs. Clinton left her with too many questions. *Her comment about the "basket of deplorables" was the last straw,* she thought. *I get that global warming is real and that Trump's reluctance to embrace it is an issue. But I have faith he'll come around, that the Paris Accord will be renegotiated, and the U.S. will, despite his promises to coal functionaries, continue moving towards renewables. After all, he's a businessman and there's money to be made in alternative energy.* Janine's digression interrupted her train of thought. After an instant of self-reflection, she returned to the topic at hand.

"You didn't answer me," Janine said, making a face as she sucked sour coffee from the bottom of her cup, "about your marital prospects."

Venla Balzar smiled. "Yes, we did get sidetracked, didn't we? Truth is, I need to find a strong, healthy Finnish man to make strong, healthy Finnish babies. Someone stout and firm and easy on the eyes like that stud you're married to!"

"Ugh. After all the passing of gas in bed last night from the spicy sausages he ate for dinner, Olavi's not as great a catch as he might seem!"

The women giggled, found empty Adirondack chairs under the eaves of the barracks, sat down, and watched rose-colored male pine grosbeaks and their duller mates flit in and out of a bird feeder.

"Beautiful," Janine said. "Reminds me of home."

Venla's eyebrows raised. "You have such birds in America?"

"In the north. Where my brother Josiah lives. In Minnesota."

The nursing student reflected a moment before continuing. "They have many Finns in Minnesota, yes?"

Janine nodded. "They do."

"And your brother, he's part Finn, like you?"

"He is. But he's a lot darker than I am. The Finn in that boy is more hidden, I'm afraid."

Seriousness imposed upon Venla's youthful face. "But he's still Finn, yes? And he knows other men who are also Finns there in America?"

Janine bit her lip and cocked her head. "I see where this is going ..."

"Perhaps a young, strong Finnish boy, even one who looks like you, can be found for a girl wanting to visit, maybe move to America? Someone who ... Josiah, is it ...?"

"Yes."

"... Josiah might know?"

Janine stood up, set her mug down on an adjacent table, and placed both hands on her hips. Slender, tawny fingers massaged the denim of her shorts. The woman's sleeveless top revealed the exotic hue of her arms and chest. The cut of her denim shorts revealed lanky legs of identical bronze. There was an air of amusement about the woman as she scrutinized the nurse-in-waiting. "Possibly," Janine said through a grin. "But I think you need to get through this year's internship, go back to school in Rovaniemi, graduate, and *then* lust after Finnish boys, or Finnish American boys, or whatever."

Venla laughed.

Janine scowled. "What? Did I use the wrong word?"

The Finnish woman shook her head and smiled. "It's just that your accent—it sounds so funny when you speak Finnish. Like an American movie star learning the language. I understand you. I get what you're saying. And I do have time. I'm not yet thirty, not yet too old to have babies with Prince Charming, or Prince Aukusti for that matter!"

"I think it's time ..." Janine paused for effect, "for lunch," she said as the noon bell chimed from the commissary. "My husband's supposed to meet me in the dining hall. He's squiring big wigs from Helsinki around the camp. Supposed to bring them by so we can eat whatever slop Katrina and Matti have in store for us," she concluded, naming the cooks whose job it was to supply three meals a day to refugee-center staff and residents.

The women began walking.

"Big wigs?"

"From Immigration and from the Security Service,"

Janine explained. "They're worried we're harboring suicide-bombers-in-the-making within the ranks of the Syrians we're trying to assimilate."

They reached the door to the commissary, a steel sided pole barn constructed on a cement slab, the building insulated and finished so as to be useable through the harsh Finnish winter. Janine grasped the doorknob, opened the door, and urged her young friend into the cool, brightly lighted space.

"Ah," Venla said, smiling. "Reindeer stew! It smells like home."

Janine didn't immediately reply. Instead, she located her husband and his guests standing in line, holding stainless-steel trays, waiting to be served, before responding: "At least it's not spicy sausages again!"

CHAPTER FOUR

Chief Inspector Alissa Utrio adjusted a leather holster on her right hip. The gesture allowed the cop to sit comfortably on a bench and pull herself closer to the table to eat. Forty-two years old, thin legged, narrow waisted, and boasting a mane of thick, flaming red hair pulled into a ponytail and held in place by a black bungee, Alissa's most striking feature wasn't her hair but her eyes: the irises were emerald and opaque, imbuing her with cat-like mystery.

Though bisexual, Alissa had settled down and married Elsa Vuolijoki, a short, black-haired, local cop six years' Alissa's junior. Both women had given birth—using donor sperm—to children during their four-year marriage; Alissa having conceived, carried, and born a daughter, Uni—two years old—and Elsa having delivered a boy, Urho, who had just turned one. A complicating factor in an otherwise unencumbered relationship was that Elsa's Uncle Leo was the Acting Director of the Finnish Security Intelligence Service—SUPO—meaning he was Alissa's boss. But the women didn't let Uncle Leo's position of authority interfere with their love for each other or their children.

"This stew is tasty," Alissa said, spooning chunks of reindeer, potato, carrot, rutabaga, broth, and sweet onion into her wide mouth.

Olavi Tanninen sat across the pine-planked table from Alissa. Janine sat to her husband's left. A bald-headed, mustached, gnome-like functionary from the Finnish Immigration Service, the man staring into his ceramic bowl of meat and vegetables as if the food was toxic, sat to Olavi's immediate right. A dull-faced, middle-aged woman—the whiskered gnome's companion from Immigration—her hands blue-veined, skeletal and in dire need of nourishment—sat next to Alissa and watched the chief inspector with curiosity.

"Better with some pepper," Olavi answered, his bowl nearly empty, his appetite, even among strangers, readily apparent.

"And where is home for you, Inspector?" Janine asked, placing her spoon on the edge of her bowl.

The man from Immigration snickered. "That's *chief* inspector, to you," he said tersely. "The chief inspector's in charge

127

of the entire Kainuu District," he added, "and doesn't let anyone forget it!"

Alissa smiled as she swallowed a lump of potato but did not reply.

"Stop it, Markku," the little man's companion scolded. "Chief Inspector Utrio is only asking for the respect her hard work and long career in SUPO warrant."

Markku from Immigration muttered something indecipherable. Olavi and Janine glanced at each but did not engage the man.

"So, without giving away state secrets, *Chief* Inspector, where are you from?" Janine asked again.

Alissa smiled more broadly. "A little place called Hossa, on the far-eastern edge of Oulu Province, not far from Suomussalmi."

Janine shook her head. "Never heard of it, have you, Olavi?"

The engineer grinned. "I'm intimately familiar with Hossa."

Alissa stopped eating. "How so?"

"I was posted there with the Finnish Defense Forces as an intelligence officer in the reserves. My unit was stationed in Suomussalmi but there was a girl, a blue-eyed, blond, Bekka, Bekka Hatajärvi ..."

Janine punched her husband's left bicep. "See how incorrigible this man is? Listing off his conquests in front of strangers. The nerve!"

Olavi rubbed his arm but continued grinning. "Conquest? I'm afraid you give me far too much credit, dear wife. Bekka's virtue was an impregnable wall that, try as I might, I was unable to breach. I spent four months wooing that girl to no avail. Still, I sometimes think of her when I'm alone in the forest. Dense trees remind me of the wilderness of Hossa, call me back to my ill-spent youth."

"Enough, husband! Do you think I haven't laments and longings for the men of my past? Especially when trying to sleep with a man who insists on having seconds of peppered sausage for dinner?" Janine asked. "I mean, women are fully capable of making comparisons as well. Am I right, Chief Inspector?"

Alissa shook her head. "I've been in government service long enough to know when to keep quiet."

Olavi slurped broth from the bottom of his bowl. "Have you found anyone, any of the Syrians in camp, Chief Inspector, worth watching?"

Alissa stiffened. "Now that, Mr. Tanninen, would be seeking classified information. I'm not at liberty to reveal my impressions in a specific way. But I'll say this: we've had our issues with the Afghanis and the Somalis and—with the murder that took place last year right here in Kajaani—with Iraqis. But so far, the Syrians haven't caused any problems. These people seem, for the most part, well educated, oriented to their Sunni faith, loyal to their families, and driven to succeed in a place they couldn't possibly have imagined living. The first Syrians arrived in April of 2016. Most of them are still living in camps. Even with the delays in resettlement, they've not caused a lick of trouble for us. Not a single incident worth noting."

The woman from Immigration tilted her narrow face. "Murder? In Kajaani?"

Markku guffawed. "Elisabet, you really do need to get out of Helsinki more often. Or at the very least, watch the evening news. Two Iraqis robbed two Finns in Kajaani. Killing one by beating and stomping him to death. For what? The dead man's ATM card which, because they murdered him without obtaining his PIN, was useless. They killed an innocent citizen for, in essence, no reason. They are nothing but animals."

Olavi's brow furrowed. His eyes locked on the little man. "I get the sense, from your remarks, that, despite working for Immigration, you're not a fan of bringing foreigners into our country."

Markku smiled wickedly. "You've got that right. I say, 'Leave things be. Let the bastards kill each other off.' We'd be doing the rest of the world a favor. Just look at what happened because of that Moroccan, the guy who stabbed those Finnish women to death in the Turku market. Wounded a dozen more. For what? For who? Allah? Revenge? Ha! Animals, I tell you. Nothing but animals. Animals who're plotting our demise as we sit and eat this awful stew."

Alissa Utrio shook her head and pushed herself away from the table. "That's mistaken thinking. The women and

129

children and men in this camp have been triple-vetted by my agency and yours. Every one of them has been cleared of ties to terrorism or ISIS or Assad. They're the innocents, the victims, of a brutal war that they want no part of. Where's your Christian charity, man, that you'd turn your back on such people?"

Markku squinted his small black eyes, put his spoon in his now empty bowl, and thought before answering. "I'm no Christian, Chief Inspector. I have no faith of any kind. Never did. It's one of the reasons I'm able to look at these people without misguided empathy. They're victims of a mess of their own creation. That they also worship a god brought to them in a fable from the cloud—a story no more reliable than tales about Aladdin's Lamp or flying carpets—is another matter. No, you'll not engender tears from me about the state of affairs in Syria. The more they kill each other off, the less we need to worry about laptop bombs on Finnair."

Janine looked at Olavi. There was so much she, a woman of color in a country filled with blond-headed, blue-eyed, pale-skinned Finns wanted to say about race and religion and faith and forgiveness and charity. Her husband reached beneath the table and touched her hand, alerting her that now was not the time or place for political debate.

"I've got patients waiting for me at the infirmary," Janine said, standing up from the table and stretching to her full height. Sunlight glorified her angular face as she collected her cup, bowl, plate, and spoon. "I've got to tend to my flock," she added, hinting at the religiosity that compelled her to volunteer, to provide medical care to strangers whose faith was different from her own.

CHAPTER FIVE: The Warrior's Story. June 2014 (Bangui, Central African Republic)

I'm marching along a dusty, dry, gravel road leading from the EUFOR RCA (European Union Force/Republic of Central Africa) camp outside of Bata, a 7.62mm Sako RK-62 assault rifle banging against my sweat-stained uniform from its shoulder strap, a black and brown P99 sidearm snug in its holster on my right hip, a full campaign pack weighing me down, straps annoying my skin, my desert fatigue shirt chafing my nipples, as I lead a column of Finnish soldiers towards a minefield. Two ancient Sisu Pasi armored vehicles that are supposed to be carrying us to our destination are, like most things on this mission, fucked. The transmission on one of the Sisus is hatched. The other has a blown radiator. The French mechanic assigned to work with us in Bata has ordered parts from Finland, but no one can predict when, or if, the parts will make it here. And so, we walk.

My unit is a collection of boys is what I think as we move through unfamiliar country. This region of Central Africa is not the jungle one perceives to be Africa, but is, rather, a broad grassy savanna, which, if it wasn't so damn hot, might be pastorally scenic. During our first three months' in the country, the thirty Finns in my unit haven't seen a lick of exotic wildlife; no Marlin Perkins moments have occurred. You think I didn't watch reruns of that old American show growing up in Finland? Ha.

An armored car displaying French insignia kicks up dust ahead of us. The Eland is one of the military assets provided by France to stabilize this place, a place that, until 1960, was a French colony. Today, the ground we traverse is under the jurisdiction of the United Nations. The UN agreed to allow EU troops (of which I am one) to augment the commitment France made to send paratroops, armored cars, tanks, helicopters, and other material to defend the defenseless. French aid was meant, along with the EU's contingent, as a stopgap measure until forces from the African Union arrive to restore order in a nation that has seen nearly two hundred thousand Christians displaced by Islamic aggression.

In addition to the Eland, there is a platoon—forty-eight Frenchmen strong—marching ahead of my whiskerless, barely-out-of-puberty mates. Together, we make a formidable force; one that no misfit Muslim outfit would dare take on.

I cannot understand a word Lieutenant René Renier, the Frog leader of our patrol, says. I must rely upon Erno Rikala, a corporal from Kauppi and one of the only veterans of a past deployment other than myself, to translate from French into Finnish. I'm fluent in English and German but Renier understands neither. *I wish the damned Estonians, or the South Africans had stuck it out,* I think, kicking a stone with my boot, the rock skittering off into the parched underbrush. *At least we could understand each other. Estonian is close enough to Finn for us to communicate and the South Africans spoke pretty decent English, despite most of them being Afrikaners. But the Estonians—never much of a force—pulled out early and the Afrikaners left after fourteen of their soldiers died in a firefight in Bangui. Can't really blame them. The folks back home in Johannesburg were up in arms, wondering what the hell their brothers and fathers and sons were doing in Central Africa in the first place. They're right to question this mission. This place is a hopeless mess. But I will do my duty and trust in God to keep me safe. Whether I can keep these brats under my charge from getting themselves killed, well that's the question now, isn't it?*

Despite the weight of my pack, filled with my bedroll and bottled water and dehydrated rations and clean underwear and fresh socks for a two-day trek, I consider myself to be lucky. *At least I'm not carrying a mine detector and a prod. I'm glad I'm not charged with poking around to see what the Muslim rebels have buried in the dirt!* The poor grunts assigned such duty are members of a mine removal platoon. I am not. I was selected by Colonel Poutvaara, plucked from the Utti Jaeger Regiment, extracted from my soft, cushy job as a firearms instructor, and sent to this hellhole to lead these whippersnappers. *Last tour,* I think wistfully as we tromp north towards the suspected minefield, *before I retire.*

As I walk, I'm not thinking about settling down in Finland, finding a girl, marrying, and starting a family. That's not the sort of life I envision. I'm thinking about how to wake up the politicians and military leaders and security operatives in Helsinki to the reality of their disastrous decision to take in Muslim refugees. I know, I know ... Immigrants aren't being brought to

Finland from Central Africa, where the Islamic Sélénka Rebels are mounting a deadly incursion against the Christian majority. The shit here in Central Africa hit the fan when President Michel Djotodia, a Muslim, lost control. Djotodia was ousted from power when he failed to restore order. He was followed in office by Catherine Samba-Panza—a well-meaning Christian and Central Africa's first female leader—and things calmed down a bit. But a succession of inept presidents after Samba-Panza eventually led to the place descending into madness. Islamic gangs returned to raping and murdering and torturing Christians and burning their villages. It was this resurgent unrest that sent the Afrikaners and Estonians packing.

The Muslims claim they are only retaliating for historic atrocities inflicted upon them by Christians. I doubt that very much. In my experience, Muslims are known to lie or, at the very least, exaggerate. But even if Central African Muslims once had reasons to seek retribution, what's happening *now* isn't related in any way to what happened *then*. The hypocritical Muslims running roughshod over this country are enjoying the chaos and murder and disaster they have wrought, and in this way, they are no different than ISIS or Boko Haram or Al-Quaeda. As I walk, my eyes constantly surveying the terrain, I come to this thought: *Why the hell are we bringing Muslim vipers into our cozy little Finnish nest?*

"Sarge," Lasse Leppälä—a young private, calls out—interrupting my daydreaming as he points to a plume of black smoke rising ahead of us, "what the hell is that?"

The lad is struggling to carry the same heavy pack I'm lugging but has the added burden of humping a collapsible Vallon VM4 metal detector and prod. The demining equipment carried by Leppälä and the other Finns, with the exception of Aapo Antonen—my radioman, who has his own burden to bear—add another ten kilograms to their rucksacks. We're only fifteen kilometers from base camp and already skinny, pimply-faced Leppäla is exhausted. Our target for mine removal lies off this road, up a rough trail through low hills and down into the valley of a small creek that may, or may not, have water in it. French intelligence reports that four children in a Christian village to the north and east of the creek have been killed—and three others maimed—by mines buried in ancestral pastures used for

133

generations by Christian herdsmen. The placement of these explosives serves no strategic purpose. Muslim guerrillas planted the landmines to render the tasks of daily living impossibly dangerous. Our mission is to find the village and remove the mines.

We march on. The French do not rest. Renier is a tough sonofabitch. Nearly fifty, having been demoted for insubordination at least twice, he's my kind of no-nonsense soldier. He's near pension and, because of his reduced rank, retirement will require Renier to find civilian work when he leaves the French Army. I'll be forced to do the same once I'm back in Finland and muster out. My pension, earned for more than twenty years' service, while sufficient for my daily needs, will not allow me comfort. I also intend, once I retire, to engage in protest. I want to express my dissatisfaction with Finland's crazy immigration policy. I want to send a message to the big shots that allowing Muslims into Finland is a mistake. To do so will require that I live in Helsinki, a place too expensive for a retired soldier. So, I'll need to find work to supplement my pension. But I feel that such sacrifice is my duty: I will have, as an eyewitness to the atrocities in Central Africa, credibility to make my argument against Finnish immigration policy. How I'll call this foolishness to the attention of those in power, I have no earthly idea.

"Leppälä, let the French reconnoiter the smoke. You worry about the job we're being asked to do. Renier says there are several mines placed in and around the village," I reply, bringing my attention back to the scene in front of us. "Concentrate on your job, keeping your cool, and not setting off one of those fucking mines. I don't want to send you back to your momma without legs, or worse, in a pine box draped with a Finnish flag."

Leppälä doesn't respond. I know he's afraid. He's been afraid since we landed in Africa. *I'll need to keep a close eye on that one,* I think, glancing furtively over my left shoulder, taking in the private's girlish face. Eyes forward, I wipe sweat from my jaw with the back of my shirtsleeve and tilt my steel pot off my forehead. Perspiration weeps from the helmet's webbing onto my cheeks. My underarms are soggy. I can feel my drawers crawling up my ass. *If I wanted to take a sauna,* I think, *I'd have stayed home!*

The plume dissipates as we close in on the village. We follow tire tracks and boot prints left in the gray, dry soil by the French as we skirt shallow hills and stunted shrubs before descending onto a treeless plain. The creek bed is bone dry. The sun burns down. At the edge of a scraggly pasture, the grass shortened by overgrazing, the landscape flat as a plate, the Eland halts. Renier walks ahead of the armored car accompanied by his communications man. The radio crackles. Rikala stands next to Antonen and translates Renier's message.

"He wants you to join him at the head of the column," Rikala says.

I nod, unsling my Sako, and move out with Rikala by my side.

Thin clouds, too light and too high to carry rain, shadow the land. Renier stands at the edge of an unfenced pasture, surveying what lies ahead. I stand next to the lieutenant. I'm a head taller than the Frenchman. Rikala, who is even taller than me, joins us. Rikala and I are both blond headed and blue eyed, though, given I'm now in my early forties, my hair is speckled with gray whereas my radioman, being only twenty-two, sports no age on his head. But because we're wearing helmets, Renier doesn't see this distinction. The Frenchman wears a red beret with the insignia of his elite unit prominent in the center of the cap. His hair, black but flecked with pewter, flows long and unencumbered, a hairstyle distinctly at odds with military decorum. His nose, angular and pitched like that of a hawk, sits regally above a thick, black, handlebar mustache, the whiskers also too long and too unruly to meet regulations. The man's grooming says it all: his hell-bent-for-leather personality—his lack of pretense—is why I would wade into a river full of crocodiles to do Renier's bidding.

"They have killed them all," he says tersely. Rikala translates as the officer points his right index finger at a cluster of what had once been mud and straw huts, thin smoke rising from the remnants of a demolished village.

I study the scene. "All of what?" I ask. As I speak, my eyes focus on dark humps dotting the pasture, the decaying remnants of the villagers' cattle. *The bastards killed the entire herd!* I think, envisioning the economic catastrophe that will result from such barbarism. But from the tremor in the lieutenant's voice, I suspect something far more sinister has occurred than the indiscriminate destruction of cows. "All of what?" I repeat.

Rikala translates.

"All of everything," Renier replies curtly, pointing to a wake of buzzards circling the village. "All of the men. All of the women. All of the children. All of the elders. All of the chickens. All of the swine. And all of the cattle. They have killed them all."

I send the minesweepers ahead. They find no explosives in the road. *They want us to see. They want us to know what they are capable of,* I think as I follow my men, the French paratroops, and the Eland into what had once been the home to forty or fifty families. White-backed African vultures picking away at the dead note our approach and retreat. Row crops have been burned to the ground. The bloated, bullet-ridden bodies of dark-skinned Africans lie randomly throughout the village. Some of the dead women have their cotton skirts hiked above their heads, their dark pubic hair and their vaginas and buttocks exposed to flies. A grandmother leans against the charred ruin of a hut, her blouse ripped, both breasts dissected, a look of empty fear in her still open eyes as maggots crawl in and out of her mouth. On the ground next to the old woman, next to a dead dog, we find an elderly man's body. Given his age, the dead man is likely the woman's husband. Cotton trousers and drawers are bunched around the dead man's ankles. A stub of flesh that was once the man's penis is caked with dried blood.

"It was not enough to kill them," Renier says venomously, "they had to humiliate them as well."

"Rape?" I ask, noting that the old woman's legs are spread akimbo.

He nods. "The little ones too," he adds, removing his beret as he moves a few paces to the right to study a girl, no more than ten, her body bruised and battered in places and in ways that demonstrate cruelty. The lieutenant barks. Soldiers check for pulses. No one remains alive.

Without hesitation, the French begin assembling the dead, lining them up in rows, knowing that the next step in our peacekeeping mission will be to dig a mass grave, say some perfunctory Catholic prayers, bury the dead Christians, and begin combing the countryside for the killers.

Understand: I've seen death before; I've been in other combat zones. I come from a family of warriors. My ancestors, including my great grandfather—who rode with Mannerheim—have always served; always been soldiers. But I immediately sense that the evil perpetrated in this quiet, hot, dusty place has inexorably altered something inside of me.

My men weep and wretch as they assist the French in attempting dignity for the dead. I unstrap my steel pot, lift it from my buzzed hair, remove a handkerchief from the front pocket of my fatigues, sit on a low stone wall, wipe sweat and grime from my sunburned face, and watch the unholy ballet being performed in the center square of that little Christian village north of Bata in the Central African Republic. I'm overwhelmed by sadness and unquenchable rage as I stumble upon this inexorable truth: talking to the politicians in Helsinki would be a fucking waste of time.

CHAPTER SIX: The Warrior's Story. February 2017. (Helsinki, Finland)

I left the army and took a job driving a cab. As my civilian life in Finland resumed, I found a pattern, a rhythm to life that made me seem like any other forty-something, single Finnish man. I didn't seek out nationalist chat rooms on the Internet or make attempts to agitate other Sons of the Raven, the social group I joined after mustering out of the Utti Jaegers, signing up for my pension, and moving to Helsinki. After a few nights spent at the *Ravihuone*, the club's meeting hall in the Käpylä neighborhood of Finland's capital city where I listened to the ranting and raving of my Finnish brothers about the "Muslim problem" over a cold beer and greasy pizza, I formed a plan.

At first, I conceived a grand operation. I envisioned a thickly muscled, very fit, warrior (me!) organizing like-minded men and women who'd seen the cruelty of the Islamists, leading my comrades against a refugee center, taking hostages, and killing all of the Muslim men and boys to make our point. But as I watched the television news and saw the tactics of my enemy, the lone wolf suicide approach adopted by ISIS in the wake of the United States' use of drones, I thought, *Yes! That's how it must be. One man, one mission.*

So I drove my cab, collected my thoughts, bided my time, and, when I had enough money saved up, found a brother-in-arms across the border in St. Petersburg, a German dealing arms to Russian gangsters who could be trusted to provide the armament I needed to make a splash. I did not want to die. I did not want it to be this way. But nightmares of brutalized black Christian women and children, and a forever portrait of that African grandfather—dickless and rotting under the Central African sun—and my own personal demons involving my dead brother compelled me to confront my fear of the unknown, trust in Christ's message of a better life after death, and move forward.

I also became convinced, watching the American presidential race, that Hillary Clinton—no friend of Islamic extremists—would easily defeat Trump. I'd long admired our greatest modern leader, Urho Kekkonen, who was President of Finland for over two decades and who managed, through cunning, political acumen, and intellect, to craft a middle course for my homeland between NATO and the Soviet Union. I felt that Hillary being elected President of the United States was a foregone conclusion. Then, as I listened to Trump's speeches and noted the rabid engagement of his followers as he addressed America's most significant issue—hordes of illegal aliens flooding across the nation's southern border—I found something to admire in the man. *He's a straight shooter, says what's on his mind even if it's not politically correct. He reminds me of Kekkonen. Direct. To the point. I like that in a leader.*

My girlfriend, Irina Juuso, a secretary in a downtown law firm, doesn't think much of Mr. Trump. "He lies about everything, even the size of his penis," she said one night after we'd made love and were watching the news on television in the bed we share. "Just look at his hands. Short, pudgy, and pink, like those of a little girl," she added.

I can't say that I *love* Irina. If I did, I would confide in her what I'm up to. But I do *like* her. Why? Well, she makes love like no other woman I've ever been with. Her body is curvy and taut and supple and agile and accommodating in all the right places. But it's wrong of me to kiss and tell. And so, enough.

Irina has thick, blond hair that teases the tops of her shoulders. She's short; the top of her head barely reaches my chin. She's a runner; exercise keeps her tummy firm and her butt tight—attributes that serve her well in the bedroom. She has me jogging with her most mornings before work, an enterprise I loathe but an inconvenience I accept to keep the peace. Irina's eyes are a washed-out dull hazel—the least exceptional thing about her. I find that this one, insignificant failing is but a small price to pay for being in a relationship with a woman whose physicality is exquisite.

"My hands aren't all that large," I had said in reply to Irina's critique of Trump, displaying my hands and fingers above the quilt on our bed. "But I've never heard you complain!"

Irina giggled and snuggled against my left hip, moving suggestively, as if she wanted more. And so, I obliged.

The weaponry I've assembled in the basement of our flat on Untamontie is formidable. I've made sure no one in this apartment complex of ten units, including Irina, has any suspicion about what I'm keeping behind lock and key. So far as my

139

girlfriend knows, that steel locker in the cellar is where I store camping equipment, fishing rods and lures, and personal items—uniforms and such from my time in the army. In truth, after being introduced to the German—Manfred Bayer—by my Russian contacts, I put together enough firepower—a Sako TRG-42 sniper's rifle equipped with a night-vision scope, an Arsenal semi-automatic handgun, six hundred rounds of ammunition, four bricks of C4 with electronic detonators and a remote transceiver—to make my mark.

Irina is only twenty-four. She knows nothing of who I really am. It's not that she's empty-headed. Far from it. She's taking classes at the university just a few blocks from where we live, studying law with an eye to becoming an international lawyer. Get this: she wants to specialize in immigration law and help folks, including Muslims, become Finnish citizens! I've not debated her on this topic nor played my hand regarding my upset and disgust with the current policies of our government. I value our nights in bed too much to start an argument that might lead to me being kicked out onto the curb by my politically misguided girlfriend. To say we make strange bedfellows—Irina the socialist, do-gooder and me, the conservative, closet Islamophobe—well, that would be an understatement. But I keep my own counsel and let her express her vividly unrealistic worldview all because the sex is so unbelievably good and because overall, outside of my one dark secret, we're compatible.

At least Irina is a Christian, albeit a passive, twice-a-year Evangelical Lutheran, whereas I'm a serious and devoted adherent to the more pious brand of Lutheranism expressed in Awakening theology. I've tried to get Irina to attend Sunday service with me at *Herääminen Kirkko* just around the corner from our flat. But so far, she's refused, saying, "I don't need any of your mumbo-jumbo to know God is on my side!" I'm afraid she misses the point. My church doesn't pontificate about salvation through works or deeds; that's Catholic heresy and not fit for a Lutheran to believe. Rather, the Awakening pastors, like Rev. Lagus of my church, emphasize that man is forever sinful and that nothing we do here on Earth will guaranty our salvation. It's all about God's grace and not at all about what good or bad works we might do. Irina is smart enough and well versed enough in the ways of the world that we could debate such concepts in the context of what I'm about to do. But engaging in such conversations would only upset her and make her a co-conspirator in the eyes of the authorities. That said, I'm also pretty certain Irina has no interest in being the girlfriend of a martyr.

It would upset Irina—no, that's not right; it would *infuriate* her—to know my true feelings on the subject of Syrians and Afghanis and Iraqis being allowed into our country. It would also devastate her to know that come December 6, 2017, I will ride a train from Helsinki to Kajaani in search of my destiny.

CHAPTER SEVEN: October 2017 (Kajaani, Finland)

"Could you hand me a number ten scalpel?"

Janine Tanninen asked the question of the nurse assisting her in the surgical suite of the Kajaani Refugee Center Infirmary. The nurse—her brother Josiah Aristotle Tate—was standing alongside the operating gurney, staring into space, his attention riveted on something other than the bowel obstruction his sister was attempting to alleviate.

"Ari!"

Janine's voice startled Josiah. *I'm not sure this was the smartest decision I've ever made,* he thought, his body and mind still numb from the eight-hour flight from Minneapolis to Amsterdam to Helsinki, the six-hour train trip from Helsinki to Kajaani, and the four hours of sleep he had managed before being roused by his older sister to assist her in surgery. "Whatdayaneed, Thena?" he asked.

"A number ten."

"Ah."

Josiah reached into a pan of sterilized instruments and winked at Doaks Hampton, who, though an internist, was functioning as an anesthesiologist during the surgery. Hampton returned the wink. The Brit was monitoring the vital signs of a heavily sedated four-year-old Syrian girl—Nooda al-Hafiz—as Josiah retrieved the lancet and provided it to his sister.

"Thanks," Janine said, staring at the operating field, the child's belly exposed and illuminated by white light. "Let's see what we can do to help this poor child."

"That went well," Josiah said, his use of Finnish a struggle despite having learned the language from their mother. "I'd never scrubbed in with you, Thena. You're damn good."

Janine sipped hot herbal tea, her need for caffeine dissipated, Nooda being their only surgical case of the morning, and smiled. The doctor considered the scar disrupting her brother's upper lip, a reminder that Josiah had been born with a cleft palate.

Her brother's circumstance, the randomness of his defect, had haunted Janine as a child. But from an early age, she'd also recognized Josiah's life had been made better through medicine. That realization was the driving force in her choosing to become a plastic surgeon. "Your Finnish is rusty," Janine noted, averting her scrutiny before Josiah noticed it. "Better practice some or the Finns around camp will tease you six ways from Sunday."

"I give you a compliment," Josiah quipped, rallying from weariness to spar, "and you repay me by insulting my knowledge of Mother's native tongue?"

Janine grinned at her brother. "Mother was born in Duluth. Her native tongue was English."

Josiah drew heavily on his coffee, the steaming brew cut with two sugar cubes and a pinch of whole milk. "Understood. But she grew up with Grandma Elin speaking Finn from the time she could walk. We learned the language filtered through Mom's Minnesota and Brooklyn accents. Not exactly the traditional Finnish brogue, you know."

They hadn't had the chance to talk much since Josiah's arrival. He had pulled in from Helsinki at a quarter-past ten in the morning. By the time a driver from the camp picked him up, delivered him to the Kajaani Refugee Center and he'd met Janine, completed paperwork, found his room in the former barracks, took a quick shower, and crashed, it was after ten in the evening. Due to jet lag and general malaise caused by Josiah's emergent realization that his marriage to Maggie Ann was likely over, the nurse slept in fits and starts. Despite the possibility of a full night's sleep, he'd only managed four restless hours in the rack.

I haven't told Thena yet, Josiah observed. *Better to broach that topic when we're alone and we have time to discuss why I did what I did: why ending a thirty-year commitment seems to be the only way to preserve my sanity. For certain, it wasn't all Maggie's fault. I had an equal hand in our decline. But an in-depth dissection of my conjugal failings can wait.*

"You seem preoccupied."

Janine's comment startled Josiah. "Indeed. Got a lot on my mind. Retiring so suddenly. Leaving the family behind. It was all pretty unexpected. For them. For me."

The doctor nodded her long, angular head and closed her coal-black eyes in consideration of pursuing the matter further.

He's not ready to tell me about Maggie Ann, Janine thought perceptively. *He needs to be the one to bring the topic up. I can't force such a difficult conversation on his first morning in Kajaani. After all, we just saved a little Syrian girl's life!*

"How's that big ox of a Finlander you're married to?" Josiah asked, interrupting Janine's contemplation. "I haven't seen him yet. He's still working here as a volunteer in charge of the physical plant and the grounds, right?"

Janine nodded again.

"And his health? It's good?"

"Very. A little hip and back trouble from his time in the reserves but beyond that, he's fit as a fiddle."

"Enjoys working here?"

Janine smiled. "As do I, Brother. As I hope you will."

Josiah laughed, exposing capped teeth, his one bow to vanity. He was a few inches shorter than his sister, well-muscled and in shape, his fitness a natural attribute. Unlike Janine, who worked hard to maintain her figure and stamina, Josiah had a metabolism that allowed him to eat whatever he wanted, laze around, and still remain trim. "You tossed me into the fire pretty quickly," he observed, diverting the conversation from the personal. "I haven't assisted in surgery in over a decade and you had me right in the middle of it without a refresher course."

Janine stood up, reached for her cup and saucer, and cocked her head. Morning sunlight touched her kinky hair as dust motes drifted to the ground. "My regular assistant, Venla Balzar, is off on holiday." She paused, setting up the punch line. "You were the best I could find on short notice," she teased. "But I knew you'd be ready," she added, to reassure her brother of her confidence in him. "Shall we check on young Miss al-Hafiz? She should be awake by now."

Josiah stood up, collected his own cup and saucer, and nodded. "I'd like that."

The recovery room was small, a few degrees too warm, and crowded with monitors and other instruments of healing. The doctor and the nurse stood next to the child, her brown skin cool despite the warmth of the space, her vital signs perfect, her infantile fingers grasping a crisp, white linen sheet as she slept. Josiah knew, from talking with Nooda before she slipped beneath the heavy gauze of narcotics, that she had brown eyes with irises so dark that they made the pigmentation of his own eyes seem pale in comparison. She had spoken perfect English, having learned only a few perfunctory phrases of Finnish during her six months at the center.

Prior to surgery, Janine had confided that the girl's mother and father were Syrian journalists who had vanished during one of Assad's purges. Tal Afar—the girl's hometown in northeastern Syria—was now occupied by ISIS. More civilians, primarily men and boys, including Nooda's older male relatives, had disappeared, leaving the girl to fend for herself. She had been lucky. Neighbors took pity on her and helped her leave Syria. In Turkey, Nooda joined other refugees in a leaking, dangerously overloaded fishing trawler sailing for Greece. Upon their miraculous arrival in Athens, the newly arrived lived in a makeshift camp until they were accepted by Germany, where they spent several months in another internment compound. Nooda filed for asylum in Finland and was vetted, accepted, and placed at the Kajaani Refugee Center. The harrowing nature of the little girl's journey reminded Janine, who'd read and reread her grandmother's memoir, of Elin Gustafson Peltomaa's near death at the hands of the Gestapo in Estonia during the Continuation War. The doctor didn't have the time to explain this deductive connection to her brother in the brief interlude between his arrival and the little girl's surgery. *That's something I'll share with Ari when we have time, once we've cleared the air about what the hell happened between Ari and Maggie Ann.*

"She's sleeping like an angel," Josiah observed, placing his fingers on the girl's wrist, the gesture seemingly medical in purpose but more an affirmation of his admiration for the child. "I hope this is the only bad thing she has to face in Finland."

Janine looked at her brother. "Most Finns are tolerant and willing to accept folks from a different race, a different faith. But not everyone is so understanding. I'm afraid little Nooda has other hurdles to overcome. But she's smart, resilient as hell. She'll be fine."

"You sure of that, sister?"

Janine smiled wearily. "I am."

CHAPTER EIGHT: The Warrior's Story.
November 29, 2017 (Helsinki, Finland)

It's a quiet night in the club. Only a few disgruntled, right-wing, nationalistic-thinking ex-soldiers, retired policemen, and pensioners are spread out across the mildewed interior of the *Ravihuone* in Helsinki's Käpylä neighborhood. I'm sitting on a stool at the bar, a shot of Finlandia and a pint of stout—a brew I'd grown to admire when stationed with Irishmen in Bosnia a few years back—in front of me, minding my own business when a redheaded hottie walks into the bar with a short, spiky-haired, flat-chested, thirty-something brunette who appears to be the redhead's partner. *Lesbos*, I think, glancing at the women as they find a table in the corner and sit down. Sanna Antonen, the bartender, the only person working the club, a short, rotund bundle of flesh whose chest merges gravitationally with her potbelly, saunters over to the strangers, takes their order, and meanders back to the bar.

"What the hell?" I say with rancor. "You just serve anyone who walks in off the street? I thought this place was for member's only!"

"And open to former military or police. The redhead was in the navy. The brunette? Served as a border guard: search and rescue," Sanna explains as she pours two glasses of red wine from a dusty bottle of Merlot, wine being a beverage rarely ordered in the club. "They qualify as guest members in the Sons of the Raven despite the fact you might not like their lifestyle," the barkeep adds. "Besides, who made you king of the fuckin' world, Alhomäki?"

I turn my head, stroke my chin—the skin rough from two-days' growth, my slovenly appearance the result of Irina being out of town for a long weekend with her sister—before picking up the shot glass and downing the vodka. "Another," I say, slamming my empty glass on the bar.

I focus my attention on the redhead as Sanna pours me a second shot. The woman is attractive and wearing black jeans so tight little is left to one's imagination. The couple talks quietly, not disturbing anyone, as the crowd dwindles to the two women, the morose and uninteresting Sanna, and me. Despite their unobtrusiveness, the women's presence annoys me. *Something's not quite right with those two*, I think. *Especially the redhead. She doesn't know it, but every time she sneaks a peek in my direction, thinking I'm watching football on the television or engaged in conversation with Sanna, I sense her attention. Curiosity? Interested in me? Doubtful. No, there's something untoward in the way she's checking me out.*

"What's eating you?" Sanna asks as she serves me another shot.

"Huh?"

"You keep inspecting the new merchandise. Give it up. Irina will kick your ass if you step over *that* line!"

I laugh, down the second shot of Finlandia, slide the empty shot glass to Sanna, and concentrate my attention on the stout. I raise the pint and take a swig. "That's damn good."

Sanna smiles, revealing two missing front teeth, the sort of decay that, along with her unimpressive physique and bad breath, makes her uniquely unalluring. "You done staring at the girls, Mr. Hot Stuff? From the looks of the designer jeans on their tender little asses, the two-hundred-Euro shoes on their royal feet, and the Coach purses hanging from their chairs, I'd wager you couldn't afford to say hello, much less spend a night, with either one."

"Not looking for trouble with Irina," I reply, downing the Guinness. "Not looking to upset that apple cart."

Sanna pats the back of my left hand with fleshy fingers. "Good boy. Your lady would be proud of your restraint," she says, odors of onion and gyro emanating from her mouth as she speaks. "By the way, when you gonna make Irina an honest woman?"

The strangers finish their wine, stand up, collect their purses, and leave through the front door. Sanna waddles over to the empty table. "Damned dykes!" she hisses, collecting wine glasses and money before making her way back behind the bar. "Should have known they'd go light on the tip."

"Bitches!" I agree.

"You never answered me," Sanna says as she opens the bar's antique cash register and deposits bills and change in a drawer. "When you gonna 'pop the question' to that lovely lady you live with?"

I remain quiet. Not because I don't want to answer but because I would have to explain my answer, an answer that is too dangerous to share with the barkeep. *I have things I need to do, things that will likely not see me coming back from Kajaani alive,* is what I'd say if I was free to talk. But Turku, the recent deaths of the two Finnish women in the city marketplace, and the wounding of ten other innocents by an Islamic madman occupy my thoughts.

Instead of answering, I turn my attention to the big picture window overlooking the street. From my perch at the bar, I watch the women walk towards a light rail stop through glass obscured by condensation. The redhead drapes her right arm around her lover's shoulder and kisses the brunette on the cheek. It's a tender, touching moment but my suspicions remain.

CHAPTER NINE: December 1, 2017 (Kajaani, Finland)

In five days, the country would celebrate its centennial, a momentous occasion that the entirety of Finland was preparing to embrace. The devastating effects of the worldwide recession that began in late 2007 had subsided. Though many of Finland's corporate giants weathered the economic storm, some, like cell-phone innovator Nokia, all but disappeared. Nokia's demise alone led to the loss of over 1,300 jobs.

But as Janine, Olavi, and Josiah sat in the *Kullattu Hirvi* (Gilded Moose), a popular bar in downtown Kajaani, sipping Voruta black-currant wine imported from Lithuania, things were looking up for the Nordic nation and its people. Yet, even with the economic turnaround, political uncertainties abounded, a topic of much concern at the round wooden table occupied by the doctor, her husband, and her brother.

"Bullshit," Josiah said, scrutinizing Janine, taking in her rare beauty, the angular and striking cheekbones, her slender, commandingly fit, physical presence as guitarist Mika Kuokkanen, fiddler Ninni Poijärvi, and dobro player Olli Haavisto livened up the place with a traditional Finnish jig. "Your man Trump has made things far more dangerous by his embrace of that asshole, Putin."

Janine thought before responding. *Truth is, I voted for the man by absentee ballot from Finland because, well, Comey's revelation right before the election that there was more to the Clinton e-mail scandal, coupled with Hillary's godawful, full-throated defense of abortion as birth control, her "deplorables" comment, and my general disdain for all things Clinton pushed me to hold my nose and vote for The Donald. After witnessing the disastrous beginning to the man's reign as president, sure, I have regrets. Even so, I don't know that I would have checked the box for Madame Secretary. I'm well aware that too many young women use abortion as birth control. Such a practice, given my Baptist faith, is a non-starter for me. A fetus is, so long as not the product of rape or incest, one of God's souls who needs the same nurturing, love, and protection an infant deserves.* Janine considered her train of thought, took a long draw of wine from

149

her glass, stared off into the crowd of Finns dancing and twirling to the music, and nodded.

"I can't argue that point. Mr. Trump *has* been a disappointment," Janine admitted, touching her right index finger to her lips as she considered a further response. The music slowed. Kuokkanen began to sing in English. His wife's soaring fiddle added texture to "Waterbound," until two voices chased the melody in exquisite harmony. Couples, already enraptured at the thought of celebrating Independence Day, clung to each other and swayed to the multi-textured music as Janine considered her words. "But I remain hopeful."

Feeling the wine, Olavi leaned in and enveloped his wife in a hug. "Your sister is an idealist, Ari. A true believer in the eventual redemption of Man. Even a man as misguided and narcissistic as Trump." The Finn released his wife, raised his glass, and instituted a toast. "To the president," he said gleefully, giddy from alcohol. "May he finally pull his head out of his ass!"

Janine frowned and did not raise her glass. Josiah chuckled, exposing the remnant scar from his cleft, his eyes dancing, his mind racing, and clanked the rim of his wine glass with his brother-in-law's.

"Agreed. For the sake of Estonia, Lithuania, Latvia, and Finland, let's hope The Donald becomes astute in matters of diplomacy!"

"Seriously? You two think that Trump is worse than Hillary? How many world stages did she trash when she was Secretary of State? Libya? Syria? Those are just two I can think of off the top of my head," Janine replied.

"Syria?" Olavi posited. "It wasn't Clinton who wanted to stay out of that fight. She was ready to roll up her sleeves and engage. It was Obama who didn't want to go back on his campaign promises to the left. He had no desire to get back into a hot war in the Middle East."

Ari nodded. "The big guy's got a point, sister."

This discussion could go all night, Janine thought. *It's time to change the subject.* "At least the wine is good and the music stellar. Makes up for my boorish, know-it-all companions."

Olavi laughed. Purple spewed from his mouth onto the table. "Resorting to personal insults isn't fair, dear wife. We are too easy as targets!"

Josiah smiled and accepted Janine's redirection. "So that little boy, he's doing well?"

"Asu al-Alamen?"

"Yes."

The band took a break, making it easier for patrons to talk. As the musicians walked past the physician and her companions on the way to the bar, Janine reached out and touched Ms. Poijärvi on the bare arm. The fiddler stopped and smiled. "Yes?"

"I just wanted to tell you how much we're enjoying your music," Janine said in Finnish.

"Thanks. We have another hour to go so hopefully, you will like the songs you will hear as well as the songs already heard," the musician replied.

Olavi, now clearly drunk, embraced Mika Kuokkanen in a bear hug. "Wonderful stuff, brother," he chirped. "Simply the best!"

"Thanks," Mika answered. "As Ninni says, 'more to follow'."

"Let these people get to the bar, would you?" Josiah urged, intervening physically, forcing Olavi to release the guitarist.

Janine watched the musicians navigate the crowd.

"The boy?" Josiah said, returning to his earlier line of inquiry.

A waitress stopped at the table. She was barely old enough to serve alcohol and certainly not twenty, the age for buying hard liquor. Her fawn-colored eyes and auburn hair complimented her stark, alabaster skin. "Another bottle?" she asked.

Janine looked at her husband, whose eyes were clouded and his smile perpetual. "Another glass for me. And coffee for my husband. How about you, Ari?"

The nurse held his glass up to the light. "Still have some left. I'll pass for now," Josiah said, escalating his voice as the crowd roared at the hockey game being broadcast on televisions around the bar. Finland's national team had scored a goal against the Swedes, prompting an outburst of pride. "On second thought, since the Finns scored, I'll order another."

"Two then? Of the Vortua?"

Janine's eyes diverted as the musicians clambered onto the wooden stage, placed their beverages on amplifiers, retrieved their instruments, and tuned. "Yes."

Olavi's eyes had closed.

"Husband!"

Janine's shout startled Olavi.

"What?"

A stern look crossed Janine's face. "You were asleep."

"No, I was merely taking a siesta."

Josiah laughed. "At nine o'clock in the evening? Brother-in-law, you are indeed an old man."

Olavi rebounded after a few sips of the thick, black coffee the pretty waitress set before him. "You were talking about some kid you two worked on ..."

Soft, understated fiddling began. Ninni's eyes closed as she concentrated. The other musicians bided their time, ready to join the woman as the song unfolded. As the slip of a woman began to sing *Valoa Päin* ("Towards the Light") in a breathy, husky voice—the song a lament about loss and migration—the room quieted. Ninni's plaintive voice and the soft bowing of her fiddle filled the room. There were no murmurs of upset. No one decried the song's message. As Ninni's mates joined in, bar patrons remained transfixed.

"Right. The boy had a very complicated cleft palate," Janine said quietly, not wishing to undermine the music. "His upper lip was a mess. It was one of the more complex surgeries I've done since coming to Finland."

"My sister is too modest," Josiah said between sips of wine. "She was nothing less than fucking brilliant today." He raised his goblet towards Janine. She responded in kind. Olavi slurped coffee. "That boy will have a smile that he can be proud of, one that little Arab girls will swoon over, thanks to Thena's good work," Josiah added.

The woman felt pride swell, an emergence of ego that disconcerted her. "Praise God. He's the one who guided my hand today."

"Praise God," Olavi said, placing a paw on his wife's right shoulder. "Something that Donald Trump has no idea how to do."

Janine rolled her eyes. The band soared into "You Love the Thunder," a Jackson Browne cover sung in English. "We're back to politics again?"

"Always," Josiah added. "If it takes all night, this big duffus and I are going to convince you of the error of your ways."

"Duffus. I like that," Olavi replied through a grin. "Your Finnish is much improved, brother-in-law."

The band switched gears again. Strains of a traditional Finnish tune filled the room.

Janine drained her glass, touched her lips with a paper napkin, and nodded towards the stage. "Husband, they're playing a polka. I think it's time we danced."

CHAPTER TEN: The Warrior's Story. December 2, 2017 (Rokua National Park, Finland)

The old Volvo 1800ES still runs strong.

I inherited the car from my brother, Niko, who's been dead now six years. He didn't leave the old station wagon to me by will or anything like that. His widow, my sister-in-law, Patrice, a lovely woman saddled with three small children—triplets, my nieces, who were only two years old when my brother died—gave me the car before she left Finland for Scotland, which is home for her. Dani and Rosa and Maria are now eight years old and though Glasgow is only a short flight from Helsinki, and Patrice has insisted I come for a visit, I haven't the heart. The girls remind me of Niko and the evil wrought against him in the name of Allah. Some might say that I should also mourn the other victims killed at the Domodedovo Airport on January 24, 2011. They too were innocents, having no particular quarrel with the Chechens who blew the place to bits. But I didn't know the others—the Russians, the Tajiks, the Austrians, the German, the Uzbek, the Brit, or the Ukrainian—who died in the blast. I only knew Niko.

Losing my only sibling was devastating. *Is* devastating. If I had friends higher up in the Russian Federal Security Service (FSB)—the successor to the KGB—I'd ask permission to assist them in finding the perpetrator of the deed: Dolu Umarov, the Muslim cleric who declared the Caucasus Emirate and who has engaged in a civil war with Moscow for years. But I have no such pull. Beyond the lowly field agents I met when I flew to Moscow on Patrice's behalf to retrieve Niko, I know no one in authority inside Russia. Wait. I shouldn't discount Boris and Dmitri, my contacts at the FSB, the men who handed me a cardboard box containing my brother's remains—Niko's bent and twisted silver crucifix and his discolored lumineers, together with bits of bone, ash, and charred flesh that once formed a man. Despite being functionaries, those Russians are the ones who sat with me as I grieved and then, once they learned of my mettle, put me in touch with Manfred Bayer, the German who supplied me with the tools I need to make my point.

So here I am driving Niko's rusty, red 1972 Volvo, a car my brother planned to restore but never did. The little four-cylinder pulls with strength, the new tires I put on the car before storing it in the garage at the family cottage on Lake Oulujärvi outside Kajaani, the place where Niko and Patrice and the girls once called home, slapping asphalt. I'm headed west from Kajaani to one of my favorite places in Finland: Rokua National Park. Or, more accurately, the *Rokuanjärvi kota*, one of the primitive Sami shelters located throughout Finland and maintained by the national park service to house hikers and skiers and snowshoers on a first-come, first-serve basis.

Bastards.

The word seems too mild, too tame, to express the venom that is coursing through my veins as I think about the more than twenty thousand civilians killed, the more than fifty thousand innocent noncombatants maimed and wounded in Islamic suicide attacks since the modern wave of terror began. Most folks remember 9/11. The American embassy in Beirut. The bombing of the *U.S.S. Cole.* Boston. Brussels. Paris (multiple occasions). London (again, repeated attacks). The St. Petersburg Metro Bombing. But few remember the insanity that claimed my brother's life. *Well,* I think as the afternoon quickly turns to dusk this far north though it is only half-past two, *when the* Helsingin Sanomat *and the other papers receive my manifesto, the one I'll e-mail on the Centennial, everyone will remember Niko's death. Everyone!*

I drive on. *Cowards. That is what they are. Using explosives to murder women and children and men who are simply going about life, who aren't threats to their faith or their beliefs.* As I plan my final days, I consider the political climate in Finland, in Europe, and in America.

I had such great hope in Timo Soini and his Finns Party after their surprising rise to prominence in 2011. But Soini's light quickly dimmed and now, I fail to see a viable alternative. I mistrust Prime Minister Sipilä and the Center Party. I have even less faith in the others. I'm convinced that they are deaf to the cries of the ordinary man and woman, like the hardworking, God-fearing Christians living in Tornio, the epicenter of Muslim immigration to Finland. *Sipilä and others of his stripe are too quick to appease the EU, too interested in putting on a good face for Germany, Britain, and France. Hell, he's talking about joining NATO, for chrissake, which would undo sixty years of Finnish*

155

non-alignment and put us in the same boat as Estonia, making us a target for Russian aggression. He's also the asshole who put Paula Risikko in charge of the Ministry of the Interior. Why is that an issue? Well, I think, Risikko selected former MP Tarja Saariaho as Finland's Assistant Director of Immigration for Refugees and Migration. Forced Director General Vuorio to accept Saariaho's appointment. It's Saariaho's misguided advocacy of an "open door" policy for Muslims that has endangered Finland from within. She's the one. She's got to go!

For all his faults, not the least of which was his pandering to the welfare state, Soini stood firmly against such nonsense. He wanted tighter borders, better vetting of immigrants. And with the fat man, it's Finland first. Just like Trump's "Make America Great Again." Simple. Direct. To the point. But the Center Party and its lackeys? They want us to give up our sovereignty and be part of a common "European experience," become an ethnic and religious hodge-podge with no thought to Finnish history and culture. No thank you, Mr. Prime Minister! None of that for me.

"Shit!" I exclaim, nearly hitting a cow moose lumbering from the left ditch onto the road in front of the Volvo. "That was close," I mutter as the big animal trots into the woods, kicking up newly fallen snow as it disappears.

"And those damned Muslims we welcome to Tornio," I say aloud, continuing the thought formed before the moose's intrusion, "telling the press that they are leaving, going back to Sweden because 'Finland sucks: it's too cold and boring.'" I pound on the Volvo's steering wheel with gloved fists. "They insult my country? They kill my brother? They butcher innocent Christians on my watch in Africa? They murder and maim shoppers in Turku? They rape Finnish girls after being welcomed and provided new lives? Fuck them. Fuck them all!"

Adrenaline is taking over, clouding my mind, making me too amped up to be an effective tool of the Lord. *Discipline,* I think. *You're a warrior. You're a Son of the Raven.* I regain composure. I grin. The thought that, as a Finn, I'm calling upon mythology that has roots in a Norwegian god, Odin—whose symbol is the raven—amuses me. My digression also makes me consider family history.

There was an ancestor, a nephew of Great-Great-Grandfather Alvar, who lived for a brief time in Norway, in Røros, before moving to the States. Family myth is that he was a miner and an American Marine in the Great War. But he's not a relation of importance to my heritage as a soldier. No, it's Alvar—who fought with Mannerheim—and his son, my great grandfather, Kari—who fought in the Finnish War of Independence as a teenager and in World War II as a seasoned veteran—and Kari's son, my grandfather, Onni—who was too young to see combat but served in the army as well—and my father, Oskari—who joined the Finnish Navy before becoming a career man in the army, retiring as a captain, never experiencing combat but having served his country with distinction—from which I claim my military lineage. Brother Niko broke the chain of the oldest Alhomäki male child serving; he was exempt from the military due to a bad back. So, *I* took up the familial mantle. The truth is I come from a long line of warriors; a long list of heroes I dare not disappoint. Niko is the one who investigated our ancestry and made me understand the length and breadth of our family's dedication. It is my duty to ensure my country knows that such loyalty includes personal sacrifice.

I arrive at a parking lot. I exit the car, the Volvo's engine gurgling, cold and darkness surrounding me, and pull the drawstring of my parka tight. Some might question why I am here in the middle of the forest many kilometers from Kajaani, the place I will make my mark. The answer is twofold.

First, I must pray. I need quietude to clear my mind and open my soul to the Lord before I approach the Kajaani Refugee Center and do what needs doing. My Awakenings Bible is in my rucksack. Pertinent passages are underlined in red. I will study scripture to ready myself. And I have my gear: the duffle bag carrying my tools—including the disassembled Sako—arrived safely from Helsinki and was stored innocently by Herbert Weise, an old Jewish man and family friend, in his garage in Kajaani. There was no risk that Herbert would peek inside the duffle, though I made sure it was padlocked to keep out prying eyes! After the taxi picked me up from the Kajaani railroad station, I had the cabbie wait outside Herbert's little bungalow—just a short drive from my family's lake cottage—while I retrieved my gear.

At the family cottage, I opened the place up, ignited the propane furnace, unlocked the garage, and charged the Volvo's battery. Early this morning, I loaded the station wagon and turned the key. The car started on the first crank. Those Swedes! This is a long-winded way of saying that I'm coming to the Sami kota on the shores of Rokuajärvi to meditate and refresh my soul. It's not an easy thing I'm being asked by God to do and I must be prepared to explain myself to Jesus when we meet.

Then there is this: my family—my father Oskari, my mother Lotta, and Niko and I—used to come to this park over Christmas holiday to ski. Though we lived in Helsinki—where father worked as an accountant after his military career ended—the family cottage, a place handed down through the years dating back to Grandfather Onni buying the land and erecting the little frame cabin, garage, and sauna building after the war, was always the place we spent Christmas. This was true even after my brother and his family took over the cottage and made it their home. It was only natural that, given how much Mother loved to ski, that we spent the holiday break skiing the eskers and woods of Rokua. Many times, we celebrated Christmas Eve in the little, unheated kota by the lake, just the four of us enjoying each other's company and singing hymns praising Christ's birth as father strummed an acoustic guitar. They are all gone now. Father to ALS. Mother to breast cancer. And Niko, well, you know what happened to him. Memories of better times compel me to trudge through ankle-deep snow, the heavy straps of the duffle tight to my chest, my rucksack dangling from my gloved left hand, a headlamp strapped to my stocking cap lighting the way, as snowshoes kick up newly fallen powder along the trail.

"Everything seems in order," I say later that evening, flames from a campfire leaping above the rim of the steel fire pit, a myriad of stars and planets and galaxies and satellites soaring above the insignificant ring of light announcing my presence to the universe. An unending vault extends to infinity above the forest, the frigid night accepting sparks from crackling pine like new stars being birthed into the fabric of time. My fingers are numb. I've removed my gloves to assemble the Sako and oil the pistol. I want to ensure that all is ready. The four packages of C4, electronic receivers, and transmitter sit on the picnic table. *Diversions.* I'll place the explosives in strategic places. The bombs will create distractions that *might* allow me to take out my target with impunity. *Not likely*

I'll survive, I muse, knowing that the place will be crawling with cops, *but at least I'm giving myself a chance.* A pang of guilt stabs me as I think of the woman I will kill. I know she is young—only thirty-two—and the mother of three girls.

Stop. Do not let emotion interfere with duty. I take a deep breath, reach for my travel mug—the coffee inside cooled to lukewarm—and sip. *Tarja Saariaho is supporting the immigration of Muslims, the people who killed Niko.*

I consider alternative arguments, the tired old adages about Islam being a religion of peace. I shake my head, put down the mug, disassemble the rifle, and slide the weapons back into the duffle bag. *Bullshit. What other faith encourages its adherents to gleefully blow themselves to bits to achieve paradise? The bastards even carry out their atrocities in houses of worship! How many bombings have Shiite martyrs accomplished in Pakistan and Iraq while Sunnis prayed? I'll tell you: dozens. The same is true of suicide attacks against Jews in synagogues and Christians in churches. No, Islam is not a religion of peace.* I stand up from the pine bench I'm sitting on and swing the heavy duffle onto my shoulder. *I've read the Quran: it's anything but peaceful.*

I walk towards the hut. Light from a propane lantern leaks from gaps around the door. I ruminate further. *Of course, the Old Testament isn't much better,* I concede as I open the door, enter the cold space, set my heavy burden on the wide planks of the floor, and wander back outside. *But we have Jesus,* I add. *He's the ultimate peacemaker. I do what I do in his name.*

I stand outside. The Aurora appears. Undulating greens and reds and violets overwhelm me. A tear forms and slides down my right cheek. *Irina,* I think, remembering the note I left on the kitchen table, my life-insurance policy and pension documents naming her as the beneficiary beneath my handwritten apology. *I was smart enough to take out the suicide rider,* I think, wiping away the wetness on my face with the sleeve of my parka. *I wish things were different,* I lament as a shooting star slashes across the evening sky.

CHAPTER ELEVEN: December 3, 2017 (Kajaani, Finland)

"**What** the hell do you mean, 'we lost him?'" Alissa Utrio asked, glaring at the object of her derision over a pile of surveillance reports, photographs, e-mails, and other documents related to the investigation. "Officer Salmela, kindly tell me where 'we' fits into *your* dereliction of duty?"

Junior Constable Teemu Salmela, less than five months on the job and posted to Kajaani out of the Oulu Police Department, sat across the desk from the chief inspector, his eyes downcast, his face, chalky. He was being dressed down privately, out of the hearing of his brother and sister officers, including Utrio's wife, Sergeant Elsa Vuolijoki, Salmela's immediate superior.

Damn newbie, Alissa thought, studying the clean-shaven, crew-cut blond, blue-eyed, stocky cop in front of her. *See how he sweats. See how he shakes. He knows that he fucked up. Now we have no idea where the hell the madman is!*

Her seemingly innocent visit to the *Ravihuone*, the Sons of the Ravens' social hall—posing as a military veteran out on the town with her lover—had convinced her: *The FSB is right. This guy is dangerous.*

Her contact in the terrorism division of the St. Petersburg office of Russia's security police, Andrei Melindov, someone she'd worked with over the course of their respective careers and someone who—despite his loyalty to Putin and the Russian oligarchs holding the reins of power inside Russia—Alissa had come to trust when it came to international terrorism, was perfectly clear on one fact. Two FSB agents sympathetic to the Finnish man's obsession with Islamic extremism had provided a name, the identity of an unsavory German arms merchant willing to supply the Finn with everything needed to replicate the homicidal chaos Breivik had unleashed in Oslo. Upon hearing the scuttlebutt, Melindov had made discreet inquiries and uncovered uncollaborated, but reliable intelligence that unspecified firearms, ammunition, and a small quantity of explosive material and detonators had changed hands and were likely somewhere in Finland. The FSB agents who assisted such skullduggery?

"I am afraid I am not at liberty, Chief Inspector, to divulge what discipline, if any, my agency has undertaken against those two."

Alissa had pushed the Russian for confirmation of the rumors that both men had been arrested and sent to Siberia, which, in Putin's Russia, meant they would die in prison. "Come on, Andre. How long have we known each other? Ten years? And we've worked, what, a dozen cases together? I just want to make sure justice, as the Americans would say, was done."

Andre had laughed. "I cannot confirm or deny these rumors. I will say that we continue to interrogate these men in an attempt to discover what your man purchased from the German. Regardless of what we uncover in this respect, let me assure you of this: justice in Mother Russia is swift, consistent, and harsh. Severity is the way Russian fathers teach their sons and daughters to respect authority. More than this, I cannot say."

Other agents within SUPO, agents with far more knowledge and sophistication in the use of Internet and digital tracking than Alissa, broke the identity of the suspect and gave her an address. Surveillance by the Helsinki Police Department, a sergeant with the department being willing to devote two radio patrol cars to the man's apartment, uncovered details of his life in Helsinki. His job as a cab driver. The existence of a live-in: a legal secretary attending university to be a lawyer. The suspect's long and prestigious military career. Confidential information was developed from the man's superior officers in the Finnish Army, from which he'd been honorably discharged and was on a pension after twenty-plus years of service, including overseas deployments, one of which, the man's last in Central Africa had, according to the man's commander, broken his spirit.

The investigation had also uncovered: the man's membership in the Sons of the Raven, an association that compelled Alissa and Elsa's clandestine visit to the group's speakeasy; the existence of a cottage once lived in by the suspect's brother and family on Oulujärvi; and a 1972 Volvo licensed in the suspect's name.

Searches of the man's apartment and the girlfriend's computer conducted by the Helsinki police revealed hundreds of inquires researching Islam and Syria and refugees and the history of the worldwide Jihad perpetrated by Islamic extremists against the West, including the tragic death of the suspect's brother in a suicide bombing at the Moscow airport. But all of that background was only circumstantial evidence of the man's intent. It was not until the girlfriend, Irina Jusso, was brought to SUPO headquarters in Helsinki, and the letter written by her lover was uncovered as part of a final search of the apartment she shared with the suspect, that Alissa had sufficient evidence to arrest the man.

"Your one and only job, Junior Constable Salmela, was to make your way into the garage of the suspect's lake cottage, crawl under his Volvo, and affix a tracking device. That was it. And in that one, simple task, Salmela, you failed. Do you understand what this means?"

They were talking in Alissa's cramped office in a one-story, nondescript 1960s vintage brick building housing SUPO's district headquarters in Kajaani.

"But Madam Chief Inspector," Samela replied, a hint of respectful objection in his voice, "I *did* put the tracking device on the suspect's vehicle."

Alissa frowned. "Well then, Junior Constable, perhaps you need a refresher course on how to *properly* place a mobile tracking device on an automobile." She stared hard into the man's indigo eyes. "For it seems, despite your protests, you did not *successfully* accomplish your one and only mission in this regard."

Salmela met Alissa's gaze for an instant, and then, as hardness enveloped her stare, he dropped his eyes and shook his head. "I don't understand how I could have failed, Chief Inspector."

Alissa nodded. A conciliatory look replaced her recriminatory glare. She was a hard taskmaster but one who understood humans are destined to disappoint. *Except Elsa,* Alissa thought, allowing a momentary diversion from the grind of the investigation. *She has never disappointed me!* "That will be all, Salmela."

The man stood up from his chair, hat in hand, and mumbled something akin to another apology. Alissa waved him off with her right hand, her eyes buried in paperwork. He retreated without saying another word, the shame and the disappointment in himself evident in the slouch of his shoulders.

Damn. The tracker on Alhomäki's taxi shows he didn't take that north. He's got two possible targets. Here, in Kajaani: the refugee center. That's a pretty soft target. Just a chain-link fence perimeter. No watchtowers. Only a half-dozen uniformed immigration officers on the premises. Alissa paused to consider possibilities. *Or, if the man's truly crazy, he could target the processing center in Tornio. That makes some sense. Much of the unrest and bad news about Muslim immigrants, which seems to be what he's focused on, originates in Tornio. But that's a harder target. Scores of local police and immigration officers and military providing security. Two possible targets ... but which one has he chosen?*

There was a knock. The door to the office opened and a woman in uniform walked in and stood in front of the chief inspector's desk.

"Sergeant Vuolijoki," Alissa said in a friendly tone to her wife, "how can I help you?"

"It's Kajaani. The refugee center."

Alissa cocked her head. "How do you know?"

"Helsinki police. Cameras at the railway station caught him going through the ticket line, buying a one-way to Kajaani. Used a fake ID: a driver's license. Name of Kantonen. Urho. The license didn't give him away. The footage did. He's dyed his hair and is wearing glasses but it's Alhomäki alright."

Alissa nodded. "And where is he now?"

"I checked the garage at the family lake place. He was there. Volvo's gone."

Alissa folded her hands across the pile of papers on her desk. "And?"

"He apparently took the weapons and ammunition with him. We didn't find anything in the apartment's storage locker or at the cottage."

"Jesus H. Christ."

The women studied each other.

"Agreed," Elsa replied. "Divine intervention may well be what we need to find this guy ..."

"... Before it's too late," Chief Inspector Alissa Utrio added, finishing the sentence, knowing her wife's thoughts like a child knows a mother's voice.

163

BOOK THREE: THEN

CHAPTER ONE: January 20, 1906 (Røros, Norway)

The wind sliced through Anders's coat as he stood on the edge of a yawning, rectangular pit clawed from frozen earth. Gravediggers had used pickaxes to break apart topsoil in the graveyard of the Røros Kirke, the desolate final resting place for the mining town's dead. The bell tower of the ancient church, completed by the copper company in 1784, shadowed the snow-covered cemetery as the Pöysti brothers, Anders, mining engineer Sig Olafson, crew chief Lars Pettersen, and a handful of other mourners clutched their coats in a failed attempt to defeat winter. Reverend Oddvar Sigismund prayed for the dead man in Norwegian. Poju Pöysti whispered a translation to Anders but the younger man, his left arm in a sling—the fractured radius and ulnar bones knitting together nicely in a plaster of Paris cast—was not listening. Anders's attention was focused on an ancient iron cross standing in the back of the graveyard: the towering relic covered in rust and moss and a mantle of new snow, the artifact somber and macabre in its decay.

I wonder what the story is behind that cross, Anders thought fleetingly. *Pay attention! This is your farewell to Edvin. He took his last breath on top of you beneath that terrible, terrible jumble of Norwegian stone. His body protected yours, saving your life.*

There was no way for Anders to know whether his co-worker ended up on top of him by chance or by heroism. All he knew for certain, standing in the cold, white flakes drifting over the assembled mourners and coating the shivering men (there were no women present to mourn the dead miner), was that Edvin Koivu had shielded him from greater harm. For that, Anders was eternally grateful to the sickly old Kven who had suffocated beneath the rubble as Anders fought for his life, the small pocket of air trapped inside the debris barely sufficient to sustain him until other miners came to his aid.

Anders had remained unconscious until Dr. David Finne, the mining-company's physician, wrenched the distorted bones of his left forearm into place without the benefit of anesthesia.

"Christ!" Anders had screamed as the rough-handed sawbones torqued the fractured radius and ulna into alignment. "What the fuck are you doing to me?" he had cursed, hurling the expletive as Fredrik and Poju Pöysti pinned him to the cotton sheet covering the examination table. Anders, though not particularly religious, was also not prone to swearing, so that when the curse exploded from his mouth, the Pöystis appreciated his pain. And yet, once the old doctor was finished jamming the ulna and radius into place, Anders reclaimed his standoffish manner.

"Learned the technique from *Norsk Ortopedi,*" Dr. Finne said gruffly after applying a cloth bandage and wet plaster to the patient's left arm, creating a cast to protect the injury.

Despite the negligence embodied in Finne's personal appearance, Anders marveled at the man's abilities. That is to say, Finne's level of competence was significantly at odds with his hygiene.

The physician left the room to allow time for the plaster of Paris to dry. The Pöysti Brothers and Anders remained silent, the shock of the bone setting having exhausted Anders and unnerved his friends. Finne returned carrying linen cloth. Placing Anders's forearm in the fabric, the doctor looped the sling over the Finn's head before tying a knot, securing the fractured arm in place.

"There. Good to go," the old man croaked, the horrific stench of his unwashed body nearly gagging Anders. "Have a seat in the corner so I can go over instructions with you, will you Mr. Alhomäki?"

Fredrik translated.

Anders swung his trousered legs off the examination table and claimed a stool in the corner of the cobwebbed, dusty, poorly lighted space. A solitary gas lamp illuminated the examination room, throwing barely enough light for Anders to discern the details of the physician's craggy face.

"It's difficult to get good ingredients to make a casting. Imported from France, you know," the doctor dithered. Finne removed a bottle of English gin from a drawer in his desk, uncorked it, took a large swig, and offered the bottle to Anders. The miner shook his head. "It'll take the edge off the pain," the physician said with a wink.

Fredrik relayed the offer. Anders shook his head again.

"Your choice. Anyway, the use of plaster came to the forefront during the Crimean War. Russian field surgeons wanted a better way to protect fractures. Came up with using plaster of Paris," Dr. Finne observed. "Keep the cast dry. Wear the sling when you're up and about. If your skin itches, use a stick to scratch. But be gentle—you don't want to shift the bones. Come back in two weeks and we'll see how things are progressing," he said, taking another swig before returning the gin to its hiding place, rising from his chair, and opening the door.

The burial concluded. A flutter of snowflakes turned into a snowstorm as mourners shuffled towards the town square.

"Buy you a beer?" Olafson asked in Norwegian.

"Sure," Anders replied, having learned enough of the foreign tongue to carry on a casual conversation.

The Norwegian matched the Finn stride for stride as they walked. It was difficult to see one's boot tops—much less the town's buildings—as the little troop of Anders, the Pöystis, Olafson, and Lars Pettersen ambled towards the Hammer and Pick tavern.

"Kjergata Street's just ahead," Pettersen said quietly, his mind occupied by thoughts of the dead. "You were lucky," he added, following Anders and Olafson, the miners' freshly polished work boots kicking up snow as they moved. "It could have been a lot worse."

Anders did not reply.

"I know you're disheartened about the fight, about it being postponed," Pettersen continued. "But the Englishman assures me that Swedberg is a patient man, that you will have your chance."

Again, Anders, his left arm—his dominant arm—confined to the sling, said nothing.

Fredrik Pöysti chimed in from behind the others. "He's not going to talk about it, Mr. Pettersen," Fredrik said in heavily accented Norwegian. "He was hoping to survive twelve rounds, collect the prize money, and sail to America. Now, he'll have to wait—at least until summer. Right Alhomäki?"

Anders maintained his silence. They arrived at the tavern. Olafson opened the door. The men clambered inside, stomping snow from their boots as they entered. The tavern was empty

169

except for the bartender and Gunhild Harraldsen, the town prostitute. Gunhild, who had once been a beauty but was now a broken-down, middle-aged drunk with bloated cheeks, distressed brown eyes, and innumerable folds of excess skin descending from her jaw to her wrinkled bosom, sat on an oak stool. It was unladylike for a woman to drink in a tavern without a male escort, but then, Gunhild was no lady.

"Poju!" the woman shouted, slurring her words. "It's been too long since I've seen my little Finnish bear!"

Poju blushed. "I don't know what you're talking about."

Fredrik elbowed Poju. "Sure, you do, little brother. You and Gunhild have rolled in the hay more times than a newborn calf on a warm spring day!"

Poju glared but made no reply.

"Schultzie!" Olafson shouted. "Beer for my friends!" He stepped up to the bar and stood next to Gunheld. The woman's exuberant perfume nearly gagged the engineer as Olafson waited for the German to fill mugs with room-temperature lager from a tap.

The whore sipped Aquavit from a glass. "What's your name, stallion?" she asked coyly, taking a drag on a hand-rolled cigarette as she surveyed her prey.

Olafson grunted, collected the beers, his big hands stretching to carry the mugs, and ignored the question.

"Cat got you your tongue?"

Olafson said nothing. Froth sloshed as he placed the mugs on the table.

Pettersen raised a glass of warm beer. "To Edvin Koivu, a fine man whose life was cut short."

"Hear, hear," Olafson concurred, raising his mug, the other miners at the table joining in.

"He saved my life," Anders replied. "May he rest in peace."

"You fellows friends of the *Kven* who died in the cave-in?" Schulz asked from behind the bar. "I heard he was a good man."

"Indeed, he was," Anders said glumly.

CHAPTER TWO: February 25, 1906

Anders walked towards the only café in Røros that he could afford. He was unable to work. His left arm remained in a cast, his wrist and forearm supported by a sling. Anders's life savings, a few hundred kroner, was tucked in his left shoe, his mistrust of bankers reflected in his choice of depository.

The landscape was shrouded by clouds. There was no sun. No snow had fallen for weeks. Old drifts remained, piled waist high along the wooden sidewalks and dirt streets of the town, the decaying humps turned ashen gray by the town's copper smelter. It was an exhausting scene that welcomed the miner as he walked towards the *Så og Styre* (Sow and Steer), where Anders would meet up with the Pöysti brothers to slurp bowls of gruel, gulp cold milk, sip hot coffee, and talk over the week's events before the brothers began their shift in the mine.

He arrived at a decrepit shack, the glass of the eatery's windows cracked, gaps in the clapboard siding stuffed with rags, stomped his work boots, grasped the wrought-iron door handle, pulled hard, and entered the depressing space.

The brothers sat at one of four tables in the overheated eatery, a pine fire roaring in the wood stove in a corner, tobacco smoke drifting near the crudely plastered ceiling. Every chair in the place, save one empty seat, the one saved for Anders—the spindled back of the chair held together by rusted wire and a few well-placed nails—was occupied.

"Hei," Fredrik said to the disheveled, wet-headed, out-of-work miner as Anders claimed his seat, Fredrik slurring his greeting because his mouth was full of food. "How's the arm?"

Anders sat heavily. A waiter approached, his white apron a mess of food stains. "What'll you have?" the man asked in Norwegian.

"Porridge and milk. Coffee. Rye bread and honey. One egg, hard-boiled."

The waiter nodded and left.

"You've learned some Norsk," Poju said, slapping Anders's narrow back. "Good for you!"

Despite Anders having learned rudimentary Norwegian, the men conversed in Finnish. "I'm picking it up bit by bit," Anders replied.

Fredrik risked piping hot coffee from a ceramic mug. "You never answered me."

Anders's food arrived. He awkwardly grasped a spoon with his right hand. "The arm is taking too much time. I need to train, but Doc Finne says it will be another two weeks before he removes the cast. After that, a full month before I can start using the wrist and hand."

Fredrik nodded. "What about work?"

Anders shook his head. "Can't work for two more months and I can't start hitting a heavy bag until May."

"Shit."

Fredrik's response indicated that he understood the Finn's desperate desire to fight, collect his purse, and leave Norway. "That puts you, what, leaving in the fall?"

Anders nodded with resignation.

Poju shook his head. "Bad luck, that accident."

"Worse luck for Edvin—the poor bastard," Fredrik chimed in, tilting his cup to drain the last bit of coffee before doing the same with his porridge bowl. "What are you going to do in the meantime, for money I mean?" he asked, pushing his now empty bowl away from his extended belly, smacking his lips in satisfaction.

Anders picked up the hardboiled egg, peeled it, salted it, and downed it in two bites.

"Hungry?" Fredrik asked.

"Didn't feel well last night. Didn't eat supper," Anders lied. He had determined that, to make his savings last until he could return to work, he would only eat one meal a day. Already haggard and thin, Anders was losing weight, something that, with a boxing match against a skilled opponent on the horizon, he could ill afford to do.

Poju scrutinized Anders. "Are you sure you're getting enough to eat?"

Anders nodded and, as if to emphasize that he was doing fine, slowed the pace of the meal, taking time to relish the two slices of dark, rye bread slathered with honey as if he was dining with royalty. "I am."

If I limit myself to one meal a day, I've enough cash to pay my rent at the boarding house for two months. The kroner in my shoe will see me through until I can go back to work in early April. Pettersen's holding my position despite Wirkkala's desire to sack me. There's no reason for Pettersen to show such kindness. No union protects my job. No contract requires him to rehire me. He's being more than fair. I can hold out until April and then, once I'm on the mend, get back to training and fight in Trondheim. I thought I was done boxing after being licked by Pekka Pakkanen. But one last bout won't kill me. I'll be ready, make some money, and leave for America before winter.

Anders was doing what he could to stay active. He walked the streets of Røros every morning. When the weather was decent, he took longer rambles into the countryside past the omnipresent smelter disgorging smoke into the thin, high-altitude air, past the graveyard where Edvin Koivu's body reposed, past the church and its bell tower that dominated the Røros skyline—as if the smattering of two- and three-story buildings that rose above the town's muddy streets could be designated a skyline at all. He had no money to buy beer at the Hammer and Pick and so, despite a desperate melancholy caused by being out of work and disabled, Anders did not, as so many men who are hurt on the job, fall into drink. But in a bow to the precarious nature of his situation and in hopes of restraining anxiety, Anders made the conscious decision to avoid walking past the copper mine. *That would be a mistake,* he reminded himself as he said his goodbyes, left the restaurant, pulled his decadent coat against his body, and began another day of aimless wandering.

Evenings he allowed himself the luxury—despite his meager financial situation—of reading by candlelight. The town had no library and, even if it did, the books would be in Norwegian, a language that would have befuddled the Finn on the page. He was saved boredom and despair because his sister Ronja—golden haired, thirteen years old and (by all accounts in the letters he received from his mother Marjatta) a stunner—sent him an abused copy of Minna Canth's writings, including her best-known plays *The Worker's Wife, The Parson's Family,* and *Anna-Liisa.* Ronja used money she made as a housekeeper for the Noskinen family to purchase books for her brother. She mailed thick, heavy packages from Paltamo to Røros. Her precious gifts took weeks to find their way across the Gulf of Bothnia, through Sweden, and into Norway. Anders read with such speed, he found himself devouring the same stories over and over and over while awaiting Ronja's next surprise.

The distraction provided by familiar Finnish words and phrases eased Anders's unsettled disposition as his arm healed. And his nighttime reading had a secondary, palliative effect: it took Anders's mind off his empty stomach. The books diverted Anders's attention from gnawing hunger until dawn cleared the hills surrounding his adopted Norwegian home and Anders left his rented room in search of breakfast.

CHAPTER THREE: April 15, 1906

"**Goddamn** it!" Anders cursed, shaking his left hand and wrist after striking an improvised heavy bag hanging from a clothesline in an abandoned stable on the property of the Røros Copper Mining Company. The large, open space smelled of must and horse sweat and dung and rotting hay even though the stalls had been removed and the pine boards burned for fuel. "Doc Finne told me I was good to go, but it's clear to me that I am not."

Fredrik stood behind the canvas duffle, an item he'd donated to the Finn's efforts to train for the upcoming boxing match in Trondheim against Antti Swedberg, holding the makeshift heavy bag firmly in both hands, his weight pressed against straw-filled canvas. "You're not fighting until June," Fredrik said evenly, nodding as Anders rubbed moose-hide boxing gloves—hand-me-downs sent to him by Otso Olson—together. "You have plenty of time to whip yourself into shape."

Anders dropped his gloved hands and shook his head. "It's not the getting into shape part that's the problem, Freddie. I starved myself for the better part of two months before Pettersen got me back to work. But despite eating only one meal a day, I managed to keep up my stamina by walking around Røros, gradually increasing my pace until I was trotting, then running," the boxer argued. "Trust me when I tell you that I'm in shape."

They were speaking Finnish, Fredrik's distinctive Finnmark accent making it slower going than if the tall, lanky miner had practiced their mother tongue in the homeland. Anders had no trouble discerning the man's intent: it just took a bit more concentration to ferret out meanings and nuances in phrases and words that would have been self-evident had Fredrik Pöysti spent his life in Finland.

"I meant no disrespect," Fredrik said, his eyes riveted on Anders standing in the shadow of the heavy bag, the only light in the horse barn natural sunlight cast into the room through infrequent windows. "I know you've had a rough go of it."

Anders lifted his feet, shuffled his raggedy work boots—the leather abused and lacking polish—as if in the ring, and started anew. He shook off the tingling in his left forearm and wrist and began systematically striking canvas; first with the left and then with the right.

"That's it!" Fredrik exclaimed. "That's the boy from Paltamo who is going to knock the snot out of Antti Swedberg!"

As Anders circled and danced and feinted and attacked, he remained silent. His mind wandered, focusing not on the upcoming match, but on the news he'd received from home.

Brother:

I hope this short letter from your <u>favorite</u> sister finds you in good health. Mr. Olson stopped by the farm the other day to report that you'd made a splendid recovery from the accident. That is good news, Praise Jesus! Mother and Father and Helmi are all well. Your old school mate Erno Karppinen continues to live on the farm and work for us. As I've said before, Erno is no longer the same person he once was. He stopped drinking and, as a consequence, has become a quietly confident farmer. He has also found God, taking on the mantle of Laestadianism, which, as you know, is a pretty severe faith but one, in Erno's case, that serves him well. It is also pretty evident that our hired man has eyes for Sister Helmi, though, because she and I are only on the cusp of fourteen, Mother is keeping a watchful eye to ensure no scandal erupts on the Alhomäki Farm!

The big news is that I too find myself longing for America and I am past merely wishing for such a thing to occur. I have saved enough money from my housecleaning jobs and my work at Noskinen's store such that I can afford a one-way passage. Come September, I intend to sail from Helsinki to England. I will take the train from Hull to Liverpool. In Liverpool, I will board a steamer on the Canadian Pacific line and sail to Quebec City. Once in Canada, I will take the train to Duluth, Minnesota where I have secured a position through relatives of the Noskinens to work as a domestic. Such an adventure we will have!

I write "we" because I know you too will soon join me across the ocean to begin a new life with new possibilities. Finland holds nothing for a single, young woman such as myself and I dare say, nothing for a daydreamer like you! I understand your reluctance to claim your birthright as the only son of Jorma Alhomäki. I know your heart, brother, know how you long to follow Uncle Alvar by searching for adventure in faraway places.

You could, of course, stay put on the farm in Paltamo and live the sedate life of a Finnish farmer. But that is against your nature. I know your decision to forego your legacy was once a bone of contention between you and Father. I am hopeful that enough time has passed so that rift is no longer significant. Besides, I am sure Mother is, despite her fears and frets and worries, in your corner so to speak!

I may, if circumstances permit, take up further schooling in Duluth. I have an affinity for teaching, and I understand that there are places to obtain such training in America. Sadly, teaching courses are not readily available in Finland for a girl like me.

Well, that's the news from Paltamo. Mr. Olson says you are going to fight again. I pray that you land your blows quickly, avoid your opponent's fists, and earn enough money to join me in America. Mr. Olson also explained that you are entering the ring to secure funds to leave Norway and make your way to Michigan to work in the copper mines. I'm uncertain how such a change of scenery will improve your lot but you are my older brother so I expect you know more about such things than I do!

Fondly,
Your loving sister,
Ronja

"Get your head in the game, Alhomäki!" a stern voice commanded from the depths of the abandoned building. After admonishing the boxer, the newcomer strode purposefully towards Anders and Fredrik. "Have you forgotten everything you once learned?"

Otso! Otso Olson is here in Røros! Perhaps there is something to Ronja's insistence on prayer, Anders thought as he watched his beloved trainer emerge from shadow.

CHAPTER FOUR: April 1908 (Belfast, Ireland)

Anders stood at the rail of a steamship of the White Star Line, RMS *Shannon,* watching the bawdy, strong-waked Irish Tug, *O'Neil's Jig,* release a towline and leave the ocean liner to its own steam.

She's relatively new, Anders thought, looking over the ship's railing to take in Belfast Harbour and its unremarkable skyline. *Her maiden voyage was in June of '01—only seven years of transatlantic sailing under her belt. But we were forced to divert from our route after leaving Liverpool due to a vibration in one of the propellers. Turns out, the shaft was in need of minor adjustment, a task easily completed at Harland and Wolff, the Belfast shipyard of* the Shannon's *making. That defect being corrected, oh what a magnificent piece of machinery she is!* he thought as his eyes scanned the placid bay. *Imagine: she carries over three thousand passengers and crew in her bowels. A floating city steaming for America!*

Anders's gaze settled on the lazy, circular path of Blackhead Light's beacon. *I've done it,* he thought, allowing a dollop of pride to invade his normally self-effacing persona. *I'm off on the great adventure I always dreamed of!*

Ireland became but a distant horizontal boundary of retreating horizon. A chilly wind birthed waves. The constant motion of the ship unsettled Anders's stomach. He drew his new wool coat, a luxury he'd purchased after the fight, tight against weather and fought nausea.

The training regimen imposed by The Bear had been arduous. Despite believing he retained stamina through walking and later, jogging the streets of Røros while waiting for his wrist to heal, Anders found he was easily winded when he renewed his time in the ring.

Otso had sold his tannery in Mieslahti and left Finland. "Off to South America, Lad," the growling, steadfastly engaging trainer had revealed once Anders's surprise at Otso's unannounced appearance abated. "There's a temptress, Tuulikki Vähämäki, whom I recently became acquainted with. She's an actress—just starting to make a career in moving pictures. I had the good fortune to share a carriage with her while in Pietarsaari on business. It was a chance meeting, my boy, that changed my life!"

They had been in the stable after The Bear's arrival, the trainer trying to convince Anders that, because of the weakness of his left wrist and hand, Anders needed to change his approach and lead not—as he was wont to do, with his right—but with his left. "You've got to remake your style and throw that damned Swede off his game. It's your only chance of making it through twelve rounds and claiming your share of the purse," Otso had instructed. And so, Anders commenced relearning the sport as if he'd never been in the ring. And over weeks of training, Otso related the circumstances of his falling in love with Tuulikki.

"She'd just come back from Munich where she was in talks with the Danish-German filmmaker Urban Gad about making a film. Gad approached Tuuli when she was performing a German-language version of Ibsen's *A Doll's House*, about doing a provocative—and scantily clad—version of the witches' scene from *Macbeth* on film," Otso explained as Anders struggled to find a pace and a rhythm to their training ritual in the temporary ring the trainer had erected in the old barn.

There being no local boxers available for sparring, Olson slipped on gloves and entered the ring, his considerable paunch jiggling with each step across the dirt floor of the stable, his forehead glistening, and his graying hair and salt-and-pepper beard dripping sweat as he tutored the younger man. "But she wasn't interested in the proposal, which, I dare say, likely involved Tuuli accepting the role of not only a witch on film but also becoming Gad's lover in real life."

Otso deflected a weak left from Anders with his right glove and tapped Anders on the noggin with a left jab, the speed of the blow at odds with the lumbering, out-of-shape old man's physique. "That would have been lights out if Swedberg was landing the punch. You need to move away from harm and guess his next gambit. Stay ahead of your enemy, read his mind, and plan your next move like you're playing poker, or you'll find yourself flat on your ass, looking at the ceiling of *Trøndelag Teater*," The Bear exhorted, referencing the venue where Antti Swedberg and Anders Alhomäki would fight.

The men had stopped to gulp cold, fresh water from tin pitchers located on the stable's dirt floor. "Is she beautiful?"

Anders asked shyly, his ardor for female companionship having been dampened by Anneli's rejection.

Otso looked up and smiled. "Of course. The most striking woman I've ever set eyes upon!"

Anders sat heavily on a three-legged stool and considered the moose hide of his boxing gloves. "Do tell, Otso. It's been a long time since I was in love. I need to know that such things are still possible, even for a broken-down ogre like you!"

The Bear grinned but shook his head. "I'll not breach a confidence, my inquisitive little friend. Let's just say that when our carriage arrived at my hotel in Pietarsaari, it continued on empty of passengers. More than that, I'll not divulge."

"She is expecting you ... where is she again?"

"I didn't say specifically. She's in Brazil. Rio de Janeiro. She's working in a club down there, singing Spanish tunes to the Portuguese! The woman's a marvel, speaks five languages, including passable Finnish despite being a Swede Finn," Otso added, smacking his gloves together. "Enough chitchat. Time to get back to work."

They trained every day whether Anders was coming off a shift at the copper mine or it was his Sunday off. Otso Olson was, as he had been since first tutoring Anders, a supremely dedicated coach.

"But you say," Anders continued, hopping down from the stool and joining Olson in the ring, "that she is beautiful?"

The Bear scowled, took a fighting stance, his gloves at the ready. "Show me what you've got."

"I want details," Anders said, sliding himself back and forth in front of his opponent, his dark eyes concentrating on finding an opening, his left hand leading the charge. "I want you to describe how stunning your lady friend is. I've been cooped up here," the boxer continued, "where the only women are miners' wives, widows of miners, old crones, little girls, or the town whore."

Anders dodged a slow right jab from the old man. Creating space by footwork, Anders snapped his left glove forward and caught the trainer on his bearded jaw, the blow momentarily stinging Olson.

"Nicely do—"

Before Otso could finish his sentence, Anders feigned another left and delivered a sharp, brutal right uppercut to the older man's chin. The punch knocked The Bear back on his heels.

Olson shook his head and blinked to clear his brain. "That's what I'm talking about! You do that to that goddamned Swede from Finnmark and you'll not only make it to the bell, you just might win the fight!" he said, lowering his gloves, signaling that the session was over.

The theater had been crowded with patrons hungry for blood sport. The men of commerce and industry who controlled Trondheim deigned to attend the event of the summer despite the sport's uncouth reputation. The men were accompanied by pretty wives or coyly seductive mistresses decked to the nines and ready to cheer for the man predicted to be the next All Scandinavian Lightweight Champion and a likely participant in the 1908 Olympics in London. The big money was on Antti Swedberg, who had been the lightweight champion of Sweden and who, had the Swedes not decided to ban the sport, would have cleaned the clock of any Swedish boxer sent his way. No one in attendance expected the twenty-three-year-old Finn—his arms gangly, his legs well-muscled but thin, his dark eyes shaded by an unruly mane of black hair that wasn't combed or confined in place by the hair oil he typically slathered on his scalp—to last a round, much less the duration of the fight. And yet, he had done just that.

"Don't let that bastard get inside your head," Otso had admonished, decked out in the finest, new, black three-piece suit Trondheim's best Jewish tailor could fashion on short notice. Olson sported a lavender bow tie, lavender suspenders, and shiny black and lavender spats, the shoes dyed to match the suit. Anders wore a white, sleeveless, cotton tunic, the words "*Mahatma Suomalainen*" embroidered across the back of the shirt, white satin boxing trunks—a stripe of Finnish blue running from waist to hem down each leg, clean white cotton stockings pulled above his shins, and gleaming blue boxing shoes, the leather dyed by the same Jew who'd created Otso's attire. There had been no cheers from the crowd when Anders entered the ring; instead, the Finn's appearance had been greeted by catcalls and derisive slurs shouted by inebriated Norwegians.

"He'll make a big entrance," Otso whispered, nodding towards the doorway where Swedberg was expected to appear with his entourage. "There will be music," he said, gesturing towards a six-piece brass band sitting on wooden folding chairs behind the boxing ring on the theater's massive stage, "as if he is the king of Sweden arriving for his coronation. Don't let the hoopla distract you. Keep moving. Use your left to set up the right. Keep your hands up. You'll make it to twelve if you listen to The Bear!"

As predicted, when Swedberg strode imperiously into the packed auditorium, the band commenced a martial tune. The music swelled, compelling the crowd to rise from their seats and cheer as the lanky, blond headed Swede Finn entered the theater surrounded by a half-dozen Englishmen. Swedberg was toned muscle from his shoulders to his ankles, towered a full head over the young Finn, and outweighed Alhomäki by at least ten kilos. Swedberg's bright, serious, blue eyes stared straight ahead. He did not acknowledge the crowd or his opponent as he slipped between the ropes and claimed his corner. Three trainers, professional boxing men from Liverpool brought in to protect the Englishmen's investment in their boy, stood around Swedberg as the boxer's silk robe bearing the Norwegian flag was removed from his shoulders and folded by his trainers. Antti Swedberg stood upright, red silk boxing tunic and shorts glimmering under harsh electric lighting, his eyes fixed on Anders, a menacing scowl defining his face.

The boxers met in the center of the ring, nodded to the referee, and touched gloves. The official instructed them in Norwegian, Anders understood only a portion of what was explained. But there was no need for translation: he knew the rules of the game and knew what he had to do.

"*Yksi,*" Swedberg whispered in Finnish as they stepped away from each other. "*Et selviä yksin,*" the taller man repeated as he showed the Finn his back.

Returning to his corner, Anders placed his forearms over the ropes, breathed deeply, stretched his hamstrings, and said a perfunctory prayer.

"What did the bastard say?" Otso asked.

"That I won't last one round."

Olson's face reddened. "Fuck him. Do as I say, and y
survive. The money for your trip to America is as good as you
you follow our plan."

Anders nodded, put on his game face, and waded into the
fray.

He had not only made it twelve rounds, he had used
Swedberg's presumption of superiority to lull the Swede into a
false sense of impending triumph. Anders abided the unorthodox
style prescribed by Otso to confuse Swedberg through the first ten
rounds. And as Anders waited in his corner for the eleventh
round to begin, Olson counseled him to continue the agreed-upon
strategy, wait out the clock, collect his appearance fee, and be
done with the matter. "There's great satisfaction in staying with
Swedberg until the end," Otso had admonished. "No need to get
greedy."

Anders nodded. But the headstrong Finn had already
determined that, if he was still standing in the eleventh and had
fire left in his belly, he would fight to win. *This is my last match.*
After tonight, I'm done with this nasty business. He looked across
the ring and studied the Englishmen attending to Swedberg. *I'll*
not be part of this sort of spectacle again.

When Anders tapped Antti's right cheek with a soft left
near the end of the eleventh, Swedberg believed he saw an
opening. He loaded up a big haymaker to end the fight. But
Anders's jab was a ruse. Swedberg was tired and unable to discern
he'd let his guard down by going on the offensive. As the Swede
brought his left into position to strike a decisive blow, Anders
danced away, his wind stubbornly strong, his legs like those of a
prancing stallion, and hit Swedberg with a combination that
bewildered the man. The Swede stumbled to his corner as the bell
sounded. He was a mess. A nasty gash had opened above his right
eye. Trainers scurried to close the wound and clear blood from
his eyes.

"What the hell are you doing?" Otso asked as he rubbed
Anders's shoulders with liniment.

Anders stared across the ring at his stricken foe but did
not reply.

The Bear frowned. "Well then," Otso said with reluctant
acceptance, "you best keep at it so that damned Swede doesn't
land one of those big, sloppy haymakers he's been throwing."

Anders nodded, slapped his gloves together, stood up, and greeted his enemy with renewed vengeance.

In the end, it was a blow to Swedberg's solar plexus, a right hand thrown with all of Anders's meager weight that did the man from Finnmark in. As Swedberg tried to reclaim his breath, Anders leveled another right and then a brutal, end-it-all left hook, the force of the blow hitting the Swede's chin with such force that Anders felt his left index finger snap. The punch brought the crowd to its collective feet as their darling staggered forward, his gloves poised as if to deliver a response, only to collapse.

There was no need for the referee to count Antti Swedberg out. Anders returned to his corner. Otso slapped the boxer's slender back in jubilation. The broken finger was momentarily forgotten as Anders considered Swedberg reposed on canvas. The Swede did not move. It was unclear if he was still breathing. *Christ*, Anders thought, *get up, man!*

But Antti Swedberg did not rise of his own accord. Medics were summoned. Norway's hope for an Olympic boxing medal was placed on a stretcher and hurried by horse-drawn ambulance to the Trondheim Hospital. His jaw broken, his cheek fractured, his brain addled, Antti Swedberg remained unconscious for an hour. When he finally awoke, the Swede Finn—who claimed Norway as his home—was finished. He would not fight in Copenhagen or London or anyplace else. He was done with the "sweet science."

And so was Anders Alhomäki.

CHAPTER FIVE: April 1908 (Atlantic Ocean)

He wanted to leave for America immediately after he bested
Antti Swedberg, but circumstances conspired against him.

June 14, 1906
Paltamo, Finland

Dearest Anders:
*I write to you with sadness. Your father has passed away. He was
working in the fields with Erno when he was stricken by apoplexy.
There was nothing that could be done. According to Henri
Nevonen, a blood clot found its way into my dear Jorma's brain,
paralyzing him and, because the infarct was so severe and medical
intervention was so far distant, Jorma died in the rye field you
once worked together. The crop is knee high and likely the best
we have ever seen on the farm, a circumstance which makes his
passing all the more tragic. Erno was there—working Aake in
harness—and was able to comfort your father as God claimed his
soul, which, praise the Lord, came swiftly. I say this not to be cruel
but because Henri advised that my dear Jorma would have been
unable to walk, talk, speak, or care for himself had he survived.
His passing has left a deep void in my heart, but I can bear the
pain of it knowing that had he lived, he would have regretted
surviving. The sort of existence predicted by the doctor would
have been no life at all for a man of the soil, the sky, and the
world like your father.*

*I have been neglectful in our correspondence because of
my stubborn pride. For this, I apologize. I am your mother and I
should not have let my disappointment over your choice to work
in Norway, with eyes set upon America, affect my love for my
firstborn child. And so, I write the words that are always difficult
for we Finns to say: I ask your forgiveness. That having been said,
I must ask you one favor before you sail off on your grand
adventure.*

*There is no will. Jorma, being of middle age and fit, saw
no purpose in anticipating the unthinkable. And yet, that is exactly
where things find us. By the time you receive this letter, Jorma's
mortal body will be in the ground and his soul will be in Heaven. I*

am not asking that you return to Finland for his burial. I am asking that you return to the farm in Paltamo because, given you are his heir by law through adoption and given there is no will, you will need to renounce your claim to the farm and transfer your interest to Ronja in writing. But such a transfer cannot take place until she marries Erno. Yes, I know that revelation is quite a shock! We were all expecting Erno and Helmi to marry. But love has a strange way of taking its own course, which, once the initial infatuation between our young border and your dark-haired sister dissipated, is exactly what transpired. And so, it is your fair-haired sister who, in the end, is to marry Erno.

This is a long-winded way of asking if you would delay leaving for America until after your sister turns sixteen and becomes Erno's wife. That's a little less than two years away. I know, I know. At the tender age of twenty-three, two years seems to be a very, very long time to wait. But in addition to these legal issues, I could use you by my side to help me bear up through this tragedy. I could use your inner strength to support me through my grief.

I realize that my request is selfish and may cause you distress. Please remember this: you are the apple of my eye and the person I feel I need by my side in this uncertain time. Besides, working closely with Erno (someone who is not, shall we say, one of your favorite people) would give you a chance to assess him as a man and decide for yourself whether he is worthy of your sister. This too is something you likely never expected to be asked to do given that Jorma would have been the one to scrutinize the young man and, if appropriate, stand up for your sister in the church parsonage at her wedding. That is impossible now, but Ronja would be thrilled to have her big brother fulfill that role.

Please consider what I have asked and advise me as soon as possible if you are willing to assist me in my time of need.

Your loving mother,
Marjatta Anna Alhomäki

He agreed to return to the farm to examine the fitness of Erno Karppinen as a potential husband and, if Anders found that Erno had changed sufficiently to win his favor, Anders was prepared to deed his interest in the farm to his sister, say his goodbyes, and catch the next steamer out of Hanko for England. But this plan, while well intended and in keeping with Anders's goal, was amended by the pain and grief and upset he encountered from spending time with his mother, his sisters, and most surprisingly, Erno as well.

The nasty, bullying nemesis who had made Anders's childhood hell had been replaced by a caring, sober, thoughtful adult whose love for Jorma, hearty affection for Ronja, and clear and unwavering respect for both Marjatta and Helmi all convinced Anders that people are capable of transformation. "The leopard has changed his spots," was the shop-worn cliché that manifested over and over and over again in Anders's head as he rolled up his sleeves and went to work on the familial farm beside his former antagonist.

Anders stayed through the wedding ceremony, having exchanged the Norwegian kroner he'd won for besting Swedberg for English pounds. His savings were more than enough to pay the cost of a one-way ticket on a transatlantic steamer and provide "walking around money," a treasure that he secured in a pouch kept beneath the straw mattress of his bed. Two years after arriving in Paltamo at his mother's request, Anders escorted his slender-waisted, golden-haired, sapphire-eyed, milky-skinned sister into the parsonage of St. Thomas Lutheran Church, uncharacteristically beaming with pride. He found his place beside Erno (Anders had been asked by his future brother-in-law to be the best man) with Erno's two cousins (the same boys who'd watched Anders deliver Erno his comeuppance) serving as groomsmen. He witnessed Ronja and Erno recite their vows. Helmi—equally beautiful given her dark features, long flowing black hair, and ebony eyes—and two of Ronja's childhood girlfriends stood statuesque and poised across the room from the men.

There had been little money left after Jorma's funeral. Most of the family's remaining savings were dedicated to paying for Ronja's modest wedding-day dress—purchased at a discount from Noskinen's store, the dress having been a return from someone else's botched wedding. The bridesmaids wore their finest everyday dresses. The groomsmen were modestly attired in the best jackets and neckties their respective wardrobes contained. There was scant coin remaining in Marjatta's purse to fund fanfare. The flowers displayed inside the church social hall in the couple's honor were cut from Marjatta's garden and from the gardens of friends. The women of the congregation provided roasts and side dishes for the wedding dinner. Beverages served at the reception were limited to lemonade and thick Finnish coffee. The pastor would not allow strong drink inside the sacred walls of his church, though some of the men managed to sip strong liquor from flasks hidden in their coat pockets, hiding beneath the concealing shade of trees outside St. Thomas to commit their sins.

At the wedding reception, Anders renewed his admiration for his uncle Alvar, met Tatianna and his cousin Kari for the first time, and heard enthralling details concerning the Elf Warrior's time in the Orient. As revelers whirled and spun to Finnish reels, waltzes, and polkas, Uncle Alvar attracted an audience. Curious listeners—both men and women—crowded the soldier to hear him spin yarn after yarn concerning his harrowing adventures at Mannerheim's side fighting the Japanese. No one made mention of Tatianna's unfortunate dead husband or her past. No one in attendance would have dared to question her honor in front of the man who had made her an honest woman.

At the end of the reception, the deed to the farm had been signed, goodbyes were said, embraces were exchanged, tears were shed, and the young miner left home on his great journey.

As he made his way from the open air of the RMS *Shannon's* promenade deck, Anders left behind churning waves, frigid wind, and a darkening sky. He was in desperate need of the marginal comfort of his third-class cabin, a space he shared with three other men. His stomach remained unsettled; his mettle tested by seasickness. As Anders descended into the bowels of the ship, he thought of Ronja, how she had yielded her dream of leaving Finland, succumbing to her affection for a man who once taunted and abused her only brother. *I hope she is happy,* was the singular thought that manifested as Anders found his cabin, opened the door, noted with weary satisfaction that the chamber was empty, climbed into his berth, pulled a scratchy wool blanket around his body, and tried to gird himself against an inhospitable sea.

CHAPTER SIX: May 1908 (Duluth, Minnesota)

A Great Northern locomotive pulling a coal tender, five passenger cars, a dining car, an observation car, a baggage car, and a caboose crossed the Interstate Bridge connecting Superior, Wisconsin, and Duluth, Minnesota. Below the bridge's deck, whitecaps whipped the muddy waters of St. Louis Bay into a frenzy as the train rattled over creosoted ties. It was a bright, cloudless, late-spring day.

Anders stood on the rear platform of the train's last Pullman and braced himself against the train's herky-jerky movement by grasping a railing with his right hand. The Finn shielded his eyes from the anger of the open sun with his left palm as he studied the Minnesota hillside. He wore no hat and his inky hair was plastered in place with hair tonic.

Why in God's name, Anders wondered, looking at the brown brick, red sandstone, blue gabbro, and wood-frame buildings hugging denuded hills rising above the lakeshore, *did they choose to build a city on the side of a mountain?* The Finn realized his use of the term "mountain" was an exaggeration. He'd been amongst snow-capped, ruggedly constructed, spires of foundational stone in Norway. *There are no mountains in Finland,* he observed ruefully as he recalled the Norwegian countryside surrounding Røros, stroking his chin with his left hand, keeping a firm grip on the brass rail with his right. *I've seen and worked amongst real mountains enough to know that these hills do not measure up. But still. They are impressive, climbing as they do from water to sky, terraced from top to bottom with buildings and roads.*

He watched as a tram ascended the hillside while another car, acting as a counterweight, plunged towards the harbor. Anders was unknowingly observing the Incline Railway carry passengers and freight from the city's downtown to a new suburban development, Duluth Heights, located on a plateau above the lake.

The miner studied the abused landscape. Sulfurous, black smoke poured from yellow brick chimneys. Factories and foundries and lumber mills crowded the soggy shoreline of the St.

Louis River estuary, spreading south—paradoxically—towards the neighborhoods of West End and West Duluth.

Not many trees remain, Anders thought, noting that, here and there, charitable loggers had left a sentinel white or Norway pine towering above the slash and debris cluttering the ground, the litter evidence of the old growth timber harvesting that had once dominated the region's economy. Anders itched his muttonchops with his left hand: he'd grown the sideburns since leaving Norway, believing the whiskers gave him a distinguished air.

In the week that it took to travel from Ellis Island to the Twin Ports by train—from New York to Chicago to St. Paul to Duluth—he'd changed plans. There was, according to a mine recruiter he'd encountered at Finn Hall in Harlem—the nucleus of Finnish immigrant life in New York City—no work presently available in northern Michigan. A glut of copper from Arizona and Montana had slowed mining operations in the Upper Peninsula, leaving recently immigrated Finnish, Slavic, Cornish, and Italian miners idle.

"It's temporary, you understand," the recruiter for the best-known of the mines in Hancock—the Quincy Mine—a rotund, nattily dressed gentleman had advised with a dour look, "but right now, I don't have anything for you. Try Johnson's booth across the way. He's recruiting for Tower-Soudan, in Minnesota. Iron, not copper. But still underground at the same rate of pay—$2.25 a day, less supplies." The man had blown his nose into a white cotton handkerchief and nodded. "Yes, if I were a young man looking for work," the recruiter continued in passable Finnish, "I'd head to the Iron Range. Plenty of jobs there, my boy."

And so Anders had altered his intentions. Instead of making his way to the Keweenaw Peninsula to sign on with the Quincy Mine, he'd spend time in Duluth, find temporary work, investigate employment in Tower-Soudan, and if an opening could be found and the terms were acceptable, he'd head north to the Vermillion Iron Range. He had enough money to survive—conservatively but without danger of starving—for a month.

Thirty days to find work, he reiterated as the Great Northern train pulled into Duluth's elegant Union Depot, an iconic building constructed in a style that appeared—to Anders's uneducated eye—European. Coal smoke roiled from the

190

locomotive's stack as the train came to a stop and disgorged its passengers. *Thirty days before I am in jeopardy of failing at my new life in America.*

He took lodging on St. Croix Avenue in Finntown, a Duluth neighborhood crammed between the retail shops and department stores of Superior Street—the city's main east-west thoroughfare— and the iconic Aerial Ferry Bridge. The bridge, Duluth's best-known landmark, spanned the navigational channel leading from the St. Louis River to Lake Superior and connected Finntown with Park Point, a spit of sand inhabited by some of the city's poorest citizens. Steel towers rose above unsettled water on either side of the shipping canal, the bridge's superstructure connected by horizontal spans of steel. A gondola, suspended above the outflow of the river and powered by electric motors brought to life by direct current, slid back and forth across the canal, ferrying people and automobiles and wagons and streetcars and horses and mules from the mainland onto The Point and back again.

Anders's first room in Duluth was at Henri Haakinen's boarding house. His lodging overlooked an alley, the Tempest Tavern, and the bridge. Through the window of the room Anders shared with five other men on the rickety frame building's third floor, the immigrant had a view of the Ferry Bridge's gondola as it moved passengers, freight, and vehicles back and forth across the canal. When bulk freighters or passenger boats or low-slung whalebacks passed through the narrow shipping channel, the gondola would move to one side, leaving enough room for vessels to navigate the turbid passage.

It was at Haakinen's, where he lodged from May through August of 1908—when he left Duluth for a job as a hard-rock miner in the Soudan iron mine—that two events of significance took place in Anders's life.

His roommates at Haakinen's Boarding House were all fellow Finns, which, since the newcomer from Paltamo knew less than a dozen phrases in English, was a comfort. Perhaps comfort is too strong a word as most of Anders's roommates—men older, gruffer, and far more recalcitrant in their speech than the younger Finn— said little to the new immigrant. The exception to this unnatural silence was Matti Peltomaa—who for convenience shortened his

191

first name to "Matt" and dropped the last "a" from his surname. Peltoma was a talker, a man, who like Alhomäki, had come to America for the long haul and whose nondescript physique concealed tenacity.

"Matt. Matt Peltoma," he had said, extending his right hand in greeting when Alhomäki claimed the bunk above Peltoma's. "Where you from?"

The innocent, opening question, asked in Finnish—Matt's speech not yet affected by his time in America—began a steady and honest friendship. It was Matt who introduced Anders to Jerome "Buzz" Albert, the foreman of a day-labor outfit, Forsyth's Employment Agency. Forsyth's hired Alhomäki to work the quays and wharfs and docks of the Duluth-Superior Harbor. For a dollar a day, Peltoma, Alhomäki, and men of their station were expected to put in a solid ten-hour shift unloading crates and kegs from boxcars, hoisting them onto hand trucks, pulling the cumbersome flatbeds across the docks, and loading the cargo onto pallets to be lifted by crane onto boats where the crew would secure the load for transport to Milwaukee, Chicago, Cleveland, and other eastern cities on the Great Lakes. And when a boat came in bearing goods for the people of Minnesota, Wisconsin, and the Dakotas, items that would leave the Twin Ports for Minneapolis and St. Paul and Fargo and Rapid City and Wausau by train, the cargo would be unloaded by the ship's crew and the reverse would be true: Peltoma and Alhomäki and their mates would place the goods onto handtrucks, haul the heavily laden carts across the docks and piers, and load the goods into boxcars. The securing of temporary employment was the *first* event of significance Anders experienced in Duluth.

The second event highlighting Anders's arrival in America was more personal and, if truth be told, not something a good Lutheran boy from Kainuu was eager to share with strangers: Matt was the man who introduced Anders to prostitutes.

It happened three weeks after Anders arrived and was settled into his new position with Forsyth's. With American dollars—Anders's first two weeks' wages paid in silver coin, twenty dollars cash on the barrel without deduction—in his pocket, augmenting the small savings remaining after his odyssey to and across America, Anders, normally sober and reflective but one who, when invited to share a cold glass of beer with his only true friend in America after a hot, sweaty June day working the docks, agreed to a night on the town with Matt and two other Finns.

The evening began at the Mercury Café in Finntown. Anders, true to his thrifty nature, had the special: beef stew, a dinner roll, a slice of cheddar cheese atop apple pie, and coffee. His meal cost seventy-five cents—nearly a day's wages. Anders's mates splurged on flank steaks—thin slabs of beef cooked to the consistency of shoe leather, accompanied by boiled potatoes and carrots, and apple pie smothered with freshly churned ice cream—leaving Anders's companions with a tab of over a dollar when it was all said and done.

"Let's get a bump at Finnegan's," Matt had suggested, gesturing towards downtown Duluth where the well-known Irish pub was located. "Beer is only five cents and it's always cold."

"Sounds good. Tomorrow's Sunday so, if I have too many, I can always sleep in," Anders replied.

"You'd miss church to nurse a hangover? I thought you were a churchgoing man," one of the other Finns, a big, burly, bearded man by the name of Hintala, said. There was a twinkle in the man's eye as he looked at Peltoma, somehow knowing that the escapades of the evening were just beginning and, if truth be told, their young friend would likely need more than just one sermon to redeem his soul.

"I was confirmed," Anders said quietly, not rising to take the bait. "But I haven't been much of a Christian since then."

Peltoma winked at Hintala. "Well, I think we have a way of reinvigorating your faith, at least your faith in the power of love. Stay close and pay attention. You might learn something."

It was after midnight when the four men, tipsy and loud and singing Finnish folksongs, knocked on the front door of Sadie Salminen's brothel. The brick building, three stories tall and, listing like a sailing ship in a brisk wind, crouched below Superior Street, the sort of introduction to Finntown that church Finns and Duluthians of a more sedate and conservative nature abhorred.

"Whosehouseisthis?" Anders said through a thick tongue, his eyes glassy and glazed over by the four shots of vodka Matt had coaxed into him. "Whatawedoinhere?"

The older men giggled. The door opened. Sadie, her eyes retracted into her skull, her face powdered and white, her formerly golden, luxuriant hair listless, stared at the drunks with derision. "What the hell do you assholes want?" she asked in Finnish.

"Sadie, it's Matt. Matt Peltoma," the dockworker said, taking off his hat to expose his face and balding head.

"Ah. Come for another romp with the Sadie girl, have you?" the woman said, her face beaming with recognition.

"Not tonight. I'm afraid I've shot my wad—at least, my cash—already. I'm more interested in you finding a nice, young, Finnish girl to help my friend here," Peltoma shoved Alhomäki forward, the newly arrived immigrant barely able to stand, his eyes slowly closing as if to fall asleep on his feet, "lose his cherry."

Sadie studied Anders. "Are you sure he can even perform? He looks about ready to crash on his head."

"You got coffee? Pour him a few cups and then, given he's young, I'm sure with the right 'persuasion' from the right girl, things will work as they should."

"Five dollars. For the coffee, the girl, and a bed so he can sleep it off."

Matt nodded, pulled out his coin purse, dug deep into the leather pouch, found a five-dollar Liberty gold piece, and handed it to the woman. Sadie held the coin up to light emanating from a nearby gas street lamp and smiled.

"We have a deal. And I've just the girl for your boy's first romp in the sheets," Sadie mused, turning in the doorway and yelling, "Sun, come down here! You have a customer!" The woman stepped aside. "Get the boy inside. You're letting in mosquitoes," she added in a commanding tone. She looked at the two Finns standing with shit-eating grins on their faces in the shadows. "You two want girls?"

The men shook their heads.

"So just the one then?" Sadie asked as Peltoma helped Alhomäki inside.

"Just the one," Matt replied, propping up Anders as they waited for the girl. "Maybe later this week I'll come back for a slice of Sadie pie!"

The woman scowled. "Do you have to be so damned crass? How long have you been coming to me, spending time in my bed? A year? You should treat me with more respect, I should think, after what we've shared."

194

Matt nodded. "Agreed. I apologize for being rough. You're a sweetheart, Sadie girl," he said, leaning over and pecking the woman on her powdered cheek. "You've never caused me to have to see Doc Heikkinen, and for that, I'm truly grateful!" he added as he shut the door, leaving Hintala and the other drunk outside.

"Pff. You pay me a compliment and then talk about the clap. I'm not sure what to make of you, Mr. Peltoma."

Before Matt could reply, a young woman, short, thick of leg and arm but stunningly poised, her complexion exotically bronze, her long black hair trussed up in a bun and held in place by silver hairpins, her brown eyes dark and mysterious, made her way down the staircase and into the foyer.

"This is Sun. My newest girl. Half Finn, half Ojibwe."

Matt gulped. "Wow!"

Sadie frowned. "Don't get any ideas, Mr. Peltoma. She's fresh to the trade and I won't have her being spoiled by the likes of you!"

Anders slowly opened his eyes. "Pleasedtomeeetcha."

The girl bit her lip. "Is he able ...?"

Sadie smiled. "We'll get him into shape to do what needs doing. Mr. Peltoma has paid for the young man to get sobered up, spend some time with you, and stay the night."

Morning Sun Karvonen scrutinized Anders. "Are you sure? I mean, he looks ready for the crypt," she said in Finnish.

Matt smiled. "Well, ma'am. This will be his first time. Seems to me that you'll need to be patient regardless of his condition. Maybe spending time with him, shooting the breeze, sobering him up with coffee will ensure his first visit with you is a memorable one."

The Indian girl raised her hand to Alhomäki's face and stroked his sideburns. "I'll do the best I can, but I make no promises." The girl took Anders by the hand. "Come on, Mister ... what's his name, anyway?" she asked in English.

"Anders. Anders Alhomäki. And you'll need to keep conversing and instructing your new pupil in Finnish," Peltoma added through an inebriated, impish smile. "His English is poor."

"As are his lovemaking skills, apparently," Sadie interjected. "Take him into the kitchen and pour him a cup of that tar we call coffee. I'll be in after I see Mr. Peltoma to the door."

Morning Sun led Anders out of the foyer, bracing his weight with her right hip as she directed him towards the kitchen. Sadie Salminen and Matt Peltoma stepped into the foyer, where the madam opened the door.

"Sure you don't want to stay? I'd give you a discount. I could use the company."

"I'm afraid I'd be a great disappointment to you in my present condition. I'll take a rain check, maybe stop in tomorrow night."

Sadie shook her head as Matt stepped out into the warm evening. Clouds of insects swarmed towards light leaking from the brothel. "Tomorrow night, you pay full price," Sadie said. "Pick up your boy before eight. He should be sober by then," she added with firmness.

Matt nodded and joined his drinking companions as the madam shut the door. The men began walking towards the Aerial Ferry Bridge, Finnish songs sung in bad harmony echoing through the stifling night, having left a virgin in the care of whores.

CHAPTER SEVEN: December 1908 (Soudan, Minnesota)

"**Finlander**," a raspy voice called out, "you're not paid to loaf: you're paid to work. Get that ore to the elevator and be quick about it."

Anders Alhomäki considered a response to the harsh rebuke of his foreman, Ivan Preblich, a Croatian immigrant who'd spent years in the coal mines of the Austro-Hungarian Empire as little more than a slave. *Preblich's a bastard*, the Finn thought, bracing himself behind the fully loaded ore cart, his weight and strength barely sufficient to budge the load, *but I need to hold onto this job. Stanley Cukela—another Croatian but a far better man than Preblich—is looking for a position for me at the Pioneer Mine in Ely. He's got connections there. Maybe he can get me out of this shithole.*

Anders, his muscles bulging beneath the sleeves and shoulders of his wool work shirt, his legs bowed and powerful from years of heavy labor, his brown wool trousers mended with patches from discarded rags—his stitchery sloppy but formidable—fought off the chill of working three thousand feet beneath the northeastern Minnesota landscape. "I'm on it, Ivan. I've got 'er movin'!" he called out in English, the candle on his soft cap casting a hesitant, yellow light on the narrow-gauge rail leading to No. 8 Shaft.

"Good thing, Finlander," Preblich chided, emphasizing the slur, "or I'll sack your ass and send you topside to collect your wages."

When he awoke on that Sunday in Morning Sun's bed, his head pounding, his mouth parched, his tongue thick from too much beer and vodka, the girl was sitting in a rocking chair holding an infant bundled in expensive swaddling at odds with Morning Sun's station in life. "Good morning," she had said, a hot cup of coffee steaming on a rickety nightstand between the rocking chair and the bed, the sleeping child snuggled against the mother's bosom, the girl's body modestly covered by a cotton nightgown. "How did you sleep?"

Anders raised his head from the soft, clean sheets, propped his neck up with a pillow, and tried to understand his circumstances. "Where the hell am I?"

The girl, not much older than sixteen by the looks of her childish face, tittered before asking. "You don't know?"

He shook his head.

"Sadie Salminen's."

Though Anders had never stepped foot in the whorehouse before the previous evening, he had walked past the notorious structure at the corner of St. Croix Avenue and Michigan Street many a time. On his sorties past the brothel he'd resisted the whores leaning out the establishment's front windows, smoking cigarettes, their exposed cleavage heaving, their "come hither" voices filled with double entendres and teasing. But it was pretty apparent, as the young man's eyes focused, as he understood where he found himself, that his staid Lutheran upbringing had likely been bested by desire.

"How did I ...?

"Your friends brought you here," the girl offered, her smile kind and gentle and not at all harsh or judgmental, "and left you with me for the night."

Anders pulled the crisp, starched white sheet up to his chin. Beneath the covers, he was naked, as naked as a newborn chick. "Did we ...?

The girl shook her head, reached with her free hand, lifted the cup from its saucer, and took a long draw of coffee. "I'm afraid you're still a virgin, Mr. Alhomäki. Try as I might, I was never able to, shall we say, 'rouse' you. At least not to where you were actually awake and interested in what I was proposing."

His face flamed. "What time is it?"

She put the cup down and shifted the sleeping child into her lap. She was dressed respectfully, not at all the sort of costume Anders expected a whore to wear in her bedchamber. Her hair was down, shiny as velvet, framing her face in ebony. "Six in the morning. The sun is up but I've kept the drapes and shades drawn to let you sleep. Your friend, the outgoing, the talkative one ..."

"Peltoma. Matt Peltoma."

"Yes. Well, he'll be here at eight."

Anders studied the woman and child as he pondered a question.

198

"Something on your mind?"

He hesitated, organizing his thoughts. "Where did you learn to speak Finnish?"

She smiled. "My father. He's from Turku. My mother is Ojibwe. I'm what some call a 'Finndian.' Half Finn. Half Indian. I'm not so fond of that label myself but who am I to change what others say or think about me?" she asked, regret infecting her voice.

Anders had nodded and tried hard to think of something conciliatory to say to the girl. But another thought intruded: *I'm naked! Where the hell are my clothes?*

"Sadie has one of the girls, one who used to work in a laundry, cleaning them," Sun interposed, reading his mind. "Your shirt, your trousers, your union suit, and your stockings were all pretty nasty after your night out. They all should be done shortly."

The dockworker rubbed his muttonchops, trying to rid himself of the pain emanating from his facial hair. "Got anything for a headache?"

The girl giggled. "I'll find some powder. That should do the trick." She stood up, walked to the bed, and handed Anders the slumbering child.

"Hold Little Red Hawk while I open the curtains and find you some medicine."

The Finn's eyes grew wide. He hadn't held a child since his twin sisters were babies. He didn't know the first thing about children. "I don't really ..."

But the infant was already in his arms, snuggling into Anders's bare chest, as the Indian maiden ripped open the drapes and snapped up the shade flooding the modest bedroom in light. "I'll go get you a cup of hot coffee and some of that headache remedy," she said, leaving the room with swift elegance.

Sun was back within minutes, placed a glass of water and a cup of hot coffee on the nightstand between them, and handed Anders a packet of Teca powder before reclaiming her child and the rocking chair.

When Sun handed Anders the medicine, their hands—his large and rugged and calloused, and hers small, dainty, and soft, her thin fingers tipped with neatly trimmed nails—touched ever so briefly. It was a moment of intimacy between them that left Anders wondering. But before he could act or say anything to the striking girl with the baby in her arms, the laundress, a tall, thin, emotionless woman whose days as a sporting lady were history, entered the room, stacked Alhomäki's freshly laundered clothes at the foot of Sun's bed, and retreated without speaking.

The moment for Anders to say something of significance passed. Instead, he opened the foil packet, emptied powder into the palm of his left hand, lifted the medicine to his mouth and swallowed it before chasing the dry elixir—a combination of aspirin and caffeine—with water. He replaced the empty glass on the nightstand, grasped the handle of the coffee cup in his left, took a swig, and marveled that the medicine seemed to immediately work its magic on his throbbing skull.

Anders studied the whore, curious as to why such a lovely, lovely girl felt compelled to service drunks and coarse old men to put food on her table, clothes on her back, and a roof over her head. But he knew it would be impolite to delve into his companion's personal history, so he kept the conversation perfunctory and light. "What's your name, anyway?"

She smiled again, exposing needle-like teeth unblemished by stains, fillings, or cavities. "Morning Sun. Last name is Karvonen. Morning Sun Karvonen. But you can call me 'Sun.'"

He took another long draw of coffee. "How old are you?"

A frown crossed the girl's forehead before vanishing as quickly as it manifested. "Eighteen."

She's no more eighteen than I am forty, the Finn thought. *It's a pity that she's here, in this place, and not in school with boys and girls her own age.*

"I don't really like talking about myself with customers," she added. "It's best to separate business matters from personal things, don't you think?"

He pursed his lips and nodded. "But you say we never ...?"

The same grin that greeted Anders when he'd first awoken reappeared. "Sorry to say, I failed you, Mr. Alhomäki. I'd offer to try to make amends, right here, right now, but well, you see I have my son and ..."

He shook his head. "No, no, that's fine. Probably better to leave things be. But let me ask a favor of you, if I may."

Her face turned fretful. "I don't go in for that sort of thing, the oral, you know. That's not something I do."

Anders had an inkling of what she was referring to but being unschooled in lovemaking, he didn't completely understand the mechanics of the act repulsing her. "No, no. Nothing like that. I just want you—if asked by Matt or Sadie or anyone else as to how things went—to make up a story. Tell them it went just fine; that I did my duty."

The last sentence, a phrase that wasn't common to the girl's understanding, stumped her for a moment. Anders watched Sun's face as she tumbled the sentence over and over and over in her mind until her face brightened.

"Oh yes, Mr. Alhomäki. Last night will be our little secret. Of that, I can promise you!"

"Alhomäki!" Preblich yelled as Anders moved the ore cart towards the mine's central shaft. "I warned you that I don't pay you to daydream. I pay you to work your fucking Finnish ass off and not waste time thinking idle thoughts," the man continued in English. Preblich refused to speak Finnish even though he was fluent in the language. He'd supervised countless Finns at the Soudan mine over the years and had learned the basics of their tongue. He'd endured the strike of 1907, when most Finnish miners were sacked for trying to organize, only to be replaced by new immigrants from Oulu and Turku and Helsinki. Preblich knew the language of Alhomäki's homeland—the birthplace of many a union agitator—but the foreman was not about to speak Finnish. To do so would undermine the Croatian's belief that every miner in his charge needed to learn English and learn it quickly; not only so as to be uniform within the mine but also as a means of assimilation, compliance, and obedience.

"I heard you the first time, Ivan," Anders replied, his arms extended to their limit, his shoulders aching from effort as he shoved the cart full of red ore down narrow steel rails. "I'll get a move on."

The Slav stood where a drift from a distant stope intersected with the main chamber of the mine, his belly straining against the waistline of his dungarees, his crisply laundered blue wool shirt, and his red suspenders. The man tilted his cap upward—creating a clear line of sight—before imperiously placing his hands on his hips. "You do that, Finlander. Or, as I said, you'll

201

be on the first Duluth and Iron Range local back to Two Harbors!"

Anders didn't reply. He simply willed his tired legs towards the elevator, a vision of an Indian princess—or was it an image of a similarly exotic and sensuous *Kale* girl from his past—occupying his thoughts as he struggled to understand the choices he had made.

Damn, he mused, nodding to the elevator men as they accepted the cart. *I could have had the farm! What the hell was I thinking, casting my fate to the wind, thinking that leaving Finland for America would result in a better life?*

The wages were, when one subtracted the costs associated with tools and blasting caps and dynamite and candles and other equipment supplied by the mine, for shit. There was no way an ordinary miner could accumulate wealth sufficient to buy a home, much less acquire acreage upon which to build a farm or save capital adequate to start a business. He was one of millions of immigrants who had listened to the siren call of the recruiters in Helsinki, Oslo, Stockholm, Berlin, London, Paris, Rome, Belgrade, and other European cities: predominantly single men who, upon leaving their homelands, found themselves trapped by low wages and long hours in a life of hell, a life no better—and in Anders's case, far worse—than the life left behind.

But I'm here now, the young miner thought, returning to the stope, grasping his shovel, and dumping newly mined ore into an empty cart by candlelight, *and that's the truth of it!* As a trammer, the lowest rank of miner, Anders's job was simple: fill an endless succession of wooden carts with iron ore. Each broken shovel, each burned-out candle was an expense against his wage, a wage paid monthly on Payday Saturday, which, for Anders, given he worked the night shift, meant he needed to mind his money and not blow his paycheck between payday and his last night shift of the week, which ended on Sunday morning.

I won't admit to my mistake, won't pack it in and head back to Paltamo. No, I'm not about to do that. Anders's stubborn pride would not accept, would not accommodate, giving in and admitting error. Instead, like a scientist puzzling over an incalculable problem, he studied his situation, dissecting his new life, evaluating possibilities. *Prayer won't help,* he thought as he grunted and sweated. *I have no one to blame and no one to turn to except myself. If I am to be successful, I will have to make it on my own.*

He bent at the waist, retrieved a flask from a Poirer packsack, removed the cork, and drank heartily. As Anders gulped water, he studied the other men working the tunnel. The miners working the Soudan were universally Finns, mostly from Oulu and the surrounding region of Ostrobothnia—steady, quiet, and stoic souls like Anders Alhomäki. Men who rarely, if ever, revealed personal details about their lives or their future dreams. They had all, like Anders, been hired after hundreds of Finns and other immigrants were blacklisted following the failed strike of 1907. The walkout had been an attempt by Minnesota miners to join the Western Federation of Miners. The immigrants' effort to organize for better pay, conditions, and treatment had led to their firing, a circumstance that Anders had been made well aware of by his boss shortly after signing on.

"Don't be gettin' any highfalutin ideas about trying to start a union," Ivan Preblich had said before the ink was dry on Anders's employment contract. "There's no room for independent thinkers in the Soudan mine."

Despite having been raised by a mother whose politics were steeped in socialism, and a stepfather who adhered to Finnish nationalism, Anders was apolitical. He had no desire to change the world; his only objective was to save money, bide his time, and eventually go his own way. He took Preblich's admonition to heart and did not seek out the more radical Finns, men who were engaged in near-constant dialectics about their bosses and the mine owners and the investors back east who were growing filthy rich off the toil of immigrant labor.

As Anders watched others work, his diligence a drawback in that he labored faster than the men who freed the iron ore from the ground, it dawned on him that the only certainty was that, if he wished to be free of this place, this wretchedly depressing subterranean Hades, he would need land. His own land. *Goddamnit! I had a farm ready-made and in the palm of my hand! I was the heir to Jorma's place. And I turned it down! Why? Because of The Elf Warrior, that's why. Uncle Alvar filled my head with stuff and nonsense, with a sense of pride and adventure,* Anders thought as he corked the flask and returned it to his knapsack.

The shovel became heavy in his expansive hands. His muscles ached. Despite the chilly temperature at the bottom of the shaft, sweat beaded along the lining of his cap, ran down his face, and pooled in the neck of his shirt. *No. That's not fair. Alvar didn't lure me to America with his stories. I made a choice. I must live with my decision,* the miner concluded before raising his shovel and dumping scarlet, iron-bearing rock into the cart.

CHAPTER EIGHT: June 1911 (Lake Vermillion, Minnesota)

In the three years Anders labored as a trammer in the Soudan Mine under the scrutiny of Ivan Preblich, the Finn did not lose his temper despite the near-constant derision of his ethnicity and insistent hounding by his boss for being "too slow and too lazy"; though, truth be told, Anders's steady-paced diligence saw him outwork the other members of his crew just like he had outpaced his co-workers in Røros. But Anders's effort went unheralded by Preblich, a cruel, uneven taskmaster who, for whatever reason, made it his business to come down hard on the man who was his best worker.

Anders took modest lodgings in a *poikatalo,* a Finnish boarding house in Soudan where he and other Finns slept after their ten-hour days underground. The cooks at the *poikatalo* provided the men with breakfast and dinner, the night shift re-heating the evening meal left for them by the cooks when they arrived at the boarding house after their shift. Anders's only respite from the grinding, muscle-destroying, aching, boring repetitive labor were occasional Saturday night visits to the Tower Tap for a cold beer, infrequent sojourns to Sadie Salminen's place in Duluth where Anders and the Finndian girl finally arrived at an "accommodation" in the girl's full-sized bed overlooking the disgusting privies lining the shore of Lake Superior, or an occasional Sunday afternoon spent in Stanley Cukela's James Cross Guide Boat—a sleek, canoe-like double-ender built of Vermont white cedar and rowed with oars rather than paddled—fishing for walleye and perch in nearby lakes.

Month after month the Finnish immigrant saved Indianhead pennies, Liberty nickels and dimes and quarters and half-dollars, Morgan silver dollars, and the occasional silver certificate from his meager pay: a paltry wage of less than ten dollars a week after the expense of candles and broken shovels and picks was deducted by Tony DeLoia, an Italian immigrant, who, having displayed a knack for math and language, was promoted from miner to payroll clerk by the bosses.

After three years at the Soudan, all of it spent shoveling ore and pushing fully laden carts to the mine elevator, Anders had accumulated less than one hundred dollars: the coins and bills stuffed inside his leather coin purse and hidden at the bottom of his Poirer pack—the canvas knapsack that was always at the man's side—Anders's meager savings nowhere near enough to break free of being another man's serf.

"Pass me a cold one, will you?" Stanley Cukela asked.

Alhomäki and Cukela were drifting on Pike Bay, the south arm of Lake Vermilion, on a Sunday afternoon. Cukela's narrow boat, the cedar planking painted forest green, the gaps in the shiplap sealed with pine pitch, bobbed on a gentle breeze out of the northwest, the wind pushing the double-ender towards the southeast shore of the enormous lake.

Anders reached over the starboard gunwale, his left hand holding a makeshift fishing pole of freshly peeled aspen, his right hand following a rope from the gunwale of the boat into brisk water. He hauled a wicker basket from beneath the boat's keel and balanced it on the gunwale. After the water drained, Anders flipped a wire latch, removed two bottles of People's beer, set the bottles in the bottom of the boat, and secured the latch before lowering the wicker basket back into the lake. With his left hand still holding the rod, he grabbed a bottle opener tied by string to a strut, held each bottle with his knees, and opened them. Anders knelt, his woolen pants soaking up excess water, stretched to the limit of his modest frame, and handed a beer to the Croatian.

"Thanks," Stan said, his eyes focused on a cork bobber slowly descending behind the weight of a fish. "Got one!" he exclaimed, setting the hook. "Feels like a keeper!"

They were fishing for perch; schooling fish easily fooled by a simple hook and nightcrawler. They had each caught two of the small green and black striped relatives of Anders's beloved zander. The fishing line and the boat they were using had been Stan's contribution to the expedition. Anders had purchased the beer—chilled nicely by the waters of Pike Bay and brought lunch. He'd discovered the simple, complete meal of the Cornish miner and ordered pasties of beef, pork, potatoes, carrots, onions, and rutabagas from the Finnish cooks at his boarding house. The small meat pies, baked to golden perfection, were edible hot or cold. The two fishermen would, due to a lack of a place to build a fire, eat their pasties cold.

"Nice fish," Anders said, admiring the half-pound perch his partner dragged hand over hand into the boat. "That one alone would be a pretty good supper."

Stan nodded, removed a hook from the upper lip of the thrashing fish, and tossed the perch into the bottom of the boat. "One more and I'll have a feast!"

They were speaking English, a language that, at least for casual conversation, Alhomäki had mastered. Oh, there were fits and starts whenever someone with a strong accent, such as a Canadian or someone from south of the Mason-Dixon Line or Boston, tried to talk to the Finn. But for the most part, after three years of working in the Soudan Mine under a boss who insisted that everyone speak the language of the land, Anders was relatively fluent.

Anders didn't reply. Instead, he sipped cold lager, relishing the luxury he'd allowed himself, his thoughts attuned to a question, a question he was about to ask.

"Cat got your tongue?"

Anders still didn't reply.

"Hey, I'm talking at you, Finlander."

Anders's cork bobber plunged. "I've got one!" he shouted, setting the hook. "And I don't think it's a perch!" Anders fought the fish, the slender aspen rod bending until its tip touched the water. "I'm pretty sure it's a pike," the Finn said quietly, concentrating on keeping the fish away from the boat's underside. "I hope this line you brought is—"

There was a loud *snap!* The rod went limp. The fish was gone.

"Shit!" Anders said, pulling in his line by hand. "I not only lost the damn fish; I lost my hook and float."

Stan took a last swig of beer, tossed the empty bottle into the bottom of the boat next to the still-thrashing perch, and smiled. "Serves you right for not answering my question."

Anders dug into a pocket of his shirt, removed a square of wax paper, unfolded it, and extricated a hook. "You got a cork?"

Cukela reached into a small satchel, fumbled around, located a spare float, and tossed it to his friend. "What's eating you, anyway?"

Alhomäki concentrated on adding a lead weight and the cork to his line before tying off the hook. When the hook was secure, he reached into a coffee can beneath his seat, found a worm, pierced it with the hook, and tossed the rig back into Pike Bay.

"Finlander?"

Anders sipped beer as he mulled a response. "I'm thinking that I'd like to take you up on your offer to work in Ely."

Stan, who lived in Tower, the town he'd settled in when he first began working as a miner and who was lucky enough to own a horse and freight wagon and winter sleigh that he used to transport himself to and from his job as a crew boss at the Pioneer Mine in Ely, nodded. "I told you: a job at the Pioneer's yours anytime you want it. Pays the same but the bosses are a hell of a lot better men than that asshole you work for."

Anders smiled. "Prebich's Croatian like you. How can you run him down like that?"

The wind kicked up.

"You love every Finn, Finlander?"

Anders pondered the question. "No."

"Assholes are born and raised in every country," Stan continued. "Croatia is no exception. And in Ivan Preblich, my homeland gave birth to a doozie!"

Anders nodded. "That's right. You worked for him when you first came to the Range, didn't you?"

"I did. As a trammer just like you. And he was such a bastard, it was all I could do to keep from bashing his fuckin' head in with a shovel. I barely lasted two months working for that sonofabitch."

Anders set his empty bottle on the planked bottom of the boat. He watched waves lap the hull while trying to focus on his bobber. When the cork began to submerge, he set the hook. "Got another one."

The perch was ten inches long and fat—likely a female. Anders removed the hook from the fish's jaw, tossed the perch alongside the others, rebaited, and returned to fishing. As he watched a pair of loons fly overhead, he considered Stan's last statement, determined that it required a response, and replied. "I thought things would get better and, having moved from Duluth to Soudan, I didn't want to have to move again. But I've had enough of, as you say, 'that asshole.' And pushing ore carts. I'm ready to go to work at the Pioneer doing something else."

Stan placed his fishing pole between his knees, pulled out a pouch of tobacco and papers, and rolled a cigarette. "Smoke?" he asked as he struck a match against a brass fitting on the gunwale.

Anders shook his head, looked up, and studied a parade of fluffy clouds drifting from west to east. He was deep in thought when his bobber disappeared again. The aspen rod bent and the line sang in the wind. "I think that big pike is back," he said calmly, setting the hook, working the fish. Anders kept the rod tip up as his partner watched the battle from the bow of the little boat.

"Try not to fuck it up again, Finlander," Stan Cukela said, taking a long drag on his smoke, a smile breaking across his face.

CHAPTER NINE: August 1911 (Ely, MN)

Anders walked towards the carpenter's shop at the Pioneer Mine with an optimistic gait. Anders—newly employed at the mine in Ely as a carpenter's apprentice—was, at least in his own mind, in love. He had no idea whether the object of his affection, an eighteen-year-old Finnish Ojibwe prostitute, shared his view of their relationship or not.

They had spent incremental time together inside Sadie Salminen's brothel cuddled beneath the covers of Morning Sun Karvonen's bed, sleeping soundly after Anders had experienced the girl's favors. For a price. Always for a price. Sun had a child, *Agaasaa Misko Gekek*, Little Red Hawk, to raise, love, and protect and that child, as Anders learned, was the girl's foremost priority in life.

Having stumbled into trading her dignity for money at an age when most girls were shelving their dolls, Sun was, despite her youth, a realist. She knew that her body would eventually undergo metamorphosis such that her charms would dissipate, that age and gravity and the hard life of a working girl would render her a less-than-desirable commodity in the marketplace of lust. But Sun also knew that, with her meager savings from her cut of the proceeds Sadie obtained for her services, it would be years—if ever—before she would be financially independent of the woman who had, when things were dark and bleak and untenable, taken her in and saved her life. Perhaps not a life as portrayed in the plethora of women's magazines in the downtown newsstands full of articles and essays and photographs depicting flower gardens and dinner parties and big homes filled with expensive arts-and-crafts furniture, but a chance to survive and one day, if all her stars aligned, escape the life of the fallen. Sun was Sadie's most popular girl and had many customers, not because she was the best of the six whores living in the brothel in terms of lovemaking or experimentation but because, despite her lowly station, simple dress, and lack of adornment, she was patently desirable. Anders understood the Finndian's allure. It was simple: despite her surroundings and the horrific circumstances she found herself in, an evening with Morning Sun Karvonen seemed, against all odds, like an evening with a "regular gal," a beau, a sweetheart.

As Anders walked to work, he could not dispel the notion that he would be Sun's savior, that he would ask her to marry him, that he and the girl and her son would one day be a family. He did not calculate, he did not comprehend in his daydreaming, that the woman in this mythical future might not love him—or even admire him—and more than likely had other plans.

In truth, that was exactly the situation. Sun felt nothing more than commercial appreciation for the immigrant Finn. Anders was—though sweet and kind and attentive beyond any of the other men she slept with—simply a customer, someone she was fond of as a bartender is fond of a free-spending drunk.

Sun had left the Turtle Mountain Reservation in north-central North Dakota at fourteen, pregnant by her mother's brother, having been raped after Uncle Two Bears groomed her with candy and trinkets and smooth talk until he secured her confidence. When her monthly stopped and her belly swelled, her mother, Anita Goodeyes Karvonen, refused to believe the girl's story, that Anita's older brother, an elder of The People, had taken liberties with her eldest daughter. Instead, Anita blamed Sun's ruination on "that boy," Edward Olson, the son of a local Norwegian farmer who had been making mooneyes at Sun, trying to earn Anita's favor so as to take Sun on a picnic or some other such romantic outing.

"She's just a child," Anita had said when Edward, fedora in hand, his flannel shirt freshly laundered, his overalls clean of stains, his brown dress shoes neatly laced, his thick blond hair pasted into a pompadour, showed up at the Karvonens' front door. "Sun is not ready to date. Come back in a few years, farm boy."

In truth, Sun's mother was wary of non-natives when it came to choosing a husband for her eldest child. With two younger daughters coming up behind Sun, Anita, who had stepped out of her ethnicity and married Teemu Karvonen because he was the first man who'd asked and because the Finn owned his own place—four hundred acres of prime farmland just east of the Reservation—did not want her mistake repeated. While Teemu was a decent and patient man, he had no inkling or understanding of Ojibwe culture, ways, or language. Anita had made a poor choice, in her determination, a slender bargain to

211

escape poverty. She was not about to allow her daughters to make the same unforced error.

Besides, Sun was striking in ways that ensured she would have, once she turned of age, a bevy of suitors from within her mother's people. Powerful men. Men of stature within the Pembina Band of the Turtle Mountain Ojibwe.

Sun's looks, it must be said, did not come from her mother. Anita was a homely woman defined by a flinty disposition. On the other hand, Teemu Karvonen was six-two and ruggedly handsome with a blond crew cut and a golden beard that tickled his daughters' cheeks whenever he hugged them which, given the father's infatuation with his girls, was every day. Whereas Anita viewed her union with the Finnish farmer as a business transaction, Teemu—for whatever reason—deeply loved a woman who, to most of her family and her tribe, was unapproachable.

The abuse started immediately. Once the secret of Sun's sin became obvious, the girl endured verbal insults, kicks to her rear end, slaps to her face, and brutal, brutal condemnation from her newly baptized and fervently religious mother. The Papist zeal with which Anita punished Sun for what the mother perceived to be immoral relations with a Norwegian farm boy drove the girl to run away from home in her fourth month of pregnancy.

With less than twenty dollars to her name—money Sun stole from her mother's "rainy-day fund" hidden beneath Anita's unmentionables in a dresser—Sun escaped to Duluth via Grand Forks on a Great Northern passenger train. She was haggard, penniless, hungry, and homeless when she arrived in the Twin Ports. The rainy Wednesday afternoon Sadie spied Sun—obviously in trouble and in need of a friend—was both the runaway girl's salvation and her ruination.

Sadie recognized an opportunity. The businesswoman cast a discriminating eye on Sun's flowing black hair and beautiful eyes knowing that, once the baby growing in the girl's belly was born, there was money to be made in what the Finndian girl could offer the hordes of desperate, companionless working men prowling Duluth's streets in search of love.

The trade at Sadie's, while thoroughly demeaning and embarrassing, did have certain advantages over working in occupations such as housekeeping, childcare, and the other unskilled jobs available to uneducated women. First, the pay was,

212

by the standards of the day, better than anything Sun could earn elsewhere. True, she was called upon to cast aside her morals and pride and repugnance of the men she slept with. The elimination of Sun's resistance to her newfound profession transpired methodically as the other girls educated Sun in the art of fucking strangers. That was what Sadie called the act her girls engaged in for pay. It was also a description that Sun came to accept for there was no love attached to her work: a prostitute's nightly labors could not, in any sense of the term, be considered to be lovemaking. The absence of affection and caring and romance attached to coupling was something Sun grew to tolerate during her apprenticeship into the oldest of professions.

Additionally—unlike the low-rent, dangerous houses of ill repute established in the other neighborhoods of Duluth—Sadie treated her girls fairly, supplying them with food and shelter as part of their employment and providing vulcanized condoms imported in violation of the Comstock Act—a federal law prohibiting pornography, abortions, and birth control devices. Supplying condoms to the girls served two purposes: it kept them in the trade because "rubbers" reduced the chance of pregnancy, and the devices also prevented the transmission of syphilis and gonorrhea—diseases that could end a girl's allure if word got out.

Sadie imported the condoms from London. The devices were supplied by an English physician she had spent time with on her journey from Tampere to Duluth. The doctor risked violating U.S. law because he retained a remembered affection for nights spent in Miss Salminen's bed as she accumulated the price of her passage to America. Dr. Spencer Munsterman—the love-struck physician—hid condoms inside hollowed-out books he mailed to Duluth on a monthly basis. The seemingly innocent packages passed the scrutiny of U.S. postal inspectors and arrived at Sadie's brothel as regular as clockwork.

Anders Alhomäki only knew bits and pieces of Morning Sun Karvonen's story. Over the three years he draped his pants on Sun's bedpost, the girl did not offer details about Little Red Hawk's conception or her childhood in North Dakota. Given the Finn's introspective nature, he did not pry. Of course, he knew about the condoms, though he'd been completely unfamiliar with the process of donning a rubber since he'd never been with a woman until that auspicious afternoon when he and Sun

213

undressed each other, climbed beneath bedcovers, and Sun provided Anders with an education. The miner did not know the back-story of the devices nor appreciate that every time he coupled with Sun, he violated both Minnesota and Federal law by consorting with a prostitute and by using a condom.

"Gotta get some beams down to level fourteen," Seymour Greene, the Englishman in charge of the mine's carpenter shop said as Anders walked into the carpentry shed. "Grab those eight footers," Greene said, gesturing to lumber stacked alongside a wall of the building, "cut them to fit," he added, handing the Finn a scrap of paper with dimensions written on it, "and get down there. Boss of the crew, Logan, is having a bird because the roof seems unstable. Engineer isn't convinced but, given the men behind the picks and shovels have a better understanding of what they're dealing with, let's be cautious and give Logan what he wants."

Anders nodded. Because he'd spent the better part of three years in the Soudan Mine as an ore trammer, he knew the daily grind: the waltz of placing charges, blowing rock; the constant whine of the newly installed steam-powered drills; and the arduous chipping away at loosened screed with pick and hammer so that the rich ore of the Vermilion Range could be pried from the earth.

It was still early enough in the history of iron mining in Minnesota that each miner was responsible—under contract to the mining company that paid his wages and took deductions from those wages for dynamite, caps, candles, and broken or lost tools—for personally setting the charges that freed precious ore from adjacent bedrock. Later, as mining became more regimented, men trained in blasting would set the TNT, light the fuses, and shout out the warning "Fire in the hole!" taking over that dangerous and sometimes fatal job from everyday miners.

But at the time Anders sawed white pine beams to specification and loaded an empty mine cart with the heavy timbers and his carpentry tools for the long, dreary descent from fresh air to squalor, each miner still placed his own TNT, lit his own fuses, and called out his own warning.

At the bottom of the fourteenth level, Anders opened the wire cage door of the elevator car, shoved the ore cart onto an adjacent track, and pushed the cart towards his destination. As he shuffled along the horizontal drift joining the main shaft, cold water dripped from the low ceiling in a constant parade of earthen tears, the water an invasive problem addressed by steam-powered pumps churning away in the sump hole at the bottom of the mine. If the steam engines stopped, if the machinery of dewatering ceased, groundwater would reclaim the mine within weeks.

"How's it goin'?" Bruno Polanski, a big-backed, Polish kid of eighteen, asked as Anders stopped at the terminus of the rails. "Got some lumber for us, Finlander?"

Though having worked only three weeks in the Pioneer, Anders was used to the youth's teasing and shrugged off the slur. "Ya. I got what you need."

Emil Logan, a Cornish miner and boss assigned to supervise work in the new sector, stopped picking at loose ore and nodded. "You can set the timbers against the far wall. I'll get the boys to fit them in place."

Anders unloaded the roughly planed timbers from the ore cart. "I brought my tools in case you need to make adjustments. I cut them with the band saw to the lengths you asked for, but I can't guarantee they're exact."

Logan shook his head. "No need. I have my own saw. Brought it from home. We lose so many tools, I figured it was better to bring my own and keep a close eye on 'em."

In truth, company tools weren't lost but stolen: every miner had a collection of hand tools taken from the Pioneer, secreted somewhere in their rented quarters, each purloined item savored and saved for that glorious day when a miner found stumpage, purchased deforested land, and built a farm.

"On second thought, maybe you can lend a hand," Logan said, hoisting a timber. "Once Polanski and I get these posts in place, you can see if the cap fits."

Anders nodded. The acrid, dynamite-infused air at the bottom of the mine made him cough. The candles affixed to the miners' caps dimmed from the low levels of oxygen found at the depths. After clearing his lungs, the Finn picked up the beam and waited for the miners to wedge the vertical braces into place. When the timbers were set, Anders manhandled the cap, snugging it into notches cut into the bedrock above the braces so that the ceiling's weight was transferred onto the wooden arch. "That good?" he asked.

"Perfect. You know your way around the business end of a ruler," Logan said, the compliment unusual; crew bosses were men of infrequent praise. "Better get back up top and see if there's more work for you in the shop."

A shrill whistle sounded. "Shift change," Polanski noted in a relieved voice. "Time to get the hell out of here."

Anders knew the routine by heart. The night shift would ascend in the wire cage to the dry house. As the day shift waited to descend, the tired night-shift miners would exit the cage, enter the dry, remove their wet, muddy, soggy overalls and shirts, and hang them on wires strung across rafters. The miners would then remove their union suits and, standing naked as jaybirds, wash the grime and grease of work from their bodies with cold water before donning street clothes. The men of the night shift would leave their work clothes hanging on clotheslines in the warm, steam-heated building to dry, shuffle out into the cool air of morning, wander home to eat breakfast, fall into the deep sleep of exhaustion, wake in the late afternoon, go about their daily chores, eat dinner, pack a lunch, and make ready to descend all over again.

Anders left the carpentry shop bone weary and tired, his time at the mine coinciding with that of the night shift. But the routine of backbreaking, soul-crushing manual labor of being a miner or trammer was distant now: he'd learned a trade, something he could carry with him back to Duluth. He had a plan, a plan to leave the Pioneer after only a few months' employment. He did not confide in Stanley Cukela—the man who'd put in a good word for Anders with the superintendent—that he was a short-timer.

No reason to tell Stan that I'm going back to Duluth to marry a girl, he thought as he retrieved a letter from his sister Ronja from a cigar box beneath his bed. *Cukela will be pissed that I'm quitting so soon after being hired. But love cannot wait*, Anders mused as he studied the feminine cursive of his sister's hand by the flickering light of the *poikatalo's* kerosene lantern.

CHAPTER TEN: November 1911 (Duluth, Minnesota)

Anders found work in Duluth through his cousin Raimo Maki. He had departed the Vermilion Range, not because he witnessed a mining tragedy for the second time in his life, but because he was intent on asking Morning Sun Karvonen to marry him and he did not want to bring a lovely, mixed-race mother of a toddler into the wild and wooly world of underground mining.

"Alhomäki, the boys at level fifteen need more shoring," Seymour Greene had advised. "Fill a cart with timbers from the stockpile and hustle down there. Sounds like things are unstable after the last round of blasting."

Anders had looked up from his workbench. He was repairing the hinges on a door that a belligerent, drunken Serb had kicked in trying to enter the paymaster's office on a day other than Payday Saturday. The drunk had ripped the door's iron hardware completely out of the wood such that the damage could not be repaired on site but rather, required the door to be removed. The absence of a door between the mine's payroll and the miners left the office vulnerable to both weather and desperados. Only an oilcloth tarp tacked to the lintel above the doorway prevented entry to the building that held the mine's safe. "I need to get this door fixed and hung before dusk," Anders replied. "Kobe will have a bird if he has to spend another night sleeping in the office with a scattergun on his lap," Anders explained, referring to Joe Kobe, a Slovenian and a low-level clerk who'd been tasked with guarding the payroll by the office manager in lieu of being able to lock the door against vagrants, drunks, and thieves.

"You'll have plenty of time to get 'er done," Greene said, "it's not even three o'clock. Get a move on and get that lumber down where it belongs. Are we clear?"

Greene wasn't often curt. Anders noted the impatience in his boss's voice, nodded, and placed the screwdriver he'd been using on the workbench. "Right away, boss."

Anders had switched from the night shift to day shift when Seymour Greene himself changed hours of work. It was less

217

disorienting to work from dawn to dusk than to arrive on the job at the cusp of evening. But despite the relief the Finn felt at being able to work during daylight and despite a fondness for both his job and Greene, Anders Alhomäki was a determined man. *End of the week and I'm out of here. I've given my notice. Raimo has a position lined up for me in Duluth. There's only one more task, delicate and daunting— "popping the question" to Sun—left to give me a new start. God,* he mused as he loaded heavy timbers into an ore cart, *I sure as hell hope she says "yes."*

When he exited the rattling, cantankerous elevator cage, his mind full of expectations of romance and tenderness and quiet nights spent with the Finndian girl, it was already too late. Between the time he'd entered the elevator and begun his descent and the time he arrived in the drift where bone-weary miners had cut steps into the bedrock and were extracting soft, red ore, hell had let loose on the fifteenth level.

"What happened?" he asked, watching miners scurry, the men wild-eyed, panicked, and running towards him to escape a roiling cloud of dust.

"Cave in!" a miner shouted as he ran past Anders. "Poor bastard is buried under tons of sand and gravel. Why the hell did it take you so long to get here with that shoring?" The man asserted the allegation against Anders without any factual basis, without knowledge of how and when the Finn was directed to descend with the additional shoring.

Miners began pushing empty ore carts along narrow gauge rails towards the accident site. Anders stood open-mouthed, not knowing what to say, not knowing what to do.

"You can pitch in, you know!" another miner, tall, reedy, and speaking English in a Surrey accent so thick Anders had difficulty understanding him, shouted. "That poor Polish kid likely only has a few minutes of air!"

Polanski! "Wait. Bruno's trapped?"

The miner stopped, looked up, tilted his soft cap to study the Finn, and asked, "You know him?"

Anders nodded. "Used to work the night shift with him."

"Well then, lend a hand. If we don't get to him soon, he's a gonner."

Anders followed the Englishman into the maelstrom. Air thickened with particulates from the cave-in stifled his breathing.

Working at a feverish pace, Anders helped others move rock and sand and gravel by the shovelful and by hand. The frantic workers removed cart after cart of debris and dumped rock and gravel and sand down an adjacent ore chute where, at the bottom of the chute, the waste would be stockpiled for use as backfill. The men worked with dedication and fury until Polanski's blond head was free of the cave-in. But it was too late.

Anders did not attend Polanski's funeral. The boy's death was too reminiscent of the tragedy that had befallen Edvin Koivu in Norway, an event that had shaken Anders's already unsteady faith and belief in a kind, benevolent, Creator God. Instead of paying his last respects to the young Polish miner, Anders packed his knapsack with his belongings, said "adieu "to Ely, and caught the first Duluth and Iron Range train to Two Harbors.

When a locomotive pulling a coal tender, passenger cars, a freight car, a flatbed loaded with white pine logs, and a caboose arrived at the Union Depot in Duluth (Anders having changed trains in Two Harbors) he walked east, towards Finntown, his pack on his back and high expectations in his heart.

I haven't been in town to see Sun since I took the job in Ely, the immigrant thought. *She'll be surprised to see me but more surprised by my question!*

The gold band in the left front pocket of his dress trousers, the wool shabby from use but the best he could afford, had been acquired from another miner, a Serb whose wife had run off with a Swedish butcher. "Never trusted that bitch," David Kokotovich, the aggrieved husband lamented, as he turned the wedding band his former bride had tossed in his face—as she left the flat they shared on Chapman Street with her suitcase and smug disdain—over and over in his right hand. "My brother Emil was right. I never should have fallen for that woman."

Anders had been sitting on his bunk, trying to console his friend, when a notion struck him. "Hey, Dave. You wanna sell that ring?" Anders asked after a suitable period of time had passed.

Kokotovich flung the gold band towards Alhomäki. The ring caught sunlight and sparkled as Anders snatched it out of the air. "It's yours. On the house. I want no reminders of that good-for-nothing skank."

The insult was lost on the Finn. He had no reference for the demeaning English term muttered by Kokotovich. Instead of seeking clarity, Alhomäki had protested, had tried to shove a five-dollar gold piece into David's hands. But the Serb would have none of it.

Walking with vigor, Anders fingered the ring inside his trouser pocket and pondered how he was going to approach the girl. Too direct a proposal might spook Sun, might cause her to rush upstairs and slam her bedroom door against him. Too subtle a request might leave her baffled and unable to discern his intentions. *My English is good but not perfect. I would like to propose in English, the language of my new home. But I fear I am not up to the task. Finnish? Yes, she knows the language in small ways. But she is not as adept, as fluent, as might be required to appreciate what I'm asking. English. I'll stick with English and hope for the best.*

"Mr. Alhomäki, what a pleasant surprise!" Sadie Salminen said, opening the brothel's front door to Anders's hesitant knocking. "It's been, what, three months since you last visited?"

"Yes ma'am," Anders mumbled.

"I'm sorry. What did you say?"

"You're right, ma'am. It's been three months. I left Tower for work in Ely three months ago and haven't been by since."

Sadie nodded, though her brittle blond hair, pinned in place, did not move. "Won't you come in?"

"I'd rather talk to Sun outside, on the porch, if I could."

The woman's eyes narrowed. At first, Anders believed she was angry with him, that he had crossed some unwritten line or said something mawkishly untoward in English. But such was not the case. Sadie's eyes turned sympathetic as she patted the miner's left forearm.

"Sun is no longer here."

CHAPTER ELEVEN: December 1911

Anders considered his new circumstances: his lodgings in the Finntown boarding house run by Charles Talonen where he'd taken up residence, his new job at the Great Lakes Storage warehouse that his cousin Raimo Maki had found for him, and the shocking disappointment of learning that Morning Sun Karvonen was no longer in Duluth.

"What do you mean?" he had asked, believing at first, as the madam spoke to him at the front door to the whorehouse, that he had misunderstood. "I have a question to ask of her, an important, personal question."

Sadie evinced empathy both through the tone of her voice and her expression while maintaining a steady grip on Anders's left wrist with her right hand. "Oh, hon," she had said consolingly, "I have a pretty good idea why you are here, hat in hand, seeking to see the most beautiful girl in my house. But she's gone, I tell you. Gone."

The Finn shifted his weight, his dark eyes never wavering from intensity as he fought upset, nerves, and remorse. *I waited too long*, he thought. *Someone else, a suitor of money and power and prominence made Sun an offer.* He wanted to confirm his suspicion, but the woman shook her head and interjected before he could speak.

"You misunderstand," Sadie explained in Finnish, "Sun did not run off with another man." She paused. "At least, not in the manner you suspect."

Anders's face expressed confusion. "What then? Why is she no longer here?"

Sadie gently moved Anders out of the doorway and onto the front porch. The November air was cold and light snow was falling; lake effect snow: snow created when the warmer water of Lake Superior meets sub-Arctic wind from Manitoba. The madam wore a thin, nearly opaque housedress, silk stockings, high heels, and a hand-knitted wool shawl, the only piece of her clothing offering protection against weather. Sadie maintained a hand on Anders's left wrist as she explained. "Her father. The farmer. Do you know about him? Did she ever talk about her family, her past, why she came to Duluth?"

Anders shook his head. "I know that she had a child—Little Red Hawk—with someone. Out of wedlock. That something bad happened back home. That she was from North Dakota. That she was Ojibwe and Finn. That her mother was not a nice woman. But about her father, she only said that he was a farmer and a good man. Nothing more."

White settled on Sadie's scarfless head, but she made no move to brush the snow away. "That's all true. But what she didn't tell you is that the baby was fathered by her uncle: her mother's brother raped her. But Sun's mother didn't believe the girl's story. She thought the child was the product of Sun sleeping with a local boy. Sun swore to me that nothing ever happened between her and the farmer's son. Not so much as handholding or an innocent kiss. It was her uncle, the bastard."

Anders removed Sadie's hand from his wrist and stroked his sideburns with his left hand. His eyes remained locked on the madam, but his surprise at learning Sun was gone had been replaced by sadness. "What does this have to do with her leaving Duluth?"

Sadie smiled weakly. "Sun's mother passed away but, on her deathbed, the woman finally confided to Teemu—Sun's father—that she'd been wrong; that her horrific treatment of her eldest daughter had been a mistake."

"How so?"

"It seems that Sun's youngest sister—Angel, who's ten—came to Anita, the mother, when Anita was recovering from surgery to remove a tumor from her female organs and spilled the beans."

Anders's eyebrows rose.

"Ah. Sorry to use an American expression while speaking Finnish. 'Spilled the beans.' It means, 'she revealed a secret.'"

"Oh."

"Anyway. It seems that the lecherous uncle was using the same tricks on Angel he'd used on Sun. He was plying her with treats and gifts and kindness so as to make her vulnerable and do things with her and to her that no adult man should ever do to a child, much less to kin."

"Bastard!" Anders shouted the word in English, forgetting that they were conversing in Finnish.

Sadie wrapped her arms around her shivering body and nodded. "That's putting it mildly. In any event, once again Anita doubted her daughter. Until ..."

"Yes?"

Sadie looked up into the gray, swirling sky filled with descending flakes, and returned her gaze to the Finn's beleaguered face. "Until the second daughter, Betsy, came forward and admitted Uncle Thomas had tried to pull the same shit on her. Betsy claimed to have fended him off—that he never laid a hand on her. Because Betsy is a straight arrow, an 'A' student, Anita believed her. Once she believed her middle child, it wasn't that big a leap for Anita to believe the other girls and to finally come to grips with the fact that her grandson was also her nephew."

"God!"

Sadie bit her lip. "I doubt He has anything to do with the whole sorry mess," she whispered. "Anita begged her husband to find Sun and bring her back to North Dakota so Anita could swallow her pride and apologize."

Tears welled and descended. Anders was not sobbing. His body was not convulsing in grief. Instead, his soul was methodically washing itself of the sadness Sun's disappearance and newly revealed history had caused. Sadie reached into a pocket of her dress, removed a clean, white, linen handkerchief, and dabbed the man's cheeks with tenderness.

"But Anita was too late. By the time Teemu arrived here, convinced Sun to come with him, and they returned to their farm with the baby in tow, Anita had passed. I know this only because Sun sent me a letter, likely the only one I'll ever receive from her now that she's engaged to that Norwegian farm boy. I doubt he'd accept his proper wife corresponding with someone who convinced the love of his life to fuck strangers for money," the madam said, using the curse for effect, to highlight the finality of it all.

Anders placed his wide-brimmed fedora on his black hair, pursed his lips, and whispered. "She wrote nothing of me?"

Sadie shook her head and looked away.

"Nothing at all?"

"Anders," Sadie said softly, her voice filled with tenderness as she returned to studying Anders's face, "you were

223

her customer, not her beau. You may have thought otherwise. In fact, given how you showed up on my doorstep with love in your eyes and gaiety in your heart, I'm quite certain you were going to ask her to marry you. But understand, whatever you felt for Morning Sun Karvonen, whatever you thought there was between you, was fantasy ... a whore doing her best to bring a customer back to her bed and nothing more."

Anders's face reddened in anger. But the truth? The truth was obvious even to a lovesick immigrant from Paltamo.

He set about rebuilding his ego and his life. He grappled with what he'd felt for Sun, how he had misled himself into believing that his love for her, a prostitute he procured with his hard-earned money, was real, not an illusion. He struggled to understand what it all meant.

Perhaps I put too much stock in Uncle Alvar's miraculous tale of finding love in a Siberian brothel, he thought as he worked backbreaking ten-hour shifts for a dollar and a half a day at the warehouse owned by Great Lakes Storage. *Or,* he mused, stacking barrels of beer in a dank building, stock from Duluth's Fitger's Brewery that would eventually be loaded into boxcars and shipped north to the Iron Range, *maybe my childhood infatuation with Anneli colored my perception of reality. Maybe Sadie is right. Maybe there was never any chance that Sun was going to have affection for me, a customer she spent time with simply to survive and feed her child. Why Alvar's experience in this regard differs from my own, I'd love to be able to ask my dear uncle. But he is an ocean away. And I am left here, in America, to put one boot ahead of the other and move on.*

Which is exactly what Anders did. By reuniting with his cousin Raimo Maki, and his fast friend Matt Peltoma—who in turn introduced Anders to fellow immigrants Olli Kinkkonen and Oskar Ketola—Anders began the slow, determined process of healing from a wound that seemed untreatable.

Frequenting local taverns, taking walks on the snowy boardwalks of Finntown and the cement sidewalks of downtown Duluth, attending cheap matinee silent movies at the Temple and the Lyceum and the Lyric, and listening to music and attending dances and athletic contests and plays at the local workers hall,

Anders began to recover from the self-inflicted hurt of falling in love with an unattainable woman.

He stopped after shift for a beer. The tavern was crowded with single men, mostly Finns, boisterous and noisy and drunk.

I am nobody's savior, Anders decided as he sipped foam off the top of a newly poured glass of People's lager at the Tempest Tavern just a stone's throw away from his lodgings. *I was a fool to ever think that I could redeem the fallen,* he concluded, focusing his attention on a heated political debate between Matt Peltoma and a conservative Finn sitting at the bar.

CHAPTER TWELVE: February 1912

Elin Gustafson was twenty-three years old when she met Anders Alhomäki. She was college-educated, having obtained a Bachelor of Arts in English from Northern Indiana Normal School, an institution founded by Methodists in Valparaiso, Indiana (later acquired by the Lutherans and renamed Valparaiso University), the alma mater of both her parents. Elin had also earned a master's degree in English Composition from the University of Michigan, the institution where both her father and Oskar Larson, another prominent Finnish attorney living in Duluth, had attended law school. She began her teaching career as an English instructor at the Duluth Normal School in the autumn of 1911. She first met Anders Alhomäki at a dance held in February of 1912 to raise money for the Finnish Women's Suffrage Society, a group organized by Elin's mother, Laina Gustafson.

Following the lead of their counterparts in Finland, educated Finnish American women like Laina Gustafson began to vocalize demands for suffrage. The dance where Elin Gustafson fell in love with the quiet Finnish bachelor was held at the Work People's College in Riverside. The school was a nurturing place for Finnish radicalism in the city.

"Who's that handsome young man?" Elin asked her friend Wendla Heikkonen.

"Anders Alhomäki," Wendla responded. "You're not thinking of swooning over him too, are you?"

Elin's impulsive nature was legendary amongst her friends. "Oh, hush," Elin whispered. "I only want a dance."

"With you, it's never just a dance," Wendla observed. "With you, every dance is a prelude to something more significant."

Elin laughed. "He's awfully striking."

"They're all awfully striking," Wendla said. "He looks like a laborer. Not the type of man your father would approve of. And he's at least thirty. He's likely only looking for an easy mark."

The women stood near a table displaying a punch bowl and assorted sweets in a dark corner of the school's meeting room. Couples and pairs of single Finnish women danced nearby, traversing the hardwood floor of the hall to traditional Finnish music. A guitarist, a fiddle player, and an old woman playing a button box filled the space with song.

"Give me a nip," Elin whispered.

"I think you've had enough," Wendla replied, clutching the sash purse dangling from her shoulder.

"I've only had a few swallows. Just one more taste," Elin urged.

Wendla glanced around the room. Though it wasn't yet Prohibition, the Work People's College was filled with temperance adherents. No one in authority appeared to be watching them. As Wendla's fingers worked the flap of her purse, her eyes remained focused on the crowd. Her left hand withdrew a slender sterling flask filled with brandy from the bag. Elin grasped the flask with clean white gloves, opened the cap, turned towards the wall, and drank greedily.

"That's enough," Wendla cautioned. "You don't want to be sick when that old man asks you to dance."

Elin smiled. "Now I'm ready," she said in Finnish, securing the cap, returning the flask to her friend, removing a handkerchief from a pocket, and dabbing her lips.

"Your father would tan your behind if he heard you speaking Suomi."

"My father isn't here," Elin replied as she began walking across the room. "And neither is yours."

Anders stood at the far end of the hall. The band played another waltz. The slight Finn watched in amazement as the most beautiful woman in the room floated towards him.

She must know someone in this group, Anders thought, *likely Oskar Ketola. He's been a consistent letter writer to the* Tribune *and* Herald *on behalf of women's issues.*

Ketola was a large-faced, broad-chested Finn who worked far less and talked far more than any other friend of Anders Alhomäki. Thick blond hair cascaded across Ketola's shoulders in Bohemian fashion, making the sometimes-employed stevedore look like a hero out of the *Kalevala*. Oskar's clear blue eyes fixed on the short, attractive woman striding towards the men. Oskar was certain, as was Anders, that Elin Gustafson was intent upon a dance with Oskar Ketola.

"Hello," Ketola said in English, his hand extending to greet the woman as she stopped in front of the cluster of Finnish men engaged in a heated debate.

Elin accepted Ketola's hand without conviction. Her eyes measured the faces of the others before settling upon Anders. She ended the exchange with Ketola and returned her gloved right hand to her side.

"I'm Elin, Elin Gustafson," she said demurely, her eyes never leaving Anders's face.

Anders's cheeks flushed. He shifted his weight nervously before offering his hand to the woman.

"Anders. Anders Alhomäki," he mumbled.

Anders knew, as every other male in the place knew, who Elin Gustafson was: the daughter of Karl Gustafson, one of Duluth's most prominent Finnish conservatives, and Laina Gustafson, a radical feminist, whose political and social ideals were directly and concretely at odds with those of her husband. Elin was considered to be one of the most fetching and most desirable women at the dance. Her best friend and confidante, Wendla Heikkonen, was a close second: whereas Elin was robust, buxom, and fleshy, with an inordinately handsome face, Wendla was delicate, thin and, despite her apparent edges, pleasingly sculpted, with long blond hair tied up off her shoulders, and penetrating brown eyes set deep in her face.

"Pleased to meet you, Mr. Alhomäki," Elin replied, shaking the miner's hand.

There was an interval of awkward silence. Olli Kinkkonen, a logger and stevedore who shared Alhomäki's dark complexion and jet-black hair, leaned over and whispered, loud enough for the woman to hear, "I think she wants to dance."

Anders turned in puzzlement. "With me?" he asked Kinkkonen in Finnish.

"With you," Elin interjected in their language.

Anders's face flushed again.

"Go on," Matt Peltoma urged. "You'll never have a better offer."

"He's right, you know," Wendla encouraged after joining her friend.

Anders sheepishly extended his right arm to Elin.

"Don't step on her feet," Olli chided as the couple moved out onto the crowded dance floor.

They danced two straight waltzes, whirling and twirling across the hardwood. Exhausted, they retreated to the punch bowl.

"You dance well," Anders said in English as he poured a cup of cranberry cider for the woman.

"So do you," Elin agreed, downing the liquid in one swallow.

Sweat leaked from the miner's scalp and dripped down his neatly trimmed sideburns. Unlike many of his companions, Alhomäki did not wear a mustache. His face was cleanly shaven except for the muttonchops. Although Anders's chin was exceedingly narrow, Elin found the overall effect of the miner's features to be handsome.

"Would you like to get a bit of fresh air?" she asked. "You look like you could use it."

"I am a bit overheated," Anders acknowledged. Certain that his innocent remark was about to be misconstrued, he quickly added, "From the dancing, I mean."

Elin laughed. "I knew what you meant, Mr. Alhomäki. I can tell you're a gentleman and not some cad."

Anders smiled, the first hint of emotion he'd displayed since asking Elin to dance.

The two talked quietly, finding easy familiarity in their discourse as they walked along South 88th Avenue West, passing construction that would eventually become United States Steel's factory town, the Model City (later renamed "Morgan Park" in honor of J.P. Morgan), a community being built to supply housing for workers at the company's steel plant in Gary-New Duluth. Anders impressed Elin with his knowledge of world politics, women's issues, and Finnish history. He was deeply passionate about his beliefs, views that transcended easy labels.

In addition to being a union man, he was an occasional Lutheran and a Populist who believed, after benefiting from the aftermath of the ill-advised labor strike of 1907, that the working man's best hope for fair treatment was to organize and gain access to the political process by electing sympathetic men into office.

Their long walk that first evening together, both of them bundled in winter clothing against the cold wind sweeping down from Barton's Peak, a prominent bluff of exposed gabbro overlooking the far western edge of Duluth, convinced Elin that Anders was a kind and thoughtful man, a man who supported efforts to improve the political and social status of women.

Laina Gustafson witnessed her daughter's flirtation with the little Finn from a distance. She stood in the shadows of the Work People's Hall and scrutinized the couple's interaction when they returned from their walk and resumed dancing. Laina, though exceedingly liberal in the raising of her daughter—a trait that annoyed her socially rigid husband to no end—understood the dangers presented by Elin's interest in men of lesser standing. *One never knows a man's motivation*, Laina thought, watching her daughter and Anders dance, linked as if they were one, their bodies pressed tightly together. *Elin knows the dangers of revealing too much of herself to a man before she's certain of his intentions. I've at least taught her that much.*

"This is Mr. Anders Alhomäki. Mr. Alhomäki, my mother, Mrs. Laina Gustafson," Elin said as she presented the Finn to her mother later that evening.

"Pleased to meet you, Mrs. Gustafson," Anders replied, extending a calloused hand.

"Likewise," Laina responded, offering her hand to the miner.

"Mr. Alhomäki is a firm believer in a woman's right to vote and to work outside the home," Elin continued, her words rushing out breathlessly as she attempted to convince her mother of her new friend's worth.

"I see," Laina answered, her faint blue eyes locked upon Anders's dark irises. "And what does Mr. Alhomäki do for a living?" the mother asked, switching her inquiry to Finnish.

"Right now, I'm working a temporary job in a warehouse with my cousin. But that work will eventually end. When it does, I plan on traveling to Houghton, Michigan to work in the copper mines," Anders answered in Finnish.

Laina studied the man's face as he answered her questions. *He seems genuine. He's articulate*, Laina thought. *Still, Karl would have a heart attack if he saw his little girl dancing intimately with a laborer!* "It was nice to meet you, Mr. Alhomäki. I'm afraid it's late and my daughter needs her rest. Tomorrow is

Monday. Elin needs to be fresh and alert to teach her students at the Normal School," Laina advised, reverting to English.

"I understand," Anders replied. "May I escort the two of you to the streetcar? It's snowing. You never know when you might need a strong arm to lean upon."

The mother looked at her daughter. Urgency and expectancy were clear on Elin's face.

"I'm the head of the clean-up committee," Laina answered. "I'll be staying long into the night. Why don't you walk my daughter to the trolley stop? You never can tell what sort of fellow might be lurking in the dark after a dance."

"It would be my pleasure. Is that all right with you, Miss Gustafson?"

Elin smiled. Her white teeth reflected the heightened lighting of the hall.

"That would be very nice, Mr. Alhomäki."

Light snow fell. The wind ceased. The temperature was timid for February. The miner and the teacher stood in near-perfect darkness at the trolley stop. There were no street lamps nearby. No automobiles or carriages braved the slippery streets.

"It's a lovely evening," Elin said as they waited for a trolley beneath a sentry white pine, a remnant of the forest that once covered the St. Louis River Valley.

"I'm glad you introduced yourself," Anders replied, his eyes focused on his black dress shoes, the toes of the footwear covered with snow.

"Would you have walked across the floor to ask me to dance?" Elin asked coyly.

The Finn thought for a moment before responding. "I'm afraid I don't have that kind of courage," Anders answered through a weak grin, his eyes fixed on his shoes.

CHAPTER THIRTEEN: June 1912

It caused a rift between father and daughter as wide and deep as the Baltic Sea. Romance blossomed after Elin Gustafson and Anders Alhomäki met at the Suffrage Dance. Despite obvious disparities in social status, income, and education between them, the schoolteacher and the miner became inseparable. However, the first meeting between Anders Alhomäki and Karl Gustafson was nothing short of disastrous, the aftermath of which drove a wedge between the lawyer and his only child.

"I forbid you to see that illiterate vagabond of a man," Karl Gustafson hissed at his daughter following a family dinner in their palatial home during which Anders first became acquainted with the attorney. "I absolutely forbid it."

By inviting Anders to the Gustafson Mansion for an evening of roast beef and conversation, Laina Gustafson sought to soften the blow of her daughter's liaison with someone her husband believed was socially and intellectually inferior to his only child. Despite Laina's attempted intervention, upon Alhomäki's arrival Karl Gustafson retreated to his study where he remained, unwilling to acknowledge the immigrant's presence, until the evening meal was served.

"He'll warm to you, Mr. Alhomäki," Laina said. "Once you two get to talking, he'll warm to you. He'll see that there's more to you than meets the eye."

"I hope so, ma'am. Right now, I feel more than a bit awkward," Anders replied in his native tongue.

"Oh, Anders, please don't speak Finnish," Elin interjected. "Father will explode if you speak Suomi."

"Sorry. It was an inadvertent lapse, a bad habit from working in the mines. You either speak Finn or Serbo-Croatian. Only a few of the men speak English—though it's encouraged by the bosses—and most of that's troublesome to understand," he said apologetically, reverting to English.

"Dinner is served," the cook announced from behind a closed door leading to the kitchen.

The door to the study opened. Karl Gustafson walked to the head of the table. Sofia Wirtanen, the family's maid, a striking single woman of twenty, bustled in and out of the dining room with plates heaped with food. Anders watched with covert understanding. Karl Gustafson grinned involuntarily as he studied the girl.

There's something between them, Anders thought. *Maybe flirtation; maybe something more. I wonder if Mrs. Gustafson knows. Probably not. If she suspected that her husband was interested in a servant Elin's age, that servant would likely be on a boat back to Helsinki!*

"Thank you, Sofia," Laina said tersely as the maid left the room and the table guests claimed their seats.

There's an edge to her voice. There's knowledge behind that tone.

Karl's face resumed scowling. Anders couldn't discern whether the grimace was due to Anders's presence or the accusatory edge to Laina's voice.

"Let us pray," the lawyer began. "Dear Lord Jesus, please accept our thanks for this bounty, for the Grace revealed in your suffering, for the precious gift of salvation, and for this gathering of family. Amen."

There was no mention of the dinner guest in Karl's prayer. His slight increased the tension in the room. Throughout the meal, Karl Gustafson made it a point to direct his comments towards his wife and daughter. The patriarch ignored remarks made by Anders in response to conversation around the table. Finally, his dessert plate scraped clean, his coffee cup empty, Karl Gustafson retired to his study, never having said a single word to Anders Alhomäki.

"That didn't go well," Anders offered as he and Elin stood on the mansion's front porch. "And I didn't even speak Finnish," he added wryly.

It was June. They'd been together as a couple, never intimate but on the verge of intimacy, for several months.

"He's an old fuddy-duddy," Elin remarked, tightening her grip on the sleeve of Anders's suit coat, the garment newly purchased from Dove Clothing, a shop on Superior Street owned by Alex Kyyhkynen, a local Finnish merchant. There was quality in the stitching and the fabric of the coat and trousers. Still, Alhomäki's off-the-rack purchase had been no match for the hand-tailored pinstriped business suit worn by Karl Gustafson, the product of hours of diligent labor by Finnish tailor Peter Sikkio, clothier to the wealthiest elite of Duluth.

"He's your father. I doubt he'll let you see me after tonight."

"I'm twenty-three years old. I can make my own decisions about whom I should and should not see."

Anders looked down the hill towards Lake Superior. The avenue's paving bricks glistened. Precipitation lingered above the city; not enough to make an umbrella necessary but enough to wrinkle Anders's carefully pressed suit. The Finn's eyes refused to consider the woman standing next to him as he watched drops of cold rain strike the warm pavement.

"I'm leaving for Houghton tomorrow," Anders disclosed.

"Tomorrow?" Elin asked, her eyes widening. "Because of tonight?"

"No. My job in the warehouse is finished. There's no work around here. A Croatian fellow I know from Soudan, Stanley Cukela, dropped me a postcard. Stan says there are jobs in the copper mines if a man's willing to work hard and put up with the bosses. I connected with the managers of the Quincy Mine. They've extended an offer for me to work as an underground miner in Hancock," the man said, refusing to engage the woman's eyes as he spoke. "It's not work that I relish, but the pay is better than what I can make on the waterfront. I've done it before, mining copper. I can do it again."

"What about us?"

Anders refused to succumb to the pleading tone of Elin's voice. "Us? After what we just went through, you still think there can be an 'us'"?

"You must have wax plugging your ears. I told you I don't care what my father thinks. I love you; that's something even a dull-brained immigrant Finlander should understand," the woman whispered, no rancor in her voice, the use of the derisive "Finlander" meant to add emphasis to her words.

Anders kicked the toe of his dress shoe against the concrete stoop.

"Well? Don't you have anything to say?" Elin asked.

Anders tilted his head to appreciate the woman's beauty. "I need to work. You know why. I've told you I want to have enough saved up to buy a farm, like we've talked about. I need to work."

"Then take me with you."

Anders's eyes widened. "You're crazy! Your father will hunt me down like a dog."

"I'm an adult woman. My mother will support my decision. She likes you. Karl will just have to get used to the idea of us being together."

"El, I'm not ready for marriage," Anders said, switching the conversation to English. "You know my history with Morning Sun. I've been plain and open about what that did to me. It's not that I want to be with someone else. You know how I feel about you. But I'm not ready to marry you unless I can make a life for us away from laboring in the mines. I need time to put together enough money to buy land. I don't want a little forty carved out of some swamp. I want at least two hundred acres, if not more, of good, level farmland. That'll take time."

Elin moved closer, raised her right hand to Anders's face and stroked his sideburns.

"Did I say anything about marriage? I'm a modern girl. We can live together until you're ready. It'll be all right."

Karl Gustafson remained impassively rooted behind his oak desk. His voice, though full of anger and hostility, never increased beyond a conversational tone as he addressed his daughter once Anders Alhomäki was gone. "You will not, under any circumstances, ever see that worthless piece of cow dung again, understand?"

Elin sat in an oak side chair in front of her father. Her mother stood at Elin's side. Laina Gustafson's considerable strength of character proved to be utterly useless against her husband's venom. "As you say," Elin replied, her voice quiet, her hands folded across the lap of her dress.

"My sources tell me he's a Syndicalist."

"That's not true. He doesn't belong to the IWW, though he has talked about joining a union."

"Same thing. Unionist, Communist, Syndicalist. You know I represent mine owners and timber interests. You know how sensitive those folks are to the threat of organized labor and the attempted uprising of the ignorant unwashed."

Elin's cheeks flushed. She pursed her lips but held her temper. "Anders isn't ignorant. He's intelligent."

"He's a filthy, uneducated laborer who will never amount to a hill of beans," the lawyer responded, choosing an American expression to emphasize his rancor.

Elin turned her head and sought her mother's support. There was only a blank, defenseless look on Laina's face. Riled but unwilling to reduce the discussion to a shouting match, Elin relented. "As you say."

"As I say," Karl repeated, his eyes turning to his wife. "And you, Mrs. Gustafson, will in no way countenance or encourage any further communication between our daughter and that loathsome immigrant."

Laina's eyes averted as she obediently nodded acquiescence.

"Good. That being understood, Elin, you may retire to your bedroom. I've got some other matters to discuss with your mother."

Early the next morning, a magenta sun climbed above the Wisconsin shoreline across the calm, silver waters of Lake Superior. An open window in Elin's bedroom overlooked the lake and the roof of the carriage house. Elin dropped her valise onto slate roofing, waited a sufficient interval to ensure that her departure wasn't detected, and eased herself out the window. It was a short distance to the carriage house's roof, an easy drop to the ground, and an exhilarating walk down Lake Avenue to where Anders waited.

A few days later, after a voyage across Lake Superior, the lovers arrived in Copper Country: Upper Peninsula Michigan. They rented a small bungalow in Hancock and began living together, a scandalous situation that caused an uproar in the Gustafson mansion.

CHAPTER FOURTEEN: December 1912 (Hancock, Michigan)

She wore the ring that he had intended for Morning Star Karvonen and went by the *nom de plume*, Elin Gustafson Alhomäki. They were not married and, other than a brief discussion of matrimony—when Elin made it clear she would follow Anders to Michigan to escape the claustrophobic constraints of her father but had no immediate intention of marrying Anders—there was no further discussion of the subject.

They forged a good life in Hancock. The underground copper mine, which saw Anders work huge reserves of conglomerate ore (native copper and pebbles fused together by pressure and heat), provided the Finn with steady employment. Elin's application to teach English at Suomi College, a Lutheran seminary and college founded by Finnish pastors, had been readily accepted.

The cottage Elin and Anders rented stood atop a hill overlooking the Keweenaw Waterway, the channel separating the cities of Houghton and Hancock. The modest one-story dwelling, constructed and owned by Anders's employer (as were most of the surrounding clapboard-sided homes) was within walking distance of both the Quincy Mine and the College, and boasted running water, a coal stove for heat, a new privy in the fenced-in backyard, a wood-fired range in a quaint kitchen, a parlor, two bedrooms, and affordable rent. Despite the couple creating an air of domesticity inside the bungalow, intimacy had been a problem for the quiet, introspective miner.

When the couple shared a cabin on the *Christopher Columbus* as "Mr. and Mrs. Rikala," it had been Elin, not Anders, who had left her berth for his on the second night of their voyage from Duluth to Marquette. Having been surreptitiously educated from an early age by her suffragette mother about human reproduction and sexuality, Elin had been a curious but careful young woman as she reached maturity. An affair with a married professor in Valparaiso, Indiana while obtaining her English degree had left Elin educated in more than just vowels and consonants. Dr. Victor Pula had been a kind and gentle lover. Concerns over unwanted pregnancy had compelled them to explore the twists and turns of innovative *amore* until Elin was fitted with a "womb veil," an early form of diaphragm. The awkwardness of the device and the difficulties she had encountered in obtaining one from a doctor recommended to her by another girl at the Northern Indiana Normal School had compelled Elin to begin her own personal study of woman's rights and birth control.

During their nearly two years together in Hancock, Elin educated Anders, as she herself had been educated by Victor Pula. The miner offered no recriminations or inquiry as to where Elin had obtained her knowledge of human love. He simply accepted her gifts, the wonder of her mouth, the rounded curves of her breasts, the salty taste of her nipples, the fiery heat of her thighs, and learned.

As Anders and Elin settled into a routine, the Finnish immigrant was impressed by the bustling industry of the Keweenaw. The discovery of native copper found on the surface of the Peninsula and in underground veins so pure that the extracted ore needed no stamping, refining, or processing of any kind (the find being of such geological rarity that it intrigued geologists around the world), fueled a stampede of Easterners to the Keweenaw in the early 1840s. Simple pit and side-cut mines sprang up overnight wherever wayfaring prospectors found shiny rock. Most of these early efforts to extract unadulterated copper ended in financial failure. Of these rudimentary operations, only the legendary Cliff Mine paid dividends, returning money to the banks and East Coast interests that financed the exploration and development of the Cliff.

This initial and largely unsuccessful run on native, unblemished copper was followed by the discovery of vast stores of conglomerate ore—known as pudding stone because the deposits of pure copper embedded in the surrounding waste rock reminded geologists of raisins in English pudding. The discovery of conglomerate was a bonanza that would keep the mines of the Hancock area, including the Quincy, in business well into the mid-twentieth century.

But the most impressive geological discovery on the Keweenaw was the uncovering of amygdaloid ore deposits in Calumet Township north of Hancock. Similar to conglomerate, but containing vastly more copper content, amygdaloid ore, despite its desirability, did have one important downside: the stubborn gabbro entrapping the copper nuggets required more powerful stamping mills.

To be sure, stamping mills were essential to processing *both* conglomerate and amygdaloid ores: the mills used pressure to crush the excavated rock and release valuable copper from the surrounding waste, which was then smelted into ingots for shipment. But the stubbornness of amygdaloid ore required more expensive and more sophisticated machinery than conglomerate ore.

By the early 1900s when Anders and Elin made Hancock their home, copper mining on the Keweenaw not only included mining but stamping, sorting, and smelting operations as well. And though the original fissure veins were played out by the time Anders and Elin arrived in Michigan, the Keweenaw of the early 1900s remained alive with extractive activity. The landscape crawled with work-hungry immigrants who descended beneath the earth to mine copper or disappeared into the woods to log steady supplies of pine, spruce, tamarack, and hardwoods. These immigrants, largely single men desperate for work, came in droves from Germany, Canada, Slovenia, Serbia, Montenegro, Croatia, England, Italy, and Norway—and most importantly in terms of sheer numbers, Finland—with bright eyes, curious ambition, and dreams of better lives: dreams that often never came to fruition.

Because he'd signed on as a miner and not as a trammer or a carpenter's apprentice, Anders's work life in Hancock was markedly different from his time spent in Soudan and Ely. Hard-rock copper mining was, in simple terms, backbreaking labor requiring little brains and tremendous brawn. But the pay—$2.50 a day—was adequate and far better than the wages he'd made working the docks in Duluth.

The details of Anders's work in the Quincy also differed in another important respect from underground work in northeastern Minnesota. No longer did Anders descend outfitted with a candle to light his way. Instead of candles, the miners at the Quincy Mine were provided wide-brimmed caps fitted with lanterns. Illumination was achieved when a miner turned a switch on his carbide lamp, allowing water and calcium carbide to mix.

239

The resulting chemical reaction created a controlled flame reflected by a crude mirror mounted behind the lantern on the miner's soft cap. Though primitive, carbide lamps were an improvement over the candles Anders and his fellow miners had relied upon in Norway and northeastern Minnesota. In addition, electric lighting was being installed in the main drifts and shafts of the Quincy, but had not yet been strung throughout the entirety of the serpentine mine, a complex that wormed through miles of subterranean copper deposits and reached eight thousand feet below the surface. This lack of a central source of light made the individual lanterns carried by each miner essential to safety.

Additionally, the wood-sided ore cars—hand powered by trammers during Anders's employment in the Quincy—were, over time, electrified throughout the Keweenaw, reducing the number of men needed to move ore from stopes and chambers to the skip. But as Anders said goodbye to a slumbering Elin—a perpetual snowfall burying Hancock—his lunch pail containing a cold pasty, an over-ripe apple, and a steel bottle filled to the brim with hot coffee, Anders ruminated on the fact that his time spent in the mine, though sufficient to pay their rent and groceries, was unchanging, boring, and lacked mental stimulation.

Entering the dry, Anders kicked new snow from his boots, disrobed, found his miner's clothes hanging from a wire strung across the room, removed the clothing, and dressed for a day in the mine alongside the other men working his shift. Anders was part of a three-man crew. His two mates were there, in the dry, dressing as well. Nothing was said between the men as they methodically suited up for work. Anders and Raiko Pinkkonen, a small, perpetually energetic and wiry man—whose blond hair tended to gray and whose mustache and beard were always neatly trimmed—manned twelve-pound sledgehammers. The third member of their crew, a huge, silent, and hulking brute, Sami Nyberg—his head as bald as an egg, his arms and legs twice the girth of an ordinary man's, his strength legendary (exceeded, it was said, only by the virility of Lauri "Big Louie" Moilanen, a seven-foot-nine-inch timber trammer from the Franklin Junior Mine outside Hancock who'd once toured with Ringling Brothers as the Tallest Man on Earth and was now serving as Hancock's Justice of the Peace and celebrity bar owner)—worked a six-foot chisel, holding the steel bar firmly against rock as Alhomäki and Pinkkonen took turns slamming their hammers into the butt of the chisel, rendering masses of conglomerate into small, moveable chunks that trammers loaded into ore cars and pushed down steel rails to the skip.

Necessary to preparing the ore field was the driller, Oskar Mikkanen, a man of considerable experience who used a stream-powered Ingersoll pneumonic drill to bore holes into stubborn Keweenaw rock. Once sufficient holes were created, Mikkanen stuffed them with dynamite, rigged fuses, and detonated the explosives to liberate ore. It was the larger chunks of ore that Anders's three-man crew battered into smaller pieces suitable for transportation to the surface, the rock house, and eventually, the Quincy stamp mill on the shores of nearby Torch Lake.

But things were changing for the miners working the Quincy. The three-man crew, which, when the driller was added into the equation was actually a four-man unit, was slowly being replaced by single-drill crews where one man, working an improved Ingersoll steam drill, did all the work. This change meant fewer and fewer jobs were available for immigrants and also meant that, whereas formerly, the men on a crew were able to account for each other's safety, one miner, working on his own, had no one to rely upon in case of accident or emergency.

Though Anders had steadfastly avoided becoming involved in labor agitation or organizing, he found, as he began his work in the Quincy, that such impassibility of conscience was impossible. All around him, the changes in mining technique and the resulting elimination of jobs fomented unrest—unrest that led to men joining the Western Federation of Miners, an organization of resistance and protest that the higher-ups in the mining companies could not abide. For the first time in his life, Anders found himself being drawn into a debate between labor and management. Like his crewmembers, he paid his dues and joined the union's local affiliate. He did not publicly vocalize his support for the union or seek positions of importance or prominence in the local: he simply accepted what was happening around him and went with the crowd.

Despite the organizational changes taking place in the mines, the day-to-day schedules of men like Anders working underground in the Keweenaw remained static. There was a dull sameness to the labor the miners endured. Each day in the Quincy began, once the miners were suited up for work, with the descent. Unlike the mines in Tower and Ely, where workers clambered aboard man cars that dropped on cables from the shaft house to the lowest levels of the mine—the wire-mesh cages being crude, industrialized versions of the elevator cars found in hotels and office buildings—miners and trammers and drillers and bosses of the Quincy rode to and from their jobs in far less regal fashion. The man car that lowered and raised the Quincy workforce was a nearly vertical, open-faced carriage in which thirty men at a time, three to a row—a complete crew—sat on wooden benches affixed to a rickety carriage that moved up and down on steel tracks. There was scarcely a foot of free board between the miners' faces and the wall of the shaft, making a miner's first ride into the Quincy Mine one that most men, including Anders Alhomäki, never forgot. Over time, like any repetitive, industrialized activity, this daily journey became routine. After a week of descending and ascending, Anders overcame the feeling of dread and death and the grave that such an inhumane experience imprinted on its victims. Ultimately, the Finn learned to sit patiently, his back firmly against the steel frame of the man car, his lunch pail in his lap, his eyes closed, thinking of Elin.

For her part, Elin, despite the deep snow that topped her black leather, lace-up winter boots and wetted her stockings, enjoyed her morning walk down the hill from the couple's company house to her office at Suomi College. Whereas Anders was off to work while the sky was pitch black, Elin's day began closer to dawn. After washing her solidly configured body with hot water from the wood stove and a bar of store-bought Ivory soap, and dressing, Elin sipped hot coffee and welcomed the sun as it rose over the hills blocking her view of Torch Lake. Every morning, her routine was the same. After dressing for the day, Elin would judiciously contemplate her surroundings from a wooden chair at the kitchen table before heading off to teach. As dawn advanced, the shaft houses of the Quincy Mine would cast ominous shadows across the company-owned neighborhood, the industrial silhouettes cloaking the miners' homes in darkness despite the open sky and the advance of the sun.

Elin taught English in a classroom down the hall from her office in Old Main, an ornate sandstone building considered the center of learning on campus. Several dozen young men and a handful of young women attended Elin's daily lectures. Her students were Finnish immigrants—or the sons and daughters of Finnish immigrants—who had completed courses of secondary education in the public schools either in Finland or America, or at Suomi Academy—a private preparatory school sharing the physical plant and instructors with the College. Elin's bright-eyed and eager students were yearning to advance themselves by obtaining seminary degrees or business training. In later years, Suomi College would become a nursing school, expanding further still to become Finlandia University, a private liberal-arts college attended by both Finns and non-Finns. But at the time Elin taught her students in Old Main, the school's primary focus was preparing Lutheran pastors to lead Finnish congregations throughout the Midwest. Suomi's secondary goal was to educate young women in the details and practicalities of office work. As to both aspects of the college's mission, Elin taught her students uniformly, without deference to any individual student's eventual placement after matriculation. And, despite her suffragette leanings and modern thoughts concerning the role of women in society at large, Elin held no disdain and voiced no recriminations for young women hell-bent on working as secretaries, bookkeepers, or stenographers. *Out of these young ladies*, she thought as she surveyed the blue-eyed, blond-headed girls in her class, *will come the first Finnish American lawyer without testicles!* The indiscrete nature of Elin's musing was at odds with the propriety imposed upon her by her overbearing father but wholly in keeping with her mother's fiery, liberal spirit.

Together, the man and the woman, working daily, sacrificing time for wages that barely allowed them to make their rent, buy food and fuel, and save a few meager dollars for a silent movie or play or musical performance at the palatial Kerredge Theater on Quincy Street or athletic events and theatrical performances at Kansankoti Hall (the Finns' local social hall that also housed *Työmies*—a labor newspaper published in Finnish), forged a life that was typical amongst the families struggling to make ends meet in the Keweenaw.

Even so, Elin was one of the few professional women in the co-joined cities of Hancock and Houghton and, despite the reluctance of her partner to voice his political and social views aloud, Elin Alhomäki—as she was known about town—knew no such constraint. She became intimately familiar with the women's auxiliary supporting the union's efforts to organize miners, took up the mantle of the Bull Moose Party—finding in former President Roosevelt a kindred spirit when it came to social causes such as women's suffrage, industrial safety, the eight-hour workday, and limitations on corporate corruption and graft—and worked feverishly, when not engaged in the brief, sweet interludes of romance and courtship with Anders that their busy lives allowed, for the overall betterment of mankind.

In her support of the former president and his progressive ideals, Elin found herself at odds with both her father—who, as a true conservative, supported President Taft's re-election—and her mother, a noted pacifist, who supported college professor Woodrow Wilson based on his promise to "keep America home" during the impending war between European powers.

With regard to Ellen's social and political involvement, Anders, who had taken his American citizenship and was eligible to vote, remained impassive yet uncritical.

"I have no desire to be involved in civic affairs or politics," was the mantra he repeated when Elin raised an issue, whether it was suffrage or European intrigue or Roosevelt's attempt to break up familial trusts. "I only wish to be left alone, to make enough money to buy a farm, and live out my life in peace."

This dream of the immigrant, to break free of his daily toils beneath the yoke of the corporate master—whether in a factory or beneath the earth in a copper mine or in the forested wilderness of the far north—and seize individual destiny and fate by the throat, ate away at Anders every day he descended into the Quincy. The impact of his unfortunate decision to forego ownership of his stepfather's farm and leave Finland for America beguiled his mind and shrouded his soul—upsetting what should have been a bucolic life with the woman he loved, just as moldy berries spoil an appetizing pie.

It was stupid of me to let my pride and my belief in my abilities affect my decision-making, he mused. *I once blamed Uncle Alvar's romantic notions for influencing my choices. But he is gone, having passed on in September from a bad heart. And even when he was alive, filling my head with tales of military service and glory in the service of the czar, he did not force my hand. I decided to go to Norway and then to America. That is the truth of it. And I must live with the choices I have made.*

CHAPTER FIFTEEN: February 1913

In the depths of a stubborn winter on the Keweenaw, with drifts piled so high that the wooden sidewalks of downtown Hancock resembled the tunnels Anders and his fellow miners carved from the earth, Anders and Elin tried to keep the coal bucket full and the wood bin in the kitchen piled high with maple, using both the small stove in the parlor and the cook stove in the kitchen to heat the rickety, hastily constructed, uninsulated frame dwelling they called home. So long as temperatures remained above zero and the wind remained at bay, the couple was cozy, warm, and content to spend their limited free time—evenings after work and before slumber and their blissfully open and unconstrained Sundays, when both Anders and Elin were not at work—together. Elin was also off Saturdays (Suomi College did not hold classes on the weekends) but spent that time correcting papers and planning lessons or working for the various organizations she relished being a part of.

Women's suffrage was Elin's *cause célèbre*: the issue dearest to her heart and the one that compelled her, when she had the notion and the time, to donate her precious off-hours promoting the right of American women to join their Finnish cohorts in achieving the right to vote, Finnish women having attained universal suffrage in 1906.

In addition, Elin began to submit—under the pen name "A Concerned Modern Woman"—essays in Finnish to *Työmies* relating the struggles of the fairer sex on the Keweenaw. Her identity as a social commentator remained concealed from the conservative administration of the college and consequently, Elin was not chastised or disciplined by her superiors for her audacity. Similarly, Anders's bosses did not know of Elin's economic and social apostasy, meaning Alhomäki kept his job as a miner for Quincy.

Beyond the great personal uplifting of Elin's soul such brazenness allowed, there was another, far more important consequence attached to the teacher's putting pen to paper as an essayist for *Työmies*: her modest success as a writer in Hancock began her life-long divagation as a reporter, a journey that would see Elin—decades later—returning to her parents' homeland on the heels of the Great Depression to chronicle an episode in Finnish American history known as Karelian Fever.

For his part, when Anders wasn't making improvements to their rented house, toting coal or chopping firewood, he spent evenings exploring the wonders of Elin's body, finding that a climax inside his beautiful companion led to the most blissful, restful sleep he'd ever experienced. Resolution after his own release and attempting—sometimes successfully, sometimes not—to bring his partner to her own pinnacle of carnal satisfaction was, to Anders, the most exquisite of slumbers in the most perfect of beds despite the imperfections of the couple's day-to-day existence.

Theirs was a hand-to-mouth subsistence with little room for mishap, disease, or injury. In this respect—despite Elin's education and intellect, and the fact that, after seven years in America, Anders was able to read English, giving him the singular ability amongst his peers to read Mark Twain's wonderfully American novels—they were like any other working-class couple in the Keweenaw in that their existence was dictated by markets and economic forces beyond their control.

Though he had obtained only an elementary-school education, Anders relished the words he deciphered and discerned late at night after the sheen of their lovemaking had grown dim and Elin was fast asleep next to him beneath the goose-down comforter warming their full-sized bed. As Anders read by kerosene lantern, recalling—as the English words filtered into his mind and portrayed the personages of Tom and Huck and Becky and Anders's personal favorite, the slave Jim—the still, cold nights he spent in the loft of his parents' farmhouse outside Paltamo, the Finn's thoughts invariably turned to the journey he had made.

It was during such moments of self-reflection when Anders would close the Twain and read letters from home. He saved correspondence in a cigar box kept on the floor beneath the bed he shared with Elin and would, when nostalgia struck, open the box, remove old letters, and reread them.

October 12, 1912
Helsinki, Finland

Dear Brother:

247

I will start by confirming that our mother is doing well despite her age and the infirmities living beyond the age of sixty entails. She continues to reside on the farm with Ronja, Erno, and their child, Aalia. The little girl is now two years old and, as I reported in my last letter, suffers from Mongolism. Cruel gossipers say that her affliction is just the roots of our ancestors surfacing; that we Finns are descendants of Kublai Khan. Linguists and historians dispute such nonsense, but you can't believe the ignorance of some people! Though delayed by her malady, Aalia is beginning to walk around furniture and has learned a few words, the most important being "milk," which she says loudly as she points to Ronja's bosom. Our sister is determined to nurse the child until age five as the local healer has convinced her that nursing until that age will improve the girl's condition. We shall see.

As I wrote back in June, Ronja is expecting another child and we are all hoping and praying that the new baby will not be afflicted with such challenges.

The big news in the family is also the saddest. Uncle Alvar died last month of a weak heart. Aunt Tatianna is now left to care for three children on a pension. I have not seen her since she and Uncle and the eldest two children visited the farm a year after Ronja's wedding.

As you know, I moved away from Paltamo, having taken a job in Helsinki as a nursing assistant while attending nursing school. I was lucky enough to earn a scholarship with my grades. With the small wage I earn, augmented by the scholarship stipend, I am able to afford an education. Otherwise, the cost of school would be beyond our family's meager resources. It goes well and within the year, I will be "pinned," which is to say, I will officially be a registered nurse.

My work in the hospital adjoining Imperial Alexander University in Helsinki is rewarding, taxing, and illuminating. I think that, given the research going on here, if Uncle Alvar had consented to come to the city for his care instead of remaining in Viipuri, he might have had more time. He would not have been cured, you understand, because so far as I am aware, heart disease is incurable. But the care here would have allowed him a longer life. Of that, I am certain.

No, I do not hold it against you or think anything less of you because you and Miss Gustafson are living together. My

248

younger, more foolish, more limited self would have been judgmental on that score. But having moved to the city and seen the reality of life, even having my heart broken a time or two (sorry, but I must spare the details of those events even from you, dear brother!) I choose not to adjudicate the failings or shortcomings of others when I myself am far less than perfect. In this way, I am hoping to emulate Christ, who, if you will remember, judged only liars and hypocrites and ministered to the poor, the hungry, the diseased, the less fortunate, and the whores without recrimination. I am not pretending to be like Him: only hoping that I can, in some small way, follow His example.

At present, there is no beau courting me, and I fear that I may well remain a single woman. If that is to be so, I hope I can find happiness in my work and in my doting affection towards my niece and the expected baby.

I will end this letter by saying that I miss you, brother. I send you my love and my concern and ask only that, when you are able, you reply with news from America.

    Your loving sister,
    Helmi Alhomäki

The bad news had leveled him like a roundhouse to the chin: The Elf Warrior was no more.

To say that Anders Alhomäki loved another man—whether the perceived target of such emotion was his stepfather or his boxing instructor or his favorite uncle—would be attributing affection to the Finnish immigrant that, upon closer inquiry, the examiner would be hard-pressed to confirm. And yet, the loss that Anders felt when Helmi's words sunk in, verified such a connection, such a bond. Anders, despite his steadfast *sisu* and his internal resolve to remain unaffected by the comings and goings inherent in being, *loved*—not only the women in his life but those male role models who had helped form Anders's personality and stubborn resolve. But he had not wept or mourned openly due to the loss revealed in his sister's letter. Even during the quiet moments spent with Elin alone in their wind-clattered cottage on the ridge, he had maintained the steady demeanor that defined him.

When he was finished rereading the sad news from home, Anders simply nodded his head, folded the letter, placed it carefully back in the cigar box, and remembered all that Alvar Alhomäki had meant to him.

"Damn, it's fucking cold," Raiko Pinkkonen, Alhomäki's sledgehammer-wielding friend from the Quincy said in Finnish. The two men were crouched over holes cut in the ice of Portage Lake, watching corks bob in black water, waiting for hungry perch to snap at suspended minnows. Though the bait was long dead, having been netted in the summer, frozen, and kept for the miners in the big freezer in Henry Sakari's grocery store in Hancock, the gentle rocking action of the lake beneath the ice caused the inert minnows to waltz suggestively on their hooks. "I've got every damn piece of clothing—except my work clothes hanging in the dry—on me and still, I'm freezing to death!" Raiko said, his teeth chattering, his face ruddy from the wind. "Who the hell came up with this damnable idea to try to catch fish in below-zero weather anyway?"

Anders, who knew full well that his friend was blaming him for choosing such a horrific day to fish, remained mute. His attention wasn't on Raiko's diatribe, or on the cork bobbing in the small circle of open water in front of him, but on a memory from the past summer.

First goddamned elephants I'd ever seen, he recalled, his mind wandering back to a lovely Sunday in July he'd spent with Elin in a huge canvas tent on the outskirts of Hancock, marveling at the exotic animals and well-proportioned athletes who'd come to town on the train from Marquette. *There was a hell of a lot of hoopla when that Duluth, South Shore, and Atlantic locomotive pulling the Ringling Brothers Circus arrived.*

He and Elin had spent the entire afternoon at the show, marveling at the huge pachyderms waltzing majestically in time to the ten-piece circus band; the acrobats tumbling and jumping from shoulders to the sawdust-covered ground and back onto another set of broad, strong shoulders; the uproarious clowns delighting the children; the death-defying acrobats on the high trapeze amazing the crowd with their near-fatal exchanges in mid-air done without the benefit of a net; and finally, being left gape-mouthed as the slender, attractive lion trainer, her hair wound tightly in a bun, her body nearly bursting from her less-than-modest sequined costume, made huge, savage cats obey her every command with no more than a bullwhip for protection.

That was as amazing an afternoon as I've ever spent, Anders thought, the sudden disappearance of his cork bringing him back to the present.

"Nice one!" Raiko said in Finnish as Anders pulled his braided fishing line hand over hand until a thick-bellied, perch was flopping on snow. "Fish dinner tonight at the Alhomäki house for certain," the smaller man added.

"English," Anders said, using the language of their adopted land without casting a glance at his companion. Anders removed the sharp hook from the fish's upper jaw. "You need to spend more time speaking English if you hope to take your citizenship, my friend."

"I've got another one!" Raiko replied in heavily accented English, pulling in his third fish. "I only wish I had a Mrs. Pinkkonen to fry these up for me and keep my bed as warm as Elin keeps yours!"

Dusk approached. The men gathered up their frozen fish, collected their lines and tackle, and trudged uphill towards downtown Hancock.

"Time for a beer at Big Louie's?" Raiko asked as the men stopped and watched a streetcar rattle onto the swing bridge spanning Portage Lake, the car carrying passengers from Hancock to Houghton.

"No. I told Elin I'd be home by dark. I'll have to pass. Have one on me, though," Anders said through a smile, his dark eyes adjusting to the gas street lamps and focusing on the walls of snow lining both sides of Quincy Street.

The omnipresent Keweenaw blizzards were temporarily on hiatus. But past storms had created snowdrifts taller than a man throughout the adjoining towns. Electric streetcars mounted with snowplows had become mired in inexhaustible piles of fluff, requiring teams of Belgians, four to the harness, to free the helpless trolleys.

"Here's my turn," Anders said, slinging a gunny sack of frozen perch over his left shoulder as he began to climb towards the Quincy Mine.

"I'll have two on you, my friend," Raiko said in Finnish. "See you tomorrow in the dry!"

"English!" Anders called out in his adopted tongue, never looking back at his friend. "You need to speak English!"

CHAPTER SIXTEEN: August 1913

"How long will the strike continue?"

Elin Gustafson asked the question of Anders as they sat at their kitchen table, rain beating a cadence against windows overlooking the industrial buildings of the Quincy Mine. The woman sipped a second cup of coffee as she spoke. Her hair was piled high on her head, held in place by a jeweled hairpin—a gift from Anders that had set him back a full week's wages at Isaac Friedman's jewelry store on Water Street—as her patrician hands grasped the battered cup, a piece of blue and white porcelain that would have been tossed into the trash of her parents' home.

There was an edge of concern, of hesitant uncertainty, to the woman's voice that caused Anders to look up from yesterday's *Mining Gazette*, where the travails of the striking miners—who'd voted to go out on strike on July 23 over issues of wages, the work day, and the implementation of the one-man drill rig—were characterized by the paper's editor as being the result of "the slovenly greed of an uneducated, immigrant, socialistic mob."

In truth, while there were socialists, communists, and members of the IWW amongst the strikers, the vast majority of the men who walked out of the Keweenaw copper mines were not motivated by political ideology but by pragmatism: they were not being paid a living wage and were offended that other men—men working the Montana and Arizona copper mines—were.

Anders was in this latter camp. He adhered to no political or philosophical creed other than he believed in a fair shake for all. And with the decline of available jobs due to the crew changes in the Quincy, the rising cost of living as the world lurched towards global war and the unexpected and unjustified increase in expenses charged against miners' wages—for lanterns, fuel, soft caps, tools, and the like—Anders did not hesitate to join his more political union brothers in striking. But the Finn's decision to join the protesting workers came with a price: the meager savings he and Elin had deposited in the Detroit and Northern Michigan Building and Loan were running out. The economic reality of the situation was that, even with Anders picking up odd jobs for cash, including working the docks in Hancock and Houghton as a day laborer, or, on occasion, joining his friend Sami Nyborg on a logging crew cutting cedar in the Keweenaw swamps, the couple was relying almost exclusively on Elin's meager salary to survive.

As their income plunged and prices soared, a pained look on Elin's comely face, a look of panic, a look of dread at the decision she had made to accompany Anders to Michigan, replaced her former, steadfastly loving expression. When she asked the question of him at their kitchen table, it was not an inquiry made out of the ether: it was an inquiry based upon the stark reality of a relationship in trouble, trouble caused not because of a lack of mutual respect or affection but caused by economic woes.

"They say it may drag on through winter," was the best answer Anders could abide, making his reply while focusing on the shaft house of Quincy No. 3 and the parade of rock doves circling the imposing building as he avoided his partner's gaze.

"How will we survive?"

Anders shook his head. *You ask a question that has no answer.* Anders did not reply, and Elin did not provoke an argument by continuing her line.

It was Sunday. The sun was up but it was still early.

"We haven't been to church in a while. Perhaps prayer might help," Elin offered in a conciliatory tone as she reached across the table and placed a soft, warm palm on the back of the miner's left hand. "Let's go to church and see if God doesn't provide answers."

Neither Elin nor Anders was particularly religious; but, on occasion, when spiritual cleansing seemed appropriate, they made the long trek into town and attended services at what would later become St. Matthew's Lutheran Church. In their time, the congregation was simply known as the Finnish Evangelical Lutheran Church of Hancock, with worship conducted—and all of the familiar hymns sung—in Finnish. Though most of their close friends and acquaintances, including folks who called the Finnish church their home congregation, understood that Elin and Anders were not legally married but were in fact "living in sin," that dicey bit of information was not shared with the more devote members of the parish whose faith tended towards the judgmental. Still, every time Anders entered the little frame building, removed his hat, and bowed his head in piety, due to custom and not personal belief, he felt like a charlatan and, more importantly, experienced a twinge of fear that their secret might be exposed. Thanks to the discretion of those who knew, such a revelation never occurred. The fear Anders experienced, a trepidation Elin apparently did not harbor, was palpable. But because he loved her, Anders could not deny Elin her spiritual due even while harboring an expectation of exposure.

"Alright. I'll go. I'm not sure the Almighty gives a good goddamn about the plight of the masses, especially miners on strike. But if you want to go hear a fable or two from Pastor Pesonen, I won't make you go alone," he replied.

Elin nodded but held her tongue. It struck Anders as odd that Elin did not, given the context of their discussion, criticize him for taking the Lord's name in vain. But as he focused on the clarion eyes and finely edged cheekbones of the woman seated across from him, Anders noted that Elin had rouged her cheeks and applied lipstick. It was then he understood that he'd been had.

Elin is already dressed for church!

CHAPTER SEVENTEEN: December 1913

Anders sat on a crude pine bench, his eyes closed, his body sweating. He was alone. His woman had left him. That was the simple truth of it.

Because the leadership of the Western Federation of Miners refused to negotiate terms, holding out for a glorious, complete victory regarding their demands, the strike fund that had been hastily collected during the summer was nearly empty. There was little in the kitty to tide the miners or their families over until the labor dispute ended. Governor Woodbridge had mustered the Michigan National Guard and sent citizen soldiers to keep the peace. Additionally, the mining companies had hired Waddell-Mahon men—private detectives who were little more than thugs—to escort miners loyal to Quincy and non-union strikebreakers across the picket line, to work. With Hancock and the surrounding countryside turned into an armed camp, there was little union men like Anders could do other than watch self-interested co-workers and newly hired scabs work the mines and the mills and the smelters while the strikers and their families starved.

Violence erupted in Hancock when out-of-work immigrants smashed windows in the passenger cars of the train carrying scab workers into town. Soon thereafter, a mob of disgruntled unemployed miners attacked a replacement worker in his home, beating the poor man bloody in front of his wife and children.

Thirty men were arrested for that little escapade, Anders ruminated as he dribbled water over hot stones with a wooden ladle. Steam rose towards the tongue and groove cedar ceiling of the newly constructed sauna. *If that's what this strike is about, I want no part of it.*

The Waddell-Mahon detectives had also engaged in their own brand of retaliatory violence. On August 14, two strikers—John Kalan and John Stimac, Slovenian immigrants who worked for the Copper Range Mine—trespassed on company property. The offense was observed by security guards, but the Slovenians escaped apprehension. A platoon of lackeys went looking for the miscreants with the intention of bringing them to the mine's superintendent for a "chat." John Kalan was confronted by a throng at his residence but refused to step outside and accompany the mob to the mine office. When Kalan shut his front door, vigilantes shot into the house, killing two renters where they slept. The deaths of two innocent miners—men uninvolved in the trespass incident—did not sit well with the strikers. Though a criminal jury trial was looming, disenchanted union members and their families held out little hope that justice would prevail given the enormous sway mining company executives held over the region.

Anders's own confrontation with Waddell-Mahon men came earlier in the week, after he'd finished tacking tarpaper to the roof of the log sauna he built with Raiko Pinkkonen's and Sami Nyborg's help in the rear yard of the home Anders shared with Elin. The men hadn't fired up the stove once the building was finished because Anders wanted to christen the sauna with Elin: just the two of them in the altogether, taking in the heat and the cleansing power of steam.

While Anders had waited for Elin to return from her charity work, his days laboring in the forests and on the docks having dwindled to little more than a half-day here, a half-day there given the plethora of unemployed men available in the Keweenaw, the three miners had walked to town hell-bent on drinking at the tavern once owned by Big Louie Moilanen. They were in a mood, despite the dismal circumstances leveled against them by the prolonged strike, for celebration.

"It's a grand day in America," Raiko Pinkkonen noted as the trio passed leafless maples, naked birches, and stunted oaks, the remnant trees clinging to the largely deforested hillside spilling into Hancock, "when a poor immigrant comes into enough of an inheritance from his dear, departed father to treat his friends!"

Pinkkonen's observation was in reference to the fact that Sami Nyborg—the big, hulking Finn who'd worked the business end of a chisel with Alhomäki and Pinkkonen in the Quincy Mine without complaint—had received a fat envelope from home, from Pooskeri, Ostrobothnia, a village north of Pori on the Gulf of Bothnia, the body of water separating Finland from Sweden. Inside the package, Sami had discovered his father's sterling-silver pocket watch, a letter from a Finnish attorney advising Sami of his father's demise, and a bank draft in an amount sufficient to tide the unemployed miner over for as long as the strike would last.

Sami had shared little about his upbringing with his companions, leaving much to the men's imaginations as to who his father was and how he'd accumulated the tidy sum he bequeathed his only child. All that Sami shared with Raiko and Anders was that his father had been a shopkeeper, a trade the elder Nyborg attempted to enlist Sami in, a trade that Sami Nyborg had no interest in pursuing.

"You speak the truth, my little friend," was all that Sami said in reply, patting the thick wad of greenbacks in his front pocket to emphasize the point. "I've more than enough for the three of us to get good and drunk!"

When the Finns arrived at the saloon, the sun sinking in the west, its subsiding image reflected on the calm, flat surface of Portage Lake, they left autumn's crispness behind when they entered the stifling confines of the smoky bar. The tavern was crowded with out-of-work miners and strikebreakers and Waddell-Mahon men and off-duty National Guardsmen all clamoring for refills from the two barmaids on duty. The lone bartender, a brusque man with blond hair, a full beard, and knuckles that cried out "enforcer" worked the beer taps and liquor bottles at a feverish pace.

Anders spied a spittoon resting on the floor and expelled a wad of phlegm and tobacco. Patrons were three-deep to the bar in front of Alhomäki, making it impossible for him to order a beer. Seeing his friend's dilemma, Raiko Pinkkonen took a long drag off his hand-rolled cigarette, impolitely shoved his way through the crowd, and made room for his companions at the bar by shoving an inebriated man aside with an elbow. The drunk grunted annoyance but, upon sizing up Sami, thought better of making a scene. Soon, the three friends were raising glasses of Empire amber to the ceiling.

"To Big Louie," Sami said reverently, "may he rest in peace."

Nyborg's impromptu toast was not lost on his companions. Though a beloved character in Hancock after taking over the bar and being elected Justice of the Peace, Louis Moilanen did not live long enough to cherish his new, respectable life away from the mines, the circus, and the gawking public. As

258

the summer and the strike of 1913 progressed, the giant experienced more and more frequent bouts of unpredictable behavior, culminating with Big Louie being placed in the Hancock City Jail for his own safety. In early September, Louie's demons got the better of him and he turned into a raging lunatic. He was transferred from jail to St. Joseph's Hospital in Hancock, where he died from an illness unrelated to his madness. The funeral for the quiet, kind-hearted, world-renowned celebrity—in a town turned upside down by labor strife and anger and violence—was attended by over a thousand Keweenawians, though only a fraction of that number crammed into the Finnish Lutheran Church to hear Pastor Pesonen's eulogy. The three miners did not gain entrance to the church but were part of the crowd that followed the giant's coffin to its place of final rest in Lakeside Cemetery.

"Here, here," Raiko added in Finnish, tossing back his beer.

"You best slow down, friend," Anders said quietly, taking in the noise, the crowd, and the bosom of the pretty little bartender bending in front of him to wash glasses in the sink. "Drink too fast and we'll have to carry you back up that bastard of a hill!"

Raiko blinked, wiped foam from his lips, and smiled. "I can handle my liquor. Don't you worry about me!"

Sami gestured to the barmaid with his empty glass. The woman—no more than twenty and shorter than Raiko but with dazzling ice-blue eyes, nearly white, shoulder-length hair, and an elfin smile—nodded, retrieved the miners' empty glasses, turned, and handed the empties to the bartender. When the glasses were refilled, the barmaid retrieved them from the silent, ever watchful barkeep and placed them in front of the Finns.

"Sixty cents," the barmaid said, eyeing up Sami with interest.

The big man didn't return the flirt as he dug into his front pocket, pulled out his wad of cash, peeled off a dollar bill, and handed it to the woman. "Keep the change," Sami replied in Finnish.

"Thanks. It's good to see someone around this town still has manners," she said, speaking their mother tongue with a noticeable Keweenaw lilt. The barmaid lingered in front of Sami awhile as if trying to make a connection.

But Sami's attention was drawn to an argument fomenting at a table in the center of the room. He did not engage the woman in small talk. Noting Sami's apparent disinterest, the barmaid moved on.

"What the hell's going on?" Sami whispered.

"To the new sauna!" Raiko yelled off-handedly, raising his glass and showering them with beer.

"To the sauna and the men who helped build it!" Anders said, placating his soon-to-be-drunk friend, before addressing Sami's question. "I think that Waddell-Mahon man, the bald, baby-faced one, is trying to goad those down-on-their-luckers into a fight," Anders whispered, pointing at a table of strikers who'd clearly had too much to drink.

Sami nodded. "I think you're right."

"To the Western Federation of Miners!" Raiko yelled out, a slur beginning to affect his speech. "Those stupid-ass sons of bitches in charge have got us in one hell of a mess, got our tits in a wringer, I'd say," the little Finn added.

The Waddell-Mahon man turned his attention to Raiko. "Watch your mouth, Finlander!" he shouted, his big cheeks puffing, his whiskerless face glowering. "There are ladies present," the detective said, advancing towards the bar. "Tell that laggard to keep his voice down and his comments civil," the private detective said, addressing Anders in a superior tone.

Shit, Anders thought. *He and his crowd are itching for a fight. I just want to drink my beer, be left alone, and eventually make it back up the hill to Elin. Beautiful Elin. The two of us naked and sweating in the new sauna. Who cares that I didn't get permission from the bosses at the Quincy land office to build it? What can they do? Fire me? Ha!* Instead of engaging the detective, Anders turned to Raiko and said, "Keep it down, friend. We don't want trouble."

"Whaddyamean? I didn't say nothin' to nobody!" Raiko yelled. "Whatthefuckareyoutalkin' about?"

The curse, delivered in English, caused the barmaid to flinch. But as the detective moved towards the source of the outburst, she tried to defuse the situation. "I take no offense. It's not like I haven't heard *that* word before! How about another whiskey water on the house?" she asked in a placating tone, her blue eyes locked on the Waddell-Mahon man.

"I told you," the detective said, thrusting a finger into Alhomäki's chest, "to shut your friend's pie hole. Don't you understand English, Finlander?"

Sami turned to face their accuser. He and the detective were of equal height, but Sami Nyborg had worked at physical labor his entire adult life whereas the Waddell-Mahon man's once solid body had gone soft. "There's no need to insult us, friend," Sami said quietly, placing his empty beer glass on the bar. "We were just leaving. Isn't that right, Anders?"

Alhomäki nodded and set his glass down. "That's right. We were just leaving."

"I'm not your friend," the detective replied.

Anders was not prepared for the fist that slammed into his face. There was no warning—Anders had no premonition—that the detective would sucker punch him. The blow dazed Anders but rekindled long-dormant instincts and memories, including a frame-by-frame recounting of the Swede being knocked to the canvas in Trondheim. Anders shook off the punch, returned to the moment, and raised his hands to defend himself. But, inexplicably to patrons witnessing the encounter, Anders did not immediately strike back.

"What the hell was that for?" Sami asked, trying to get at the instigator. Sami found he couldn't move, that two men—companions of the Waddell-Mahon detective who'd punched Anders—restrained him. "What did this man do that deserved you lashing out like that?" Sami asked angrily in English.

Raiko stared through glazed eyes at two additional Waddell-Mahon detectives who had joined the confrontation. The newcomers took up positions in support of the provocateur. Raiko reached behind the bar, and without missing a beat, grabbed a bottle of Canadian whiskey with his right hand. Before the Waddell-Mahon man closest to Raiko perceived danger, the bottle crashed into the man's skull and dropped him to the floor. The bottle shattered upon impact, leaving Raiko defenseless. A Waddell-Mahon reached out, grabbed the Finn by the throat, and lifted him off the floor.

"That'll do!" Anders said, his dark eyes flashing menace, his attention having been drawn from the instigator to the detective choking Raiko. "Let him go."

The man squeezing the life out of Raiko did not comply. Raiko's body went limp.

I promised Elin I'd never fight again. She knows what happened in Norway, knows why I no longer box. I won't be responsible for a man's death. But what choice do I have but to engage? Raiko's defenseless. Sami is occupied and of no help. Damn it to hell!

Most male Finnish immigrants to the Keweenaw carried *puukkos*—wood or bone handled knives used for skinning animals and for self-defense. Anders did not carry a knife. *Too likely a chance I'd resort to it and kill someone. Better to rely on my wits and The Bear's training than to pull out a* puukko. It was either let Raiko go down or resort to his fists. *I'm sorry Elin. I have no choice.*

A solid right to the big detective's jaw was the only punch needed. The man who'd started the altercation collapsed without a word. The main antagonist down and useless, Anders flicked a right at the man choking Raiko. The blow befuddled the detective and gave Alhomäki the opening he needed. He unloaded a haymaker into the man's midsection. The detective released Raiko, who slid to the floor. Anders followed up with two jabs, one right, one left, to the stunned detective's chin, setting the man up for a left hook that toppled him.

The mêlée caused the detectives holding Sami to loosen their grip. The big Finn took advantage of their inattention, spun on his heels, and banged their heads together, knocking them out. Men aligned with the private detectives—National Guardsmen and scabs—began crowding the Finns. Catcalls and insults were hurled towards Sami and Anders in English as the mob grew in size. Only the sudden appearance of a phalanx of Hancock policemen, their wooden batons drawn and ready, staved off the inevitable.

Sami bailed them out using his inheritance. The bartender and the barmaids verified the story told by the Finns: the Waddell-Mahon crew had started the fracas. The miners were minding their own business until the detective caused trouble. The testimony of the bar employees and from folks who knew the miners from past trade saved them from spending more time in jail. But their candor could not heal Anders's black eye and bruised face. When he finally made it home after a night in jail, Anders had been forced to confess to Elin that he'd been involved in a bar fight.

Sitting in the sauna, sweating the residue of a laboring life out of his pores, Anders thought back to Elin's wounded expression, and how, when she saw his swollen cheek and blackened left eye, she'd wept. No amount of Anders explaining, "It wasn't our fault: the Waddell-Mahon goons were gunning for us," made any difference. He understood that, the moment he admitted to brawling, something changed between them. A hint of mistrust was newly sewn into their relationship because of his, as Elin described it, "boorish, uncouth behavior."

It was not that Elin immediately grew cold and aloof. No, the alteration of their relationship was subtler than loud arguments and fighting and a sudden cessation of passion. But Anders recognized the shift in their connection for what it was: a deep and serious rift in what had once been a near-perfect romance. Because of Anders's behavior in the bar and the economic strain placed on the couple by the strike, their relationship was already in jeopardy when Elin received devastating news from home.

October 1, 1913
Duluth, Minnesota

Daughter:
Regardless of how you feel about my rules or how I feel about your unspeakable relations with that illiterate miner, you must return to Duluth immediately. There is no kind or soft way to tell you this. Your mother has been diagnosed with the cancer. It has spread from her female organs to her brain and it is unlikely that she will survive the winter. If you wish to see her and comfort her before she passes, you will be on the next train out of Houghton for Duluth.
Sincerely,
Karl Gustafson

Elin had been stunned by the news, and Anders had been incapable of addressing her upset. The Finn was not emotionally equipped to be a shoulder for the grief-stricken woman to cry on. It wasn't that he was incapable of feeling another's sorrow—he was able to appreciate the pain and anguish of someone struck down by awful news. But true to his imperturbable nature, Anders did not easily express empathy.

Still, as Elin had packed her valise for the trip home on a Duluth, South Shore, and Atlantic passenger train, Anders made an effort to support her.

"I'll go with you," he offered.

"No. This is something I must face alone," Elin replied. "Besides, there's no telling what Father would do if he learned you were back in town. It's best that you stay here for now. The strike will end, and you'll return to your work. You can save money for that farm you're always talking about. I'll write to you. I'll keep you up to date on what's happening. But it's best that you remain here with your mind focused on the future."

That had been it. They had come together one last time in the small bed they shared, a sweet, slow, tender coupling that reminded them both of the adoration they once professed for each other. Neither Elin nor Anders could know, as the sun peeked through shabby curtains drawn across the frosty window of their bedroom, as Elin made ready to catch her train, that it would be the last time, the very last time, they made love.

Anders stood on the platform outside the Hancock railroad station as a steam locomotive connected to a string of passenger cars, a dining car, a baggage car, and a caboose rolled south on tracks towards the Houghton swing bridge. He waved at the train. Elin returned the gesture in perfunctory fashion. As the train's caboose disappeared from view, Anders did not know—he could not know—that while he and Elin would meet again, they would never rekindle the desire they once shared.

After Elin departed, the troubles on the Keweenaw continued. Out of kindness—and concern for the children of the strikers—the Western Miners Auxiliary organized a Christmas Eve gathering for out-of-work Calumet and Hecla miners and their families. At the Italian Hall in Calumet, hundreds of miners, their wives, and their children came together for a celebration. Someone—no one knows who—shouted "Fire!" in the crowded hall, causing a stampede that led to seventy-three men, women, and children being crushed by the partygoers' frantic attempt to exit the building. As early as the next morning—Christmas Day—there were rumors circulating that the "warning" was a false alarm perpetrated by a Waddell-Mahon man.

In a letter Anders sent to Elin immediately after the Italian Hall disaster, he repeated the innuendo that a Waddell-Mahon detective had started the panic. The anguish such speculation caused Elin—a strong-willed woman whose belief in the goodness of humanity had been jaded by Anders's unexpected behavior and her mother's terminal diagnosis—cannot be overstated. Anders's revelation of the alleged cause of the tragedy in Calumet was an additional blow to Elin Gustafson's optimism and her faith.

"What the hell?" Anders asked aloud, recalling the events of the past months, reflecting upon the declining affection Elin had displayed towards him before leaving. Anders Alhomäki did not answer his rhetorical question as he climbed down from the sauna's top bench opened the door—the hinges creaking from subzero cold—and exited the steam bath to confront a frigid, black, starry, moonless night, naked to the world.

BOOK FOUR: NOW

CHAPTER ONE: The Warrior's Story. Independence Day (December 6, 2017) (Kajaani, Finland)

Ida Elina's version of *Myrskluodon Maija* is playing over my Samsung Galaxy. My music app is set on random. The song is perfectly suited to my melancholic mood and my vision of what will happen. I know that security around the Kajaani Refugee Center will be tight, that I'll need to draw upon all my experience as a veteran to deliver my statement. I'm a warrior, a descendant of a long line of Finnish soldiers whose military heritage can be traced back to my great-great-grandfather, Alvar Alhomäki—known to generations of Alhomäkis as The Elf Warrior—and I know I'm well equipped for this mission.

As I clean parts of the disassembled Arsenal spread out on a towel in front of me, the newly oiled and re-assembled Sako sniper's rifle leaning against the paneling of the living room in Cottage C of the Kajaani Cottages at Jormua, I hum along to the kantele piece, mindful that, in Heaven—the likely destination for me, Jere Gustav Alhomäki, on this Centennial Independence Day—there will be music far sweeter than any earthly tune. My body remains flush from the invigoration of the cottage's sauna as I consider the trigger mechanism of the semi-automatic pistol and ruminate on a distracting thought: the cost of my lodging. My stay at this lakeside resort is an extravagance that, along with the bottle of imported Italian red I drained last night, and the tender reindeer steak, imported scallops, potatoes, carrots, and onions I fried in a skillet on the cabin's gas stove and savaged, I can't really afford.

But it may well be my last meal, I think as I re-assemble the pistol. *There is no harm in eating a fine meal in a quaint lakeside cabin before one confronts death.*

I'm dressed in blue jeans, Nike runners, and a Rush T-shirt. My winter uniform and matching camouflage boots are packed in a garment bag hanging in the cabin's bedroom, ready to go. I assemble the Arsenal, aim down the barrel of the handgun at a photograph of the iconic Helsinki train station tacked to the wall above the living-room couch—the image adorning a poster promoting an architectural symposium a decade in the past—and mouth, "Bang!"

I stop and look at my reflection in a mirror. *My dye job is terrible!* My crew-cut, usually blond, is as black as night, courtesy of coloring bought off the shelf from a Helsinki convenience store. *Bootblack,* I think as I turn my head—the pistol still in my right hand—and study my profile. I place the Arsenal on the towel and pick up a pair of eyeglasses, the frames made of thick, brown plastic with lenses of clear glass. *Not perfect but it'll do,* I think, hoping my inexpensive and hasty disguise buys me time, time to get within striking distance of the assistant director undetected by the authorities.

I return the pistol to a black leather holster resting on an end table. The holster is attached to a belt holding pouches bulging with magazines filled with ammunition for both the Sako and the handgun. "A hundred rounds should be enough to make my point," I muse, stroking the leather with contentment. "I'll not be indiscriminate in fulfilling my duty," I add. "I'll take out Assistant Director Saariaho and no one else," I promise aloud as I turn the music down.

My plan, one that I've been mulling over, amending, improving, and considering for the better part of a year, is simple. I'll lose the Volvo, commandeer another vehicle, load my weaponry and explosives into the stolen truck or car, and dress for combat. I'll ditch my borrowed ride a few blocks from the target, hoof it to the refugee center's perimeter fence, place the C4 and detonators in strategic locations, and take up a position on a hill I've reconnoitered on Google Earth as being the best place to establish a base of operations. From satellite imagery, the hill's summit appears heavily forested but affords a good viewpoint from which to scrutinize the camp.

I'll e-mail my manifesto to the newspapers from my Galaxy just before I begin the operation, I think as I stare out a frost-framed window at the burgeoning morning. *That will put everything in perspective!*

My advantage will coalesce after dark, when Independence Day festivities reach a fever pitch. Assistant Director of Immigration for Refugees and Migration Tarja Saariaho, a former member of the Finnish Parliament and now in charge of supervising Muslim immigration to Finland, is scheduled to address the camp's refugees and staff in the camp's amphitheater. *Damned Leftist,* I think, considering Saariaho as I wander into the kitchen, grab a can of Diet Coke from the refrigerator, and open it, *coddling Muslims trying to destroy the Christian fabric of our country.* I sit on the couch, shut off the music, remove my earbuds, turn on a flat screen, and scroll through the menu. *And now I hear she's considering a run for fucking president! That woman has as much right to lead Finland as a drunk sleeping in his own piss in downtown Stockholm has to be crowned king of Sweden!*

I consider that Saariaho is married, has three children—little girls, if I remember correctly, all under the age of ten. *True,* I reflect judiciously, *her death will bring them sadness. But in the big scheme of this world, there's much to be sad about. Just ask my sister-in-law and my nieces living husbandless and fatherless in Scotland because of the Muslim bastards Saariaho seems hell-bent on bringing into Finland. I can't let emotions stay my hand,* I think, evaluating the woman's impending death.

I sip Coke, the hazy effect of last night's wine only a memory, my mind clear headed and open to the future, as I search for a football match or a hockey game on television. I'm unsuccessful. I turn off the flat screen. I glance at my phone. "Half past eight. Time to get moving."

I disassemble the Sako and place it, the holstered Arsenal and utility belt and cartridge pouches, a Kevlar vest, boxes of extra ammunition, four squares of C4, four electronic detonators, and a remote transmitter into my duffle. I select a Sibelius concert by the Helsinki Philharmonic from the Galaxy's music library and pop my earbuds in. As lush violins sooth my nerves, I stop to consider the path I've chosen.

Some might say I am overreacting to the violence that Muslims have wrought here. Ha! This is the thanks we get for taking in refugees who profess a different faith? See here now, even Finnish citizens have become contaminated, I argue, standing in the middle of the kitchen, my bags packed, my anger rising. *The state prosecutor just brought charges against three Finns for trying to assist ISIS by sending money to the terrorist group* and *by joining its terrorist operations! I experienced Muslim handiwork in Central Africa. Old men, women, and children. All butchered and debased. Good for Toiviainen—the*

271

state prosecutor—for bringing charges against Finns seeking to perpetrate such enmity. Good for him!

Though I'll not likely live out the day and there's little reason to be careful, I remove a handkerchief from a back pocket of my Levis and wipe down every surface I've touched. I collect the Coke can and other garbage and toss it into my daypack, ensuring I've left no trace of my presence in the rented room. I put on my parka—zipping it tight against weather, slip my hands into gloves, slide the straps of my pack over my shoulders, retrieve the garment bag holding my camo from the bedroom, return to the living room and snatch the duffle bag holding my weaponry and daypack from the carpeted floor, and move out.

I stop at the cottage's front entry, set the day pack on the tile, open the door, glance around the clean, pine-paneled space, turn off the lights, reclaim the pack, and step into the pink light of emergent dawn. Tired of Sibelius, I search for and find *The Cranberries Live in Paris.* Dolores O' Riordan's voice, hard-edged, raspy, and colored by age, fits my melancholic mood and makes me smile as she sings the opening lyrics to "Linger." *Nothing like Irish music to get the blood boiling.*

It's Finnish Independence Day. My moment has come. I feel the need to be prophetic despite the fact that I'm speaking to an audience of one. "Like the Oglala leader Low Dog once observed," I say as I close the cabin door and admire the timid sun rising hesitantly above Oulujärvi's frozen surface, "'today is a good day to die.'"

CHAPTER TWO: 9:00 a.m. Independence Day

"**You** need to intervene, to call her off!" SUPO Chief Inspector Alissa Utrio shouted into the receiver of a landline. "With all due respect, Director, this is an untenable situation. This man— Sergeant Jere Alhomäki—the terrorist we've been tracking, is here. In Kajaani. And we have credible intel that he's about to attack the refugee center. He's a cagey veteran—was a firearms instructor in the army—not some high-school kid who's decided to take out his fellow students with his father's hunting rifle because he was bullied!"

It was nine o'clock on Independence Day morning. Sergeant Elsa Vuolijoki watched her wife's eyes. Alissa's diffuse green pupils were wide and urgent. Elsa also noticed that Alissa was fidgeting with a migrant strand of thick, scarlet hair dangling off her left temple. *She's worried. Can't blame her for being upset. What better way to hit pan-Europeanism and Finland's immigration policies than to assassinate one of Finland's most liberal political leaders?*

"Fuck!" Alissa's voice was edged with exasperation as she slammed the remote into its charging cradle. She stood up from her desk. Her eyes maintained the pique that Elsa had detected during the telephone exchange. "Her handlers won't call her off. Say she's not about to let the threat of an extreme nationalist causing a 'scene' at the center dissuade her from speaking her mind. Her SUPO security detail from the Helsinki office has its marching orders from Director Vuolijoki himself."

"Which are?"

"Do whatever Saariaho asks them to do and keep her safe."

Elsa unfolded her legs, stretched, pushed against the back of her chair, stood up, and looked at Alissa. "That's plain crazy."

The chief inspector nodded, grabbed a mug off her desk, and sipped green tea. "Worse yet. That was the director I was talking to. Your uncle insists on personally leading the security detail. He's taking the rumors of Alhomäki's planned attack personally. Says to me, 'Not in my Finland! There'll be no Breivik moment in Kajaani as long as I'm the director of SUPO!'"

Elsa shook her head. "Uncle Leo is a stubborn cuss. Very good at his job. But as unbending as a mule when his mind is set."

"You know him well."

Elsa grinned. "That I do. So, if we're gonna try to stop this madman, what's our plan?"

"Local police tracked the Volvo to Kajaani Cottages on the lake. Seems a stranger with good manners rented a cabin there yesterday. The description of the renter isn't an exact match. Dark hair. Wearing glasses. But the build, height, and the fact the stranger paid cash for one night in a lakeside cottage in the dead of winter caused the manager to pause. He'd seen the television alert and thought there was a resemblance."

"Good God, did we ..."

"We were too late. He's already left. Cleaned out the place. Wiped everything down. With one exception. He forgot about the toilet handle. He's good but not perfect. Got a match of his thumbprint. It's Alhomäki alright." Alissa took a deep breath. "Manager says he left in the old Volvo. Thing isn't about to outrun a squad car. Every cruiser and plain-clothes unit and SUPO agent in Kainuu is on the lookout for that antique. It's not like he can just drive into Kajaani in a 1972 Volvo 1800ES and remain invisible!"

Elsa shook her head. "He won't be driving the Volvo for long. He must be planning on ditching it. Likely some place away from the refugee center so as to remain off the radar," she said. Elsa turned her head from side to side. Vertebra cracked in her neck; the "pops" audible in the close confines of the office.

I am so glad we found each other! Alissa thought as she watched her wife unravel kinks and knots in her spine. *I am such a lucky woman.* "I'd say it's time I got to the refugee center to supervise, to ensure things are secure," Alissa said when her partner stopped fussing. "You ready to take a ride?"

Elsa nodded.

As Alissa donned her coat, gloves, and stocking hat, she thought about the one and only encounter she and Elsa had with Alhomäki. *The club in Helsinki. We had him in our sights but, because this isn't* Minority Report, she mused, buttoning her coat, *all we could do was observe. We couldn't pick him up and hold him without evidence of a crime, or at the very least, proof he was planning to commit a crime. At that point, we had nothing concrete. Now we do. Now we have the letter to his girlfriend and evidence—through Russian intelligence—that he's in possession of illegal weaponry. But we have no fucking idea where the man is beyond the fact that he's somewhere nearby!*

They exited Alissa's office and entered the bullpen where a dozen local cops and SUPO agents milled around, antsy as hell to receive direction. "Saddle up, boys and girls," Alissa said calmly, the nerves and excitement of the hunt held in check as she assumed command. "Defense ministry has a platoon from Kainuu Brigade's 1ˢᵗ Jaeger Company—kindly loaned to us by General Virtanen—already patrolling the camp. But they're soldiers, not cops. We'll be the ones who need to be diligent, who need to catch Sergeant Alhomäki before he does harm."

The cops stopped talking, put down their cans of soda and cups of coffee and mugs of tea, and listened to Alissa. "One SUPO, one local police officer at each gate," she said, nodding with sincerity. "Just like we went over yesterday. Everyone vested?" she asked, looking around.

The cops nodded or tapped their chests in response.

"Good. You all know your assignments?"

"Yes, Chief Inspector," the group responded in half-hearted fashion.

Alissa shook her head. "Not good enough. Not nearly good enough." She drew in a breath, stood as tall as her frame allowed, and bellowed, "DO YOU KNOW YOUR ASSIGNMENTS? DO YOU HAVE THE SUSPECT'S PHOTO WITH YOU?"

"YES, CHIEF INSPECTOR!"

Alissa nodded. "From surveillance footage at the Helsinki rail station, we know he's dyed his hair black and is wearing glasses. The photo isn't an exact match. But he can't change his profile or his stature," she continued. "So, stay diligent and radio in anything suspicious. Don't try taking him out yourself. Got it?"

The men and women, the local cops in uniform, the SUPO agents in plain clothes, nodded. Alissa decided not to invoke another cheerleading session as she disbursed the officers.

"Alright then. Let's get to work." Alissa almost added, "and let's be careful out there," a reference to her favorite American police drama, *Hill Street Blues*, but thought better of diminishing the moment with an off-the-cuff reference to

American pop culture that would be lost on the younger cops under her command. Instead, she drew on her faith and prayed silently: *Lord, keep them safe from harm.*

CHAPTER THREE: Noon Independence Day

Dr. Janine Tate Tanninen studied the Syrian boy sitting next to her in the Kajaani Refugee Center's infirmary. *That's one nasty cleft*, she thought, examining the teenager, Ibrahim Al-Saad. *It's far worse than Josiah's before his second surgery at age six. But despite the complexity of the Syrian boy's case, there's no question: I can repair his cleft and leave only a minimal scar.*

"Ibrahim," Janine asked, using her scientist-turned-healer voice to draw the boy out of his shell, "are you willing to let me try to help you?"

Paula Mohammad, a dour, tensely proud thirty-something woman provided to the camp through the United Nations, translated from English into Arabic, doing so with accuracy but without enthusiasm. The Arab American woman, her family embedded in the culture of its adopted land for generations, her father having served in the U.S. Army as a translator during the First Gulf War, could not help but show her disdain for the teenager. She had, in prior conversations with Janine, made it clear that she did not approve of Finland—or any other nation—accepting refugees from the Syrian Civil War. More than once, she had plainly stated, "My family waited years to get to America and then, when my ancestors made the journey from Damascus to New York City, they arrived with money and skills. My great-great grandfather Abdullah was a healer, a physician just like you, Dr. Janine, a man ready to serve the people of his new home." She would pause during these conversations, remove her eyeglasses, and focus her deep brown eyes on Janine. "He did not arrive under darkness, or by climbing over a fence, or after being deposited illegally on some beach. He followed proper procedures and came to America with something to give back to his adopted country. These people," she would add with a hint of disgust, "arrive without going through appropriate channels, with only the clothes on their backs, starving, and without skills. They should have stayed in Syria, fought for their freedom, and tried to make their homeland a better place." But as Janine waited for the woman to translate, Paula didn't offer her standard lecture, likely because, though she had shared her opinions on the subject with the doctor, her views had little impact on Janine.

The boy nodded.

"Good. We can do the surgery later this afternoon if you like."

Paula Mohammad translated.

"Oh yes," Ibrahim replied in Arabic. "I have waited many years for someone to repair my smile. Today would be fine for such a miracle to happen, Allah be praised!"

The translator delivered Ibrahim's response accurately if somewhat sedately.

"God is indeed great, my child," Janine replied, smiling. "I'll notify the surgical team. I have nothing scheduled after lunch. Be here with your parent or guardian at two so I can go over the proper forms with him or her."

As the child listened, his bitterly disfigured upper lip quivered.

"What's wrong?" Janine asked Paula.

For the first time in their exchange, the younger woman, five inches shorter and appreciably huskier than the slender physician, showed a hint of sadness—or perhaps more accurately, sympathy—for the teen sitting unaccompanied in the examination room. "His parents are still in Syria, at least, that was the last word. They escaped ISIS but, so far as anyone is aware, have not been able to leave the country. He is alone. There is no one to sign papers on his behalf."

It was not a unique or unusual circumstance to encounter a refugee child orphaned either in fact or by situation. Janine nodded. "We have waivers that can accomplish what needs doing," she said, looking directly into the uncommonly blue eyes of the dark-skinned boy, the tint of his irises likely the result of some English or Irish or French soldier intersecting with one of Ibrahim's female ancestors. "The camp administrator can sign the appropriate papers."

The words, when translated by Paula Mohammad into the familiar, caused an imperfect smile to spread across Ibrahim's brown face. "Thank you, Madam Doctor," Ibrahim whispered in Arabic.

Though Janine did not understand the boy's words, she needed no translator to comprehend his gratitude.

CHAPTER FOUR: The Warrior's Story. 3:00 p.m. Independence Day

Manifesto

To: The Finnish People
Date: 6 December 2017
My brothers and sisters in Christ:

My name is Jere Gustav Alhomäki. I am a twenty-year veteran of the Finnish Army, having retired honorably after achieving the rank of master sergeant in the Utti Jaegers. I served my country in combat zones, most recently having been part of a United Nations peacekeeping mission to Central Africa. During my service in Africa, I witnessed first-hand the incredible cruelty of Jihadists. I personally encountered the aftermath of a brutal atrocity committed by Muslims against Christian men, women, and children in an African village. Let me be very clear. What I saw was not an isolated, rare occurrence. What I saw was a small piece of a far larger global war wrought by the Islamic faith against the Christian faith in every corner of the world. This truth, the fact that Islam is not a religion of peace, but is in fact, a religion of conflict and terror, is something that liberal public officials want to sweep under the rug. Those in charge of our beloved homeland's immigration policy seek to convince you, despite firsthand evidence of atrocities committed right here in Finland, that the things I witnessed in Central Africa, or the bombings and killings across the world committed by Islamic terrorists, are aberrations of the faith of Mohammad. They are not. They are the rule—not the exception.

Today is the day we celebrate Finland becoming an independent, democratic nation. Today is also the day that I avenge the death of my brother, Mikko who died in the Moscow airport bombing that claimed so many in the name of Allah. It is also the day that I right the wrong done to our nation by liberal politicians allowing the unfettered entrance of Muslims into Finland. There can be no rest, no peace, no moment of security for our people until this abomination is stopped once and for all.

And so, when you watch the news tonight or read the newspaper tomorrow morning, know this: what I do today, I do for Mikko, for the innocents butchered in Central Africa, for all *the other victims of Islamic Jihad, and for Finland. As it is written, so it must be.*

Look, the storm of the Lord!
Wrath has gone forth,
A whirling tempest;
It will burst upon the heads of the wicked.

The fierce anger of the Lord will not turn back
Until He has executed and accomplished
The intents of his mind.
In the latter days, you will understand this.
(Jeremiah 30:23-24)

Master Sergeant Jere Gustav Alhomäki (Ret'd)

I stare at the screen of my Galaxy. There is something about reading text on a digital device—be it a phone, a tablet, a computer, or a Nook or a Kindle or a Kobo—that seems surreal. In contrast, there's a tactile connection between readers and paper, a connection that is vastly different, somewhat nostalgic, to reading words on a screen. As I consider my message to Finland and decide whether or not I should send my words out into the world, I'm reminded of the enchanting smell of fresh-brewed coffee mingling with the odor of thousands of newly printed books awaiting discovery in the vastness of the Academic Bookstore in downtown Helsinki. *Despite the advance of technology,* I think, reading and rereading "Jere's Epistle to the Finns"—the informal title I've given my manifesto—*there remains something elemental and timeless inside the covers of printed books, something that cannot be replicated with ones and zeroes. But the convenience of the Internet age! Now that is something that cannot be duplicated in print.*

I managed to "liberate" the Ford panel van I'm sitting in from two Finns taking a piss on the side of the road. *Good luck, this,* I'd said to myself as I slid the 1800ES alongside the idling van, popped the Volvo's hatch, grabbed my gear, opened the sliding door of the van, tossed my bags into the Ford's cargo hold, slid into the driver's seat, slammed the manual transmission into first, and roared away from the stunned plumbers who'd turned around, dicks in hand, just in time to see their van heading into town. *At least I wasn't an asshole*, I ruminated as the Ford bounced along the rural gravel road leading towards city center: *I left them the Volvo with a half-tank of petrol and the keys in the ignition. They'll get their van and tools and parts back when the day is over*, the sour finality of that thought nagging me as I sped off, *unless I get stopped between here and there.* But the police, SUPO, and Finnish Army units (I'd listened to *Yleisradio, Yle Puhe* and learned that the local base had contributed troops) were concentrated near the refugee center.

Closer to the camp, security had tightened. I checked my phone, looked at Google Maps for a place to ditch the van. I located a private school just a few blocks away from the hill I needed to climb. I drove to the school. There wasn't a car in the parking lot or a light on inside the building. I couldn't believe my luck. *It's Independence Day. A holiday. Schools are closed!* I parked the van behind a dumpster. The Ford can't be seen from the street and with no custodians or teachers or other staff working, it will be hours before someone stumbles upon the vehicle.

I ponder my manifesto sitting in the driver's seat of the parked van. There's no traffic. No pedestrians walk about. It's as if the entire city is intent on saving its celebratory glee for Saariaho's arrival, her speech, and the fanfare—including fireworks—slated to follow her remarks.

I reread my words. The "to" line on my e-mail lists the online addresses of the ten largest newspapers in Finland, including *Helsingin Sanomat.* I press "send." I hear the comforting "swoosh" of my message being released into the world. *Now all of Finland will know who I am!*

I dress inside the van. I slip into insulated long underwear, followed by a uniform shirt, fatigues, utility belt and holster, Kevlar vest, jacket, toque, and gloves, wool socks, and cold weather boots. I remove weapons and explosives from my duffle, reassemble the rifle, load the firearms, affix a night-vision scope and bipod to the Sako, slide the Arsenal into its holster, step out of the van, close the sliding door, leave the schoolyard, and enter forest. It's four in the afternoon but night is omnipresent. I follow a hiking trail through piney woods without the aid of a flashlight. Footing is difficult.

Tarja Saariaho is due to speak at half-past six, I think as I labor up the brambly hillside. *I need to be in place and ready.* At the pace I'm climbing, timeliness will not be an issue. I'll be snuggled in, my post protected by deadfall stacked around me, long before the assistant director begins her address. The Sako TRG-42 will give me command of the amphitheater. Though a metal roof covers the stage, I'll have a clear shot. *There should be nothing obstructing my view of her as she takes the podium.*

At the top of the hill, I stack logs around a natural depression, set up the Sako, lie prone on cold ground, and sight the rifle in. After establishing my overwatch, I descend the hill to affix two packages of C4 and remote detonators equipped with micro-receivers to power poles outside the chain-link fence that encloses the camp. I tape the explosives to creosoted poles with duct tape, activate switches on the receivers, remove my gloves, retrieve a pair of wire cutters from a pocket of my trousers, and cut a hole in the fencing. *At some point, I may have to enter the camp and finish the job.* The hole in the fence will allow easy entry. I spin on my haunches, note that no one is nearby, complete my task, and return the wire cutters to my pocket. I slide my toque above my hairline and scan the area. *No one: there is no one walking the perimeter! All the assets must be either at the gates, inside the camp, or patrolling nearby streets.*

I climb through forest. A safe distance off the trail, I select two pine trees. I tape the last two bundles of C4 to their trunks. *If anyone gets too close, I'll blow the C4 and give the intruders the fright of their lives. The distraction will allow me to retreat or head for the amphitheater to finish the job, depending on the circumstances.* I activate the receivers.

I return to my outpost and settle in. I hunker down. Cold seeps into my joints. I keep the transmitter close at hand. *Hopefully, my aim is true and I won't need to blow the C4. But if I fail at taking out Ms. Saariaho from distance, I'll light up the C4 to give me a chance to get inside the wire.* The detonations *will* cause panic. If my shot from distance fails, I have an alternative plan. Dressed in my uniform, the appropriate unit patch in place, I'll descend, blend into the mob, and confront Madam Assistant Director Saariaho with the Arsenal. *Two shots to the head should do it.* By assassinating Tarja Saariaho, I'll claim justice for all the innocents murdered by Islamic terrorists across the world and send a warning to my Finnish brothers and sisters: *No More!*

But for now, I wait.

CHAPTER FIVE: 4:30 p.m. Independence Day

She had surveyed the operating field. The boy, Ibrahim Al-Saad, was sedated. Dr. Tanninen held the scalpel in her right hand and concentrated on Ibrahim's deformed upper lip and palate. *As severe a case as I've seen*, she had thought. Though she knew the boy's surgery would be difficult, Thena believed she was up for the challenge.

"You ready?"

Ari smiled. "Yes, Doctor."

"How about you, Doaks?"

Dr. Doaks Hampton, the English internist serving as the team's anesthesiologist, grinned behind a surgical mask. "Yes, ma'am."

"Venla?"

The nurse-in-training nodded.

"Then let's fix this child's smile."

"That was exhausting," the black woman whispered as she reclined later that afternoon, her spidery arms stretched above her head.

Olavi studied Janine's naked body like a farmer inspecting prize livestock.

"It shouldn't be so hard," she added wistfully, ignoring Olavi's leer.

Following the Al-Saad boy's surgery, Janine and Olavi found themselves with an hour of free time. There had been no planning behind their tryst. Suggestive glances over coffee in the mess hall after Janine finished her case had led to the woman excusing herself to "freshen up." Her husband also left Ari, Doaks, and Venla in mid-conversation, saying he "needed to check on security" for the impending arrival of Assistant Director Saariaho.

Afterward, they sprawled across crisp, cotton sheets in the bed they shared in their apartment, unabashed and spent. An odor of musk mixed with perfume and cologne permeated the bedroom. Olavi's penis—wet and limp—nudged Janine's bare thigh as the couple spooned. She breathed heavily, her ribs rising and falling in a pattern that made it clear Janine had run a race, a race to that culminated in a satisfactory finish.

"Agreed," Olavi said, playfully nibbling his wife's skin. "When we were younger, things seemed to be less onerous, less difficult. And yet, we are still here, making love like youngsters," he continued in Finnish. "For that, we must thank God for our good fortune and our good health!"

"Would you stop gnawing on me like a Labrador with a bone?" Janine asked, gently pushing her husband's face away from her leg, tugging at the sheets until her body was covered. "You know how I don't like to be touched afterwards."

Olavi raised his head and smiled. "I was just thinking ..."

Janine shook her head. "No time, husband. You have much work to do before the assistant director and her entourage arrive. The camp is crawling with police and SUPO and soldiers. All of them are looking to you for direction, seeking your wisdom as the operations manager."

Olavi swung his body, his legs muscular and covered in downy hair, off the mattress. "You're right, of course. Though I can't reveal the details, there's a threat against Saariaho being monitored by the SUPO. A credible, serious threat."

Janine's eyes widened. "I've heard the rumors. You're saying that they're true, that some madman intends harm to the assistant director? Today? Here?"

Olavi ignored the question, walked into the adjacent bathroom, and turned on the shower. Stepping into a cascade of hot water, he washed the residue of lovemaking from his body, shampooed his fading blond mane, rinsed, turned off the water, exited the shower, and toweled off, all within the span of a few minutes.

"That was quick," Janine quipped as Olavi re-entered their bedroom, slipped on underwear, and began to dress. "Are you ever going to answer me?"

Olavi shook his head. "Can't confirm anything you might have heard. Sworn to secrecy by Chief Inspector Utrio. You remember her, right?"

Janine considered Olavi's profile. Day had closed; night was upon them. The bedroom lamps were off. Light leaking into the space from streetlights outside the apartment allowed her to scrutinize her husband. *He's put on weight,* she thought distractedly. *But he's still one striking man. I did well when I said "yes" to Olavi Tanninen!* "No, I don't recall the name," Janine finally replied. "Have I met her?"

"A while back. At lunch. In the mess hall. She was with people from immigration, real tools who weren't particularly impressive."

She thought a moment. "Ah. The gay policewoman."

Olavi shook his head.

"Oh, she's gay alright," Janine argued.

"That's not what I meant," Olavi answered. "I meant she's no policewoman. She's SUPO, a chief inspector, in charge of the entire Kainuu."

"Oh."

"Anyway. That was lovely, dear," Olavi said cheerily. He tied his necktie, slipped a blue blazer over his arms, slid stockinged feet into a pair of black loafers, leaned over, and kissed his wife on the cheek. "I'll be thinking about what we did while listening to Madam Assistant Director's boring speech."

"You'd best keep your head in the game, make sure things are running smoothly for the bigwigs," Janine said quietly.

"Why so serious, Thena? We're married and still in love so what's the harm in daydreaming instead of listening to a politician?" Olavi asked, stopping to consider the suggestion of his wife under the sheet. "We are, aren't we?"

"How's that?"

"In love?"

Janine grinned. "Go. You're going to be late."

He didn't move.

"What?"

His tone grew serious. "We're still in love, aren't we, Janine?"

She nodded.

Olavi beamed. "I'll see you at the amphitheater? At six?"

"Yes. I wouldn't miss the hundredth anniversary of Finland's independence for anything."

"Alrighty then," Olavi said before walking across their bedroom, opening the door, and leaving his wife to shower and dress.

CHAPTER SIX: 5:30 p.m. Independence Day

"**What** the hell do you mean, 'We haven't found the stolen van yet'?"

Chief Inspector Alissa Utrio asked the question, her complexion matching her scarlet hair, as she dressed down Senior Constable Erik Heikonen. They were conversing in Utrio's satellite office located in the security building of the Kajaani Refugee Center as Heikonen listened to Utrio and stared at his shoes.

"Well, what do you have to say for yourself, Heikonen?"

The man, who towered over Utrio like a dead birch, mumbled in reply. "We're trying, Chief Inspector. We're trying. I have two of my best teams on it. Plus, three uniform squads. I've brought in everyone," he continued, glancing at Utrio's wife, Elsa, who was standing in shadows sipping herbal tea, "including Sergeant Vuolijoki. She's supposed to be off today and yet, here she is."

Utrio's ire did not abate but the color in her face returned to baseline. "Heikonen, come over here and look at this photograph."

The tall man, his skinny jeans too tight, the lining of his sport jacket frayed, his powder-blue dress shirt open at the neck and tieless, claimed space next to Alissa.

"What do you see?"

The cop placed his right hand on his chin and furrowed his eyebrows. "Well ..."

"Out with it."

Elsa joined them.

Heikonen examined the photograph. "If he's after Saariaho, we need to figure out his thinking."

"Tell me something I don't know."

"Boss, it's Melindov," a nondescript young Finnish woman—a receptionist—said, standing at the threshold with a remote phone in her hand.

Alissa left the others, stepped out into the hallway, accepted the telephone, and mouthed "thank you". The receptionist returned to her desk without reply.

"Andre."

"Madam Chief Inspector."

"We're a bit frazzled here, my Russian friend. We think Alhomäki is making his move. He's slipped through the cracks and we may well have a disaster on our hands if I can't figure out what his game is. Stubborn politician is making my job damn near impossible!"

There was silence on the line from St. Petersburg.

"Melindov, did you hear me?"

"I did. I have information that may help."

Alissa tensed, tried to forestall her upset at the game playing that always seemed part of her interactions with Russian authorities, pursed her lips, and replied, "Then get to it, goddamn it, before he takes out his target!"

"The weapons. We finally tracked down the German who sold Alhomäki the weapons."

"Yes?"

"He bought a Sako TRG-42 equipped with a night-vision scope, an Arsenal, four packs of C4 with remote detonators and a transceiver, and several hundred rounds of ammunition. Does that help narrow it down?"

"It does. Thank you, Andre." She hung up the phone without saying goodbye, walked over to the receptionist, handed the woman the phone, and returned to her office.

"He's going to kill from distance," Alissa said firmly as she re-engaged her wife and Heikonen.

"How do you know?" Heikonen asked.

"That was my Russian contact. They tracked down the German arms merchant and got him to talk. Alhomäki's armed with a Sako TRG-42 fitted with a scope, an Arsenal, a shitload of ammo, and C4 that can be triggered remotely."

"Damn," Elsa muttered.

"The Russians put a Sako with a scope in his hands?" Heikonen asked.

Alissa nodded.

"Does it really matter what sort of firepower he has?" Elsa asked.

Before Heikonen could answer, Alissa interrupted. "It does."

"How so?"

"The Sako's a sniper's weapon," Heikonen said with confidence.

Alissa nodded. "Right. How would you proceed, if you were Alhomäki?"

"I'd take her out when she was speaking, in the amphitheater," Heikonen said. "She'll let down her guard once she's in front of the crowd."

"Which means?" Elsa asked.

"He'll shoot from elevation," Alissa observed, straining to find locations on the photograph matching her theory.

"Three choices. Here, here, and here," Heikonen interjected, pointing out locations on the photograph. "All have clear sightlines to the stage and the podium."

Elsa's face evinced skepticism. "Are you saying he's going to take a shot from what, a thousand meters away, give or take?"

Heikonen nodded. "He was trained for this. His service record indicates he's a sharpshooter. None of these shots would be impossible for a man of his training and skill." The detective paused. "Especially if the Sako is equipped with a bipod and a scope. Not a piece of cake but doable."

Alissa looked at Heikonen. "We find the van, we find where he's shooting from."

"True enough," Heikonen agreed. "I'll redirect my teams, narrow their focus to these three areas—"

Alissa raised her hand, silencing the detective. "You hear that?"

Heikonen and Vuolijoki tilted their heads.

"What?" Elsa asked.

"Choppers," Alissa whispered. "Assistant Director Saariaho and Uncle Leo are here."

CHAPTER SEVEN: The Warrior's Story. 6:00 p.m. Independence Day

I watch two French-made NH90 Tactical Transport Helicopters, circle, hover, and land in tandem. The cargo doors of the Finnish Army choppers open. The rotors stop. I am prone, eyeballing the helicopters as the lead bird disgorges its passengers. Mrs. Tarja Saariaho, Assistant Director of Immigration for Refugees and Migration, exits the chopper closest to my position.

Ah, I think, the Sako resting in its bipod, the two-legged platform providing stability as I view the scene through the Sako's scope, *this speech is of such importance that Director Leo Vuolijoki, the head of the SUPO, is here in person!*

There's too much cover for me to get a good view of the dignitaries as they walk towards camp headquarters. Someone with less experience might chance a shot while the Assistant Director is distracted by the crowd waving and screaming at her. *But that's iffy at best,* I think. *Patience is the best tool in a sniper's toolbox.*

I know the biographies of the great ones by heart. *Simo Häyhä,* the most celebrated sniper in the history of modern warfare—and a Finn—*had that trait in spades. The White Death killed over 505 Russians during the Winter War—259 confirmed long-distance kills using only a Mosin-Nagant with iron sights.* I consider the man's remarkable story. *His face blown to bits by a counter-sniper's explosive round and he retired from this nasty business early, but lived to the ripe old age of ninety-six! What a hero!*

I watch Acting Director Vuolijoki and his SUPO agents swivel their heads in nervous anticipation. *Of me. They know I'm out here. They're anticipating me!*

I ruminate on the exactitude required to be an effective sniper. *The Russians had some great ones. Like Roza Shanina, a beauty—if the old photographs are accurate—who fought on the Belorussian and East Prussian Fronts: 59 confirmed kills. She left a diary—a memorialization of her service, her fears, and her loves—published after she was killed in action. Such a woman!*

The second chopper empties. *Good! The press is here in force. When the Assistant Director topples from behind the*

290

podium, one clean shot to her forehead ending her pathetic life,
there will be plenty of witnesses with laptops and pens and pencils
and recorders and cameras to preserve her death for posterity. I
watch newsmen and newswomen waddle across snow dusted grass
following Saariaho and her detail until all of the visitors are inside
the camp's main office.

I lift my cheek from the stock, find a piece of tissue in a
pocket of my jacket, clean the scope's lens, and consider the
weather. *There's a breeze from the west,* I surmise, gauging the
gusts to be fifteen kilometers an hour. *I can adjust for that. The*
scope's elevation and windage marks are easily matched to the
terrain and weather. I'm a bit more than a thousand meters out.
Definitely not an easy shot but, given the Sako's accuracy when
firing .338 Lapua Magnum cartridges loaded at .250 grams, one I
can make. I itch my nose and consider other clandestine heroes of
World War II.

I've watched *Battle for Sevastopol,* a Russian flick
honoring the life and military career of Lyudmila Pavlichenko—a
historian turned sniper who took out 309 Germans—more than a
dozen times. Lyudmila rose to the rank of major, was befriended
by Eleanor Roosevelt, and, like The White Death, survived the
war, returning to her work as a scholar when Germany
surrendered. But she did not escape combat unscathed. She was
wounded in 1942: a circumstance that—along with her deadly
accuracy as a killer of Germans—caused Woody Guthrie to honor
her in song.

The wind kicks up dirty snow. *Damn. God surely is*
testing me this day! I retrieve the tissue again, wipe down the
scope's optics, and ponder the last of my heroes. *Five hundred*
and thirty-four kills! That Georgian knew his way around a rifle!
My reference is to Vasilij Kvachantiradze, who, because of his
ability to eradicate human targets from afar, was awarded the title
"Hero of the Soviet Union." He too survived the war but died
young, aged forty-three. *Any of those men and women could*
make this shot with their eyes closed!

I am not them. I am not a trained sniper and I've never
killed anyone. Not in battle. Not in civilian life. Not ever. In all my
deployments, I've never seen real combat: only its aftermath. Like
the scenes I witnessed in the Balkans and Central Africa. *That's*
true, I reflect. *But did I not win every shooting competition in the*

Jaegers? *It didn't matter if the target was at 50 or 100 or 300 meters. I hit it, dead center. God is with me today. God will ensure my eye is clear, my finger is smooth, my nerves are calm, and my breathing is steady.* I pull up the left sleeve of my jacket, look at the illuminated dial of my wristwatch, and nod. *Fifteen minutes.* I retrieve a pair of binoculars from a jacket pocket and survey the camp. "The Kajaani Jaegers are here," I say through a smile, lowering the field glasses and patting the Kajaani Jaeger unit patch affixed to my sleeve. *If I have to, I can fit right in.*

I remove my gloves and place the binoculars on top of them. I feel inside my jacket, locate a flashlight, turn it on, find my Bible, flip to a dog-eared page, and study a verse underlined in red.

The parents have eaten sour grapes
And the Children's teeth are set on edge.
But all shall die for their own sins;
The teeth of everyone who eats sour grapes
Shall be set on edge.

Good Old Jeremiah! I close the book, shut off the light, slip the flashlight and Bible into my jacket, pick up the binoculars, and watch Muslim men, women, and children exit former army barracks and stream towards the amphitheater. *They cannot fool me*, I think as I study the Syrian men—dressed in suits and ties and dress slacks and dress shoes escorting their wives, the women's heads concealed in hajibs or their faces covered in niqabs or their bodies wrapped from head to toe in burqas. The younger, more Westernized women scorn such limitations but still appear in modest dress with no skin displayed. Then there are the children, skipping alongside their parents, being dragged to a speech they will not understand. *No, they are not us. They are the spawn of Ishmael, Abraham's illegitimate son. Their line sprang from the loins of betrayal and deceit and adultery. But despite their inequity, I will not harm them: they have been granted safe passage by my government and I will honor that promise. But I will most assuredly send a message to the liberals and to the world—by cutting off the head of the snake, by assassinating Tarja Saariaho. From that one death, all will know that Muslims are no longer welcome in Finland.*

I lower the field glasses, set them on my gloves, wipe the sweat off my forehead with my sleeve, and settle in behind the Sako. Through the rifle's scope, I watch as Acting Director Vuolijoki, Assistant Director Saariaho, and a cadre of SUPO agents exit the camp's main office.

It's time.

CHAPTER EIGHT: 6:35 p.m. Independence Day

Assistant Director Tarja Saariaho waited in the blue room behind the stage of the Kajaani Refugee Center amphitheater. Her face was ashen. Her hands trembled as she sat in an upholstered chair, drinking from a glass tumbler. Water spilled as she raised the glass to her lips. The woman, young, tall, imperious, and professorial, was dressed in a white blouse, blue business suit, white nylons, black pumps, and a green winter coat. Her rail thin body was scrunched into the chair as she went over her speech—saved on an Android phone clasped firmly in her left hand—the glass of water shakily held in her right.

"It will be fine, Tarja," Acting SUPO Director Vuolijoki said quietly, "we have our best men and women on this. No harm will come to you."

The politician blinked and sought calm, but her cinnamon-colored eyes revealed uncertainty. She did not answer Vuolijoki immediately. Acting every bit the social worker—her chosen profession before running for office, winning a seat in Finland's unicameral parliament, and later, after she'd tired of electoral politics, accepting a position inside the Ministry of the Interior—Saariaho deliberated before responding. "I know. But a wiser woman would have canceled the event or appeared via TV," she said. She studied her speech one last time, closed the app, and placed her phone in a coat pocket. "But on this day, the one hundredth anniversary of our country, I must stand up for what I believe in." She paused. "Isn't that right, Leo?" Tarja touched Vuolijoki's thick, bare wrist with long fingers, seeking reassurance. "I've pushed hard for Finland to take in Muslim refugees and so, I must be here today, to speak to them, to reassure them that they are safe, that there is a place for them in Finland."

Leo stood next to the woman, listening intently to her rationalize why it was she was not turning tail and running back to Helsinki. *I don't agree with the woman's politics,* he thought. *Never agreed with the premise that it was a good idea to take in Somalis. And I sure as hell don't agree with taking in thousands of Muslims from another country torn apart by civil war.* The acting director's head was as bald as an egg, his formerly blond hair present only as faint eyebrows and a pencil thin mustache. Light reflected off his head as he considered his mission. *But despite our political differences,* he thought, *she's part of the government. I'll be damned if I let that asshole Alhomäki take out one of our own.*

Olavi Tanninen opened the door, entered the green room, and walked across the carpeted floor before stopping in front of Tarja. "It's standing room only," the operations manager said cheerily. "Every staff member and camp resident, along with a crowd of reporters and local dignitaries are waiting to hear from you, Madam Assistant Director, on this greatest of days for Finland. The Community Band is warming them up with patriotic music. It will be a wonderful night for you and for our country!"

The woman smiled ineffectually and rose from her chair. Her left hand snatched black leather gloves from the end table and stuffed them in a pocket of her coat. "May I leave my purse?" she asked, her stature towering above Leo and the two other SUPO agents in the room—one man, one woman—functioning as sentries. "Will it be secure?"

Olavi smiled down at Tarja. He was the only person in the room taller than the assistant director. "It will. I'll lock the door behind us."

Leo turned to his agents. "I'll lead. You two flank the assistant director. Tanninen can bring up the rear."

Olavi and the agents nodded.

"Alright then. Here we go," Vuolijoki said, leading them out the door.

As the group climbed a set of stairs onto the stage, the crowd cheering madly, the band playing a strained, uneven version of *"Maamme"* ("Our Land"), Olavi glanced towards the VIP section. Seats reserved for his wife, her brother, and Dr. Hampton remained unoccupied. *Where the hell is Thena? I can't believe she's about to miss the centennial celebration of Finland's independence. Something must have come up.*

The camp director—Jussi Orpo—was already behind the podium, the microphone adjusted to his slight height. The man beamed with pride at the arrival of Tarja Saariaho and Leo Vuolijoki. As Orpo returned his gaze to the crowd, the bright lights of the venue shining across a sea of Middle Eastern faces, camp staff, reporters, and local people of importance, Orpo felt confident and reassured despite the manifesto that Jere Alhomäki had released into the world. *This place is crawling with soldiers and police and SUPO agents. That man would be a fool to try anything here!*

Tarja and Leo advanced, stopped, shook Orpo's hand, and claimed two folding chairs behind the podium. Olavi sat as well. The SUPO agents providing security took up positions on either side of the seated officials.

Still no Thena or Ari or Doaks, Olavi noted.

Orpo exhorted the audience to sit. The crowd complied. The camp director began his address by reciting a short history of Finland's War of Independence; how the Germans aided Mannerheim and the Whites and how the Whites defeated the Reds championed by Lenin. How afterward the new nation, torn apart by unrest, took decades to heal before unifying to stop Stalin. For brevity—as much as national pride—the camp director skipped over the part where Finland aligned with the Nazis against the Soviet Union during the Continuation War, concentrating his rendition of the nation's story to achievements occurring since 1960. Education. Industry. Technology. Security. National Resources. Neutrality. These topics were briefly touched upon by Jussi Orpo as he cleverly avoided wading into the difficult choice Finland made to side with Hitler during WWII.

Orpo also reflected upon how Finland had changed for the better thanks to the men and women and children coming to Finland as refugees. "You have brought much culture and innovation and perspective to the Finnish people, giving us a diversity that we have never, until now, possessed. For that, my friends, I thank you and I thank Allah!"

The salutation to the God of Islam caused Leo Vuolijoki to wince. He was not a religious man. He'd long ago left the Lutheranism of his youth, choosing to spend Sunday fishing or hiking or hunting or skiing rather than listening to long-winded pastors expound on concepts of salvation and grace that, quite frankly, did not fit in with his worldview. *What a load of horseshit!* Though appalled by Orpo's appropriation of Islam's version of God and the camp director's praise for Muslim immigration, Leo held his tongue and concentrated his attention on the crowd, the hills surrounding the camp, and the undeniable certainty of danger.

When Orpo concluded his remarks, he introduced Tarja Saariaho. In cursory fashion, so as not to belabor the matter or prolong their time on stage, he briefly recounted the assistant director's educational and political career. When he was done providing a snapshot of the woman's professional life, he simply said, "Please welcome Assistant Director Tarja Saariaho."

The crowd rose to its feet, waving, cheering, and shouting accolades in Arabic and Finnish. Tarja stood, steadied herself with a hand on the back of her chair, and walked to the podium. Jussi Orpo gave Tarja Saariaho a pat on the shoulder, wished her well, and left the woman—her eyes large and open behind the thick lenses of her eyeglasses—alone and exposed.

CHAPTER NINE: 6:50 p.m. Independence Day

"**Shit.** How the hell did I miss this?"

Janine, Doaks, and Josiah were back in the operating room of the Kajaani Refugee Center Infirmary. Their patient, Ibrahim Al-Saad—the boy they had worked on a few hours earlier—was again under general anesthesia. His facial skin was open to his palate, the bright lights of the room illuminating a significant, uncontrolled bleed.

"Don't second guess your skills," Doaks said quietly, monitoring the child's respiratory and blood pressure and pulse numbers on electronic equipment. "He's strong, stable, and will survive any correction, Love," the Englishman said through his surgical mask. "Complications happen. You're a great surgeon, Janine. But even the great ones have to go back in from time to time."

Ari stood by his sister's side, a complete inventory of surgical tools at his disposal, ready to provide whatever Thena needed. The boy had done well, been discharged shortly after coming out of general anesthesia, and had been resting in his bed in the orphaned children's building when he started coughing up bright, red blood. His friend, Yana Nader, had helped him from their living quarters to the Tanninens' apartment and upon arrival, had pounded on the doctor's front door.

"My friend is dying!" Yana had shouted over and over and over again in English.

Janine opened the door, took inventory of Ibrahim's condition, grabbed her cell phone, called her team, and led the boys back to the infirmary, dressed in a red satin blouse, a hip-hugging black skirt, ebony nylons, and spiked scarlet heels that made her nearly as tall as her husband. Janine had been ready to go to the amphitheater and hear Mrs. Saariaho's remarks, her hair neatly combed, her makeup nearly finished, only needing to pull a tube of red lipstick across her lips to complete the look when Ibrahim Al-Said appeared at her door.

She had been thinking about her marriage, reflecting on her life with Olavi, when the pounding began. The commotion caused her to put down the tube of lipstick, clatter across the tile in her heels, open the door, observe Ibrahim, and lead the patient and his young friend back to the medical clinic, forgetting her overcoat and thoughts of seduction and touching and completion in her rush to save a life.

Now, here she was, re-stitching sutures that had proven insufficient to resist the boy's coughing, the jags a result of Ibrahim coming out of anesthesia.

"Not me, Doaks. I don't make these kinds of mistakes," she said softly, her gaze concentrating on her work, her feet aching from standing on concrete in stiletto heels.

In truth, the repair was not complicated. In a matter of minutes, Thena had opened up the boy's facial flap, found the problem, requested the proper thread, needle, needle holder, and forceps and stopped the bleeding. She put in a couple of extra sutures just to be sure but in relatively short order, the boy was out of danger.

"Good work, Thena," Ari said as they removed their surgical gloves, tossed them in the trash, stood side by side at the double sink in the prep room, and washed their hands. "You got that done in record time."

She smiled wearily, rubbed the left side of her chin against her blouse to calm a twitching facial nerve, and nodded. "We need to get a move on if we want to hear Saariaho."

Before she could wipe her hands with a paper towel, before Ari could reply, Doaks burst through the door. "There's been an attempt on the assistant director!" the Englishman blurted out. "She's been shot!"

"Oh my God!"

Doaks stared at the tall, black woman with pity.

"What? Is she dead?" Ari asked, drying his hands.

The Englishman dropped his gaze.

Janine's eyebrows knit into a frown. "What is it, man? What's happened?"

"Olavi was also hit. Same bullet. Passed through Saariaho's shoulder and entered Olavi's left chest."

Thena's eyes widened. Her lips pursed. Her fingers dug into the skin of her cheeks. "Is he ...?"

The Brit placed a hand on Thena's left shoulder. "He's hanging on. They're bringing them both in now so we can stabilize them for the chopper ride to Helsinki." Hampton paused. "Can you do that? Under the circumstances, I mean. Can you work on your own husband?"

Janine shut her eyes against the world. She thought about the afternoon, what they had shared, the love that she still felt for her Finnish husband. "I'll try," she murmured without opening her eyelids, tears washing her cheeks.

CHAPTER TEN: 6:45 p.m. Independence Day

Sergeant Vuolijoki found the Ford. "The van's here, parked behind a dumpster at a private school. About three hundred meters from the hill," Elsa said, steeling her nerves, speaking slowly and deliberately to Alissa over the shoulder mic of her portable radio. "We jimmied the door and checked inside. Empty except for a pile of clothes and a duffle bag. Duffle's empty too. Alhomäki must have changed clothes before dumping the van. Nothing else of evidentiary value. We're on our way to the trailhead. Going to check out the hill overlooking the camp. I think it's our best chance to find the guy ..."

Alissa nodded as she pictured her lovely, determined wife methodically inspecting the Ford for evidence. "Just keep yourself and your team safe," she whispered, concern edging into the exchange.

"Roger that."

Elsa followed three Jaegers, each soldier wearing standard winter camouflage, Kevlar helmets, Kevlar body armor, and carrying fully loaded Sako RK 62 assault rifles, and extra magazines. Elsa herself was armed with a Walther P99 semi-automatic 9mm handgun. She was wearing a standard-issue Finnish Police Department Kevlar vest over her department-issue jacket.

She liked the short, brawny feel of the pistol in her hand and was deadly accurate with it up to thirty meters. The Walther was equipped with a sixteen-round magazine and she carried two extra magazines on her utility belt in leather pouches alongside the Walther's black leather holster. In addition to the Kevlar vest and her jacket, she was wearing Sorels, wool socks, Thinsulate long underwear, a black turtleneck, blue jeans, a black watch toque, and black leather gloves against the cold.

"Looks like someone has been here today, ma'am," the lead Jaeger, a slack-faced Finn with razor-cut brown hair and brown eyes said quietly, pointing at boot prints on the ground. "One man, by the size and depth of the track. In but not out," he added as the soldiers and the policewoman stood at the trailhead.

Elsa nodded. "Let's hope it's our guy," she replied, "and that we get to him before he can take his shot."

The lead soldier—a corporal—led them up the steep, slippery trail. The Jaegers wore headlamps illuminating the rugged path. The soldiers carried their assault rifles loosely as they climbed. Sounds of the Kajaani Community Band playing the Finnish national anthem leaked from behind the hill. Stars punctuated the night sky. There was no moon. The wind came and went in gusts. The ground was covered in a thin layer of old snow insufficient for skiing but sufficient to reflect stars. The corporal held up his hand. The group stopped.

"Someone's speaking into a microphone," he said. "Can't make out the words, but it sounds like it's coming from the amphitheater."

Elsa nodded. "That would be the camp director, guy named Orpo. He's likely introducing the assistant director to the crowd. We need to find our guy. She'll be standing in the middle of the stage, out in the open, and vulnerable. How much further?"

The corporal stroked his whiskerless chin. "Not far. We're almost there," he said, before shifting his weight and moving out.

Thunderous applause echoed from somewhere over the crest of the hill. "Quickly," Elsa urged. "I think she's taking the microphone."

They were moving as fast as the mud and slop and melting snow would let them. Their boots slipped as they climbed. There was no sound to be heard save for the distant crowd, their own labored breathing, and the intermittent hooting of a male Ural owl roosting in a tree.

Hoot-hoot-hoooot.

"It seems ..."

Craack!

The corporal's observation was cut short by a gunshot.

"Shit!" Elsa said loudly, her caution destroyed by circumstance. "We're too fucking late."

CHAPTER ELEVEN: The Warrior's Story. 6:45 p.m. Independence Day

"**Damn** it to hell," I mutter.

It happened in the blink of an eye. I was calm. My breathing was controlled. My cheek was tight against the stock and my eye was fixed on the assistant director, the windage and elevation perfectly adjusted for the shot. *One goddamn shot!* I had Saariaho's head centered in the crosshairs and was squeezing the trigger to the point of no return when the big Finn tapped the woman on the shoulder. My target turned her head just as the rifle went off. Instead of striking the assistant director in the temple, blowing her brains out the back of her skull from a thousand meters and toppling her sorry ass onto the plywood stage, the bullet hit Saariaho below the collar bone and went straight through, tearing a hole in the left side of the big man's chest.

"Fuck!" I said as I watched both Saariaho and the stranger fall to the stage. "The point of this mission was to send a message by killing that miserable woman, not taking out some stupid Finn who couldn't stay out of the line of fire!"

I consider my next move. A twig snaps. *Might be a mountain hare or a roe deer.* I turn my head towards the noise to listen. *Footsteps!* I'm fairly certain that the police or Jaegers are coming for me. *Unlikely folks are out for a stroll in the dark.* I concentrate. *Three. No, four. Moving quickly. Must have heard the shot.* I gauge distance by the sound of boots crunching frozen leaves and debris. *They're on the trail.* I reach for the transmitter. I flip the safety, count down in my head, and blow the first package of C4.

Boooom!

I hear scurrying and yelling and surprise. I don't want to hurt the intruders, just disorient them. *They're only doing their jobs. Can't fault them for following orders.* I wait until my company reorganizes before blowing the second package.

Boooom!

"Shit!" The expletive comes from less than a hundred meters away. "He's tossing grenades at us!" The voice, though husky, is distinctly female.

303

"No, Sarge," a male replies. "That's the C4. It's just a diversion."

I tuck the transmitter in my jacket, leave the Sako behind, and bug out. *They'll be trying to get the wounded on a chopper. Doubt the Finn will make it. Looked like he took the bullet center mass. Shit. Too bad. Nothing can be done about it. But Saariaho still needs addressing.* I pat the holster holding the Arsenal. *Two shots to the head,* I remind myself, repeating the mantra of my planned alternative scenario. *Doesn't matter what happens to me.*

I hear my pursuers crashing through the woods. I scurry down the hillside. I discern disappointment in the voices of my foes when they realize I've slipped away. At the fence enclosing the camp, I crouch. I hear screams and yelling in Arabic and Finnish, but I can't discern one voice from another in the panic. I find the hole I cut earlier, scan the area, assure myself that there are no cops or Jaegers close at hand, remove the transmitter from my pocket and blow the remaining C4.

Boooom!
Boooom!

Power poles crash to the ground. I hear pops and arcs as the transmission lines come into contact with the perimeter fence. The refugee center's lights remain on. *That's fine,* I think, unsnapping the holster and liberating the Arsenal. *Hadn't intended on taking out the power—just causing a disturbance.* The handgun is cold in my bare hand. I realize I've left my gloves behind. *Don't need them,* I think as I duck through the hole in the fence, *not for what I'm about to do.*

The blown power poles have accomplished what I intended. The scene inside the camp is calamitous. Syrian men, women, and children stream towards the amphitheater's exits. *Perfect.* I slip the faux eyeglasses out of my jacket pocket, adjust my toque to lessen my profile, and join the throng. Ahead of me, I see four SUPO agents carrying two stretchers loaded with the wounded. Acting Director Vuolijoki—easily the second-most famous person at the event—barks orders and directs his agents: not towards the waiting choppers but towards a one-story building across the street from the amphitheater.

Didn't even know the camp had an infirmary. I ponder why, after hours of researching the refugee center online, that little detail failed to register. *Makes it a hell of a lot easier! She'll be like a skunk inside a trap once they make the building!*

I watch Vuolijoki scream at panicked civilians. An ocean of frightened Muslims parts to let the acting director and the stretchers pass. *Moses commanding the sea,* I observe as the SUPO chief obtains compliance in a shit storm. I stand across the street from the clinic in my Jaeger uniform. No one questions me. No one confronts me. Refugees and reporters and dignitaries and camp staff scurry past. I keep the pistol at the ready. *But I won't use it on a Finn, not a SUPO agent or a police officer or a Jaeger unless they fire first. I'm after that goddamned woman. She's the only one I want.* The crowd thins. The stretchers enter the clinic. Two SUPO agents assume positions outside the infirmary entrance as sentries.

What to do?

A clatter arises from behind me. I see three Jaegers following a woman in plainclothes, likely someone of rank and importance, running towards me. The woman is screaming at civilians to "Get the fuck off my road!"

Shit. I thought blowing the power poles would delay them. But that woman is one determined cop.

I look around, adrenaline rising, my nerves raw. I feel trapped, without a strategy. Then it hits me. *The clinic must have a rear entrance where they take out the trash and receive supplies.* I move towards the building, avoiding eye contact with the sentries. I round the corner and smile. *The back door is unguarded!*

I edge along the building's brick wall, the Arsenal's safety off, the weapon ready to fire. I arrive at the rear door and try the handle. *Unlocked.* As thorough as Leo Vuolijoki is, he's preoccupied with saving the victims. He's failed to ensure that the clinic's second entrance is manned or that the door is locked. I crack open the door and peer inside. *An empty hallway.* I cock my head and listen. I hear voices coming from behind closed doors. But before I can enter the building, the crunching of boots on gravel draws my attention outside.

"Drop the weapon! Get down on the ground!" the policewoman commands from the across the road. "Do it now or I'll shoot!"

One chance, I think, not moving, not turning my head to address the cop. I jerk open the door and dive onto cement.

Bang-bang-bang!

Bullets strike drywall inside the building. I reach up with my left hand, slam the door shut, and slide the deadbolt in place.

Knowing the commotion will draw attention from agents inside the clinic, I regain my feet and move towards the sounds of doctors and nurses trying to save lives.

I clear myself of emotion and try to remember the "why" behind what I'm about to do. *Madam Assistant Director, your time has come.*

CHAPTER TWELVE: 6:50 p.m. Independence Day

Alissa heard the detonations while providing security at the amphitheater. Once the melee erupted, she moved to assist local police and elements of the Kajaani Jaegers in evacuating the venue. "Leo, you take care of the wounded and I'll see to it that these folks are safely out of danger," Alissa said as she watched SUPO agents pull stretchers out of an ambulance parked behind the amphitheater stage. "I'll join you at the infirmary when things settle down."

Leo nodded towards the choppers. "After the docs have checked them out and tell us they're stable, we'll get them on the birds and in the air. Pretty sure both will need surgery in Helsinki."

"Good luck," Alissa said as she waded into the crowd, leaving her boss to attend to the fallen. "Private!" she barked at a square-jawed Jaeger standing wide-eyed in the middle of chaos, "make yourself useful. Direct people to the exits. Ensure that order's maintained, that no one gets hurt."

The soldier snapped out of his funk, nodded, and joined his comrades directing traffic. An army sergeant approached Alissa and stopped by her side as people streamed by. "What the hell happened?" he asked in a controlled voice, the man obviously well trained and, by his gruffness and even-keeled nature, a veteran.

"What happened, Sergeant, is exactly what we didn't want to happen. That bastard was able to take out Assistant Director Saariaho. Also hit Mr. Tanninen, though I don't think he was a target. Just unlucky."

"One of our own did this?"

Alissa nodded.

"Fuck." The soldier watched civilians, now organized and protected by a full platoon of Kajaani Jaegers and dozens of local cops and SUPO agents, move towards the front gate. Realizing that he'd just cursed in front of a federal agent, the sergeant sought to make amends. "Sorry about that, ma'am."

Alissa ignored the curse. "Can you keep this crowd moving? I'd like to follow up with Director Vuolijoki." Though she was speaking directly to the soldier, her eyes were following the stretchers and the SUPO agents as they entered the infirmary across the gravel road.

"No problem, ma'am. We've got this."

Alissa spun on her heels and moved out at a near run. She nodded at the sentries—who recognized her—grasped the handle and opened the front door to the clinic. Before she could step inside, she heard three distinct "pops" from the rear of the building.

"Gunfire!" she shouted, unsnapping a flap and removing a Belgian-made, Browning Hi-Power BDA 9mm semi-automatic from its holster. She held the handgun, standard issue for the Finnish Army but utilized by the chief inspector as a matter of pride and preference—it was her father's pistol, one that he carried as an officer in the army—in her right hand as she assessed the situation. "You two go around back. It sounds like that's where the commotion is coming from."

"Yes ma'am," the closest agent, a lanky, dark-haired Sami, said, nodding to his companion. "Let's go, Niemi!" The second agent, a woman, her dull hazel eyes confident, her blond hair cropped short, her curves confined by the Kevlar vest she was wearing over her wool coat, "SUPO" clearly stamped across the protective gear, also nodded but did not reply as the two agents headed towards danger.

Alissa entered the building. The foyer was bathed in LED lighting. She shut the door and moved down a hallway, stepping lightly, trying to avoid making noise.

"Utrio, do you read me?"

The chief inspector recognized Elsa's voice.

"Roger, Sergeant," Alissa whispered.

"Where are you?"

"Inside the clinic. Just past the foyer and headed towards the surgical suite."

There was a pause. "He's coming your way. Alhomäki is inside the building and headed your way."

Alissa glanced at the Browning to ensure the safety was off. It was. "Roger that. Is he hit?"

"Negative. I missed him. He made it inside and then locked the door. There's a squad of us back here—three Jaegers, the two SUPO agents you sent to assist, and me. I'm sending the

Jaegers and the agents back 'round front. I'll keep an eye on the rear door in case he backtracks."

"Got it. Stay safe. No hero bullshit."

"I think you mean 'no heroine bullshit.'"

Alissa grinned nervously at the correction. "Roger that."

The radio went silent. Alissa Utrio heard sounds of discussion and debate from somewhere in front of her. "Examination Rooms and Surgical Suite" was neatly stenciled in Finnish and Arabic on the door closest to her. She recognized Leo's voice coming from behind the closed door. As Alissa reached for the doorknob, she heard grit scratching tile. *Footsteps.* She turned towards the noise and raised the Browning. Alissa's right arm trembled as she raised the heavy pistol, slipped her index finger inside the trigger guard, and waited.

CHAPTER THIRTEEN: 6:50 p.m. Independence Day

"**Goddamn** it to hell!" Janine had said, placing the business end of her stethoscope against the left side of her husband's throat. "There's no fucking pulse!" she screamed, her professional demeanor and Baptist upbringing destroyed by the facts apparent in front of her. "Get the paddles and a syringe of adrenaline," she commanded, trying to reassert professional calm, trying to sound more controlled, more in tune with her role as healer, not wife.

Her brother didn't move.

"Damn it, Ari, are you deaf? Olavi has no pulse! We need to act now; use the defibrillator to bring him back."

Thena's words rushed out. Her hands trembled. She bit her lower lip. Blood leaked from behind her surgical mask and onto her husband's inert body as she stood over Olavi, ready to do battle with God.

Julie Chambers, the Canadian OB-GYN—whose tour in Kajaani was nearly up—and Doaks Hampton stood across the gurney from Janine, shaking their heads.

"Janine," Chambers said quietly, "he was gone before he hit the deck. Look at the wound. The bullet ripped through the middle of his heart and took out the aorta for good measure."

Doaks touched the woman's left wrist with pasty, dainty fingers. "Jules is right. There's no heart left to pump."

Janine had wanted to protest, to object. But even in the depths of despair, she was a scientist and, looking at the gaping wound in her husband, the truth could not be denied. *Bits and pieces of his great heart exploded upon impact and are plainly visible in the exit wound. Fuck.*

She placed her head on her husband's chest. Olavi was not breathing. The reality of him being taken suddenly, with no chance to say goodbye, drove her to her knees. She bawled and wailed and hit her face with her fists. *There was no reason for it. None. The madman's beliefs had no basis in reality. He had no business targeting Assistant Director Saariaho. These people are not a danger. They pose no threat to the Finns, their country, or their way of life. They are simply here, trying to escape death and destruction and persecution in their own homeland. Olavi's death accomplishes nothing. It was a senseless act of violence that cannot be reconciled with my belief in a loving, caring God.*

Rather than fall into a rabbit hole of apostasy, Janine concentrated her thoughts on the fact that the man who had done this was still at large. *I hope SUPO finds him and makes him die a slow, painful death for what he's done.*

Minutes later in Exam Room No. 2, the surgical team—minus a distraught and inconsolable Janine who remained in Exam Room No. 1 with her husband—provided care to Tarja Saariaho. Though Tarja's were wounds sutured and bandaged and her fractured clavicle was stabilized, the woman continued to moan in agony despite the hypo of Demerol Ari had injected into her thigh and additional, non-narcotic pain medication infusing into her body by way of an IV bag and line. Though the fracture had been reduced, the damage caused to the clavicular bone and adjacent tissue required surgery beyond what the refugee center's infirmary could offer. However, the choppers could not leave with Jere Alhomäki still at large and so, Tarja waited in the infirmary until the would-be assassin was either neutralized or eliminated.

Leo Vuolijoki stood beside the stricken woman's bed. His sidearm remained holstered. Two SUPO agents manned the door to the exam room with pistols drawn. An additional agent remained with Janine in Olavi's room, her handgun also free of its holster. Two more SUPO agents stood guard at the doorway allowing entrance to the suite: their handguns locked, loaded, and ready to block Alhomäki's access to his target.

"How are you feeling, Tarja?" Leo asked, his voice even and without sympathy. The man was dedicated to duty, to serving the assistant director, but he was not about to expound or elaborate or empathize or engage in idle conversation.

"Terrible. The pain's getting worse," Tarja moaned, her left shoulder splinted, the arm in a sling, the bullet wound bandaged, Dr. Chambers having worked quickly to provide basic triage care. "Can't you give me something more for the pain?"

Doaks Hampton, a surgical mask dangling from his neck exposing his uncommonly bland features, stood over the woman, slightly irked that she was complaining about pain when Olavi Tanninen was dead. "You've already had enough Demerol and IV Tylenol to deaden a moose," the Englishman said, his Finnish infected by having lived his life within sight of the Thames. "I can't risk Nurse Tate giving you another hypo. You'll just have to grin and bear it until you get to Helsinki, I'm afraid."

"Have you been able to reach my husband?" Tarja asked, gritting her teeth as she spoke.

"No, ma'am," Leo replied. "Headquarters is on it, but we're having a bit of an issue reaching him in Norway."

She had told Leo where her husband was staying in rural Norway on holiday with their children. The girls and their father were enjoying fresh, deep Norwegian powder snow as they downhill and cross-country skied. "I was supposed to join them after giving my speech," Tarja lamented.

Bang-bang-bang!

"What the hell?"

"That's gunfire!" Leo yelled, unsnapping the flap of his holster and pulling his 9mm Glock 17 free of leather. "From the rear of the building. Sandstedt and Nevonen!" he barked at the two agents protecting Tarja, "stay here. Don't let anyone in except me. Got that?"

The two agents, Nevonen short and wide with black hair and brown eyes, forty-something and on the verge of pension; and Sandstedt, nearly the same height but younger and female, nodded.

"Got it, Sir," Sandstedt replied with certainty.

"And Doc, you stay put, understand? As long as you're inside this room, no harm will come to you."

Doaks nodded.

As the acting director left the room, he encountered Dr. Chambers sitting in a chair, staring at her lap, tears wetting her cheeks, and trembling. The two agents securing the outer office swung towards Leo, pistols at the ready, as he entered the space unannounced.

"I heard it too, Boss," the taller agent said, relaxing a bit, his eyes seeking permission to confront the killer. "Want backup?"

Leo shook his head. "Stay here," he said with authority. "We've got plenty of folks outside this suite. Dr. Chambers stay with these men. Understand? Do not leave this room."

The Canadian doctor pursed her lips. Her face was ashen. Her eyes denoted fear. "Is he inside the building?"

"Don't know. And for your sake, I don't want you to find out. Stay put, alright?"

Chambers nodded but did not reply.

Leo noticed that the doctor's hands were shaking, that she seemed incapacitated by circumstance. As he walked past Dr. Chambers, he touched her lightly on the left shoulder. "You'll be fine. I'm not about to let that asshole hurt anyone else on my watch," the SUPO director said with confidence, reaching for the doorknob, opening the door, and stepping into the unknown.

CHAPTER FOURTEEN: 6:50 p.m.
Independence Day

Inside Exam Room No. 1, the disturbance sounded like china plates being smashed on the floor.

"What the hell was that?" Janine asked sitting in a plastic chair across from her husband's corpse. Olavi's skin had grown cold and foreign to her touch. Not her touch as a physician—for she had placed hands on her share of dead folk during her training and her practice—but her touch as a wife, lover, and friend. Janine had been unable to continue holding Olavi's hand once his body cooled. And so, she had taken up her vigil in an uncomfortable chair. Waiting. Waiting for it to be over. Waiting for the danger to pass. Waiting for Olavi's body to be taken to the medical examiner for the official and redundant determination of the cause of his death. And later, waiting for the undertaker, waiting to select a coffin, and waiting to determine the when of Olavi's funeral. She knew the where. She knew she would meet with Pastor Filip Berge, the Norwegian-born preacher who spoke professorial Finnish while leading the congregation of St. Bartholomew's Evangelical Lutheran Church, the steepled, clapboarded country church that Olavi and Thena attended, there being no Baptist preacher in town to Janine's liking. Her husband's funeral service would be in the sanctuary of St. Bart's and he would be buried in the town's cemetery across the road from the little white church.

"That's gunfire, ma'am. Director Vuolijoki has it under control," a SUPO agent, a nondescript, thirty-something, round-faced dirty blond said. "We're on lockdown until he gives the all clear."

"How do you know this?" Janine asked, wiping tears from her face, straightening up in the chair as she addressed the man.

The agent shifted his eyes to his shoulder mic. "Radio, ma'am. Director Vuolijoki gave those very instructions before he left to check on things."

I must be completely out of it, must have lost my mind. Understandable given Olavi is stone-cold dead, his eyes closed, and his hands placed across his body in supplication by my brother. I didn't hear the radio. Didn't hear the officer speaking to anyone on the radio. But there it is.

Her mind wandered. In what seemed a tortured digression but was, in reality, only a brief interlude—perhaps a minute, perhaps a few seconds—Janine examined and considered the fact that her husband was dead because they had returned to Finland, the place of his birth, to aid and comfort Syrian Muslims. After milling around the circumstances of how she and Olavi came to Kajaani, her attention fixed upon discussions she had with a Muslim cleric.

It was a bucolic summer day. She'd just finished her morning ride. She was walking, pushing the Trek to cool down. The sun had climbed above the pines bordering the camp's perimeter fence. The sky was cloudless, open, endless, and suggested heat. As Janine pushed her Top Fuel 9.8 along the sidewalk, she found herself in front of the camp's mosque, a modest, single-story building without adornment—save for a sign in Finnish and Arabic proclaiming the structure to be a sacred space. A Syrian flag flew in the mosque's front yard on a pole that once held the unit insignia of a company of Finnish reserve infantry.

As Janine passed the mosque, immigrant men who had been kneeling and facing Mecca were rolling up their prayer rugs and speaking to each other in Arabic. The tone of the discourse was respectful, as one would expect after engaging in a dialogue with God. Janine stopped, admired the solemn, dignified men and boys and noticed, as she resumed pushing the Trek, a group of Syrian women and girls also rising from prayer rugs spread over dewy grass. Her gaze fixed on their flowing, modest, colorful clothing. As she watched the women, Janine didn't appreciate a wizened man, a Syrian of slight build, standing next to her.

"Madam Doctor," the ancient one said, his voice serene, his Finnish clipped. "I see you are interested in our ways," he continued politely, switching to English, a language he had learned in his native Syria while attending university. The man's teeth were exposed by a sincere smile—the brilliance of his teeth matching the immaculate white *kufi* on his head.

Though his almond-shaped eyes exuded respect, kindness, and curiosity, his unsolicited approach caught Janine off guard. She was startled and, truth be told, slightly embarrassed by the man's manifestation. Still, she managed to be respectful in her

315

reply. "I am. I too am a believer, though my prophet of choice is Jesus the Christ," she replied.

"And yet," the craggy-faced man observed, "you are interested in learning about Islam?"

Janine nodded. "I've been working with you folks for over a year," she said. "I've read parts of The Quran, tried to research the faith online, tried to come to a place of understanding."

As the old man tilted his brown head, thin strands of white hair escaped the brim of his kufi. He stood against the early morning light in a white muslin suit, his feet covered in black leather sandals in a style not far removed from footwear either The Prophet or the Son of Man would have preferred. "And so, you have questions?"

Janine had been exhausted from her ride. Her bike helmet hung from the Trek's handlebars by its chinstrap. Her springy black and gray hair glistened from perspiration. She sipped from a water bottle, looked away from the man, trying to figure out a way to disengage. *I respect Muslims as people of deep faith*, she thought, still avoiding the holy man's intense gaze, *but I'm not about to convert!* But she found the elder's kindness and empathy, traits that poured off him like rain shed by a slicker in a storm, compelling. She nodded.

"I am the imam of this congregation," he said softly, his teeth clicking as he spoke, "and I would be happy to answer your questions about my faith over tea in the office of the mosque whenever you like."

And so, their friendship had begun. Janine spent hours sitting in the imam's office, reading and dissecting and discussing verses from both The Bible and The Quran with Imam al-Khalid. She found, after months of study and dialogue, more common ground with the cleric than she thought was possible given the constant drumbeat of media reports of Jihadist violence wrought by ISIS and other radical Islamist groups. She came to appreciate that much of what drives modern terrorists is a misguided twisting of The Quran. After spending time with the imam, Janine understood that ISIS and its ilk pluck verses from their Holy Book out of context, appropriating The Prophet's words to fit their own agenda and worldview in a manner akin to how judgmental, Xenophobic Christians select verses of The Bible in support of their self-appointed moral authority.

In the end, what Janine was left with, after months of conversations, cups of hot herbal tea, and Muslim hospitality, was the knowledge that one *sura*, 25:63, encapsulates the Prophet's theology in a way very similar to Jesus' "one commandment":

The worshippers of the All-Merciful are they who tread
gently on the earth,
and when the ignorant address them,
they reply, "Peace."

Days before Olavi's death, Janine had sipped tea with the imam and talked openly and frankly about the pain the events of September 11 had caused America. She revealed the emptiness in her heart and her anger and rage at Islam that welled up when she visited the 9/11 Memorial in New York. She had made that pilgrimage several times—alone and with Olavi—when she lived in the city. "Each time," she confessed to Abdul said al-Khalid, "I found that I could not forgive. I felt nothing but hate. Not just for the men who flew the airplanes and killed innocent men, women, and children. But all of those who profess The Faith of Muhammad."

The imam had touched the brown skin of the top of Janine's right hand like a father, his eyes filled with tenderness. "I understand. It is like how I felt when the Americans invaded Iraq. My Sunni brothers and sisters suffered much for the sins of men who were, in truth, radicals raised and educated and indoctrinated in Saudi Arabia and Iran and Yemen and Afghanistan and Pakistan." He stopped and looked away from her, the pain of remembering too great. "And then, to make matters worse, the civil war started in Syria and, despite the fact I am Sunni—the majority branch of Islam—I found myself and my family persecuted by the Alawites and Shiites—minority sects who control the reins of power and, as a consequence, the tanks and airplanes and guns. We held on, kept out of sight, until the *Mukhabarat*, Assad's secret police, began detaining, torturing, and ultimately killing my congregation, my friends, and my family. It was then," Abdul said quietly, his voice having grown as delicate as a child's, "that we chose to leave. Unfortunately, my wife and my son remain in Germany. I am hoping they will be allowed to

317

immigrate to Finland. That is our dream. But separation is, for now, our reality."

Janine had lowered her head. Tears dripped onto the imam's desk. "I am so sorry," she said, her own voice as fragile her teacher's. "I had no idea."

"We will survive. Our faith and our nation will survive. Time is not impacted by human caprice. It was once said," he continued, standing to his full height to place The Quran back in its proper place on a shelf behind his desk, "by a Christian, no less: 'Never fear the future since God is already there.'" The holy man smiled and nodded as Janine closed her dog-eared Bible and her paperback copy of The Quran, slid the books and a notebook and a pen into her green canvas satchel, and stood up to take her leave. "These have been good discussions, Dr. Tanninen. Good for me," he said wryly, "and I hope, good for you."

"They have been of great benefit to my understanding of Islam, Teacher. I no longer hate the people who are truly guided by The Prophet—only those who have misappropriated Islam for their own purposes."

He nodded and opened the door. Outside, they had been greeted by rain. Janine was not dressed for weather, so the imam loaned her his raincoat. They had not seen each other since. She still had the imam's slicker hanging on a hook in the front hall of her apartment.

Bang-bang!

Two shots. Louder than the first three. Not like the sounds of plates breaking but clearly gunfire and close at hand!

Silence ... The crackling of a radio ...

The SUPO agent guarding Janine whispered into his shoulder mic. All Janine Tanninen heard was "Roger that." There was an interlude—a moment of silence—before the young agent closed the radio connection and looked at her. His face relaxed and the tension in the room vanished when the SUPO agent turned to Janine and said, "They got him; They got the sonofabitch."

Alissa did not wait. She did not alert Jere Alhomäki to her presence. The assassin rounded the corner holding the Arsenal semi-automatic in his right hand, but his apparition did not

318

intimidate her. And she made no attempt to take him alive. When Alhomäki presented himself as a target, Alissa identified him—despite the artificial hair color and the stage prop glasses and the fake unit patch on his winter fatigue jacket—as the threat she was duty bound to neutralize.

It dawned on her, as she aimed her Browning at the former soldier, that Alhomäki likely recognized her from her visit to his social club in Helsinki. *He remembers.* But that was it. There were no speeches. No discussions of morality or politics or religion were held. There was only an instant of clarity and understanding between them before Alissa pulled the trigger.

The bullets hit the man with force, causing Alhomäki to drop his weapon and collapse. Alissa kept her Browning aimed at the assassin. Blood leaked from two neat holes in the man's forehead as he twitched unnaturally on the floor. Alissa kicked the Arsenal away, bent down, noted the ever-enlarging pool of scarlet pooling on the linoleum behind the man's head, looked into Alhomäki's unfocused eyes, and whispered, "I got you, you sonofabitch."

After checking the man's carotid and confirming he was dead, Alissa realized she was not alone.

"You should have waited for backup."

Alissa was startled until she recognized the voice chiding her. "Acting Director ... "

Leo Vuolijoki slid his Glock into its holster, snapped the flap, and pointed to the unit insignia on the dead man's uniform. "Bastard covered every detail. Brilliant. Too bad he went off the rails. Happens, you know, to folks who hold too tightly to their own version of faith."

Others joined them in the hallway.

"That him?" Doaks asked.

Leo nodded.

"He say anything before someone put two in his noggin?" Elsa asked. "Your shooting, Uncle Leo?"

The acting director shook his head. "Afraid not. On both counts. Your better half took him out before he could offer up a confession."

Elsa considered the people assembled in the corridor. "Where's Mr. Tanninen, his wife, and Mrs. Saariaho?"

Alissa's face slackened. "Mr. Tanninen didn't make it. His wife is with his body."

"Shit," Elsa muttered. "And Saariaho?"

"Exam Room No. 2. She'll be fine."

"No bloody sense to it," Doaks added in English. "No fucking, bloody sense to any of it."

Leo removed a red handkerchief from his jacket, picked up the Arsenal, wiped Alhomäki's blood from the grip, and handed the pistol to Alissa. "I believe this is yours."

Chief Inspector Utrio shook her head. "No, you keep it. I don't want anything to remind me of what happened here."

EPILOGUE

January 1945 (Papoose Lake, Minnesota)

Andrew Maki sat in a homemade tamarack chair beneath the snow-covered roof of his cabin's front porch. The modest structure—constructed of logs joined with dovetailed corners—overlooked the frozen surface of Papoose Lake north of Duluth. It was dawn, the beginning of another day in the old man's long life. A diminished sun climbed above scrubby forest. New growth aspen and birch and balsam trees merged to create an irregular black wall along the lake's far shoreline.

Maki was sixty-one years old, having immigrated to the United States as a young man from Paltamo, Finland in search of adventure. He'd come to America with experience hard-earned and ingrained in his young back and limbs from working the mines of sub-Arctic Norway. During the immigrant's search for a new home, he had labored on the wharves and docks of Duluth, sweated in the dusty iron mines of Soudan and Ely, and struggled to make a life with his truest love, Elin Gustafson, a college-educated teacher, writer, and suffragette, in Hancock, Michigan. When their relationship soured, Maki returned to Duluth and took jobs in northeastern Minnesota's mines and forests before leaving America to fight Germans in France.

After the Great War, his soul permanently scarred but his wounds healing, Anders Alhomäki— who Anglicized his name from Anders Alhomäki to Andrew Maki—had settled down with a tall, angular widow, Heidi Genelli, the mother of an eight-year-old son. Together, they built the farm abutting the marshy shores of Papoose Lake and ran the Wolf Lake Logging Camp until the good timber was depleted and Andrew's considerable strength was spent. With the pine forest gone, the logging camp was shuttered, then razed. The couple sold off the desolate stumpage to eastern speculators who believed there was iron ore beneath the topsoil. In truth, there was no treasure located on the former logging camp—only gravel and sand and rocks and muskeg and peat and water were discovered between open sky and the land's foundational Canadian Shield. The big shot speculators paid a premium for disappointment, but the sale of the logging camp, along with Heidi resuming the management of a café in Aurora— an enterprise she once shared with her Finnish father, Jerome

Seppo—Jerome having passed from a stroke after reading the headlines of the *Duluth News Tribune* on December 8, 1941—gave the Makis money to live independently and allowed Andrew to raise crops, cattle, pigs, and chickens without fear of economic catastrophe.

Andrew scrutinized the veil of snow covering the adulterated land with full knowledge that he had been part of the army of men who had logged northern Minnesota's old-growth timber like ants devouring an unattended sandwich. *Sisu*, he thought. *Fortitude. Guts. Perseverance.* The old man considered the Finnish laborers and miners and dockworkers and loggers he had worked with in Finland, Norway, and America. *There really is no one word in English that equates to "sisu." But we Finns seem to have, from the quiet to the boisterous, from male to female, plenty sisu to go around. Sometimes,* the old man thought, *our ability to tough it out turns into simple insanity. The melancholia and inward reflection that fuels us also can isolate us and make us crazy.*

The case of Thomas Sukanen—an immigrant miner from Biwabik who abandoned his wife and children, traipsed off to Saskatchewan, failed as a farmer, and spent years trying to build a steamboat in the middle of the prairie he planned to launch in a nearby river and sail back to Finland—was an extreme example of sisu run amok. *Plumb nuts, that Finn was. Died insane, in a Moose Jaw sanitarium. Penniless, starved, and alone but confident that he could build an ocean-going ship and single-handedly sail across the North Atlantic. Now that's sisu!*

After ruminating on the nature of Finnishness, Andrew turned his attention to news of the day.

Damn Germans, he thought. *I was sure once the Allies landed in Normandy, Hitler's boys would pack it in. How wrong I was!*

The *Duluth News Tribune*—Andrew had the daily paper mailed to the post office in Brimson, which required him to drive fifteen miles of potholed, gravel roads in a world-weary 1935 Ford pickup to retrieve his mail and a day-old newspaper before retracing his route—was full of dispatches detailing a last-ditch Axis offensive in the Ardennes.

They're calling it the Battle of the Bulge. It looks like Hitler threw everything he had, except what's tied up on the

Eastern Front, against our boys. I doubt he'll succeed. I hope to God Timmy makes it out alive. I lost Heidi. I can't stomach losing our son.

Timmy—named after Tim Laitila, a friend and co-worker of Maki's who died in a logging accident thirty years earlier—was in the 101st Airborne. He'd been due to come home, his time in Europe over. *But then the goddamned Germans sprang a surprise and the 101st was ordered to Bastogne. Soon after Timmy and his mates arrived in Bastogne, the city was surrounded, cut off from the Allies. But our boys held! Now the tide has turned, and the Germans are on the run. But I've heard nothing from Timmy. I can only hope that he's unharmed.*

Their daughter Lila lived with friends in Aurora during the week while attending high school. Every Friday afternoon, Andrew drove the Ford into town, parked in front of the school, and waited for his daughter.

Two winters earlier, Heidi Maki had slipped on ice outside an Aurora grocery store, fell, hit her head, and died of a swollen brain in Duluth's St. Mary's Hospital. Until her mother's unexpected passing, Lila had been the most cheerful, carefree of girls. *Now,* Andrew considered, standing up from his chair, the tendons of his aging legs as tight as piano strings, *my little girl is sad, mournful, and depressed. The loss of her mother changed Lila's outlook on life despite the Catholic faith her mother instilled in her.*

Andrew leaned over, picked up a cup, and downed the last dregs of coffee. *I wish I had Heidi's belief in a supreme, benevolent, creator. Or that His son is our intermediary: the path through which eternity may be secured. Or that the son's earthly mother holds some special, unique place in the hierarchy of the universe such that petitions to her can improve our lives.*

Andrew opened a pine door and entered the cabin, intent on rinsing out his coffee mug and dressing for an early-morning ski.

The cup cleaned and turned upside down on the kitchen counter, he padded in stocking feet into his bedroom. The bed was unmade. A dresser stood along a log wall, its top crowded with bills and ledgers and papers, including stacks of letters: letters from Finland, from Andrew's two sisters and his mother that had once been secreted in a cigar box back when Andrew Maki was a

young man and cared about such things. Now, the old letters were
bound together by string and stacked randomly atop the chest of
drawers.

Reaching into the top drawer of the dresser for a second
pair of socks, an envelope caught Andrew's eye. He slipped the
yellowed envelope from its twine binding, opened it, removed the
letter, and reread it.

Anders Alhomäki
Duluth, Minnesota
June 30ᵗʰ, 1914

Dearest Brother:
I have not heard from you since you left Hancock and returned to
Duluth. Your last correspondence was filled with sadness
regarding Miss Gustafson. From your report, it sounds like you
were simply attempting to defend your friends and that any
brawling you engaged in was done in self-defense. Of course, I am
only a nurse, not a lawyer. What do I know of such things?

Anyway, you said that you were going to try and win Elin's
hand by returning to Duluth. I hope that you are able to woo her
back or, if that is not possible, move on with your life.

Things here remain largely unchanged except that Ronja
and Erno are expecting their second child. Their first, Ailia, is
delayed in her development though no official diagnosis has yet
been made. Despite the challenges they face with Ailia, our sister
and her husband are joyfully awaiting the big day!

Mother remains on the farm and is excited to expand her
role, Christ be praised, as a doting grandmother.

I continue to work in Helsinki in the maternity ward.
Given the difficulties Ronja has experienced with Ailia, I am trying
to convince her to come and stay with me when she is close to her
time. That way, Auntie would be able to deliver her own nephew
or niece! But so far, Ronja has resisted my suggestion.

I do have a bit of sad news to share with you. Do you
remember that Kale girl you once had an eye for? Anneli Balzar?
Well, I had forgotten all about her until I read the Helsingin
Sanomat *a few weeks ago. There, buried inside, away from the*
headlines, was an article about a Canadian ship—the Empress of
Ireland. *Seems that the ship, bound from Quebec to England, had*

a number of Finns aboard. Somehow—there remains much dispute as to the exact circumstances—a Norwegian collier crashed headlong into the Empress, opening her up and causing her to sink. 1,012 passengers and crew died in the accident. Reading the list of Finns who were lost, I came across Miss Balzar's married name (I'd heard a while back that her husband was a Tammi from Oulu) along with the names of her two children. I later learned that their bodies were recovered and returned to Finland for internment in a Kajaani graveyard. What is so upsetting to me is that this disaster got faint attention in Finland even though many Finns died in the sinking of the Empress, reminiscent of the loss we suffered when the Titanic went down. Finns, you will recall, died then as well, though far more noise was made about that tragedy.

But I digress. A few weeks after reading the article, I ran into some Gypsy women selling craftwork on the Helsinki pier and asked if any of them knew Anneli Tammi. One did. The woman explained that Mrs. Tammi had left Finland for Canada with her children to avoid Mr. Tammi's fists only to decide that she couldn't live without him. Mrs. Tammi and her girls were headed back to Finland to reconcile with their husband and father but sadly, never made it.

I am sorry to be the bearer of bad news, but I thought that, since I remember Anneli being your first love and all, you would want to know.

Please write and tell me how it goes with Miss Gustafson. And no, I do not have a beau of my own! There are several gentlemen interested in your dark-haired sister but, as you know, I am very particular and thus far, none of them have made a lasting impression.

If that changes, you will be the first to know!
Your loving sister,
Helmi Alhomäki

Andrew put on a second pair of stockings and his boots. Outside, he stomped his feet and, one boot at a time, slid the Chippewas into leather bindings. He was dressed warmly in a union suit, the socks, a flannel shirt, wool pants, a wool coat, leather choppers, and a black toque. With stout maple ski poles—the bark peeled and the shafts varnished—in each mittened hand, Andrew Maki pushed off.

"Snow's good. Fresh, loose, and not too deep," Andrew observed as he found his stride and cut a track along the bulrushes and black alders defining the lake's shoreline. Exercise was something Andrew believed he needed given that he no longer logged or mined and given that, other than feeding and watering the animals or shoveling snow or hauling wood, there was little in the way of physical work to be done on the farm during winter. As Andrew glided across the snow, his thoughts turned to his friends, his family, his history, and his legacy, such as it was.

Joey is doing so well, he thought, stopping to admire a pileated woodpecker hammering mercilessly on a dead white pine, the racket created by the exuberant bird the only noise to be heard. Andrew's reference was to his stepson, Heidi's eldest child. *And Ada. Ah! Such a beautiful, tender child!* It was unusual for the Finn to outwardly express emotion but the remembered image of Joey's daughter, the product of a near-perfect marriage to a Finnish girl from New York Mills—Inari Aaltonen, whom Joey had met at the University of Minnesota where she was pursuing a teaching degree and he was a dental student—caused Andrew to visibly tremble. *I cannot help but spoil my only grandchild!*

Joey Genelli had been a phenomenal athlete and had, at one time, considered giving up his studies to become a prizefighter. Andrew had taught his stepson to box—after the child was accosted by bullies—and once it became known that Joey could handle himself, there had been no more trouble from the thugs of Aurora.

Andrew's stepson had continued boxing for recreation, never taking it seriously until he won a regional Golden Gloves tournament and went on to finish second in the state championships, which meant promoters were knocking at his dorm-room door, trying to lure him away from the university. But Heidi had stepped in and seen to it that such foolish notions remained unrequited.

Now thirty-five years old and well established in his dental practice and in his marriage to Inari, Andrew knew instinctively that Joey fostered no regrets about what might have been. *Damn fine young man,* Andrew thought as he left the woodpecker to its hammering. *Damn fine husband and father.*

The old man herringboned up a short hill and began skiing a logging trail. Aspen and balsam and birch had sprouted alongside the trail and sought to overcome the path. But the 1941 Allis Chalmers B tractor Andrew used for farm work and its attached brush hog kept the forest at bay. As he regained a rhythm to his skiing, Andrew's thoughts returned to his son Timmy and the ugliness of war.

No one has to explain it to me, Andrew thought as he planted his poles, bent his knees, and moved over the land. *Being wounded at Belleau Wood during the Great War taught me about mortality and pain and destruction and the suddenness of loss.*

As he skied, an unexpected sensation asserted itself in Andrew's left arm. *Must have pulled something climbing the hill,* he thought, stopping to shake his left hand and wrist loose of numbness.

Without warning, a ruffed grouse exploded from a cluster of ground pine, followed by a second and a third bird, the thunder of wings causing Andrew's heart to skip a beat. *Godddamn it!* He watched the yearling birds set their wings, make for a canopy of balsam, and glide into shadow.

The partridges' sudden appearance caused the old man to momentarily forget his left arm and wrist. But once the birds disappeared from view, the discomfort returned, intensified, and advanced into his jaw.

"Shit," Andrew moaned, clutching his chin with his left mitten. "I think I'm ..."

Andrew Maki did not finish his sentence. He toppled over the tips of his skis, landing face first in unblemished snow.

As his mind retreated into darkness, Andrew saw the familiar features of Matt Peltoma—who was rumored to be with Elin, the two lovers trapped somewhere in war-torn Finland. Peltoma's face slipped away, replaced by Elin's. But Elin wasn't conjured in Maki's fading mind as a middle-aged woman that she'd become. Instead, she appeared to Andrew Maki as a long-ago object of youthful affection. And then, as quickly as she'd manifested, Elin too was gone.

The final image that appeared to Andrew—as he teetered near the veil—was that of Heidi, her face crowned in glory, her slender figure cloaked in white. Her apparition reached for Andrew with steadfast hands. A multitude—of friends and relatives and loved ones Andrew Maki had lost—stood behind the statuesque woman. The old man marveled that his wife—and those with her—had been recast without imperfection.

And then, Andrew's heart stopped. In his final moment, a period of infinite time filled with limitless comprehension, Heidi Maki smiled, lowered her hands, stepped aside, and allowed others to welcome Andrew Maki home.

Janine's Story. March 2018 (Harlem, New York)

It's a foul, late-winter day. As we walk, I can't help but feel sadness. *It's only been four months*, I think as it rains. I'm about to cry. The pit I'm wallowing in is so deep and dark and difficult, I simply want to lie down on the concrete, curl into a ball, and die. *That is not the Finnish way. Olavi, if he were still alive, would not put up with such self-pity. He would be succinct and direct in his admonition: "Thena," he would say in that serious, fatherly voice I know so well, "there is nothing that can be done about it. The man took my life. That's the simple truth of it. Oh, don't get me wrong: I was not ready to die. I was not ready to leave you. And I most certainly was not prepared for what came next. But now, what choice do we both have but to go on? I am here and you are there, and we must make the best of things until your time comes."*

I stop walking.

"Something wrong, Sis?" Ari asks.

"This is the block we lived on. That's our first house—the one we lived in before we moved to Long Island," I say, pointing to a two-story brownstone.

We're standing, the wind increasing, our jackets insufficient, our clothes saturated, our bodies chilled to the bone, in front of a row house in Harlem not far from Finn Hall. Back in the day, Finn Hall was the center of all Finnishness in New York City, a place our maternal grandmother, Elin Gustafson Ellison Goldfarb Peltomaa, frequented as a newspaper reporter. Officially, it was known as the Finnish Progressive Society Hall. We're on West 122ⁿᵈ Street, only a few blocks from Finn Hall, admiring the brownstone we once called home, as drizzle changes to downpour.

"Isn't that Marcus Garvey Park?" Ari asks, pointing through the watery curtain towards an open space covered with remnant snow. "Isn't that where we played cowboys and Indians?"

I shift my gaze and take in the park where we once enjoyed swings and teeter-totters and slides. I nod, return my eyes to the well-maintained row house and consider our childhood.

Our parents, physicians who founded and practiced at a free clinic in Harlem, were the best role models any kid could ask for. Our mom, Alexis, faithfully steady and lovingly kind, was one of the first female doctors to put out a shingle in Harlem. Dad, serious yet thoughtfully patient, instilled in his wife and his children the Baptist faith of his upbringing—a faith that has, in my case, been sorely tested by Olavi's death. There's little doubt that both Ari and I became healers because of our parents. There's also no question that the two of us went to Finland to serve immigrants because of our parents' example.

I resist the urge to walk up, knock on the front door of our former home, explain who we are, and ask to see what the current occupants have done to the place. Given the immediacy of the loss I experienced in Kajaani, I'm not strong-willed or determined or brazen enough to make such an intrusion upon strangers. Instead of moving towards the building, I pull the hood of my winter jacket—the fabric sodden and heavy—over my head in a belated effort to stay dry. "Let's go take a look at the old Finn Hall, shall we?" I say. "It's a place Grandmother Elin loved to reminisce about when we were small."

We head east on 122nd, turn north on Malcolm X, pass the intersection of Malcolm X and MLK Boulevards, walk along 126th, and arrive at our destination just as the rain subsides.

"Doesn't look like all that," Ari observes, rain dripping from our jackets. "I'm not sure I get why Grandma was so excited about this place."

I tilt my head towards what was once a haven for radical Finns. The old socialist hall is now the Pilgrim Cathedral of Harlem. "Listen."

"To what?"

The harmonies grow and grow until the air is filled with the unmistakable joy of gospel music—the music of my people. Or at least, people I identify as mine whenever I look in the mirror. I know nothing of the church's theology beyond the fact it's affiliated with Pilgrim Assemblies International, a sect of Christianity said to be Pentecostal and Trinitarian. *Whatever that means!*

"Beautiful," Ari whispers, recognizing strains of "Walking and Talking with Jesus" carried on the still-moist air. "Like how you'd expect angels to sound."

We stand next to each other, soaked to the skin and awestruck. The music stops. The sacred is replaced by the secular.

Sounds of trucks and cars and buses and the subway and commuter trains and conversations and barking dogs and cooing pigeons blend together in a cacophony of urban life.

My brother lights up a Marlboro. *I've tried.* I've chastised him and cajoled him and harangued him until I'm breathless. And still, he smokes. Ari smiles at me, knowing what I'm thinking. He inhales and holds the smoke before expelling a white ring into the pewtery air in defiance.

We walk back to Malcolm X to catch the subway. Our plan is to visit the 9/11 Memorial in Manhattan. I've seen it. Given I'm a New Yorker, I've spent considerable time there. But Ari has never been and because of what happened in Kajaani, I think it's important for my brother to contemplate a place dedicated to the victims of extremism.

I also made a promise to the imam. After Olavi's funeral, when we met for the last time, Imam Abdul said al-Khalid and I talked about fate, and life, and death, and God. He tried to offer comfort, tried to make me understand that which has been impossible to comprehend. His counsel didn't help all that much. But I thanked him for the effort. The imam did, however, offer one piece of practical advice that made sense. "As you are going back to New York to deal with your apartment, bank accounts, insurance, and other such affairs," he had said, "now that you have a better understanding of Islam, and now that you have your own reason to grieve the acts of madmen, perhaps you should make another Hajj to the site of the Twin Towers. Such a visit would allow your tears and your prayers to join those of others who have suffered loss."

Light flashes through the windows of the subway car. We stand next to each other, hands gripping steel for balance. My brother becomes emboldened and brings up politics.

"So, Thena," Ari asks, his breath soured from cigarettes, "what do you think of Trump now?"

I know what he's getting at. President Trump has, in the course of the past week, fired the Secretary of State, engaged in an ugly Twitter assault on a former FBI Director, praised Putin's phony electoral win, endorsed the death penalty for drug dealers, ridiculed the Special Prosecutor investigating the Trump presidential campaign, examined prototypes for a new border wall, and—worst of all—waded into a legal battle with a porn star.

Since taking office, the president has, by my way of reckoning, accomplished just two things of note: he successfully appointed Gorsuch to the Supreme Court (replacing a pro-life justice with a like-minded man) and passed a tax plan that will put a few more dollars in our wallets.

Being that I voted for Donald Trump as a protest against Hillary Clinton's vehement support of abortion—a procedure I cannot countenance given my faith—I fully support his accomplishments. But given the past week of political chaos, I cannot help but feel that I erred when I cast my vote for Mr. Trump by absentee ballot.

How do I answer Ari?

Josiah Aristotle Tate is a patient man. I know this. I know he'll not ask the question again. I look away from my brother. I focus on the faces of strangers crowding the subway car, faces that reflect the broad spectrum of ethnicity and status and gender and orientation that *is* America.

Truth is, I admit to myself, *I made a mistake. I knew, before casting my vote, that Donald Trump is a man without honor or principles. And yet ...*

My head pounds. I'm weary after crossing the Atlantic burdened by grief, exhausted from shedding tears over Olavi's death, and gripped by the uncontrollable rage and resentment I feel towards the man who murdered my husband. As I breathe deeply and try to think, a memory intrudes.

After burying Olavi, I took a contemplative walk in the graveyard. I was seeking answers from God but purchased nothing but silence. No bird song. No wind. No voices. I stopped walking, not lost, but unaware of where I was. From the names on the graves, I determined I'd wandered into the Gypsy section of the Kajaani Town Cemetery. A name engraved in marble caught my eye: Anneli Balzar Tammi.

From the dates carved into the family tombstone, and from an old newspaper clipping, an article written in Finnish by Grandma Elin for *Työmies* I found years ago in her writings—pieces of history handed down from grandmother to daughter to granddaughter—I knew that Anneli Balzar had once been connected to Grandma Elin's first lover, Anders Alhomäki. I also knew that Anneli and her daughters perished in the sinking of *the Empress of Ireland.* Upon finding the headstone memorializing that tragedy, I stopped, knelt in respect, and, despite God's stubborn silence, said a prayer. For Anneli. For her daughters. For all those who sought new beginnings across the Atlantic but did not live through their journeys.

Kasich, I think, my mind coming back to the present. *I should have written in my vote for John Kasich. Of all the candidates on the conservative side of things, he was by far the best choice. But his campaign never got out of the starting gate, did it?* As I ponder the "why" behind the Ohio governor's failure, my stomach churns. I'm upset because I have a secret, a secret that no one, not even my brother, knows. My secret is an unpleasant part of my past that, truth be told, makes me feel like a hypocrite: I had an abortion. In medical school. Over forty years ago.

I know—from having confronted this bit of personal history over decades of self-appraisal—that thinking a truth is not the same as speaking a truth. I look at my brother's handsome, gently aging African face and consider whether I should, after years of silence, reveal to him this ancient act of selfishness that haunts me. When it happened, I was able to rationalize the choice I made without regret. But after years of spiritual handwringing, I've found it difficult to convince myself the decision I made was the right one.

There was simply no way I was going to let <u>one</u> *slip-up, the forgetting of* <u>one</u> *pill before engaging in drunken, casual sex with a fellow student destroy my dream of becoming a doctor. I was certain then, less certain now, that bringing a child into the world as a twenty-two-year-old single mother of color would have been the death knell of my medical career. I made the difficult decision on my own. I never told the boy. Hell, that would have done nothing more than complicate my decision. I got myself to the clinic, withstood the anxiety and the dread, and, in a matter of minutes, it was over. And yet, it isn't. That unborn child remains a part of me. Not as memory, but as fact. Truth is, I don't want other women to regret their choices like I regret mine. I know, I know. Some say that women need to be able to make such choices for themselves. That no one else should have such power*

335

*over a woman's body or her destiny. But having been there,
having carried the horrible burden of my mistake all these years, I
disagree.*

My eyes close. I fight tears. Tears for Olavi. Tears for a
life-changing decision made years ago. Tears for the
impoverished, frightened immigrants Trump wants to keep out of
this country.

And then, the answer to my brother's question manifests.
"Ari," I say quietly, the wheels of the subway car rumbling beneath
the floorboards.

"Yes?"

I swallow. Our brown eyes, our father's eyes, lock. "I
made a mistake." I pause, uncertain of which error I'm about to
disclose. But the urge to cleanse my soul by revealing a long-
concealed sin has abated. "I never should've voted for that man."

My brother nods, urging me to tell.

"Never again, Ari. Never again will I let a single issue,
even the life issue, guide my hand in the voting booth." I take a
breath before continuing. "I'm sorry I had a part in getting Trump
elected. He's a disgrace. An embarrassment. A schoolyard bully
with a limited understanding of the world, its cultures, and its
people."

Ari grins, reaches out with his left hand, and touches my
right cheek. "And you just realized this now?"

"I didn't vote for Obama. But I would today," I admit.

My brother smiles. "And I didn't vote for George W. But
if it was down to 'W' or Trump, I'd vote for 'W' in a heartbeat."

We arrive at our stop. We climb from darkness into
muted light. The rain has ended but the sun remains hidden
behind steely clouds.

As we walk, we hold hands, something we haven't done
since childhood. We encounter a reflecting pond—the North
Pool—memorializing those who died in the North Tower and on
American Airlines Flight 11 on September 11, as well as those
who perished during the failed 1993 attack on the same building.
We stop and read names cut into bronze. I didn't personally
know anyone who died here or at the Pentagon or on that plane
that crashed in Pennsylvania. Neither did my brother. But in a
very real sense, Ari and I recognize the names etched in metal.
They are us.

Several thousand visitors, Americans and foreigners, men and women and children, the old and the young, the rich and the poor, Muslims and Jews and Christians and Sikhs and Buddhists and Hindus and those professing no faith; people of every shade of white, red, brown, yellow, and black—a snapshot of what America is and must be—stand in reverent silence or whisper prayers to disparate versions of the Almighty.

As Ari and I clutch hands, tears streaming down my cheeks, my brother turns to me, and whispers, "I'm going home—back to Minnesota. Maggie called last night while you were sleeping. She wants to work things out. Says Amy Lee and Dexter think we're fools for not staying together."

"Will you return to nursing?"

Ari shakes his head. "No; at least not right away. But if I do go back to work, it won't be at an assisted-living facility. I'm done with that sort of thing: I've hit the wall dealing with end-of-life stuff." My brother pauses. "I might retire. Or not. But after what we went through in Kajaani, I'll take some time to decide." My brother smiles wistfully. "Maybe I'll buy a camper and explore Minnesota. And then, who knows? If Maggie's up for it, maybe take longer trips to national parks and monuments." Ari stops, grasps my head in his big hands, tips my chin, and kisses me on the left cheek. "Maybe my big sister would like to join us."

I gently push my brother away and smile. "Me and you and Maggie cooped up in a camper? Sounds *way* too cozy for my taste."

"What then?" he asks.

Before I can reply, a Hispanic family stops in front of the bronze parapets surrounding the North Pool. Two young boys, a mother, and a father talk quietly in Spanish, a language I don't understand. Ari listens and translates.

"His sister was a flight attendant. For American. She died when the first plane hit the North Tower."

I tear up again. "Shit."

"She was twenty-three years old and pregnant with her first child."

"Goddamn it!" I whisper. "That's just so horrible, so awful," I add, empathizing with strangers as if their loss is my own.

My brother leaves my side, approaches the grieving visitors, surprises the Hispanic man with a bear hug, and whispers into the guy's ear.

The little boys blink. Their mother stares at Ari with puzzled eyes. The father nods and says, "*Gracias, señor.*"

Ari retreats. We walk on.

"What did you say to him? I'm pretty sure I heard you speaking Spanish."

"I was."

"Well, what did you tell him?"

"I told him that his sister is a hero, that she and her baby are with God, and that you, my very religious, younger sister, would pray for their souls."

I nod solemnly. "I can do that."

We continue on in silence until, just before entering the museum, Ari stops and asks me a question.

"What will you do, Sis, now that your reason for living in Finland is gone, now that you've made it perfectly clear you don't want to rough it across America in a pop-up camper with Maggie and me?"

I know Ari doesn't mean to be insensitive. I take no exception to his kidding. "There are still immigrants in Kajaani requiring medical attention," I say. "Muslim boys and girls born with clefts; and other newcomers needing care." I pause, look at Ari with love, and complete my thought. "I'm pretty sure Olavi would be upset with me if I didn't return to help them."

And so, that's exactly what I do.

THE END

Finnish Progressive Society Hall

(Now Pilgrim Cathedral of Harlem)

Resources

Books

Clements, Jonathan, *Mannerheim: President, Soldier, Spy.*
London, England: Haus Publishing, 2009.

Falkberget, Johan, *The Fourth Watch* (Translated from
Norwegian by Ronald G. Popperwell). Madison, Wisconsin:
University of Wisconsin Press, 1968.

Finnish Americana: Vol 1. New York Mills, Minnesota: Parta
Press, 1978.

Grout, Derek, *RMS Empress of Ireland: Pride of the Canadian
Pacific's Atlantic Fleet.* Gloucestershire, England: The History
Press, 2014.

Haeussler, John. S., *Images of America: Hancock.* Charleston,
South Carolina: Arcadia, 2014.

Haywood, Joseph, *Red Jacket: A Lute Bapcat Mystery.* Guilford,
Connecticut: Lyons Press, 2012.

Holmio, Armas K.E., *History of the Finns in Michigan*
(Translated by Ellen M. Ryyanen). Hancock, Michigan: Great
Lakes Books, 2001.

The Koran Interpreted (Translated by A.J. Arberry). NYC, New
York: Touchstone, 1996.

Lutheran Study Bible (New Revised Standard Version).
Minneapolis: Augsburg Fortress, 2009.

Maki, Vienna C. Saari, *Ready to Descend: The Journals of Matti
Hallila Pelto.* New Brighton, Minnesota: Sampo Press, 2000.

Meinander, Henrik, *A History of Finland.* NYC, New York:
Oxford Press, 2013.

Munger, Mark, *Suomalaiset: People of the Marsh.* Duluth, Minnesota: Cloquet River Press, 2004.

Munger, Mark, *Sukulaiset: The Kindred.* Duluth, Minnesota: Cloquet River Press, 2014.

Murdoch, Angus, *Boom Copper: The Story of the First U.S. Mining Boom.* Calumet, Michigan: Drier and Koepel, 1964.

Taylor, Richard, *Images of America: Houghton County 1870-1920.* Charleston, South Carolina: Arcadia, 2006.

<u>Films</u>
The Battle for Sevastopol. Janson Media. 2015.

<u>Print Media</u>
"An Afternoon with 'Aunt Martha.'" *The Finnish American Reporter.* (December 2015).

"Disavowed 2009 Report on Domestic Terrorism Now Rings True." *Duluth News Tribune.* (Date unknown).

"The Finnish Poikatalo." *The Finnish American Reporter.* (April 2018).

"Finns Protest Against Racism after Man Assaulted at Neo-Nazi Rally Dies." *Reuters.* (Date unknown).

"Hate Crimes on Rise in Finland, Data Reveals." *The Finnish American Reporter.* (October 2016).

"Immigrants are Facing a New Reality this Fourth." *USA Today.* (Date unknown).

"The Path to Finland's Independence: Part 2." *The Finnish American Reporter.* (July 2017).

"Protest Site Broken Up." *The Finnish American Reporter.* (Date unknown).

"Research and Documentation Confirm Discovery." *The Finnish American Reporter.* (October 2017).

"The Shipbuilder Remembered." Warchuck, Larry. *The Finnish American Reporter.* (Date unknown).

"Terrorist Attacker Gets Life Sentence from Finnish Court." *The Finnish American Reporter.* (July 2018).

"Terror Suspects Arrested." *The Finnish American Reporter.* (November 2017).

Music
The Best of Sibelius.
https://www.youtube.com/watch?v=DsLoe5LaKqU

The Best of Tchaikovsky.
https://www.youtube.com/watch?v=DsLoe5LaKqU

Jean Sibelius Megamix: Symphonies 1 to 7
https://www.youtube.com/watch?v=DYLNqoSwQO4

Finnish Folk Music
https://www.youtube.com/watch?v=j1a4bNn1FEs

"Myrskluodon Maija." Elina, Ida. Album: *Hello World.* IMU, 2015.

Powderburn. Poijärvi, Ninni and Kuokkanen, Mika. Humble House Records, 2011.

"Valoa Pain." Poijärvi, Ninni. Album: *Saman Taivaan Alla.* Playground Music, 2016.

The Very Best of Grieg.
https://www.youtube.com/watch?v=ZWG-WQDussQ

Websites
"Afghanistan: Fatalities by Year."
http://icasualties.org/OEF/By/Year.aspx. Accessed 03/22/2018.

"Allis Chalmers B." http://www.tractordata.com/farm-tractors/000/0/0/3-allis-chalmers-b.html. Accessed 04/04/2018.

"Allis-Chalmers Model B." https://en.wikipedia.org/wiki/Allis-Chalmers_Model_B. Accessed 04/04/2018.

"Alta, Norway." https://www.revolvy.com/main.index/php?s=Alta,%20Norway&item_type=topic. Accessed unknown date.

"The Amazing Story of Tom Sukanen and His *Soitiainen*." http://www.odditycentral.com/news/tom-sikanen-the-man-who-built-a-ship-in-the-middle. Accessed 03/20/2018.

"Anders Behring Breivik." https://en.wikipedia.org/wiki/Anders_Behring_Breivik. Accessed 05/29/2017.

"An Illustrated History of American Money Design." https://grzmodo.com/an-illustrated-history-of-american-money-design-1743743361. Accessed 11/22/2017.

"Awakening (Religious Movement)." https://en.wikipedia.org/wiki/awakening_(religious movement). Accessed 06/04/2017.

"Bachelor of Health Care, Nursing." http://www.lapinamk.fi/en/Applicants/Bachelors-degrees/Nursing. Accessed 05/29/2017.

"Battle of the Bulge." https://en.wikipedia.org/wiki/Battle_of_the_Bulge. Accessed 04/04/2018.

"Battle of Mukden." https://en.wikipedia.org/wiki/Battle_of_Mukden. Accessed 04/22/2017.

"Blackhead Light: Great Lighthouses of Ireland."
http://www.greatlighthouses.com/lightouses/Blackhead. Accessed
08/10/2017.

"A Brief History of the College (Suomi)." Isaac, Edward.
http:// www.genealogia.fi/emi/art/article240e.htm. Accessed
12/24/2017.

"Boxing." https://en.wikipedia.org/wiki/Boxing. Accessed
11/14/2016.

"Carl Gustaf Emil Mannerheim."
https://en.wikipedia.org/wiki/Carl_Gustaf_Emil_Mannerheim.
Accessed 03/09/2017.

"Central African Republic."
https://en.wikipedia.org/wiki/Central_African_Republic. Accessed
08/27/2017.

"Center Party (Finland)."
https://en.wikipedia.org/wiki/Center_Party_(Finland). Accessed
06/09/2017.

"Commemoration of Empress of Ireland 2014."
http://www.empress2014.ca/seelangen/testimonies.html. Accessed
05/29/2016.

"Copper Country Strike of 1913-14."
https//en.wikipedia.org/wiki/Copper_Country_strike_of_1913-14.
Accessed 12/29/2017.

"Crimean War." https://en.wikipeida.org/wiki/Crimean_War.
Accessed 11/24/2016.

"Cultural Tracks: Finnish Americans in Michigan."
http://www.folkstreams.net/context%2C127. Accessed 03/23/2017.

"Duluth, Missabe and Iron Range Railway."
http://en.wikipedia.org/wiki/Duluth_Missabe_and_Iron_Range_R
ailroad. Accessed 11/15/2017.

"Education in Finland."
https://en.wikipedia.org/wiki/Education_in_Finland. Accessed
11/11/2016.

"1854: Asak Hetta and Mons Somby, Sami Rebels."
http://www.executedtoday.com/2014/10/14/1854-aslak-hett-mons-
somby. Accessed 04/29/2017.

"Elias Lönnrot." http://kalevalaseura.fi/en/about-kaevala/elias-
lonnrot. Accessed 11/11/2016.

"The Emigration from Tornedalen."
http://www.mfhn.com/houghton/finn/s_torikka/Emigration-from-
Tornio-valley-v6.asp. Accessed 04/26/2017.

"The Empress of Ireland."
http://bessemerhistoricalsociety.com/empress.html. Accessed
05/29/2016.

"Evangelical Lutheran Church of Finland."
https://en.wikipedia.org/wiki/Evangelical_Lutheran_Church_of_Fi
nland. Accessed 11/19/2016.

"Famine of 1866-68."
https://en.wikipedia.org/wiki/Famine_of_1866%E2%80%9368.
Accessed 12/09/2016.

"Finland About to Deploy Troops in Violence-Torn Central
African Republic." http://www.helsinkitimes.fi/finland/finland-
news/domestic/9042-finl. Accessed 08/07/2016.

"Finnish Defense Forces."
https://en.wikipedia.org/Finnish_Defense_Forces. Accessed
05/29/2017.

"Finland Election: Anti-EU Right Marches onto Center Stage."
http://theconversation.com/finland-election-anti-eu-right-marches-
onto-center-stage-40504. Accessed 06/09/2017.

"Finland's No Good." https://www.yahoo.com/news/finlands-no-
good-disappointed-mirgrants-turn-back-15204206. Accessed
06/09/2017.

"Finland's Immigration Crisis." Bunikowski, David.
https://www.gatestoneinstitute.org/7559/finalnd-migrant-crisis.
Accessed 08/07/2016.

"Finland Receives Syrian and Congolese Refugees Under the
Refugee Quota for 2018."
https://reliefweb.int/report/finland/finland-receives-syrian-and-
congolese-refugees-under-relief-quotea-for-2018. Accessed
02/08/2018.

"The Finnhorse." http://hippos.fi/mutt/in_english/the_finnhorse.
Accessed 08/23/2016.

"Finnish Americans." http://www.everyculture.com/multi/DU-
HA/Finnish-Americans.html. Accessed 12/09/2016.

"Finnish Kale." https://en.wikipedia.org/wiki/Finnish_Kale.
Accessed 11/13/2017.

"Finnish Peacekeepers Head to Bangui."
http://yle.fi/uutiset/finnish_peacekeepers_head_to_bangui.
Accessed 08/27/2016.

"Finnish Security Intelligence Service."
https://en.wikipedia.org/wki/Finnish_Security_Intelligence_Service
. Accessed 05/29/2017.

"The Finns in America."
https://www.loc.gov/rr/european/FinnAmer/finchro.html.
Accessed 12/09/2016.

"The Finns in Michigan."
http://www.genealogia.fi/emi/art/article/235e.htm. Accessed
04/26/2017.

"Finns Party." https://en.wikipedia.org/wiki_Finns_Party.
Accessed 06/09/2017.

"Finns Resist Russification, End Conscription, Regain Elections,
1898-1905." http://nvdattabase.swrthmore.edu/content/finns-resist-
russification-end-conscription-regain-elections-1898-1905.
Accessed 08/27/2016.

"First Syrian Refugees Resettled from Turkey to Finland."
http://yle.fi/uutiset/news/first_syrian_refugees_resettled_from_turk
ey. Accessed 05/29/2017.

"1930-1939 Ford Trucks." https://auto.howstuffworks.com/1930-
1939-for-trucks6.htm. Accessed 04/04/2018.

"'Gentleman Jim' Corbett Knocks Out John L. Sullivan, 1892."
http://www.eyewintesstohistory.com/corbett.htm. Accessed
11/15/2016.

"Goahti." https://en.wikipedia.org.wiki/Goahti. Accessed
06/09/2017.

"Gun Laws in Finland."
https://en.wikipedia.org/wiki/Gun_laws_in_Finland. Accessed
02/08/2018.

"History of Condoms."
https://en.wikipedia.org/wiki/History_of_Condoms. Accessed
11/30/2017.

"History of Finland."
https://en.wikipedia.org/wiki/History_of_Finland. Accessed
11/17/2016.

"History of Skiing."
https://en.wikipedia.org/wiki/History_of_skiing. Accessed
12/03/2016.

"How the Rape in Tapanila Started an Outrage against Somalis in
Finland." http://finlandtoday.fi/how-the-rape-in-tapanila-started-an-
outrage-against-somalis-in-Finland.

"Islamic Clothing Requirements."
https://www.thoughtco.com/islamic-clothing-requirements-
2004252. Accessed 03/31/2018.

"Kainuu Brigade." https://en.wikipedia.org/wiki/Kainuu-Brigade.
Accessed 01/23/2018.

"Kåfjord, Alta."
https://en.wikipedia.org/w/index/php?title=Kåfjord,_Alta&oldid=7
71855756. Accessed 04/26/2017.

"Karelian Question."
https://en.wikipedia.org/wiki/Karelian_question. Accessed
04/26/2017.

"Kautiokeino Rebellion."
https://en.wikipedia.org/wiki/Kautokeino_rebellion. Accessed
04/26/2017.

"Kven People." https://en.wikipedia.org/wiki/Kven_people.
Accessed 11/13/2017.

"Lake Olujarvi, Finland." http://www.lakelubbers.com/lake-
olujarvi-1190. Accessed 08/08/2016.

"Louis Moilanen-The Tallest Man."
http://www.thetallestman.com/louismoilanen.htm. Accessed
12/23/2017.

"Louis Moilanen." https://en.wikipedia.org/wiki/Louis_Moilanen.
Accessed 03/11/2017.

"Lymudmila Pavlichenko."
https://en.wikipedia.org/wiki/Lyudmila_Pavlichenko. Accessed 02/07/2018.

"Migrant Tales." http://migranttales.net/a=letter-to-the-non-discrimination-Ombudsperson-Kirsi-Pimiä. Accessed 01/18/2018.

"Migration from Finland 1866-1970."
http://www.genealogia.fi/emu/art/article300e.htm. Accessed 04/26/2017.

"Military of the Grand Duchy of Finland."
https://en.wikipedia.org/wiki/Military_of_the_Grand_Duchy_of_Finland. Accessed 11/24/2016.

"Military Intelligence Directorate (Syria)."
https://wikipedia.org/wiki/Military_Intelligence_Directorate_(Syria). Accessed 04/01/2018.

"Morehouse College."
https://en.wikipedia.org/wiki/Morehouse_College. Accessed 05/27/2017.

"National Baptist Convention-Envisioning the Future Exceptionally."
https://www.nationalbaptist.comdeaprtments/disaster-management. Accessed 05/27/2017.

"National Baptist Convention USA."
https://en.wikipedia.org/wiki/National_Baptist_Convention_USA_Inc. Accessed 05/27/2017.

"National September 11 Memorial & Museum."
https://en.wikipedia.org/wiki/National_September_11_Memorial_%26_Museum.

"NH Industries."
https://en.wikipedia.org/wiki/NHINdustries_NH90. Accessed
03/24/2018.

"Norwegian Berries."
https://norwayconnects.org./2015/norwegian-berries/. Accessed
04/09/2018.

"Norway." https://en.wikipedia.org/wiki/Norway. Accessed
04/26/2017.

"Nearly 1,000 Killed Over 2 Days in Central African Republic."
http://www.cnn.com/2013/12/18/world/africa/car-violence-
index.html. Accessed 08/27/2016.

"Norwegian Krone."
https://en.wikipedia.irg/wiki/Noarwegian_krone. Accessed
04/26/2017.

"Paltamo." https://en.wikipedia.org/wiki/Paltamo. Accessed
08/08/2016.

"Operation Sangaris."
https://en.wikipedia.org/wiki/Operation_Sangris. Accessed
06/03/2017.

"Pechengsky District."
https://en.wikipedia.org/wiki/Penchengsky_District. Accessed
04/26/2017.

"Pioneer Mine."
http://www.virginiamn.com/mine/pioneer/article_3196b5264-f967-
11e2-abc4-0019b. Accessed 11/13/2017.

"Places that Matter: Finnish Progressive Society Hall (Now
Pilgrim Cathedral of Harlem)."
http://www.placematters.net/node/1174. Accessed 03/20/2018.

"Police Arrest Two Iraqui Asylum Seekers on Suspicion of Manslaughter, Robbery."
http://yle.fi/uutiset/osasto/news/police_arrest_tow_iraqui_asylum_seekers_on_suspicion_of_manslaughter_robbery. Accessed 05/30/2017.

"Police of Finland."
https://en.wikipedia.org/wiki/Police_of_Finland. Accessed 05/29/2017.

"Police Firearm Use by Country."
https://en.wikipedia.org/wiki/Police_firearm_use_by_country#Finland. Accessed 05/30/2017.

"Postoperative Complications from Primary Repair of Cleft Lip and Palates."
https://www.ncbi.nlm.nih.gov.pmc/articles/PMC4924396/. Accessed 03/25/2018.

"Puolanka." https://en.wikipedia.org/wiki/Puolanka. Accessed 12/27/2016.

"Ranks and Insignia of the Russian Armed Forces until 1917.
https://en.wikipedia.org/wiki/Ranks_and_Insignia_of_the_Russian_Armed_Forces_unitl_1917. Accessed 09/23/2018.

"The Rise and Fall of the New Right in Finland."
http://www.nestatesman.com/politics/2015/02/rise-and-fall-of-far-right-finland. Accessed 06/09/2017.

"RK 62." https://en.wikipedia.org/wiki/RK_62. Accessed 03/25/2018.

"RMS *Celtic* (1901)."
https://en.wikipedia.org/wiki/RMS_Celtic_(1901). Accessed 08/10/2017.

"RMS *Empress of Ireland.*"
https://en/wikipedia.org./wiki/RMS_Empress_of_Ireland.
Accessed 05/29/2016.

"Roma in Finland." http://www.erc.org/articl/roma-in-dinland/2077. Accessed 12/23/2016.

"Romani People." https://en.wikipedia.org/wiki/Romani_people.
Accessed 12/23/2016.

"The Røros Copper Works."
http://www.worldheritageroros.no/copperworks/1359. Accessed
05/05/2017.

"Røros." https://en.wikipedia.org/wiki/Røros. Accessed
04/20/2017.

"Røros Line." https://en.wikipedia.org/wiki/Røros_Line. Accessed
07/18/2017.

"Route Description (Trans-Siberian Railway)."
https://en.wikipedia.org/wiki/Trans-Siberian_Railway. Accessed
04/21/2017.

"Roza Shanina." https://en.wikipedia.org/wiki/Roza_Shanina.
Accessed 02/07/2018.

"Russian Operations in the Boxer Rebellion."
http://marksrussianmilitaryhistory.info/BoxerReb.htm. Accessed
03/26/2017.

"Sako TRG." https://en.wikipedia.org/wiki/Sako_TRG. Accessed
02/02/2018.

"Sako TRG-42." http://www.snipercentral.com/sako-trg-42.
Accessed 03/21/2018.

"Sako TRG (Series) Sniper Rifle-Finland."
https://militaryfactory.com/smallarms/detail.asp?smallarms_id=66
3. Accessed 02/16/2018.

"Security Boss: Neo-Nazi Group Should be Banned."
http://yle.fi/uutiset/osasto/news/security_boss_neo-
nazi_group_should_be_banned. Accessed 05/30/2017.

"September 11 Attacks."
https://en.wikipedia.org/wiki/September_11_attacks. Accessed
03/20/2018.

"Simo Häyhä."
https://en.wikipedia.org/wiki/Simo_H%C3%4yh%C3%A4.
Accessed 02/07/2018.

"Services in Raku National Park."
http://www.nationalparks.fi/en/rokuanp/services. Accessed
06/09/2017.

"Somali Community in Finland."
https://en.wikipedia.org/wiki/Somali_commiunity_in_Finland.
Accessed 01/02/2017.

"Soudan Underground Mine."
http://www.virginiamn.com/mine/soudan-underground-mine-
article_e96e630-5ed1-11e4.

"Species Profile-Lake Whitefish."
https://www.dnr.stat.mn.us/minnaqua/speciesprofile/lake_whitefis
h.html. Accessed 04/12/2018.

"Suomi College." http://www.collegeprifiles.com/suomi.html.
Accessed 12/24/2017.

"Swallowed in 14 Minutes." http://www.encyclopedia-
titanica.org/empress-of-ireland.html. Accessed 05/29/2016.

"Trump Backers Charged in Anti-Muslim Terror Plot."
https://www.huffingtonpost.com/entry/kansas-militia-trump-muslim-terror-plot_us5ab0f0. Accessed 03/20.2018.

"20th Century Coins." http://rrcoins.net//20th-cnetury-coins. Accessed 11/22/2017.

"Two Iraqi Asylum Seekers Sentenced to Prison for Homicide, Robbery." http://news.xinhuanet.com/english/2016-12/17/c_135911762.htm.

"2017 Turku Stabbing." https://en.wikipedia.org/wiki/2017_Turku_stabbing. Accessed 09/18/2017.

"Typhus." http://www.nytimes.com/health/guides/disease/typhu/overview.html. Accessed 03/28/2017.

"Undergound Mining (hard rock)." https://en.wikipedia.org/Underground_mining_(hard_rock). Accessed 05/05/2017.

"UNHCR: Finland." http://www.unhcr-northerneurope.org/where-we-work/finland. Accessed 08/07/2016.

"The Union's Last War: The Russian-Swedish War of 1808-09." http://www.napolean-series.org/military/battles/c_finnish.html. Accessed 11/22/2016.

"UN Report Shows Hundreds of Central African Republic Abuses." https://www.washingtonpost.com/world/africa/un-report-shows-hundreds-of-cnetral-african-abuses. Accessed 05/31/2017.

"Vasilij Kvachantiradze." https://en/wikipedia.org.wiki/Vasilij_Kvachantiradze. Accessed 02/07/2018.

"Vintage Canoe Works."
http://vintagecanoeworks.com/restored/1878_jamescross.html.
Accessed 11/16/2017.

"Voices: Anyone Who Says the Quran Advocates Terrorism
Obviously Hasn't Read its Lessons on Violence."
https://www.independent.co.uk./voices-islam-muslin-terrorism-
islamist-extremism-quaran. Accessed 03/28/2018.

"Walther P99." https://en.wikipedia.org/wiki/Walther_P99.
Accessed 03/25/2018.

"Weight Divisions."
http://boxrec.com/media/index.php/Weight_divisions. Accessed
01/10/2017.

"What We Should Learn from the Tapanila Rape Case."
http://migranttales.net/what-we-should-learn-from-the-tapanila-
rape-case. Accessed 08/07/2016.

"Where Nokia Went Wrong."
https://newyorker.com/business/currency/where-nokia-went-
wrong. Accessed 06/09/2017.

"Women as Imams."
https://en.wikipeida.org/wiki/women_as_imans. Accessed
03/29/2018.

"Woman Imam Leading Men and Women in Salat."
https://www.islamicity.org/2576/women-imama-leading-men-and-
women-in-salat/. Accessed 03/29/2018.

About the Author

Mark Munger, a former trial attorney and retired district court judge, is a life-long resident of northeastern Minnesota. Mark and his wife, René, live on the banks of the wild and scenic Cloquet River north of Duluth. When not writing fiction, Mark enjoys hunting, fishing, skiing, and reading excellent stories.

Other Works by the Author

The Legacy (ISBN 0972005080 and eBook in all formats)

Set against the backdrop of WWII Yugoslavia and present-day Minnesota, this debut novel combines elements of military history, romance, thriller, and mystery. Rated 3.5 daggers out of 4 by *The Mystery Review Quarterly*.

Ordinary Lives (ISBN 97809792717517 and eBook in all formats)

Creative fiction from one of Northern Minnesota's newest writers, these stories touch upon all elements of the human condition and leave the reader asking for more.

Pigs, a Trial Lawyer's Story (ISBN 097200503x and eBook in all formats)

A story of a young trial attorney, a giant corporation, marital infidelity, moral conflict, and choices made, *Pigs* takes place against the backdrop of Western Minnesota's beautiful Smoky Hills. This tale is being compared by reviewers to Grisham's best.

Suomalaiset: People of the Marsh (ISBN 0972005064 and eBook in all formats)

A dockworker is found hanging from a rope in a city park. How is his death tied to the turbulence of the times? A masterful novel of compelling history and emotion, *Suomalaiset* has been hailed by reviewers as a "must read."

Esther's Race (ISBN 9780972005098 and eBook in all formats)

The story of an African American registered nurse who confronts race, religion, and tragedy in her quest for love, this novel is set against the stark and vivid beauty of Wisconsin's Apostle Islands, the pastoral landscape of Central Iowa, and the steel and glass of Minneapolis. A great read, soon to be a favorite of book clubs across America.

Mr. Environment: The Willard Munger Story (ISBN 9780979217524: trade paperback only)

A detailed and moving biography of Minnesota's leading environmental champion and longest-serving member of the Minnesota House of Representatives, *Mr. Environment* is destined to become a book every Minnesotan has on his or her bookshelf.

Black Water: Stories from the Cloquet River
(ISBN 9780979217548 and eBook in all formats)

Essays about ordinary and extraordinary events in the life of an American family living in the wilds of northeastern Minnesota, these tales first appeared separately in two volumes, *River Stories* and *Doc the Bunny*. Re-edited and compiled into one volume, these are stories to read on the deer stand, at the campsite, or late at night for peace of mind.

Laman's River
(ISBN 9780979217531 and eBook in all formats)

A beautiful newspaper reporter is found bound, gagged, and dead. A Duluth judge conceals secrets that may end her career. A reclusive community of religious zealots seeks to protect its view of the hereafter by unleashing an avenging angel upon the world. Mormons. Murder. Minnesota. Montana. Reprising two of your favorite characters from *The Legacy*, Deb Slater and Herb Whitefeather. Buy it now in print or on all major eBook platforms!

Sukulaiset: The Kindred
(ISBN 9780979217562 and eBook in all formats)

The long-awaited sequel to *Suomalaiset: People of the Marsh*, Mark Munger's epic novel of Finnish immigration to the United States and Canada, *Sukulaiset* portrays the journey of Elin Gustafson from the shores of Lake Superior to the shores of Lake Onega in the Soviet Republic of Karelia during the Great Depression. The story unfolds during Stalin's reign of terror and depicts the interwoven lives of Elin, her daughter Alexis, an American logger, and two Estonians wrapped up in the brutal conflict between Nazi Germany and Communist Russia. A page-turning historical novel of epic proportions.

Boomtown
(ISBN 978-0979217593 and eBook in all formats)

An explosion rocks the site of a new copper/nickel mine in northeastern Minnesota. Two young workers are dead. The Lindahl family turns to trial attorney Dee Dee Hernesman for justice. A shadowy eco-terrorist lurks in the background as Hernesman and Sheriff Deb Slater investigate the tragedy. Are the deaths the result of accident or murder? Equal parts legal thriller and literary fiction, this novel includes many characters from Munger's prior novels. A page-turner of a tale.

Visit us at:
www.cloquetriverpress.com

SmileTrain

Changing The World One Smile At A Time.

10% of all gross sales of CRP books are donated by CRP to SmileTrain in hopes of helping children born with cleft lips and palates across the world. Learn more about SmileTrain at http://www.smiletrain.org/.

Grant funding generously provided by the Finlandia National Foundation. Kiitos!

Made in the USA
Coppell, TX
26 February 2021

50924404R00215